© Sergio Lobo-Navia/The Bend Media

BILL LOEHFELM is the author of *The Devil in Her Way*, *The Devil She Knows*, *Bloodroot*, and *Fresh Kills*. He lives in New Orleans with his wife, the writer AC Lambeth, and plays drums in a rock 'n' roll band.

Praise for Bill Loehfelm's Maureen Coughlin Series

"Rapid-fire pacing, dialogue that crackles, an artful depiction of the streets of New Orleans . . . Bill Loehfelm is a terrific writer."   —Alafair Burke

"Beautifully written . . . [New Orleans] has been the setting for a couple of outstanding crime novels, including James Lee Burke's *The Tin Roof Blowdown* and Sara Gran's quirky *Claire DeWitt and the City of the Dead*. . . . [Loehfelm] measures up to that standard and then some."
—Bruce DeSilva, Associated Press

"[Loehfelm] succeeds by placing an intriguing heroine in a fascinating city."   —*The Washington Post*

"[Maureen Coughlin] brandishes a knife as convincingly as she worries about becoming a cat lady."   —*People*

"You can't do any better than riding shotgun with Maureen Coughlin. She's hip, contemporary, and the perfect guide to one of America's most broken cities."   —Ace Atkins

"Punches are flying from page one. . . . Electric."   —*The Daily Beast*

"An absolutely original voice, and a story that grabs you by the throat and doesn't ever, ever, ever even think of letting you go."
—John Lescroart

"The most engaging cop to battle bad guys in the Crescent City since James Lee Burke's Dave Robicheaux."   —*The Times-Picayune*
(New Orleans)

"A fast, rough ride you can't put down."   —Colin Harrison

"Damaged, uncertain, and willing to pop a few Percocets over a sore ankle ahead of her shift, [Maureen Coughlin]'s a good girl who's not too good." —*The Commercial Appeal* (Memphis)

"If Jane Tennison of *Prime Suspect* had a daughter, I'm convinced it would have been Maureen Coughlin." —*Killer Nashville Magazine*

"Bill Loehfelm takes us on a deep, gritty tour of the New Orleans tourists never see. . . . [I] can't wait for Leohfelm's next." —Sara Gran

"Loehfelm meshes graceful prose with edgy suspense." —*Publishers Weekly* (starred review)

"This is timely stuff . . . [and] watching Maureen find her way makes for gripping reading." —*225* magazine (Baton Rouge)

"Bill Loehfelm writes about New Orleans with tenderness and grit, two qualities mirrored by his unforgettable protagonist, Maureen Coughlin. Compelling, whip-smart, and completely original." —Hilary Davidson, author of *Blood Always Tells* and *Evil in All Its Disguises*

"Maureen Coughlin [is] a Clarice Starling for New Orleans. Readers will rip through [this] and then curse Loehfelm for not having another heartbreaking tale at the ready." —Bryan Gruley, author of *The Skeleton Box*

DOING THE DEVIL'S WORK

DOING THE DEVIL'S WORK

BILL LOEHFELM

PICADOR   A SARAH CRICHTON BOOK   FARRAR, STRAUS AND GIROUX   NEW YORK

DOING THE DEVIL'S WORK. Copyright © 2015 by Beats Working, LLC. All rights reserved. Printed in the United States of America. For information, address Picador, 175 Fifth Avenue, New York, N.Y. 10010.

picadorusa.com • picadorbookroom.tumblr.com
twitter.com/picadorusa • facebook.com/picadorusa

Picador® is a U.S. registered trademark and is used by Farrar, Straus and Giroux under license from Pan Books Limited.

For book club information, please visit facebook.com/picadorbookclub or e-mail marketing@picadorusa.com.

Designed by Abby Kagan

The Library of Congress has cataloged the Sarah Crichton Books edition as follows:

Loehfelm, Bill.
    Doing the devil's work / Bill Loehfelm. — First edition.
        p. cm.
    ISBN 978-0-374-29858-6 (hardcover)
    ISBN 978-0-374-71171-9 (e-book)
    1. Policewomen — Fiction.   2. Murder — Investigation — Fiction.   I. Title.
    PS3612.O36 D75 2014
    813'.6 — dc23

                                                            2014014641

Picador Paperback ISBN 978-1-250-08153-7

Our books may be purchased in bulk for promotional, educational, or business use. Please contact your local bookseller or the Macmillan Corporate and Premium Sales Department at 1-800-221-7945, extension 5442, or by e-mail at MacmillanSpecialMarkets@macmillan.com.

First published by Sarah Crichton Books, an imprint of Farrar, Straus and Giroux

First Picador Edition: June 2016

10 9 8 7 6 5 4 3 2 1

For Barney

"I may be on the side of the angels, but don't think for one second that I am one of them."

DOING THE DEVIL'S WORK

1

The first bottle exploded twenty feet behind the patrol car. Maureen didn't even turn around. The next hit ten feet in front of her. She'd expected it, but she started at the impact anyway. The piss inside the bottle sprayed her bumper. She heard yelling and laughter from the people lining the sidewalk. Maureen glanced in her rearview mirror. The men couldn't help themselves. They were hunched over, leaning on each other and laughing, covering their mouths with the backs of their hands as if that would hide their mirth, as if their mothers were watching while they giggled in church. They raised their eyes to the rooftops, looking for the next missile. For the boys throwing them. She wanted to roll down her window, reach for her spotlight, and shine it along the rooftops. She wanted to drag those punks into the street by their braids and slap them senseless. She left her windows rolled up and kept the car moving forward.

The Saints had won their big Sunday-night prime-time game. Unde-feated into October. If that wasn't enough to get the streets buzzing, the

autumn parade season had started a couple of weeks ago, and a neighborhood second line had rolled nearby earlier in the day. Since before
the parade had started, people had been out in the streets of Central
City with their barbecue grills and their coolers, their massive car speak-
ers pounding out bass-heavy hip-hop and brass-band music. Now it was
eleven o'clock at night and things were not only going strong, they were
getting unruly. Maureen would've preferred to let the party run itself out.

Another bottle hit the street, not as close this time. She was pretty
sure they didn't want to hit her car. They knew that if they did she'd call
for backup. She'd have to. The other units would roll in and break up
the party for good. Then the grown-ups, the ones with weed in their
pockets, purple drank in their go cups, or guns in their waistbands would
be angry. It was all fun and games, Maureen thought, until somebody's
parole got violated. She hit the light bar to send a message. Blue and red
lights flashed over the faded gray and yellow house fronts like dance-
floor lights at a club. She waited for another bottle to hit the street. It
didn't come. Good. As long as everyone on the block was on the same
page, she thought, about when enough was enough.

The party wasn't why she was on Magnolia Street, anyway. The dead
body was the reason. She rolled down her window halfway. The music
was earsplitting. She could feel the bass notes in her chest. The piss smell
wafted into the car, along with a bouquet of marijuana, spilled beer, and
cheap charcoal briquettes. The smell of anything good to eat was long
gone. Death was dominant, though, over the odors of the block party.
Nothing smells quite like a dead body, Maureen thought.

She had picked up the scent as soon as she'd turned onto Magnolia
Street, the air conditioner pumping it through the cruiser.

She slowed the patrol car to a crawl. The smell intensified as she
moved down the block. She lit a cigarette and hit the cruiser's spotlight,
searching the block in front of her for the source of the smell. She radi-
oed her location to dispatch, telling them she'd arrived on scene, had
found nothing specific yet, and asking them to wait for more detail.

She panned the left side of the street with the spot, wishing the anonymous caller had given a more specific location, looking into the dark and narrow alleys between houses and the shallow crawl spaces underneath them. The eyes of feral cats gleamed back at her. The houses on the block were occupied, worn and weary, but kept up and cared for. Most were owned. Some were rented. A few had porch lights lit. Flower boxes and sun-faded secondhand children's toys cluttered their scraggly yards. Saints banners and signs hung in the windows. Someone had cut the music on the block. No one was laughing at her now. A group of men had gathered in the street, their matching red T-shirts peeking out from underneath their Saints jerseys, their red ball caps tilted sideways or turned backward. Hostile eyes watched her. Word had traveled about why she was there, she figured. The people on the block had to smell it, too.

Down at the far end of the block, beyond the party, the street dead-ended against a sagging chain-link fence, tall weeds growing through it. Overhead, small dark forms moved against the stars, scurrying along the power lines. Rats. Like the cats, like her, they had noses, too. Maureen felt she had the block's full attention. Every few moments the shrill whir of cicadas cut through the air. Across the empty lot, a couple hundred yards beyond the dead end, glowed the well-lit backyards of the Harmony Oaks subdivision, the new mixed-income development that now sprawled where the brick boxes of the Magnolia projects had once loomed, back before Maureen's time in New Orleans.

She'd heard stories about the Magnolia, tales about cops and even National Guard taking fire from the project rooftops in the first days of the flood.

A frightening thought clicked in her brain, and she braked the car to a stop, her taillights throwing ruby light behind her. If someone wanted to set a trap for a cop, an ambush, she thought, this block of Magnolia Street was a perfect place to do it—the dark end of a narrow dead-end street. There were fifty people, most of them men, drunk, high, some of them armed, between her and the corner. She was a cop, and armed and armored as such, but she was also five-four and a hundred and twenty pounds. Outnumbered and outgunned. Her mouth had dried up. Her pulse accelerated. She breathed deeply through her nose, staring hard into her rearview mirror, trying to settle herself and stay focused, fighting back the anxiety. They weren't a mob, she told herself, they were just a crowd, they were the neighborhood and they didn't want trouble. She was a white girl cop, and she had crashed their party. I don't wanna be here, either, she wanted to say, but one of you called us.

Tonight, like most nights, like most cops in New Orleans, Maureen rode alone in her cruiser. Solo patrols were a risky strategy, but the policy put more cars on the streets at a time when the NOPD's manpower was at its lowest since the year after the storm. The superintendent was working hard to clean up the department, a years-long project, and tolerance for malfeasance, mistakes, and the appearance of either was also at an all-time low. Unfortunately, recruitment had not come close to matching the attrition. The papers and community leaders made a fuss over it, but the situation didn't much bother Maureen. She preferred riding alone. She didn't want a partner. The idea of spending hours and hours each night in a car with another human being horrified her. She liked making the decisions. She liked the quiet. And so far, in her short time on the job, when she'd needed reinforcements, they had come when she called. Behind her, the crowd of men inched closer to her car, trying to look casual doing it.

She stuck her cigarette in the corner of her mouth, rubbed her sweaty palms on her thighs. She unbuckled her weapon, slid it from the holster, placed it in her lap, careful not to let the men behind her see. She flexed the fingers of her right hand, rolled her wrist. She wasn't afraid of her gun. She put her time in at the range. She hit what she shot at.

She put the cruiser in reverse, depressing the brake. She held the radio mic in one hand, and using the other, scanned the street in front of her with the spotlight. Nothing on the pavement. Nothing in the overgrown weeds beyond the fence. Nothing around or under the parked cars. The last house on the block. The only empty one. The body was there.

Shifting the patrol car back into drive, she rolled it forward a few yards, the engine knocking, the bald tires crunching on the gravel and grit. She exhaled a breath she didn't know she'd been holding. She rooted around the messy front seat of the cruiser until she found her pack of peppermint gum. She unwrapped a piece and put it in her mouth, cracking the outer shell with her back teeth. Once she got close to the body, a cigarette wouldn't be nearly enough of a defense against the stench. She reholstered her weapon, grabbed her flashlight and radio, and secured the radio on her belt, clipping the mic to her shoulder. She got out of the car, dropping her cigarette in the street. She lit another, grinding her gum.

The weeds in the front yard of the house stood two feet high. The green paint was cracked and flaking. The brown shutters hung at odd angles beside the windows, their hinges rusted and useless. The neighbors had tacked up large signs on the front of the house, their messages hand-lettered in red marker on the white poster board. One said, CUT THIS GRASS. Another said, BLIGHTED PROPERTY! One simply read, SHAME. Someone else, with different handwriting, had scrawled a name and a phone number along the bottom border of each sign. The property owner's name and number, Maureen guessed.

Maybe, she thought, the dead guy in that house was the guy who owned it. Counterproductive strategy, she thought. If the owner was the corpse, squaring away the property would take the city that much longer.

At the walkway to the house she turned in a slow circle, shining her flashlight into the shadows in front of and between the nearest houses, over the faces of the people watching her. She said nothing to them. None of them spoke. The streetlight over her head flickered and went out. Perfect. That seemed to happen to her a lot, the lights going out. Too much darkness on these streets, she thought. So many places for people to hide. She paused for a moment, listening for sounds from the block, from the empty lot behind a fence, from inside the house she was about to enter. Everything she heard was distant—the whine of an ambulance headed down Napoleon Avenue, the imitative howl of a dog in a nearby yard, the long, deep note from a ship on the river. The cicadas had gone quiet. People on the block murmured to one another. A couple of people talked on their phones.

She turned her back on the crowd, headed up the walk, kicking trash out of her way. She swatted away the small insects fluttering and hovering above the grass, the stench getting stronger with each step she took. She pushed thoughts of an ambush out of her mind. If someone were going to shoot her, they would have done it already. She couldn't think about shit like that. How could she do her work if she couldn't get out of the car?

The wooden porch steps creaked under her boots. Furry things scattered into the high grass from under the steps. She hoped the front door was unlocked, that she wouldn't have to search the yard or the alley for another entrance, for a back door or a broken window.

She heard them before she saw them, the ultimate signifiers, big black flies. Hundreds of them, wings beating and buzzing, crawling on top of and over one another as they crept around on the dirty window of the front door. They almost completely covered the pane of glass, which seemed to vibrate with their activity.

Flies that size, Maureen knew, collected in those numbers only around dead things. The sound of the flies, their eager, busy humming, brought on a strong wave of nausea Maureen tried breathing and blinking away. She realized she stood in something slimy. A puddle of puke. Fantastic. Most likely left in the doorway, she figured, by whoever had found the body.

Closing her eyes and mouth tight, Maureen leaned her shoulder into the door. It opened easily and she stumbled across the threshold. Flies streamed into the air around her like tiny bats from a cave. She stepped through them into the entranceway, the bend of her elbow covering her mouth and nose, and deeper into the house. At a doorway she turned right, shining her flashlight into what would've been the living room. And there he was at the end of her beam—her dead body, purple and bloated, oozing fluid into the floorboards. She sighed with relief.

It's funny, she thought, the things being a cop does to your brain.

Bizarre, the comfort that comes with finding what you were looking for, no matter how gruesome a thing it was. She hated surprises, in life and on the job.

The dead guy was a white male, Maureen saw. *That* was a surprise.

She approached the body. He appeared to be in his late twenties to early thirties, though it was hard to tell from the swelling and decomposition. He was flat on his back. He'd died wide-eyed with surprise, his mouth hanging open, his chest soaked in blood from a heinous wound slashed across his throat. She'd discovered a homicide.

The deceased's hands were sticky to the elbow with blood from his failed efforts to staunch the massive bleeding that had killed him. Blood had pooled around him on the floor, the stain looking like a dark hole opening beneath him, waiting to swallow him. He had dirty blond hair, grown long from neglect more than style, Maureen guessed. She had no idea what color his T-shirt had been before all the blood. His jeans were undone and pulled down around his pale, hairy knees, his little dick lying shriveled against his fat thigh. He had taped-up work boots on his feet and his belt had a large round buckle bearing the number 88. He looked like the kind of guy, Maureen thought, who hadn't smelled much better when he was alive than he did when he was dead.

She considered for a moment going back to the unit and getting some latex gloves. She could take some time to herself, as long as she could stand the smell, and spend a few minutes with the crime scene. She could see what she could learn, give the detective who caught the case a head start. Whether or not that was a good idea, though, depended on which detective showed up. Maureen couldn't know who would arrive to take over. She didn't need to be stepping on the wrong toes. And the reek of a body, it had a way of feeling like it was seeping into your skin. She walked out onto the porch, keyed her radio, called in her discovery, her location, and a request for a homicide detective.

Behind her on the block, she heard the shuffle of feet and the distinctive creak of screen doors. People were headed inside; they knew more cops would be coming, and asking questions. The party was over. The scent of a corner-store cigar drifted her way. Hushed voices came nearer. Other neighbors were curious and lingering, emboldened by THC and alcohol. Good, she thought. The block party meant less knocking on doors and rousing people out of bed. As soon as she got some help secur-ing the scene, she could start canvassing the block and asking questions. Until then she had to stand guard over the body.

Maureen wrinkled her nose, but not from the smell of the cheap cigar or the dead body. Thanks to her job, she was growing accustomed to both odors. She scrunched her lips into a tight bud, her brain up and running. She'd found what she'd expected: a body. But that of a dead white boy with a savage neck wound, who'd been left for days in a black, gang-troubled, working-class neighborhood like Central City—that didn't fit. That didn't belong. Not at all.

2

Ninety minutes later, the red, white, and blue emergency lights of multiple vehicles whirled in the night and spotlights chased away the shadows, casting the block in a movie-set glare. The block party had ended. Crime lab was on the scene, photographing the body and the house and gathering evidence. Three other units had arrived, as had the detective in charge. Maureen looked around. Half the Sixth District overnight shift seemed to be on the scene. She wondered who was out patrolling.

By now, most of the block's residents had been interviewed, either by Maureen or by one of her fellow officers. The interviews didn't take long. None of the neighbors had heard or seen anything useful or telling. Nothing unusual about that, Maureen knew. The interviewing officers hadn't even learned who had reported the body. Whoever had called all about the bad smell hadn't offered a name. People seemed surprised though, Maureen had noted, that it was a dead white boy who'd brought the NOPD homicide experience to their street. Some waxed cynical about it, daring Maureen to contradict their claims that, watch, one dead white guy would get more attention than a whole block of live black folk. Especially if it turned out that a black person had killed him. She didn't argue. She listened, nodding her head, writing down page after page of lies and complaints. If you listened, she figured, or at least did a convincing job of acting like you were paying attention, people felt respected. They remembered the feeling. Next time, or maybe the time after that, she came around asking for help, she might just get it.

Her share of the interviews done, a fresh cigarette in her hand, Maureen leaned against the chain-link fence at the end of Magnolia, away from the lights and action, the metal wire biting into her shoulder. Quinn and Ruiz, two officers from her platoon who had helped with the canvass, smoked with her. Quinn stood a shade over six feet tall, wiry and angular, all elbows and knees and nose. He reminded Maureen of Disney's Ichabod Crane, but with the blond hair and casual lilt to his voice and stride of a California surfer. And a growing bald spot. Ruiz, his longtime patrol partner, was a green-eyed beer keg on short legs, olive skinned, acne-scarred, quiet. He was always restless, like a large animal unnerved by a sound it couldn't identify. From a distance, he seemed kind and competent, but his size made Maureen uncomfortable. Especially up close. She had a bad history with large men.

When they worked a crime scene together, which was often, Maureen sometimes felt as if Ruiz was watching her. The attention wasn't sexual. She knew that look. He just paid more attention to her than to any witnesses or evidence at the scene of the crime. That feeling is on you, she told herself over and over. You're bringing it to the job. Don't see enemies where they aren't.

"We were shut out," Quinn said, shaking his head.

"Y'all got nothing?" Maureen said. "You work this neighborhood for ten years and they do you like that? Nobody talked to you?"

"Everybody talks," Ruiz said. "Just nobody says anything."

"Maybe everyone knowing us," Quinn said, looking back over the block, "worked against us. I saw three guys I've busted without even looking real hard. I know half the cats out here tonight by their first names."

"Maybe," Ruiz said, "it's true that nobody really knows anything."

"You talking about them or us?" Quinn said. A ping from his cell phone indicated a message. He shrugged, grinning, rolling his eyes, reaching into his pocket. "Anything's possible, I guess." He checked his message. "About fucking time." His faced darkened as he read more, his forehead creasing in a scowl. "Again with this shit." He handed his cell to Ruiz, who read the message, produced a sympathetic grunt, and handed back the phone.

"Your son again?" Maureen asked.

"Quinn's ex again, more like it," Ruiz said.

Quinn had a young son, ten or so, Maureen recalled. The boy's mother and Quinn did not get along. They hadn't been romantically involved since the pregnancy was discovered. If not for the child, they would have nothing to do with each other. The boy was undersized for his age, and got bullied badly in school. Maureen had heard a lot about the situation, as did anyone on the NOPD and the streets of New Orleans within earshot of Quinn when his phone rang. This is the price, Maureen thought, of getting to know her coworkers better.

"It's Sunday night, right?" Quinn said. "Friday afternoon his mother takes him to get his stitches out and I don't get a report from her till now. Okay, it's only five stitches in his chin, and everything's fine, but still, I'm the boy's father and I'm paying the fucking bill." He turned to Ruiz. "You saw that last bit, about the new school because he's getting pushed around? Again with that noise. Fuck that. I can afford that?" He turned to Maureen. This happened when his ex came up, Maureen had noticed. By being female she somehow became a stand-in for Quinn's ex when he got worked up over her. "There's KIPPs and charters and all that shit now," he said. "He doesn't have to go to the Catholic school. So he's a little short. He'll grow. He's a normal fucking kid, it's *her* that makes him feel like there's something wrong with him. Always taking him to the doctor, tests for this, tests for that. Jesus. Kid's a fucking mess because of her."

Not just the kid, Maureen thought.

Ruiz, himself happily married and the father of two daughters, put a big hand on Quinn's shoulder. "Like you said, bro. He'll grow up. Kids bounce back."

"He's ten," Quinn said. "He hasn't even hit puberty yet, already she's cut his balls off." He looked over at the abandoned house, shaking his head at the sirens, the lingering neighbors, the trash tumbling around in the street, the scent of a freshly sparked joint. "Those fucking schools she likes cost a fortune. Every one of them." He tossed his notepad in the tall grass. "Fuck this. Why are we standing here like a bouquet of dicks? They don't care. We don't care. Fucking pointless, the load of it. Rue, let's roll. I'm outta cigarettes."

He stalked away. Ruiz hesitated for a long moment.

"He's getting worse," Maureen said. She retrieved Quinn's pad from the grass, gave it to Ruiz.

"It'll pass," Ruiz said. "He'll smooth out. He goes through phases. You haven't been around that long." He raised his chin and narrowed his eyes at a tall figure, Detective Sergeant Christine Atkinson, from Homicide, walking their way through the red and blue lights. "Just the same, let's keep it in house."

Ruiz, not waiting for Maureen's reply, nodded at Atkinson as he walked past her in pursuit of Quinn. Atkinson was a tall blonde in her late forties, partial to old blue jeans, older cowboy boots, and faded men's button-down shirts. She had a chaotic mop of curls hovering around her head, huge hands, and the wide back and shoulders of a lifelong swimmer.

"So the dead guy isn't the property owner," Atkinson said to Maureen.

Maureen shook her head. "There's a man's name across the bottom of the signs. I did confirm *that's* the property owner. You want me to get you that number?"

"I've already got it," Atkinson said. "Thanks, though. He's on his way." She took a drag on her cigarette. "Quinn and Ruiz have nothing for me, I take it."

"Not the slightest," Maureen said. "It's been a tough canvass. The usual resistance."

"Well, damn. I'd hoped you all would make this an easy one for me."
Maureen smiled. "Sorry to disappoint."

"Was there somebody squatting in the house?"

"Nobody on the block said anything about a squatter," Maureen said.
"And judging by the signs, I don't think they were even worried about
drugs. They wanted the place cleaned up. The whole rest of the block,
it took years, but they've rebuilt after the storm." She shrugged. "They're
trying to work, put the kids through school. Normal-life shit. They're
pissed this last house has been left to rot. Like a reminder."

"Hard to blame them," Atkinson said. "You think he's a gutter
punk?"

"Nah. The clothes weren't right," Maureen said. "I didn't see any
tattoos. And they hardly ever make it this far uptown." She knew Atkinson
was testing her. The detective had already reached her own preliminary
conclusions. "It's not impossible, but I don't think so."

"Tell me, then," Atkinson said, "what you think happened in there."

"My first thought is the obvious one," Maureen said. "Sexual assault,
going by his pants being down. He gets her into the house, whips it out,
she whips out her weapon, previously hidden on her person somewhere,
and slashes him dead."

"Why go into the house with him, then?" Atkinson asked. "Why not
show the weapon before she's trapped?"

"Drugs? They went in the house to get high, he got wrong ideas,
started feeling romantic, got aggressive, and things went bad."

"Possible," Atkinson said. She dropped her cigarette in the street,
crushed it out. "Drugs are always a good place to start. That's no small
wound he's got. Ugly. Whoever cut him got him with something special.
Something she, presuming it is a she, which I'm not sold on, had on her.
Nothing found in the house could do that." Atkinson sucked her teeth.
"I'm not so sure the killer is female. There's some serious strength behind
that cut."

"You could do it," Maureen said.

"I eat. I exercise," Atkinson said. "Sometimes I even sleep. I'm not a spirit in the night like this guy. He wasn't in that house with someone he met at the gym."

Maureen shrugged. "Okay. Same narrative then, only he's in there with some guy. Maybe one of them was tricking. There was no ID, nothing on the body at all. No phone, no money. Maybe he got robbed as well. Looks like it."

Atkinson unleashed a long sigh. Squinting, she gazed over the block. "What's your take on his belt buckle?"

Maureen was surprised at the question. "I hadn't thought about it. Maybe he played high school football and eighty-eight was his jersey number. Or it's his favorite race car driver?"

"High school football?" Atkinson asked.

"He look like college material to you?"

"That's not what I meant," Atkinson said. "I thought you'd know this. In certain circles, eighty-eight means 'Heil Hitler.'"

"Excuse me?"

"It's supposed to be like code," Atkinson said. "The letter 'H' is the eighth letter of the alphabet. So eighty-eight makes 'HH,' or 'Heil Hitler.' It's a way for neo-Nazis and Aryan Brotherhood and any other wannabe groups to signal each other in public. You know, without attracting the attention of someone who might want to punch their teeth down their throat, or cut that throat."

"That's the dumbest thing I ever heard," Maureen said. "Fucking idiot. Well, no wonder he ended up dead, wearing that around here. Heil Hitler. Seriously? I knew there was a reason I didn't like that guy. Even dead he didn't look right."

"You know, you don't have to do that," Atkinson said. "In fact, it might be better if you don't."

"Do what?"

"Decide how you feel about the victims, make judgments on them."

"He was a Nazi, for chrissakes, or at least he wanted certain people to think he was."

"For our professional purposes," Atkinson said, "he is a murder victim first and foremost. You don't need to feel sorry for him, but that's how you need to think of him. That belt buckle is a lead, maybe. We need to figure out what were *this* guy, and whoever he was with, doing on *this* block? It's not like there's *no* white people up this way, but to find this corner of the neighborhood, he'd need help."

"It's second line season," Maureen said. "If he's dead a week, there was a parade last Sunday, too. Either the killer or the dead guy could've scoped the house beforehand."

"That would go a long way to explaining it," Atkinson said. "A second line hookup goes wrong. An accidental meeting. A planned rendezvous. Either one works. Get the guy back to the house, pull a weapon, then the robbery goes wrong. Maybe the vic was the original aggressor, maybe he was thinking rape or robbery. Maybe the killer acted in self-defense. I could roll with the second line playing a part. As a place to start. That introduces lots of possibilities. That's a good thought, Coughlin. Well done."

"There would've been another block party that night, though," Maureen said, "if there was a parade. Somebody might've seen something."

"If that's the case," Atkinson said, "I'm wondering how our boy and whoever he was with made it through the party to the end of the block. Would the people on this block let him get to that house? Though if he and the killer came through late at night, they could've slipped on by. Depends on the parade route, too. Looks like this block went hard tonight. I don't know if that happens two weeks in a row. Could've been quiet last week."

She turned, looking over the large empty lot behind the fence. She rubbed her temples. "This murder happened a week ago. The trail is cold, cold, cold."

"I sense you're not optimistic," Maureen said.

"He's white," Atkinson said, throwing her hands up. "That can excite people. But he's poor white trash, at least at first look." She crossed her forearms into an X. Held her arms up to Maureen. "The white and the poor, they cancel each other out. I'll look at the body after the coroner's cleaned him up and had a chance to poke around on him." She shrugged. "Maybe someone from the block will come forward when their neighbors aren't out watching who's talking to the cops. Maybe someone's been looking for him and we can get a name through Missing Persons. I'll call in his description. Maybe we'll get lucky. Finding out who he is makes finding out who killed him a lot easier."

"Can someone tell me why I need to be here?"

Maureen and Atkinson turned. A man approached them, early thirties, a shade over six feet, slender but soft, flab jiggling under his gray polo shirt as he walked. He had thin, hairy wrists and doughy arms. His brown hair was swept straight back, thinning at the crown. His eyes were light, but dull, like old nickels. His cheeks were sunburned. He wore pressed jeans and alligator loafers with no socks.

Atkinson stepped forward. "That depends on who you are."

"I'm Caleb Heath. I own this house. I own half this block. You know who I am. You called me. You demanded I be here."

"I never demand anything," Atkinson said.

"You told my father that—"

Atkinson raised a finger. "Ah, see. Your father demanded you be here. That's between you and him. I simply asked him to put you in touch with me."

He released a long sigh. "Whoever demanded it, why am I out here in the middle of the night?" He waved his hand behind him at the block. "I see the lights, the sirens, I'm sorry somebody got shot, but I'm not responsible for what these people do. I'm their landlord, not their babysitter."

"Nobody got shot," Atkinson said. "We're here about the empty house."

"Oh, for fuck's sake. So I'm out here over a bunch of weeds?" He raised his hands in a placating gesture. "Look, I'm sorry about this. I don't know who thought y'all needed to make this kind of fuss. Nobody likes their landlord, right? They're trying to make me look bad. I'm in a dispute with the city over this property. Property taxes, back taxes. I won't waste your time explaining it; it's complicated. I can barely follow it myself. But I can't touch the property until the dispute is adjudicated. That's been explained to these people over and over again. I don't have to tell you that nobody listens to what they don't want to hear." He gestured at the house. "You see how these people have vandalized my property. These signs. I should be the one calling you. I'm following the law."

"Were you renting this place?" Atkinson asked.

"Excuse me? I said I own it."

"Did you have a tenant at this location."

"Does it look like I do?" Heath asked, laughing. "I understand. You have to ask."

"Maybe you hired someone," Atkinson said. "To hang around here, keep an eye on the place. Since you were so concerned about vandalism."

"No, no, I didn't," Heath said. "Who would I hire to do that? Who would I know that would live in a place like this, on this block?"

"Did any of the complaints you got have to do with squatters or vagrants using the house?" Atkinson asked.

"I don't know," Heath said, holding up a hand as if to ward off more questions. "You'd have to ask my people. They handle the specifics. I run a big corporation. I don't handle the minutiae."

Maureen stepped to Atkinson's side. She looked down at her notepad. "A Mrs. Hunter three doors up, a tenant of yours, of your big corporation, she said she called the management office three times this week about the awful smell coming from that house."

"You lost me," Heath said, his gaze fixed on Atkinson.

"We're not here for the weeds," Atkinson said. "Or for the signs. I'm Detective Sergeant Christine Atkinson. I'm a homicide detective. We're pulling a dead body out of your house as we speak. It's been in there at least a week. That's why we're here."

Heath leaned back, his weight on his heels, looking over at the green cottage, his wet bottom lip curling down over his chin like a miniature of the fat roll hanging over his belt. "Oh, well, I certainly didn't kill anyone. We can agree on that. Anyone in that house was trespassing." He sounded amused, and relieved, Maureen noted, like he'd gotten the news that someone else's dog had shit in the neighbor's garden.

"So trespassing is a capital offense?" Maureen asked.

Heath looked at her for a long moment, as if she'd spoken to him in a language he'd never heard. He turned to Atkinson. "Can I go now?"

"Officer Coughlin," Atkinson said. "You were first on the scene. You did a significant part of the canvass. Have you any questions for Mr. Heath?"

Maureen flipped through the pages of her notebook, just to delay Heath's departure. "What's the name of your company?"

"Heath Design and Construction."

"No, that's your daddy's company," Atkinson said. "What's yours, the one that handles the rentals? Or do I need to go to your father for that?"

Heath said nothing. Maureen watched the red blotches surface on his throat. She couldn't quite read if it was anger or humiliation. With men, it was hard to tell the difference. She wasn't sure there was a difference. He would not look at either of the women.

"It does have a name," Atkinson asked, "does it not? Or should I call your daddy for it?"

"CHR," Heath replied. "Caleb Heath Residential. It's part of my father's company, a full part, an offshoot, they're really the same company—"

"I'm sure it's very complicated," Atkinson said, waving away his explanation. "I'm sure we wouldn't understand." She turned to Maureen. "Anything else, Officer?"

"No," Maureen said. "There's nothing more I need from him. Thanks, Mr. Heath. You've been very helpful. Anything else we need, we'll send for you again."

Heath looked both women up and down, stuffing his hands in his pockets. "My tax dollars hard at work."

He turned and walked away.

"You know that guy?" Maureen asked.

"Only by his reputation," Atkinson said. "Which, of course, is lousy. His father's the one everyone knows. He built the Harmony Oaks development, built the River Garden where the St. Thomas used to be. I'd bet anything, Heath Design and Construction is building at least a part of whatever will replace the Iberville projects by the Quarter. And they're building the new jail. Anything that hooks into city, state, and federal construction dollars, Solomon Heath has his hands in it. He redefines mixed income. His income comes from a wide range of sources." She shrugged. "Though, from what I hear about him, Solomon is a pretty decent human being."

Atkinson lifted her chin in Caleb Heath's direction. "I get the feeling the heir isn't quite living up to the expectations of the king, in the business or any other way. He never has. I think managing these small properties is supposed to teach him something. Whatever it is, he's not learning it."

Maureen watched Caleb make his way up the block. She waited for another urine-laden missile to arc out of the darkness in his direction. Were it her on the rooftop, she thought, she would take the shot. But nobody did. None of the people on the block, Maureen noticed, paid any attention to Caleb Heath. It took her a moment to realize why. Nobody recognized him. No one on the block, not the people who paid him rent, not their neighbors had ever seen him in person. He was just another well-dressed white guy at the scene of a crime. Hell, Maureen thought, if they noticed him at all, they probably took him for a cop.

3

Later that same night, walking through the wash of blue light emanating from her patrol car's light bar, Maureen approached a battered, dirty white pickup truck from behind. Sweat trickled down the back of her neck. Three lanes of Claiborne Avenue traffic whooshed by her left shoulder, the cars running close and fast despite the late hour, ruffling her uniform sleeve. People drove with their windows down. Laughter, cigarette smoke, and hip-hop bass notes cascaded through the air around her. The citywide Saints party rolled on. Hangovers would abound in the morning.

In her left hand, she held a flashlight at shoulder height. Her right hand rested on her weapon. Her heart beat high in her rib cage, pulsing hard and steady against her breastbone like fists on a speed bag, adrenaline charging her blood. These were her favorite moments. She licked her lips. The approach, the anticipation, an energy throbbing inside her that she could only describe, were she ever to share the sensation, as carnal.

When she'd first spied the pickup, her heart had jumped into her throat and she'd hit the lights. She'd been parked on the concrete apron of a Claiborne Avenue gas station, keeping half an eye on the traffic as she updated her paperwork from the Magnolia Street incident on the cruiser's laptop. The truck was the wrong vehicle on the wrong street at the wrong time of night. Obvious. She'd felt that right away, it was just so *wrong*, as wrong as the body she'd found earlier that night. *Always mind the anomaly*, Preacher, her training officer and current duty sergeant, had taught her. She'd pulled over the white pickup with this advice in mind. Of course, *anomaly* hadn't been Preacher's word, Maureen thought with a smile, closing in on the truck. He called it the *Sesame Street* rule: one of these things is not like the others. Her job was to find out why and decide what to do about it.

As she approached, she identified the motionless heads in the cab of the pickup truck as a man and a woman, the man driving. She'd run the plates from her patrol car. They'd come back registered to one of the more rural river parishes southwest of New Orleans. Not a common sight around town, but nothing suspicious about that fact, either.

Maureen watched the driver's reflection in the truck's side-view mirror. His eyes watched her. His hands gripped the steering wheel at ten and two, like the hands on a clock. He was a redhead, his hair cut military short, his hairline receded. He had a crooked nose several times broken, red cheeks, and small, angry dark eyes. A fat diamond stud glittered in his left ear.

"Wait on a Code Four," Maureen said, calling in to the dispatch officer. "Show me on the twenty-one hundred block of Claiborne, near Jackson Avenue, lake side."

Dispatch agreed. Maureen's channel would stay open in case she needed to call for backup. For the moment, she felt she had the situation handled. No need to make it more than it was. The line between being smart and showing fear, it was so thin.

She played the flashlight beam over the Toyota pickup, the "Y" and the "O" colored in black paint on the rusted tailgate to highlight the *YO*.

The dirty plate hung by one corner, the lightbulb above it broken or burned out. Faded Confederate battle flag stickers, one of which read, *These colors don't run*, were pasted askew on the back bumper. She thought of the dead body in the Magnolia Street house and his belt buckle. But those colors do bleed, buddy, Maureen thought. In the bed of the pickup was a red ten-speed bike, a bell and a rusty basket on the handlebars, spots of rust peppering the frame like chicken pox scars. A cheap cable lock snaked around the frame. A plastic bag had been tied over the seat to protect it from rain.

She approached the driver's side window and rapped on the glass with her knuckle. "Evening, sir."

The driver hand-cranked the window down. His forehead was shiny with sweat. Red pimples dotted his hairline. He wore a top-of-the-line, custom gold Saints jersey, two sizes too big for him. A thick platinum chain draped over the front of the jersey. He reminded Maureen of a man in a costume, or a boy in his big brother's clothes. He was a pale imitation, very pale, she realized, of the men who'd laughed at her on Magnolia Street.

The stale, acrid smell of discount cigarettes mingled with the tang of body odor floated from the cab. Maureen blinked at the funk, as if someone had blown smoke in her eyes. She surveyed the passenger, a skinny white woman with long greasy brown hair that curtained her face. She sat with her bony shoulders slumped and her hands squeezed between her knees. She wore loose black jeans and a plain blue T-shirt.

No weapons in plain sight. Nothing within easy reach of the passengers.

No one in the car said a word. No one moved. Maureen tried again. "Evening, y'all."

The driver's eyes flicked over to Maureen, then back to his hands on the steering wheel. "I wasn't speeding," the driver said.

"I never said you were."

"I'm not drunk."

"Never said you were that, either," Maureen said.

She smelled alcohol on the driver's breath. Not cheap beer, which she'd expected, but something sickly sweet, like he'd been eating rum-infused lollipops, or drinking those candied cocktails sold by the quart on Bourbon Street. Makes sense, she thought, throwing a glance along Claiborne toward downtown. They were coming from the direction of the Quarter when she'd pulled them over. It was half past three in the morning. The drive-through joints along Claiborne were long closed. And she didn't smell fast food coming from the car or the driver. No bars around. Nowhere to eat. What were they doing out here?

And the neighborhood they were in, black, working class to poor, Maureen thought, it wasn't the place to cruise around showing off your rebel flags and your red necks. Was the man taking the woman some-where? Was that why they were headed into the darker and quieter neigh-borhoods? Where numerous empty and neglected houses remained, like the one that had just coughed up a body. Start at the beginning, she told herself. Don't spook them. And mind the anomaly.

"Anything to drink tonight, sir?"

"I already told you that."

"Answer the question I've asked, please. Have you had anything to drink tonight?"

"No," the driver said.

The lie was no surprise. "Y'all a little lost?"

"We're not in a free country anymore?" the driver asked, leaning for-ward. "Can't go where we want? We gotta check in? This Afghanistan or America? We gotta go through the checkpoint?"

Maureen shined her light in the driver's eyes. "Relax, and shut up with that shit."

The woman's body, Maureen noticed when the driver spoke, had tightened like a mouse caught in the open, hoping the owl in the tree hadn't seen. Classic anticipation-of-violence reaction. Maureen's adren-aline surged again. Had she interrupted a kidnapping? Prevented a rape?

Maybe even prevented another house with fly-covered windows? The driver pumped a bad energy into the air. Maureen could feel it on her skin like static electricity.

The driver leaned to his right, reaching for the glove box.

"Whoa, whoa. Don't fucking move," Maureen yelled, taking half a step back from the car, reaching for her weapon. "What the fuck are you doing?"

The driver raised his hands. He squinted in the beam of the flashlight. "The paperwork. Registration, insurance. You're gonna need it, right? Ain't that how this bullshit goes?"

"When I need it," Maureen said, "I'll fucking ask for it. Sit back, put your hands in your lap, and don't fucking move. Right now, that's how this goes. The way I *say* it goes."

He had the tiniest curl of a smile at one corner of his mouth. His diamond glinted in the light. He'd enjoyed scaring her.

"Driver, your license, from your wallet, please. Slow."

The man pulled a squashed nylon-and-Velcro wallet from his back pocket. Maureen took note. Not exactly a match for his jewelry. He found his license, handed it over. Maureen studied it under her flashlight. Clayton Gage. The photo was him. In it he wore a collared shirt, no earring. Looked miserable, and a lot younger. He had more hair. According to the birthdate, he was in his mid-thirties. Hard living had taken its toll. The license was expired. She'd gotten a different name when she'd run the pickup's registration. That name was Jackson Gage.

"This your truck, Mr. Gage?"

"It is not," Gage said. "Not technically. Not according to you, I guess. It's registered to my father. But it's really mine. I paid for it."

Maureen heard a strange murmur from inside the truck. The woman had started singing to herself, more formless sounds than discernible words. Gage pressed back against his seat, as if instead of singing the woman emitted heat or a foul odor. The woman squeezed her hands even tighter between her knees, her face hidden behind the veil of dirty hair. Maureen wasn't sure the woman even knew she was making sounds.

"Ma'am? Are you okay?" Maureen asked.

"My girl," Gage said, turning back to Maureen, faking a smile. "Had a bit too much to drink watching the game. I picked her up in the Quarter. I'm taking her home." Another small, false smile. Like her attitude would change because he'd come to the aid of a helpless female. Mr. Gage, Maureen thought, you are a fucking terrible liar.

The situation stank, she thought, of things worse than booze and cheap cigarettes and body odor. Of false and hidden things. Drugs, had to be. Sex and the violence involved in getting it for a man like this. Only drugs and sex brought a pair like this together. She keyed her radio mic. "Dispatch, this is fourteen-twelve."

"Go ahead, fourteen-twelve."

"Be advised, I'll need assistance with that traffic stop. One vehicle, two individuals. White male, and a white female. Multiple violations."

"Ten-four, fourteen-twelve."

Gage rocked in his seat, glaring at the woman. "Jesus fucking Christ. Y'all are all the same."

"Eyes front," Maureen said. "She's not who put you here."

"No," Gage said, "that'd be you."

Maureen stepped away from the pickup. She should wait on searching the truck until she had more hands and eyes available to her. Just keep the situation under control. Don't let things escalate. Maureen tucked Gage's license in the pocket of her uniform shirt. She should make Gage sit there and stew. Then again, that woman seemed pretty frightened of him. Was it fair to make her sit there with him? She looked up and down Claiborne Avenue. And as for her part, Maureen thought, she didn't feel like waiting for the menfolk to arrive and commandeer her traffic stop. There'd be talk of how two half-in-the-bag rednecks had made her skittish. She was a woman. She was new on the force and in town. Like on Magnolia Street, like everywhere else, when she called for backup she'd better be dealing with a weapon or a body or an angry mob, she needed a better reason than *I was afraid*.

"Out of the truck, the both of you," Maureen said, gesturing with her hand. "Leave the keys in the vehicle. Mr. Gage, assume the position against the hood. Nice and easy. Ma'am, you come stand beside the door here."

No one moved.

"You wanna tell us what for?" Gage asked. "We got rights."

"Now," Maureen said, gesturing with her flashlight. "Out of the car. Let's go. That's an order."

Gage stepped out of the truck one long leg at a time, insectoid in his movements. Maureen half expected four more legs to follow the first two. He was almost sickly thin. Gage took his time moving to the front of the car, glancing around the neighborhood as if he were a tourist stretching his legs after a long drive. Instead of assuming the position with his palms flat against the hood, a posture Maureen was sure he knew, Gage crossed his arms and leaned against the grille, expelling a dramatic sigh. Maureen decided to let him have his moment of defiance, for the time being.

The woman had not moved.

"Can you please exit the vehicle?" Maureen said to her.

No direct response, though the singing had resumed.

"I told you," Gage said, over his shoulder. "She's completely wasted. She'll puke on you."

"Shut the fuck up," Maureen said. So much for his moment. "Turn to face my direction and put your hands on the hood of the car where I can see them." She turned her attention back to the woman, waved her flashlight at her. The woman refused to look over. "Out of the car, ma'am. Now."

No response. Maureen was losing her patience.

She moved to the front of the truck. Gage had not done as he was told. "Hands on the hood of the truck, sir. Now. For your own safety."

Grinning, puffing out his chest, Gage set his hands flat on the hood behind him, as if to push himself up to sit on it. His face was less than a foot from Maureen's. She hooked a hard right into his solar plexus, followed it with a quick left. His knees crumpled and he gasped.

While he was off balance, she turned him around and grabbing a fistful of his Saints jersey, shoved his face hard into the rusty hood of the pickup. She kicked his feet apart to widen his stance. Palming the back of his skull, she bounced his forehead off the hood.

"This is your field sobriety test, Mr. Gage, and you are fucking failing." She bounced his head again on the truck's hood, for emphasis, but not hard enough, she hoped, to leave a mark. She released her grip on him, stepping back. "Stay."

Being the only cop on the scene had its risks, she thought, but it also had its advantages.

Maureen looked into the truck. The woman appeared to be watching her through the windshield. She wasn't singing anymore.

Gage stayed as Maureen had left him, breathing hard. "I can't believe you fucking did that." He sounded almost amused. "Y'all cops are all the same."

"You'd rather be Tased?"

"No."

"Excuse me?"

"No, ma'am."

"*Officer* will do fine." She patted him down. "Any weapons or contraband, sir? Anything sharp or dangerous that might injure me?"

"No, Officer."

"Don't talk. Don't move."

Maureen returned to the pickup's cab. She leaned into it. "Ma'am, I need you out here with us. Now, please. Right now. Let's move this along."

The woman sniffled, dragging her forearm under her nose. She inched her way along the bench toward the open door. Maureen figured her treatment of Gage had been persuasive. The woman stepped from the truck and slumped against it, jamming her hands into her pockets. She never raised her head to look at Maureen.

"Please keep your hands away from your pockets," Maureen said.

The woman complied, letting her thin arms dangle at her sides. No tattoos, no track marks, Maureen noticed. Not much of anything but skin and bones.

"Mr. Gage," Maureen called out. "Anything in this truck I should know about? Anything I'd be interested in?"

"How the fuck should I know what you're interested in?" Gage replied. "Other than breaking balls." He spat blood on the pavement. "You got no probable cause, anyways. I ain't stupid."

Gage was brave and noncompliant, Maureen noted, as long as he was out of arm's reach. He'd been the kind of kid, she figured, that taunted from the edge of the schoolyard, that taunted girls only when he was surrounded and protected by other boys.

"Yeah, you are stupid," Maureen said, moving to the front of the truck, where she spoke into Gage's ear. "You stink like booze and weed. Your whole truck's a goddamn moving violation. Scratch that, it's a rolling fucking felony. And your escape strategy is to fuck with me? Maybe it's time I call the canine unit? We can go that way, if you want."

"Typical fucking fascist New Orleans cop," Gage said, a growl creeping into his voice. "You oughtta have a German shepherd to sic on people. It fits."

Maureen couldn't tell what he hated about her more, that she was a cop or that she was a woman. But he hated her. She was cool with that.

"This is what I get for doin' you a favor," Gage said, "for taking this sad drunk crazy lady home safe before she gets victimized."

Maureen circled around Gage's back, leaning into his face. "So you were lying to me with that girlfriend bullshit. Why would you do that? How do you really know this woman?"

Gage blew out his breath, as if Maureen's bad attitude caused him physical pain. He settled his forehead on the hood of the truck. Maureen hoped he'd finally accepted that she wasn't impressed with him, that she wasn't going away, and that this situation wasn't ending anytime soon. She hoped he'd realized that she was in charge.

"The truth," Maureen said, "is that you met this woman tonight, didn't you? Does she know who you are? Does she know where you were taking her?" She paused. She felt her temper rising. "She doesn't, does she? What'd you slip her? What's she on?"

"I ain't telling you nothing," Gage said into the hood of the truck. "Not another thing."

"So you're saying I should arrest you both," she said, "because that's when the Miranda rights and the lawyers get involved."

"I refuse to recognize your authority over me," Gage said. "You are the agent of an illegitimate and hostile government and I refuse to recognize your false authority. Fuck you and fuck lawyers."

"The war's over, motherfucker," Maureen said, shaking her head. "Your side lost." She pulled out her cuffs. "Here's my authority right here." She'd see how serious Gage was. She bent one arm behind his back, waiting for him to resist, hoping deep inside that he would, because he had the cruel stink of a bully on him and she wanted to do him real damage. If he fought, she'd have her excuse. But he didn't fight her; he let her cuff him. She was disappointed. And relieved. She knew she'd pushed things about as far as she could.

"Stay where you are, you little rebel, you."

Starting on the driver's side, she searched the inside of the pickup's cab. Right there in the console sat confirmation of her candy cocktail theory. Two tall green paper cups from Pat O'Brien's in the Quarter, but instead of bright red hurricane, the cups were half full of purple drank, a potent and debilitating mix of codeine crushed up in cough syrup. Two counts of open container in a vehicle, at least, right there, along with possession. Continuing her search, she found old food wrappers, soda cans, and empty cigarette packs. Cigarette butts. An ancient pack of Zig-Zag rolling papers and a three-pack of condoms. A couple of unpaid parking tickets. Under the trash, she spotted the leather handles of a woman's handbag peeking out from under the bench.

She leaned deeper into the truck and yanked the bag out from under the seat. It was a stained and faded denim tote with big fake leather handles, about the size of a diaper bag. Oh, Lord, Maureen thought, don't tell me there's a kid mixed up in this. But when she looked inside the bag, instead of diapers or baby toys Maureen found eight or ten smaller and much more expensive handbags, clutches, and thin-strapped purses.

Stolen, she knew, every one of them. "Dispatch, unit fourteen-twelve here."

"Go ahead, fourteen-twelve."

"Have we had a run on purse snatchings tonight? Maybe in the Eighth District, most likely the Quarter?"

"Hold on, please."

This batch looked stolen from the same party. Something formal, or semiformal, at least. Maureen wondered how either of the two people in her custody gained access to a party like that. More likely the thefts had occurred at the after-party, the women hitting a bar or club in the Quarter, like Pat O'Brien's, hazy and giddy with booze and who knew what else. Gage wasn't the snatching type. His type shoplifted, or stole packages off of old ladies' front steps. The woman was the thief. That big denim bag wouldn't attract any attention slung over her shoulder. Maureen wondered if Gage was in on it. Maybe he'd put her up to it. Even without tracks on her arms, she had that pale junkie sheen to her. She could smoke it or snort it or shoot it into the gaps between her toes. Maybe she had pills of her own that she took. Meth. Something. Maybe Gage had her stealing for a fix. Trade her some purple drank for the cash and cards in the bag. A good deal if she was hard up and dope sick.

Maureen's radio crackled as dispatch came on the line.

"Fourteen-twelve, be advised the Eighth District duty sergeant reports at this time a lobby full of angry coeds in formal wear. Seems there was a near riot at Pat O'Brien's after a sorority social. A bunch of purses went missing in the courtyard. Please advise."

Maureen smiled. "I've recovered the missing items, and I have a couple of suspects. I'll have some people in custody. Ask the sisters to sit tight."

"Affirmative, fourteen-twelve. You'll have some friends in Alpha Epsilon Pi."

"Just what I've always wanted," Maureen said.

She walked the bag over to the woman. "Is this yours?"

The woman said nothing.

"This blue bag," she said to the woman, in a lower, calmer voice, "is this yours?"

The woman slid down the side of the pickup, sitting on the pavement, her arms wrapped around her chest.

"Ma'am?" Maureen said. "Did this man hurt you? Did he force you to steal? Did he force you into the truck?" Maureen squatted beside the woman. "You can tell me. You're not getting back in the truck with him. He's going to jail tonight."

The woman said nothing, pressing her forehead into her knees.

Frustrated, Maureen walked back to her unit, leaving the woman where she sat. She tossed the bag on the passenger seat. She lit a cigarette as two NOPD units, one a beat-up patrol car like hers, the other a newer Bronco, a rank car, light bars flashing on both, parked behind hers.

Now she had numbers on her side, Maureen thought. Now the fun would start.

4

From the Bronco stepped Preacher Boyd, duty sergeant on the night tour, a rotund, green-eyed Creole who was a thirty-year vet on the job and twenty years Maureen's senior. She was surprised to see him. He wasn't often out on the streets. He hitched up his ill-fitting pants and, after easing the truck door closed, headed her way. In the second unit rode Quinn and Ruiz. They lit cigarettes and leaned on the hood of their unit, waiting for Maureen and Preacher to decide what would happen next.

"I was on my way to the St. Charles Tavern," Preacher said. "Chicken fried steak there with my name on it." He cupped his hand at his ear. "But then I heard the call, and I had to see what fourteen-twelve had cooking."

Maureen watched Preacher study the pickup truck and its two former occupants, adding up the details in his head. He caught Maureen's eyes and grinned at her.

"Officer Coughlin," he said, "you been out racial profiling white boys again? I thought we'd spoke on such things."

Maureen approached. "They call to me, Preach. Like chicken fried steak."

Preacher pulled his flashlight from his belt, played the beam over the truck, shined Gage in the eyes until he groaned in complaint, blinking at the light. "A real stunner, that one." He looked at the woman. "What about her?"

"Catatonic, it seems," Maureen said. "Almost nonresponsive. Though I can't tell if it's trauma or drugs or her natural state."

Preacher walked over to the woman. Hands on his thighs, he leaned a few inches in her direction, the closest he came to bending over.

"Can you stand?" Preacher asked. He turned to Maureen, a quizzical look on his face. "Her lips are purple."

"In the car," Maureen said. "Purple drank."

"Ah. Ma'am, you high? Are you on drugs?"

"No, sir."

"Can you stand for me, please?"

The woman stood.

Fucking Preacher, Maureen thought. Everyone talked to him. Everyone. The dealers and stick-up boys and wife-beaters he had cuffed facedown on the sidewalk, the Uptown hipsters and riot grrls making his po'boys and his coffee. She'd arrested guys, from hard-core thugs and gang bangers to fey and cheery male prostitutes, who asked after him as she drove them to lockup. People didn't always tell him the truth, but they talked to him. Getting people talking was a skill Maureen knew she needed to cultivate, for her current work on the streets and certainly for the future if she wanted a shot at making detective someday. People got their backs up around her—women especially. She needed subtler tools than barked threats and profanity, than her newfound muscle and fists and her boots and her Taser.

Back when she'd been a waitress, she'd charmed the shit out of people, men and women alike. She'd been a champion flirt. But bright red lipstick and a short skirt weren't available to her anymore. As a cop, she'd struggled to connect on the streets and around the district, and it frustrated her. She'd changed when she'd put down the drink tray, moved to New Orleans, and picked up the badge, which was what she wanted. Becoming someone else in this strange, new place had been the entirety of her plan. She felt questions forming, though, rising like mist off the river, about who and what she was becoming. And she knew Preacher and the other cops around her saw her growing pains. She worried she wasn't learning fast enough to fit in. She worried she enjoyed the violence more than she should, and that others, cops and criminals alike, could tell. She hoped Preacher wouldn't look too closely at Gage's forehead. She didn't want to be the one the others whispered about in the hallways, the girl with the bad reputation. She'd been that once before. She hadn't cared then. She cared now.

"Have you been abused," Preacher asked the woman from the truck, "or traumatized in any way? Tonight, at least."

"I'm fine," the woman said, her voice a raspy whisper. "I'm tired. I wanna go home."

"Don't we all. So you're the quiet type. What's your name, darlin'?"

The woman nodded her head. She half smiled at Preacher, her cracked lips trembling as she showed discolored teeth. "Madison. Madison Leary."

"Can you wait for us a few more minutes, Miss Leary?" Preacher said. "Just a few things to sort out."

As Madison Leary chewed a thumbnail, looking out over dirty knuckles and greasy bangs, Maureen studied her, seeing her eyes for the first time. They were two different colors, one eye antifreeze blue, the other a deep emerald. One eye, the blue one, seemed to emanate light, the green to swallow it back down the well. Creases cut deep into their corners. Alive and sharp, quivering like small living creatures balanced in the palm of a hand, Leary's eyes contradicted her loose-limbed, rag-doll body language. Her nose was small, peppered with blackheads. The corners of her mouth were cracked. The left corner bled. Leary poked at the blood with the tip of her pale tongue. She could've been twenty. She could've been forty.

"But can I get my bag back?" Leary asked.

"Yeah, about that," Maureen said. A chill shook her. "That's one of those things we need to sort out. Preacher, join me at my car a minute."

Gage called out from the front of the truck. "What about me?"

Preacher laughed. "Holy shit, son, we forgot you were even there. You coulda wandered off and we'd've been none the wiser. Officer Coughlin?"

Maureen raised her flashlight, flickering the beam at Quinn and Ruiz to get their attention. They tossed their smokes into the street and walked over.

"Where y'at, OC?" Quinn said.

"Can you hook that one up?" she asked. "I gotta handle her." She dug Gage's ID from her uniform shirt, handed it to Quinn. "Clayton Gage. Take him to lockup?"

Quinn glanced at the license, raised a pale eyebrow. "Charges?"

"Open container in a vehicle, DUI, narcotics, and possession of stolen property to start," Maureen said, "and depending on what else she says about how she got in the truck, maybe something more serious."

"You give a field sobriety test?" Quinn asked.

"Technically, no," Maureen said.

"So no Breathalyzer, either?"

"Feel free," Maureen said. "You want the stats, make it happen. But that means you get the paperwork."

"He gonna hurl in our unit?" Ruiz asked. "I'll leave him curbside, white boy or not, 'hood or no 'hood."

"Fuck it," Quinn said. "Whatever. We're already in OT for this week." He held out his fist. Ruiz, nodding silently, bumped it with his own fist. "We like to keep it simple in the Sixth. You know how we do, Cogs. Living the dream." Quinn turned to his partner. "Rue, pull the car around, homes, while I make the arrangements."

As Ruiz walked to the patrol car, Quinn, twirling one finger in the air, headed for the front of the pickup. "Assume it, dog fucker."

Gage didn't seem surprised at Quinn's orders. He didn't protest, didn't reject their authority. Fucking men. They crabbed about their rights when a woman asked for simple shit, but now that the men were here, Maureen thought, everyone behaved. Not a peep about getting arrested. But she's the fascist. Typical, she thought.

"Come to the car with me," she said to Preacher.

They walked to the unit. She grabbed the denim tote from the passenger seat. "This is her bag. It's jammed with other ladies' bags, stolen, most likely from a sorority party at Pat O's. I already talked to the Eighth about it."

"She's definitely good for it?"

"No doubt. Can you see Gage purse-snatching and getting away with ten bags? Woman like Madison, skinny, plain, poor, she's invisible everywhere she goes."

"What's she doing with that winner?" Preacher asked.

"I couldn't get a thing from her," Maureen said, watching Quinn and Ruiz load Gage into their unit. Prisoner secure, Quinn and Ruiz lit another round of cigarettes and leaned against their cruiser. Lean and smoke. It was what they did best. "I got two different stories from Gage already. I don't believe either of them. I'd like to get one from her, but she's giving me nothing. And I was nice. I promise."

"Something ain't right with her," Preacher said. "It's like there's this hum coming off her. And those crazy eyes. Weird. Had a dog with those once. That dog was crazy crazy. Saw ghosts. I'd swear to it."

"I don't want her back in that truck," Maureen said. "I want Quinn and Ruiz to take Gage in, and I'll take Madison in. If she's out stealing, if she's an addict, I can't put her back on the street knowing that. If we lock her up, even just for the night, sober her up, then maybe we can pin her down and get some answers about what Gage was up to."

"Suit yourself," Preacher said. "It's your traffic stop."

Maureen walked to the truck, leaned against it beside Madison. She pulled her cigarette pack from her pocket, offered one to Madison, who declined. Maureen lit up.

"That man giving you a ride home, Madison?" Maureen asked. "Is that true?"

"Bike had a flat," Madison said. "I wanna get that back, too. I want a receipt from you for the bike. And for my handbag."

"Did you ask for a ride or did he offer?" Maureen asked. "Did he make you get in the truck? How'd you meet him?"

In her periphery, she could see Preacher shaking his head. She could hear his voice in her head: *One question at a time, Coughlin. Let her answer.*

"You been in legal trouble before?" Maureen asked.

Madison shrugged. "I avoid cops as best I can."

"You wanna tell us about that denim bag, Madison? You wanna tell us about the other bags inside it? They yours? How'd you get them?"

"I fucking stole them, you dumb bitch. Jesus. This your first fucking day?" She turned, leaning her temple against the roof of the truck. She crossed her wrists at the small of her back. "You gonna take me in or what? I won't make you whack me around, like you did him. Let's get going. I gotta pee."

Maureen took Preacher's cuffs from his outstretched hands. "My pleasure."

"I fucked him," Madison said, licking again at the bleeding corner of her mouth, eyeing Maureen over her shoulder. "Made his eyes roll back in his head like he was struck by lightning. He nearly bit my titty off."

"I'm so proud." Maureen cuffed Madison. Usually the gears clicking excited her. Locking the cuffs on Gage had made the hairs on her arms stand up. Right then, though, what she felt was thin tendrils of guilt squirming in her gut. She led Madison by the chains to the unit. Preacher opened the door to the backseat.

"In that tiny truck," Maureen said. "That's some Cirque du Soleil shit, for sure. You're a fucking miracle worker." She palmed the top of Madison's skull, squeezing. "Watch your head." She lowered Madison into the unit.

"You believe that shit?" Maureen asked, slamming the car door shut.

"I been a cop in New Orleans for thirty years," Preacher said. "I believe everything."

"Can you wait here for the tow truck?" Maureen asked. "I would, but you know she will absolutely piss herself in my car. Just to aggravate me."

"You even call for it yet?"

"Not yet."

Preacher sighed. "You ain't even mine to train no more, Coughlin, and still you try me."

Maureen pulled the denim tote from the patrol car. She held it up. "There's a crowd of drunk co-eds in fancy clothes over at the Eighth waiting for these. I'll let you be the hero."

Preacher touched his index finger to his chin. "This a face that gives a fuck about college girls? Get a grip, Coughlin. I'll call it in, but then I'm going to the St. Charles Tavern, get some steak and eggs. I'll make Quinn and Ruiz wait for the truck and let you make it up to them later. You get rid of Miss America here and drop off the bags in time, join me at the Tavern. If not, I'll see you back at the district for shift change. Make sure your prisoner is squared away."

Maureen tossed the bag in the car. "Don't say I never tried doing you a favor."

Preacher slipped a cigar from his pocket. He unwrapped it, crumpling the plastic and tossing it in the street. "You better get going with her, you don't want a mess on your hands. She really did fuck that boy, I wouldn't wanna be the poor slob that's gotta inventory that truck at impound. Who knows what went where and what happened when it got there."

"If she fucked that moron," Maureen said, "I'm glad I'm not the one who's gotta inventory *her* at lockup."

5

The next afternoon, the rain slowed in time with her pace as Maureen jogged to the corner of Constance and Sixth Streets. As if dispersed by the wave of a magic wand, the rain clouds vanished. The sunshine tumbled down, brilliant, wet light, golden with a weight of its own. The heat returned like fog, rolling in off the river heavy and thick with moisture. Sweat mixed with rainwater trickled down her forehead and into her eyes. She wiped her face with her T-shirt, soaked from the run and the rainstorm.

Fall and its hard-earned break from the heat were coming, she told herself. She could catch traces of the change of seasons in the night breezes, a coolness that lingered on her skin for moments before vanishing. Coworkers had promised her the heat always broke. She was plenty ready for the end of her first New Orleans summer, the end of her first hurricane season. It was like counting down the days until Christmas

Across the street, a small black girl, six or seven years old, wearing pink shorts and a matching sleeveless pink top, pedaled a pink-and-white tricycle up and down the cracked and buckled brick sidewalk, her hair tied up in a riot of braids, her forehead glistening with sweat, her face scrunched in determined concentration. Maureen knew that look. The little girl's fists gripped the handlebars as she worked her bike to the corner, where she turned around and struggled back the other way. Maureen wondered what mission was under way in the little girl's head, what story unfolded.

Maureen leaned forward to stretch her hamstrings, her palms flat on the damp sidewalk. Drops of perspiration fell from her face onto the concrete. Winding bright green vines, their tiny white flowers winking from among the leaves, hung over the wrought-iron fence in front of her. She closed her eyes and inhaled their scent. Exotic. Tropical. Better than anything she encountered at work most days, though every now and again, when she slowed the unit to give some shady knucklehead the stink eye, the scent of frying chicken or a simmering pot of red beans would hit the car as hard as an ocean wave and knock her almost off balance.

She opened her eyes, leaning forward with her hands on her knees. A tiny face materialized at eye level in the vines. A small, thin lizard colored the same bright green as the leaves watched her sideways with one swiveling eye. His eye fixed on her, the lizard puffed out the bright red pouch at his chin. He did three quick push-ups on his front legs and flicked his tail.

No, this was definitely not Staten Island, Maureen thought, where she had grown up and lived her whole life until eight months ago. Not any place near or like it, which was the thing she loved about New Orleans the most. Steeped in the past as decadent ol' New Orleans was, it wasn't her past.

A light sun shower started. Just because the sun was shining didn't mean it couldn't rain. Maureen stood up straight, tilting her face to the rain, pressing her hands into the small of her back. When she moved, the lizard disappeared in a flash into the foliage.

On the other side of the fence, tall stalks of red-flowering ginger rose above the broad leaves of elephant ears. Several other green, fast-growing and flowering things, the names of which Maureen had yet to learn, formed a dense, chaotic garden swarming with dragonflies, glinting emerald bodies hovering on red-veined wings. In the middle of the garden, two plastic, wire-legged flamingos, one black and one gold, stood watch over a ceramic grotto of Drew Brees. Her own personal Breesus. The Saints. She was a fan now. A girl who'd never had more than a passing interest in team sports, New Orleans had made short work of her. That her deadbeat father had been a rabid Jets fan, she thought, had probably only helped her into the arms of another team.

Football season's opening Sunday, she'd found herself in Parasol's bar at noon wearing a brand-new Pierre Thomas jersey and screaming at the TV along with the rest of her neighborhood. There wasn't a social activity she'd ever found that asked less of her. Wear the right colors. Holler the right names. Learn the "Who Dat" chant. Talk about the big plays at work with the other cops. Maureen found the communal game watching scratched her itch to fit in, to belong in New Orleans, a feeling as new to her as her interest in football.

The house she rented was a tiny shotgun single. The rooms ran in a row, front to back. She loved the exterior colors the landlords had picked: eggplant-purple walls with bright orange shutters that closed over the lone front window and the front door, tomato-red steps leading up to the baby-blue porch. It was as vibrant and conspicuous a place as she had ever lived, and a stark contrast to the grim, tumbledown Staten Island apartment she'd left behind. And, she thought, to the tumbledown abodes Caleb Heath rented out on Magnolia Street. She half expected her house to one day sprout canary-yellow wagon wheels and roll away in pursuit of the parade that had left it behind—because the place looked exactly like Maureen's idea of an old-time circus wagon.

Inside, the house was clean and sedate. Walls and ceiling painted a quiet off-white. Bare wood floors the color of honey. The structure was original, the freestanding fireplace between the rooms, the high ceilings, the tall windows. It had been built more than a hundred years ago for and by Irish immigrants, dirt-poor people who landed on and then worked the docks and wharves of the nearby Mississippi, people with the same roots as Maureen's own New York–settled ancestors.

One of the owners had been born in the house, Maureen had learned, in what was now *her* bedroom. His mother had been born there, too, in that same room. She had died in the place less than a year ago, which was how it had come up for rent after a long renovation. The old woman died in the same bed where she'd given birth to her only son fifty-some years ago. Maureen now slept where they had slept. When insomnia tormented her, as it often did, she let her eyes drift over the moonlit ceiling and walls, and into the lightless corners. She alternately feared and wished for a ghost to visit, to teach her secrets about the new city and for her to tell secrets about the city she had left behind. She never saw a sign.

As she headed up her porch steps, legs heavy from her run, her phone buzzed in her hand. She checked the number. Nat Waters, a retired NYPD detective and her mom's live-in boyfriend. Other than the move to New Orleans, he was the one good thing to come out of her troubles in New York.

"Where y'at?" Maureen asked.

"Listen to you," Waters said. "Going local in record time. I'm out in the yard, waiting on your mother to get ready for dinner. Soon, it's gonna be too cold to sit out here. Getting it in while I can."

"How's Mom? She okay?"

"She misses you," Waters said. "She's fine. The new place coming together?"

"Bit by bit," Maureen said. "I know it's small, but it feels like a palace after six months in that studio apartment. At night, I keep walking from room to room just because I can." And because I can't sleep, she thought. But Nat already knew that. Whenever it was her calling him, it happened in the middle of the night.

Maureen sat in a wooden rocking chair, painted purple. She put the phone on speaker, set it on a small table beside the chair, and leaned forward to untie her running shoes. "I finished repainting that kitchen table and chairs I told you about."

"I remember. You got any more furniture?"

"The couch and the bed came last week," Maureen said. "The couch is brand-new. This luscious chocolate brown. So comfy. The bed's an antique. Both are gorgeous. I can't believe they're mine. I keep expecting the delivery guys to come back and take them away. Sorry, miss, wrong house."

She kicked off her running shoes and stretched her legs out in front of her. She liked watching her strong quads pop to life, though she did worry that her thighs were getting thick. She rotated her right foot. An old injury from her high school track team days meant the ankle tightened when she ran, which was often, daily if she could fit it in. Twice a day if she was feeling restless. A couple of weeks ago she'd twisted the ankle in a foot chase, hurting it worse than she'd thought at the time. She didn't need to be out running on it, not five miles at a time, but she didn't like what happened in her head when she didn't get her exercise. She got anxious, sleepless, and temperamental. Twitchy. Angry. She struggled with her impulse control. Not a good thing for a cop.

"I'll send you and Mom pictures," she said. "I financed both of them. My credit is mediocre, but both places liked that I'm a cop. Chris Atkinson's family owns the antique shop, so that helped."

"Membership has its privileges," Waters said. "You know, your mother and I could help, too. Think of it as an ongoing housewarming gift."

"The porch rocker was plenty," Maureen said. "It's perfect. I sit in it all the time. I'm sitting in it right now. I love it in the early mornings, after my shift. I watch the neighborhood get up and go to work and then I go to bed. Besides, paying these things off will help my credit. For when I make an offer on this house."

"Thinking of the future," Waters said. "Good. Do me a favor. Take a picture of you in the rocker, too. Send it to your mother. She'd like that."

"Will do," Maureen said. "I know it wasn't easy for her, sending something homey and impractical like that to me. I know she hates New Orleans."

"She misses you," Waters said. "She worries. *Hate* is a strong word.

You're her only child. She's glad you're out of that cramped studio and in a real house. After you take that picture in the rocker, call her up, tell her what you just told me."

"I painted the rocker purple," Maureen said. "It's a popular color down here. Just warn her before you show her the picture."

"She really loved the white," Waters said. "She put a lot of thought into the color."

"You saw the card she sent with it," Maureen said. *"So you don't smoke in the house*, it said."

"She's your mother," Waters said. "You know how she is." He paused. He knew when to let things go. He was especially good at stepping aside of these passive-aggressive campaigns that arose between Amber Coughlin and her daughter. Maureen really liked that about him. When to disengage was one of any number of things she knew she could learn from him.

"What else is happening?" Waters asked. "You been doing that thing we talked about?"

"Kinda. Not really. No."

"Maureen. You're putting me in a tough spot."

"I tried a shrink last month. I saw that one woman, remember? I went a couple of times. It didn't work out. She asked so many questions. And then I ran into her in the coffee shop. Thank fucking God I was not in uniform."

"Because she blurted out you were a patient?" Waters asked.

"No, she acted like she didn't even know me. Thank God. That's not the point. It was a sign. Whatever I tell her, it goes out in the world. I can't have that. You know why."

Waters laughed. "Asking questions is her job. C'mon, Maureen." She could hear him take a deep breath. "It can take a few tries to find the right person. You promised. These people are professionals, like you. They'd be out of work if they couldn't keep secrets."

"Don't tell me you told my mother," Maureen said. "I was going to do that, when I was ready. That was part of the deal. I'm gonna do it, the therapy, just not right now."

"I haven't said a word," Waters said. "But I don't like having secrets from your mother."

"There's plenty you know about me and things I've done," Maureen said, getting up from the chair, "that she doesn't know. And that you would never tell her." She went into the house, found her cigarettes on the kitchen table. She lit up and sat. She crossed her ankles under her chair. "Nobody here knows what I did up there, why I left, and I want to keep it that way." She paused. "I'm just saying, let's concede neither one of us can claim the moral high ground here about secrets."

"I'm not saying tell everyone what happened," Waters said. "Just tell *someone*. You said you needed help for the anxiety from that thing up here. For the insomnia and the nightmares. For your temper. So you could keep your job. PTSD is a real thing. Ask anyone who lived in that city in '05. Or up here after 9/11. I'm just repeating what you told me."

"I was drunk when I said all that."

"What does that tell you?" Waters asked.

"See? What do I need with a therapist? I have you."

"I'm not there. I'm fourteen hundred miles away."

"You know, Nat, I think maybe sometimes I'm better this way," Maureen said. "You ever think about that? Because I do. I'm tougher now than I was. I have sharper edges. I can be dangerous if I want to. What if I'm a better cop like this? I'm not linebacker-sized, like you. I have to compensate in other ways." Her sore ankle throbbed. She'd caught the guy she'd been chasing when she reinjured it. He'd split his temple on the curb when she'd tackled him in the street—bad luck how he fell. Didn't pain her, though, that he was somewhere in New Orleans with a swollen face etched with stitches. She stretched her legs under the table, as if that would put the pain farther away. "And I'm not a man. I have things I have to do to keep control of situations, to stay in charge. I need a lot of fuel to burn to stay humming. I have to prove myself every time

I walk into the station, every time I get out of the car. You must've seen it when you were on the job."

"I saw what it was like for the women," Waters said. "With the other cops as well as the criminals. I know things haven't changed on the job as much as they should. But I saw a lot of cops short-circuit their good careers 'cause they fell in love with the power they thought they had. They liked drawing blood. They liked how good fear looked in another person's eyes. They made a lot of excuses for themselves, too, while they circled the drain."

"You didn't like it? You didn't like what you could do with that big body?"

"I worked in a different time, Maureen. People got medals for shit that gets you brought up on charges nowadays. I'm not saying it was a better time, but it was different. Everyone didn't have a camera in their hand twenty-four seven for one thing."

"Did you get one of those medals?" Maureen asked. She knew as she spoke that Nat wouldn't rise to the bait; he never did when she antagonized him. She wanted him to know she was never afraid to poke the bear.

"That doesn't matter," Waters said. "Is there *anyone* down there you can talk to? Somebody away from the job? And I don't mean beers after work with the other cops. I mean like a friend. Somebody to take a long lunch with, shoot the shit with over coffee. You ever see Patrick anymore? You said the two of you stayed friends."

"He's been by once or twice," Maureen said. "A couple of nights. But he's not, you know, what you said. We don't have coffee when he comes over." She got up from the table, hobbled toward the bathroom. If only that dope-slinging motherfucker had stopped when he was told, she thought, she wouldn't be gimped up like this. She had another long shift ahead of her. "It's tough. I haven't been here that long. I work a lot. And the job doesn't exactly leave me feeling like socializing."

"Just think about it," Waters said. "You have to do something. Something other than work. Take a class. Join a running club. You can try yoga again. I thought you liked it. That helped, right? Maybe something more intense, like kickboxing."

"I thought I'm supposed to be trying to *stop* hitting people," Maureen said. In the bathroom, she opened the medicine cabinet, careful not to see herself in the mirror. "Classes? That's what you did to deal? What classes did you take? You did two things with your life, Nat, play football and be a cop."

Waters chuckled. "Save me the sarcasm. I haven't seen my sons in twenty years. I was a shambles when you and I met. Face it. I weighed almost three bills. I wasn't much good at being a cop anymore. And I only quit when I almost died of a heart attack. I was even worse at being a functional human being than I was at being a cop. You don't want to live like I did for my whole career. You don't. Trust me. Don't be ridiculous.

"All I'm trying to say is I remember how it was when we met, Maureen, when you were waiting tables. All you did was work. Everyone you knew, you knew from work. You didn't move as far away as you did, take the chances you did, work your ass off in the academy and training with Preacher to live the same life you had up here."

"I hear you, Nat," Maureen said. She started to settle down. She felt herself warming inside toward him, remembering how much she liked him. He took shot after shot from her prickly temper, her sharp tongue, and he never flinched, never snapped, never hung up on her. Never gave up on her. She felt a pang of something new, something she'd never felt: envy for her mother. She took an orange pill bottle from the medicine cabinet shelf, shook out two pills.

Percocet. For her ankle. She shook out a third. Additional favors from Patrick. Friends with benefits, indeed. "I do hear you. I know you're on my side. It's just hard."

"I know it is," Waters said. "That's why I keep telling you to get some help with it. I was a cop as long as you've been alive. Trust me, the job'll take everything from you if you let it. Everything. And I know it's more than the job that eats at you. People you knew were murdered. You were almost murdered yourself. You had to kill two men to survive.

"The thing I never learned, Maureen, the thing that no one ever taught me that I'm trying to teach you, is that you have to protect yourself not only from what's coming, but from things that have already happened. Something is always coming up behind you, breathing on your shoulders, chasing you. Most people get to live their lives oblivious to this fact, but you and I know different. Protect yourself. No one else is going to do it for you. I've been telling you that since the day we met."

"I'm trying," Maureen said. Her runner's high, her endorphin-laced confidence, had vanished. Her righteous anger had dissipated as quickly as it had arisen. She didn't want to talk anymore. She wanted to lie down on the floor, feel the cool tile against her cheek. "Sounds like it's gonna take more than fucking yoga."

"You need people," Waters said. "You need friends."

Sadness flooded through her. She swallowed her pills dry. She wondered when she had learned how to do that. Years ago, she figured, waiting tables. She couldn't remember not knowing how. "I am trying."

"Try harder," Waters said. "Be braver. Or you're going to lose more than your job. That's the reality, Maureen. I gotta go, your mom and I have plans. I'll give her your love."

He hung up.

Maureen walked back to the kitchen, where she poured herself a cup of cold coffee. She had been planning a nap for after her shower, but right then she needed something to wash the bitter taste of the pills from her mouth.

6

Around ten o'clock that night, Maureen smoked a cigarette and nursed a cup of cold coffee under the spotlights of the Orleans Parish Prison intake and processing center, a boxy cinder-block bunker painted the dull cream and brown of the Orleans Parish Sheriff's Office. The one-story building stood hidden behind the dirty six-story art deco shell of one of the old city jails, flooded during Katrina and abandoned in the years since. At the end of the street lay the flat, ugly expanse of the construction site that would in two years be the new intake center and jail. It might all get built, she thought, before she retired.

When she finished her smoke, she walked up the wooden ramp and pushed through the heavy green door, dropping her coffee cup in the trash as she passed the long benches and the humming vending machines in the lobby, the smell of institutional antiseptic rising from the freshly mopped floor. Her head was fuzzy from the lingering effects of the afternoon's three Percocets. She wasn't entirely sure the buzzing in her ears came from the fluorescent lights in the ceiling. She headed for the intake and information office, separated from the lobby by a wide window of bulletproof glass and a locked metal gate.

Seated at a squat metal desk on the other side of the window was a short, heavyset black woman about Maureen's age, clad in a dull green-and-gold sheriff's uniform. Her cheeks were high and square, her features reminding Maureen of an Egyptian statue. Her dark hair was pulled tight over her scalp and clipped in the back. Her uniform strained around the folds of her soft body. Maureen couldn't read her name tag. She tapped on a smartphone, not looking up as Maureen spoke.

"Excuse me, I'm Officer Maureen Coughlin, from the Sixth District."

The sheriff's deputy said nothing, fixated on her phone. The clicks of her nails on the screen of the phone set Maureen's teeth on edge.

"I'm here to see about a prisoner," Maureen said. "A woman I brought in last night. I need some additional info for my paperwork."

"I wasn't here last night," the deputy said.

"No, but that computer you're getting paid to babysit, it was here last night."

"What I meant was," the deputy said, "I wasn't here last night, so I don't remember you, or your prisoner, so I'm gonna need some information *from* you before I can help you. Did you check the screens?"

Maureen turned, reading the flat-screen monitors hanging high on the lobby wall. The names and processing status of prisoners flashed ten at a time. The city certainly had enough people in custody, she thought, working their way through the system. She didn't see Madison's name. Could she have bonded out already? Once she was gone she wouldn't be on the screens.

Maureen turned back to the deputy. "I don't see her. I'd like to get back on the street as soon as I can. Maybe you can help me?"

The deputy, expelling a long sigh, set down her phone, and rolled her chair to the computer. "Item number?"

Maureen flipped open her notepad. "Twenty-six fourteen one nine."

The deputy moved her mouse around, clicking a few keyboard keys. She frowned at the screen. "You sure it was last night?"

"I guess technically it was this morning," Maureen said. "Between three and four. Has she bonded out?"

"She'd be off the screens, but she'd be in the system. I should be able to see her. Gimme that number again."

Maureen did so, but all she got was another shake of the head.

"You lost my prisoner," Maureen said.

"Hold up. Item number probably went in wrong, is all. Let's try it another way. The prisoner's name?"

"Last name Leary. Madison Leary."

"Nope. DOB? Social?"

"Didn't have either of them. She had no ID on her. That's the info I'm here for. I thought maybe y'all could get it from her."

"She might have gone in as a Jane Doe."

"That shouldn't be," Maureen said. "I just told you her name was the one thing we did have."

The deputy lifted her hands from the keyboard as if it had burned her. "I'll unlock the gate and you can go around the other side, have a look at what we got wandering around in holding."

"I shouldn't have to. She shouldn't be in holding. I brought her in eighteen hours ago."

"This your first arrest?" the deputy asked.

"Hardly."

"Then you should know," the deputy said, "that a lot of things 'round here shouldn't be, but are. If she ain't in the computer and she ain't on the screens, then she must be in holding and hasn't been processed yet, probably because you left us with no information on her."

Another deputy, this one an obese white male with a sweaty shaved head and tiny ears, pink splotches coloring his neck, wandered over in the direction of the window. He clutched a giant plastic Saints mug in his hand. He nodded at Maureen when she caught his eyes. He waddled over to an empty desk where he started a phone call he conducted in a hushed voice.

The female deputy looked up from her computer, lips pursed and a skeptical frown on her face. "So I'm guessing no driver's license num-ber for this mystery prisoner, nothing like that."

"She wouldn't give us anything but her name. I got the impression she'd been through the system already, so I thought y'all would have information on her. I guess I was wrong."

"I guess you were." The deputy used her long nails to pick at some-thing in her teeth. She glanced at her companion, then back at Mau-reen. "Gimme what else you got. I'll call her 'scrip over to LE intake."

"White female, about five-eight, one-ten. Brown hair, long and straight, one blue eye, one green. No visible tattoos or scars. Blue T-shirt and black jeans. I brought her in on possession of stolen property and robbery charges. The eyes. You'd remember her eyes."

"Wait a sec." The deputy swiveled around in her chair. "Theriot, didn't you work last night? In the back?"

Theriot listened as Maureen repeated the description. "I remember her," he said. "She was a live one at first, screaming crazy shit when we first touched her. Spitting, clawing, like a cat in a bathtub." He shrugged. "Then the lights went out. She went limp on the floor. Like someone had thrown a switch. For just a second I thought she'd stroked out or something."

"The lights went out, or you put 'em out?" Maureen asked.

Theriot raised his hands. "I did no such thing. Neither did my part-ner. She was giving us trouble then she collapsed. Lying on the floor, staring off into space like a zombie. Wouldn't talk, wouldn't even stand up." He shrugged again, as if instantaneous catatonia made a curious footnote to an otherwise bland story. "We thought it was some kind of seizure, or, like, psychotic episode. We put her down as a ten-fifteen M, called an ambo for her. That crazy shit is above our pay grade. We don't have the resources."

He tilted his head at the computer. "Could be we never got her in there. 'Specially since y'all gave us so little to work with, information-wise." He sipped his soda, shook the cup, rattling the ice. "The EMTs strapped her down on the gurney and took her away. Paperwork's around here somewhere, I'm sure. My partner filled it out before end of shift."

"They took her to LSU Public?" Maureen asked.

"It's the only game in town anymore," Theriot said.

"Has she come back?"

"Why would she do that?" Theriot asked.

The female deputy looked over one shoulder, then the other, twisting way around in her squeaky chair as she did it. She stared right at Maureen. "You see her here, Officer?"

Outside, Maureen found Preacher waiting for her by the cruiser, gazing up at the unfinished jail like a man alone in a museum wrangling with a work that eluded him, his hands in his pockets. His Bronco was parked a few spaces away. She was surprised to see him, and not in a good way. Twice in two days he'd arrived in her orbit unexpectedly. Not only was he on the streets, this time he had left the district. She felt like he'd caught her up to no good, and like he somehow knew her prisoner had gone haywire, despite the fact she had only just learned about it herself. Like it was her fault. What was worse, she knew he could tell at first sight how guilty she felt.

As he turned to face her, hearing her boots on the wooden ramp, the ringing in her ears intensified, she felt light-headed again, and the bitter taste of her ill-gotten Percocets returned to her tongue. Like her body was trying to rat her out. Preacher could always tell, often before she could, what she was really after. She'd gotten the same "I see through you" vibe from the therapist she'd seen, the main reason she'd stopped going, no matter what she told Nat Waters.

She felt being the first to speak was of vital importance. "What's up, Preach?"

Preacher frowned. "You're listing to starboard. Your ankle acting up?"

"It's good," Maureen said, convinced she was not favoring her injured foot. "Fine. Stiffens up now and again. What brings you out here?"

"What're you doing for it?"

"Not much I can do," Maureen said. "Rest, ice. It's one of those things." She smiled, pained by how fake she knew it was. "You got someone inside?"

"I'm here for you, actually," Preacher said. "I need to talk to you."

That didn't help. "Anything fun?"

"That body from Magnolia Street," Preacher said. "We have an ID."

It was all she could do not to laugh out loud from relief at the change in subject. "That was quick. Do tell."

"Turns out, he was already in the system," Preacher said. "Edgar Cooley. Twenty-six. From out of state, originally. Last known address was a West Virginia trailer park, but that was four years ago. Let's say there are some gaps before and after in his résumé. And I don't think he was in the Peace Corps during his downtime."

"Anything that points to his killer?" Maureen asked.

"That's for Atkinson to decide. You can get more from her. You're gonna want to talk to her, if she doesn't come looking for you first."

"I don't like the sound of that."

"When I said this guy was in the system," Preacher said, "I meant the *federal* system. He was a federal fugitive. The U.S. marshals are interested in him. The FBI, too. They'll come looking for Atkinson since she caught the case. They might come looking for you since you found the body."

"Well, damn," Maureen said. "Our boy was a celebrity. And I had him pegged for some two-bit trick. What did he do?"

"He shot a bunch of cops."

"Holy shit."

"He lit up four locals in West Memphis three years ago in a traffic stop. He had some high-powered shit in his car. Military grade. Blew two units into complete junk. Left one guy in ICU for six months, another lost his left hand. Nobody died, thank the Lord. He was in a stolen car, waited until backup arrived to open fire."

"That motherfucker," Maureen said. "Man, who gives a fuck who killed him? You know, Atkinson said he was a Nazi. He had a Heil Hitler belt buckle. I saw it. So you got this information about him from where?"

"Around. I can remember hearing about the shit in Memphis some back then. We were worried about copycats here in New Orleans. It made national news when it happened."

"I wasn't up on anybody's news three years ago," Maureen said. "Sorry."

"Be careful with the feds," Preacher said. "That's mostly what I wanted to tell you. With the consent decree being finalized, we got enough heat on this department. This loser, Cooley, there's some other guys he ran with, at least back then. The feds are interested in them, too. They figure Cooley wasn't alone here in Louisiana. I believe them. His kind of coward never acts alone. What he was doing in New Orleans, it might be a lead for them. He might tie into this network of hate-group loonies they've been looking at, some shit like that. I'm hearing it might reach back to the Murrah Building bombing in Oklahoma City. Point being, this shit runs long and deep. We're gonna hear about it if the FBI or the marshals think we fouled some evidence or blew their lead. There's no telling these days. Heads might roll, yours even, since you were first on the scene, things get bad enough."

"You got nothing to worry about, Preach," Maureen said. "Everything was on point. I kept the house locked down until the detective arrived. You know Atkinson runs a tight ship, and I didn't mess with anything, didn't let anyone else mess around. There's not gonna be anything for anyone to complain about."

"I don't doubt you, Coughlin, but someone wants to jam us up, they can often find a way. We're a fallible group. How was the canvass?"

Maureen shook her head, hands on hips. "You know, like it's our fault the feds lost track of this asshole for three years. Oklahoma City was almost twenty years ago. Where they been since?" She hesitated, thinking of Quinn's tantrum. He probably hadn't done his best work. How much did that matter, though? "The canvass was fine. Typical. I mean, I did my part, I'm sure everyone else did theirs, too. It's not like I was supervising. You know how these things go, Preach. You taught me. We never get anything at the time we're asking questions. We're out making nice and making friends, hoping someone calls us later."

"Well, let's hope somebody on Magnolia Street liked you, Cough-lin." He scratched at the rough stubble on his throat. "Much as I hate to admit it, doing the feds a solid right now would make everyone look good." He met her eyes. "I'd especially be happy if that favor came straight out of the Sixth District, from cops under my command. What's good for the Sixth is good for the department is good for the city. Whatever any-body needs, the feds, Atkinson, we need to provide, with smiling fuck-ing faces."

"I'll keep that in mind," Maureen said. "Speaking of favors, I was about to call you when I saw you here. You remember Sergeant Hardin from over the Eighth?"

"Absolutely. He helped with that thing in Jackson Square."

"When I was done inside, he called me on my cell. He's on the night shift tonight. He asked me to come see him, but to keep it quiet. He's got a friend of mine, as he put it in the message, in an interrogation room. This okay with you?"

"You finally have friends in this town?" Preacher asked. "News to me. About time."

"Low, Preach. That's low."

"You're right. But I'm not wrong, am I? He say a name?"

"He did not," Maureen said.

"A blind date," Preacher said. "Fuck it. I've known Hardin forever. I trust him. If I wouldn't be cool with it, he wouldn't have called you in the first place. Go see him, and whoever he's got over there, be grateful and do what he says. I'll bet anything it's payback for getting that shriek-ing flock of spoiled co-eds out of his face last night."

"Heard that," Maureen said. Preacher's approval eased her nerves. And there was the compliment of a veteran officer like Hardin doing her a solid. A mark in her favor in front of Preacher. Maybe she wasn't making friends in the city yet, but she was making the right connections on the job. That mattered more to her, excited her more than lunch and coffee dates. She gestured at the cruiser. "I should get over there. He's already been waiting and we're one short in the district with me out here."

Preacher eased out of her way. He raised his chin at the intake office. "Before you go, what happened with that Leary woman?"

The guy was psychic, Maureen thought. She'd swear to it in court.

"Who knows about her?" Maureen answered. "She's kind of a casualty."

"Aren't we all," Preacher said. "But she's why you're here."

Maureen said nothing.

"She's why you're here," Preacher repeated, again telling and not asking. "You're not a social worker, Coughlin. Remember that. The city pays other people for that. They have degrees and shit. The one job you have is hard enough. Just try to do it right."

"That guy she was with," Maureen said. "He was no good. There's more to that story. You know I'm right. It's like when I first saw Marques Greer. I knew he was in trouble, I knew there was more to it than we were seeing."

"As I recall," Preacher said, "mistakes were made in the matter of Marques Greer. And you needed some considerable help."

"I know, I know. I'm a new cop, Preach, but I've been a woman my whole life. *Believe* me, I know a predator when I see one."

"And so you sprung the rabbit from the trap," Preacher said. "You did a good thing. But when the rabbit goes back down the hole, as rabbits do, we don't follow. It's the natural order of things. The wild animals stay wild. We don't bring them home and make them pets. Understand?"

"We might need her," Maureen said. "We want her feeling good about us if anything important comes up on Clayton Gage. And, trust me, something will. We might need a witness or something. Look at how handy a witness would be in the Cooley case. I thought looking out for her might get us on her good side. I'm trying to make friends, like on Magnolia Street. I'm trying to think ahead."

"Nice try, Coughlin. You're so full of shit. You let me know how it goes with Hardin."

"Ten-four," Maureen said, chastened. Even if she'd lied about her original motivations for pursuing Madison Leary, what she'd said to Preacher was true.

"Ten-four, good buddy," Preacher said, chuckling.

"One more thing," Maureen said. "I have to ask, how did you know to find me here?"

"You called in your twenty to dispatch like the good soldier you are," Preacher said. "I wish everyone left a trail like you do. You're so by the book sometimes, Coughlin, you kill me. You chose the right side of the law. You'd make a lousy criminal. When you come back to the Sixth, bring me a Hubig's. Sweet potato flavor."

7

After double-parking on Royal Street among a pack of other units, Maureen found Sergeant Hardin standing on the marble steps in front of the classy Colonial structure that housed the Eighth District. The Eighth, in the heart of the French Quarter, with wide white columns bracketing the beveled-glass and brass-handled front doors, outclassed in appearance the modest, scuffed, and utilitarian Sixth District home base Maureen was used to. Hardin came down the slate walkway to meet Maureen on the sidewalk.

Hardin was dark-skinned, with a smooth shaved head. He stood well over six feet tall, with a thick muscled frame. She'd dealt with him before, a real professional, calm as a glassy lake. She liked him a lot. He was high on her list of people to emulate as she learned the job. Considering the size of him, she wondered why he'd never unnerved her the way Ruiz did. Maybe because Hardin reminded her of an old friend from New York, a bouncer she had worked with at her last cocktailing job. Seemed like yesterday sometimes, her Staten Island life, the good and the ghosts. Other times it seemed a lifetime ago, or, on her best days, like someone else's life entirely.

Hardin held an unlit cigar in his left hand. He extended his right. Maureen shook it, her own hand disappearing into his palm. She squeezed extra hard.

"Saint Coughlin of the Sixth," Hardin said. "It's been a minute. How you been?"

"Staying busy," Maureen said. "Sorry to keep you waiting."

"Heard you got the piss-bottle treatment from some of the neighborhood fellas. Preacher told me."

"I did," Maureen said. "The car got the worst of it. Nothing a hose can't fix. Just some people fooling around. Nothing to it."

"You're all right, though?"

"Never better."

Hardin tapped his watch. "Good, good. Hate to be rude, but I'm up against it here. Busy night. They started tearing down the Iberville projects last week. A few people been out looking to get even. Let's get inside and get this done." He turned and headed up the walkway. Maureen followed.

"You been back to the block yet?" Hardin asked over his shoulder. "Crack some heads, get some names?"

"Doesn't seem worth it," Maureen said. "I know boys. I keep reacting to it, they're only gonna keep doing it, right? Why encourage them? All part of the rookie experience. I get worse shit from other cops."

Hardin was grinning at her, holding open the door. "That is the truth," he said, nodding as Maureen passed through the district entrance.

He led her through the lobby, through the sets of desks, and down a narrow side hallway. They stopped outside a door with one small high window. The plastic plaque on the wall read INTERROGATION 2. When Maureen reached for the doorknob, Hardin stopped her.

"That was a nice catch on those purse snatchings," he said, checking his watch again.

"Having answers to give those girls, not to mention their belongings, made life much easier around here. In gratitude, we're prepared to kick your friend loose. The arresting officer, though, he's been a cop for as many years as you have weeks on the job, so there's an etiquette to observe."

"I got you," Maureen said.

"If I'm telling you things you already know, listen to me anyway. Don't walk another officer's collar out the front door. Go out the side. And it's not a story to share with the fellas. No need to brag around the Sixth about the pull you got in the Eighth. Let's keep this close."

"You can trust me," Maureen said.

"Good to know." Hardin opened the door to the interrogation room. "You remember Mr. Marques Greer, right? Famed teenaged snare drummer and failed city homicide witness."

"Speak of the devil," Maureen said. "Preacher and I were just talking about you, Marques."

Seated at a long table on the other side of the room, slouching in a cheap folding chair, one arm cuffed to the table, was a reedy middle-school-aged boy, all arms and legs, his wrist barely thick enough to fill the cuff around it. The boy was seething, breathing hard like he'd sprinted a hundred-yard dash. He said nothing at the sight of Maureen, glancing at her before turning his eyes to a corner of the ceiling. He acted more like he was mad at her for taking so long to get to him than he looked happy or grateful she'd arrived.

"Mr. Greer tells me he's an essential part of an ongoing police investigation," Hardin said. "Any truth to this?"

"It's not *entirely* false," Maureen said.

"Perhaps he's ready to come clean," Hardin said.

Marques said nothing.

Hardin fished out his handcuff keys.

"Hang on," Maureen said. "Let me have a few minutes with him in here."

"Your call," Hardin said. "But not too long. Wherever he goes next, he's got to be out of here sooner rather than later. And make sure he understands he got there as a favor to you, not to him. He's got nothing coming to him in the Eighth District."

"Ten-four," Maureen said.

Marques rattled his chains. "Seriously?"

Maureen turned to Hardin. "What's the charge?"

"Curfew violation."

"I was working," Marques said. "We allowed to work at night. It's in the law. This is racist bullshit."

"You two have fun," Hardin said. "Holler when you're ready. Don't take too long."

He left the room, closing the door behind him. Maureen sat opposite Marques, who slumped in his chair, legs splayed under the table.

"For real, OC?" Marques said. "You the bad cop now?"

Maureen raised her hands. "What's up with this? We talked about this. Low-profile, we said. This is not low-profile."

Marques shrugged, continuing to pout. She hadn't seen him in almost two months. He'd been busy growing, Maureen noticed, both his body and his hair. His body at an almost freakish rate. He'd grown several inches, put on at least a dozen pounds. Whatever Marques had been eating, she thought, Quinn needed to get the recipe for his son. She noticed that the beginnings of braids dotted his head. Long braids were the style on the street now. She saw a lot of them. Though Marques's were in the sprout stages, Maureen didn't like the look on him. Marques had already been in and out of both the Game and the System, as a reluctant soldier for a drug dealer named Bobby Scales, as a witness to a homicide, then as a target in a drive-by. Being a young black male made him a target of the NOPD, even at his tender age. His history made him a target of other young black men, especially any looking to make good with Scales, who remained on the loose. The braids on top of his precocious résumé sure wouldn't help him avoid trouble.

"Are there drugs anywhere in this?" Maureen asked. "Tell me now. That changes things."

"Don't be like the rest of them, OC. Just don't. You know me. You know I ain't triflin' like that. I got bigger plans."

"Looks like it. How's Mother Mayor feel about your new hairstyle?"

Marques shrank into his chair at the invocation of his grandmother, trying and failing to cross his arms over his chest, his wrist chain rattling. "She don't like it."

"I'd imagine not," Maureen said. It'd be a hard, hard road for him, she thought, rebelling against a woman like Mother Mayor. "Cops hate that shit, trust me on this. It's what the gangsters are wearing these days. We look for it. She knows that. *You* know that."

"Because y'all be profilin' I gotta get a haircut y'all approve of? No thanks."

"I'm just saying, why make your life harder than it already is?"

"I don't make it harder," Marques said. "Y'all do. Who says my life is hard?"

"Then what's the story? Why are you in here?"

"Ask the fat ass that brought me up in here," Marques said. "Like I said, I was working, down on Frenchmen. Same as forty other motherfu—I mean, people out there on the street. And I ain't *even* beggin' or bullshittin' like most of them."

"Working where?"

"On that empty corner, by the old Café Brasil, where them stanky-ass gutter punks hang out, playin' them stupid fiddles." He sat up in his chair, straightened his shoulders. "I'm running a band, a brass band. A *real* band. Me and some fellas from school and a couple who graduated outta Roots of Music. We kickin' it out there now. We're gettin' good, yo. No sheet music or nothing. We puttin' a bucket out. Gettin' paid a little bit. I gotta start thinking about the future. I age outta Roots next year."

"It's a school night," Maureen said.

Marques shrugged. "We new. Weeknights the only time we can get the spot."

"It's not real work."

Marques's eyes got big. "*Don't* let my band teacher hear you say that. Oh, hell no."

"What I mean is," Maureen said, "to us, the police, it's not real work. There's no pay stub or time card you can show us when we stop you. Horns and drumsticks don't count, even if you're standing there playing them."

"Shamarr gotta show his papers everywhere he go? Shorty gotta show his?"

"They're over eighteen," Maureen said. "And pretty famous, to boot. You're *twelve*."

"Thirteen last week," Marques said.

"Happy birthday."

"Thank you. Shamarr rolls with them braids, by the way," Marques said, perking up as if he'd won an important point in an argument. "And the ladies are *into* Shamarr. You *know* it."

"Shamarr almost missed his Jazz Fest gig last year because him and his long braids got popped the night before in St. Bernard Parish. Ladies love the braids, cops not so much."

"That was straight-up racist shit," Marques said. "And everyone knows it. He wasn't doing nothing but being black in Cracker Town. Shamarr only got busted 'cause of how he looks."

"That's my point, Marques," Maureen said. "And Shorty keeps it tight. Ladies love Shorty, too."

Marques dismissed her argument with a wave of his hand, squirming in his chair, suddenly an embarrassed thirteen-year-old boy caught talking with a woman about sex appeal.

"Whatever with that noise," he said. "For real, though. How am I gonna get known if I ain't allowed to play? TBC and Baby Boyz? That's how they got gigs, club owners hearing them on the street."

He turned his eyes away from her. He was at that age, Maureen noticed, where he could go from boy to young man and back again with a single gesture. The legal system would start seeing him as a grown man real soon. On the street, his age had never been relevant. For such a young kid, he seemed to be running out of time in a hurry.

"So where are the other guys in your band?" Maureen asked. "Doesn't seem like the whole band got dragged in. Seems like it's just you."

"They ran."

"Even the tuba player?"

"We don't have one," Marques said. "At least not right now this minute. I had to fire his dumb ass."

"Oh, really?" Maureen said, suppressing a smile over Marques's frustration with his administrative duties. "And what for?"

Marques raised his shoulders high. "Kept gettin' in fights on the school bus. Can't *have* that in a band. Can't have it. We'll get a new one. Soon dudes'll be lining up to play with us, as long as we can keep working."

"And why didn't *you* run?" Maureen asked.

"'Cause I don't. You know that." Marques shifted in his seat.

"You stayed," Maureen said, "and hassled that cop so the other guys could get away, didn't you? You took the hit."

"This whole thing is some bullshit," Marques said. "I gotta have permission from the cops to play music? In New Orleans? What the fuck is up with that? A black dude can't come and go without his papers? I was *born* here. That's some Klan Nazi shit, what that is. Just 'cause we got a black president now. It's worse than *ever*."

Maureen fought back another smile. "I hear your grandmother's voice. She's well?"

"She finds out I got busted, we'll hear her voice all over New Orleans, and won't neither of us be well."

"You asked for me," Maureen said, blowing out her breath and raising her hands. "You got something for me? You heard anything about Bobby? He been sniffing around you and your grandmother? Been doing dirt in the neighborhood?"

"We moved," Marques said.

"I heard. But you never get back to Josephine Street? Not ever?"

"I wouldn't know about his 'hood, wherever it is."

"You know what I mean," Maureen said.

"I told you," Marques said, "there's two things I don't do."

"Yeah, you don't run, and you don't snitch. How's that working out for you?"

"It is what it is," Marques said. "I don't know why you so worried about that, anyway. Ain't like y'all arrested nobody. Who am I gonna testify against?"

"We couldn't chase down his hideouts fast enough because our only surviving witness to his habits and drug trade, you, wouldn't give a statement that was worth anything. No names, no places, nothing, despite everything we did for you. That's how I remember it."

"Stop. I'm thirteen, yo. You can't catch the man without me? That sounds like *your* problem. And you want me to side with *y'all* on this. Nigga, please."

Maureen paused, rubbing her temples until the echo of her own complaints about Edgar Cooley and the FBI faded away. She took a deep breath.

"A man who murdered your friend also tried to shoot you and your grandmother," she said. "Asking if that man has tried it again since is hardly asking you to snitch. Especially after the *huge* breaks we cut you. I'm not askin' who's grinding on what corner, Marques. I'm not asking for your friends' names."

"I told you I'm not into that," Marques said, frustration sharpening his tone.

"This is life-and-death stuff and you know it. Save that 'nigga please' shit for the street. And we will bring Bobby Scales in, sooner or later."

"Don't hate the playa, OC."

"I know, I know," Maureen said. "Hate the game. Whatever. So this isn't a trade, then, where you help me because I'm helping you. This is a straight-up favor I'm doing you."

"Call it what you want," Marques said.

"You try me, kid. You really do sometimes. One of these days, I'm not coming for you." Maureen stood up, her chair scraping the floor. "This room stinks. Let's get outta here." She walked to the door, knocked on it. "You owe me, Marques. Again. Still."

Hardin came in, tilted his chin at Marques. "He good to go?"

"He is," Maureen said. "If you'd do the honors."

Hardin unlocked the cuffs. He gave Marques a hard slap to the back of the head as the boy stood. "I don't want to see you here again. Not even on a school trip. Stay home sick that day. And get a fucking haircut."

At the door, Maureen grabbed Marques by the upper arm. "Let's go. Head down, mouth shut."

Honoring Hardin's request, Maureen led Marques through the building, down a flight of stairs, and out a side door, onto Iberville Street, where she ran right into Quinn and Ruiz on the sidewalk.

Quinn laughed as Maureen and Marques stopped short, the door banging closed, the lock clicking into place behind them. Marques backed up against the building.

"Is anybody left patrolling the Sixth District tonight?" Quinn asked. Ruiz loomed, dark-eyed, over his shoulder. "With all of us down here in the Eighth?"

The way the two men stood so close to her made Maureen feel cornered. She could smell the dried sweat and nicotine wafting off them. Narrow sidewalk, she told herself. That's why they stood so close to her. They'd been reaching for the door when she and Marques had emerged from it. Of course, they were right there. She'd walked into their space. She rolled her shoulders back, squared her chest, trying to reclaim some ground. Marques inched away from the trio of cops, sliding along the wall. If she felt cornered, Maureen could only imagine how uncomfortable Marques felt. Neither man gave an inch. One of them smelled of garlic. One of them had alcohol on his breath.

"Quick errand," Maureen said.

"Funny," Quinn said. "Us, too."

Maureen noticed as Ruiz slipped something into his pocket. He stared hard at Marques. "Taking out the trash, Cogs? That's what it looks like."

Maureen flinched. Sticking up for Marques in front of her fellow officers wouldn't happen. Still. Ruiz's insult irked her. They should at least show her more respect. It was Quinn who'd been drinking.

"He's a good kid," she said. "He just steps in it now and again. He's learning."

"We can take him off your hands," Ruiz said. "We can speed up his learning curve, too. No offense to you, Cogs, but he looks like a kid who might benefit from a strong *male* influence." He raised his thick eyebrows, his pockmarked face a mask of insincere concern. "Where's your daddy, son? Angola? Cemetery? Under a floor somewhere?"

Marques said nothing. He kept his eyes lowered, but he raised his chin.

"You wanna see some mug shots?" Ruiz asked. "Maybe we find one that looks like you. Maybe we get lucky and he's alive and willing to claim you, his lost little boy."

Quinn slapped Ruiz in the chest with the back of his hand. "The shit you say, dude. Damn." He'd gone pale, vampiric, Maureen thought. Or maybe it was the streetlights.

"What about your own errand?" she asked. "Don't let us hold you up."

"Yeah, there's that," Quinn said. Ruiz's aggression had made him uncomfortable. He looked at Marques. "So you've got it under control with—what did you say your name was?"

"I didn't say," Marques answered. "Sir."

"Let me get this kid home," Maureen said. "And y'all can do your thing and we can get back uptown before Preacher throws a stroke."

"Sounds like a plan," Quinn said. "We'll see y'all later."

Maureen walked away, blinking, fighting for her breath, trying to hide the spike in her stress level. Marques stuck close to her, his eyes glued to the sidewalk. She didn't need to grab his arm this time, didn't even need to talk to him.

"My car is around the block," she said, just to make a sound, "on Royal."

Maureen glanced back down Iberville Street before she and Marques turned the corner onto Royal. Quinn and Ruiz remained at the side door, both of them looking back at her. She couldn't read their faces in the dark and distance. The encounter rolled around in her stomach, sour and acidic, leaving her feeling like she had a bellyful of the cheap liquor on Quinn's breath. A key, she thought. That was what Ruiz had put in his pocket when she walked out the door. Had to be. They couldn't get in through the side door without one. Why would Quinn and Ruiz, she wondered, have or even need a key to that door? Why not walk in through the front door? Because Hardin would see them? And why wouldn't they want that?

She looked at Marques. Maybe she wasn't the only cop who'd come for him. Did Hardin know Quinn and Ruiz were coming? Was that why he'd rushed her with the boy? Was that why he'd asked her not to brag on the favor, hadn't asked for her over the radio? Maureen wondered who Hardin was crossing, letting Maureen slip out of the station with Marques in tow. It had to be someone more important than Quinn and Ruiz. He outranked them. If he didn't want them around, he could order them to stand down, send them back to the Sixth with their tails between their legs. And they knew it, which was why they were sneaking around the side door. She wondered who the cop was who'd busted Marques in the first place.

"Oh, hells no," Marques said, recoiling at the sight of her patrol car. "I can't get a ride home with you. In a cop car?"

"Gimme a break. What'd you think I'd be driving? A Range Rover?"

"Serious, OC. The whole block'll think I'm snitchin'."

"You gotta go home. That was the deal I made."

"Yeah, that *you* made," Marques said, walking away. "What I gotta do is go get my drum. Peace."

"Wait right there," Maureen said.

Marques kept walking, accelerating his pace. Maureen wasn't sure it was her he was trying to escape.

"I mean it," she said, hustling after him. "Do not make me fucking chase you. I'll call it in. I'll leave you in the box this time." She took a shot. "I've got Quinn and Ruiz down here to help me, and I know where you're going. I get the feeling they'd be happy to help round you back up."

Marques stopped. He waited for Maureen to catch up to him, jaw set as he tried to drive the fear from his face. She'd seen that look on him in the past. She wanted to know the connection between the boy and the cops. Uncovering that fact without tipping off those two would be tough. Marques would lie to her. He'd deny knowing them. And he'd never, ever trust her to take his side over other police, no matter their personal history, asshole cops or not. That was the way things worked. That was the game. She couldn't blame him. Were the situation flipped, she wasn't sure she'd trust him.

"I'm just playin', OC," Marques said. "I wouldn't walk out on you. But I do have to get my drum. For real. Officer Fat Ass made me leave it behind."

"What was the officer's actual name?" Maureen asked.

She wanted to know who had told Quinn and Ruiz he was being held at the Eighth. Certainly Preacher wouldn't give the kid up; he'd helped save him from Scales.

"I don't know no names," Marques said. "Y'all all look the same to me."

"You have to go home," Maureen said. "I made promises."

"Where am I gonna get the money for another snare drum? They ain't cheap."

"And you have no desire," Maureen said, "to tell your grandmother you lost this one. Forget the haircut, you'll need a whole new head."

"I ain't lost it," Marques said. "That cop made me leave it. There's a difference."

"None of your boys would've gone back for it?" Maureen asked. "Since you took one for the team? Seems to me the least they could do."

"By the time I track those guys down," Marques said, "if they don't have it, one a them gutter punks will have took it and probably sold it off on me. Then what am I gonna do? How am I gonna lead a band with no damn instrument?"

Maureen took a deep breath. Marques had a point. A new instrument wouldn't be cheap. His grandmother was on a fixed income. His mother was serving in Afghanistan. His father was a name nobody spoke, the few that knew it. Ruiz's insults probably hadn't been that far off the mark. Marques and his grandmother had moved since getting sideways of Bobby Scales a month or so ago. Their income was what it was and their new neighborhood, an older mixed-income development called River Garden, would stretch what they had to the limit. Maureen wanted those drumsticks in Marques's hands, keeping him from picking up anything, in an effort to make money, that would make more trouble for him than curfew violations.

"I'll make you a deal," Maureen said. "I'll take you down to Frenchmen. We'll go get your drum. It's probably right where you left it. If you've been playing down there, people will know what's yours. From there, it's home. Immediately."

"In a cab, though," Marques said.

"Marques, that's the deal. I take you to Frenchmen for your drum, then home to your grandma's, or I take you from here to the curfew hall and call your grandmother to come get you."

"Fuck that, she leave me there."

"Don't hate the game," Maureen said. "What's it gonna be?"

Marques pretended to think it over, running his tongue back and forth over his teeth. "I can ride in the front?"

"You touch anything and you go to jail."

Marques was a good kid at heart, Maureen thought as they headed for the cruiser. Exasperating, but good at heart. He just struggled with authority.

"On the real, no disrespect to you, OC," Marques said, "but *fuck* that take-out-the-trash motherfucker. Fuck him."

8

The popular Frenchmen Street, the dusky crown of an oddball neighborhood called the Marigny, with its multiple blocks of bars, cafés, and live music clubs, bustled most nights until close to dawn. Musicians like Marques and his band, who couldn't get or didn't have inside gigs, busked for change on the street. Some played solo. Others played in duos and small groups. Self-appointed chefs cooked everything from tacos to turkey legs atop various smoking mobile contraptions built from Weber grills, shopping carts, and random spare parts. Local artists hawked handmade clothes and books and jewelry from car trunks and bicycle baskets. Fedora-topped hipster poets smoking hand-rolled cigarettes perched typewriters on folding cocktail tables, scratching their beards and tapping out poetry on demand, hoping for enough in cash donations to cover their next round.

The street was noisy and dirty and casually chaotic. Most of its outdoor commerce was illegal. The city authorities talked of cracking down. Maureen ignored both facts, as did the majority of her compatriots on the NOPD, content to let it be, at least until the orders came through. The action—musical, culinary, literary, and otherwise—was self-regulated with moderate efficiency and fairness. The surrounding neighborhood concerned the police much more. With the street vendors and the servers and bartenders from the restaurants and music clubs heading home along its dark and quiet streets, cash in their pockets, the area made for a popular hunting ground for pistol-toting stick-up boys.

Among the buzzing industrious locals lived a population of street kids in their teens and twenties, almost exclusively from out of town and out of state. Travelers, they called themselves. To Maureen they didn't seem to travel much. Maybe from the front of one bar to the front of another until shooed by the next bouncer. When she came down to the Marigny for a meal or a brass-band show, Maureen saw many of the same faces in the same doorways and on the same corners. "Gutter punks" was the common pejorative for these kids, a name born out of their worn and torn clothing, their affinity for piercings and bad tattoos, their antipathy toward employment and hygiene, and the aggressive nature of their panhandling.

They hung together in packs, eschewing the solitary way of working the streets embraced by the city's older, more traditional homeless. Often the kids had surprisingly well-fed and well-behaved dogs in tow. Most cops, Maureen had learned, even those who'd roll up on a gangster-heavy corner at midnight, would bypass dealing with a thirty-pound dog in a dirty bandana, and the kids knew it, too. Maureen didn't see much of the kids in her district. The nicer parts of Uptown were less bohemian and therefore less tolerant and less lucrative than downtown neighborhoods like the Quarter, the Marigny, and the adjacent Bywater. The tougher parts of Uptown where Maureen spent most of her time would eat them alive. She'd noticed the kids played threatening to tourists or folks in from the suburbs for festivals and Saints games, but they made sure to avoid as much real danger and the people responsible for it as possible. They kept to their own.

Cops who dealt with these kids had told her that their searches and pat downs often uncovered cell phones and credit cards. Some kids were desperate runaways, fleeing real abuse or flailing in the grips of brutal addictions, packing homemade weapons they clutched in their sleep and could wield with inspired and dangerous fury. Others, most, were poseurs and dilettantes, going through a phase, Maureen had learned, living with their parents' phone numbers packed in the back of their wallets, dabbling in the minor criminal pseudo-rebellions of drug use, graffiti, and vandalism until the weather turned cold and the tourist charity dried up.

Maureen rolled up on a bunch of such kids clustered around the intersection where Marques had directed her. They loitered in a back corner of the empty lot, their backs to Frenchmen and to the patrol car. Maureen bumped the car up onto the sidewalk. She hit the driver's side spotlight and put it on the kids to get their attention. They turned to face the car, boys and girls alike looking like unisex extras from a Dickens novel, shielding their eyes and complaining about the light and the hassle as they staggered back into the shadows. They had musical instruments of their own, Maureen noticed. One boy held a ukulele with one string. An accordion sat on the ground, propped up against a battered fiddle case. A young woman with the shadow of a buzz cut covering her scalp sat wide-legged on an upside-down pickle bucket as she tuned a banjo.

"That your tip bucket she's sitting on?" Maureen asked.

"No way the fellas left cash money behind," Marques said. "Ain't you learned nothin' yet? That bucket's hers."

Before getting out of the car, Maureen leaned toward Marques. "Anything I should know here? You had problems with these people before? Has there been fighting over this corner?"

"Not with me and my band," Marques said. "We usually share pretty good. Some of the other bands?" He shrugged. "Bunch of black kids makes everyone nervous, yo. They on their best behavior."

"Ever use that to your advantage?" Maureen asked.

"Don't hate, OC."

"Wait here, playa," Maureen said. "I mean it."

"Ten-four," Marques said.

Maureen climbed out of the car. The air smelled of cheap weed, unwashed bodies, and patchouli oil. A couple of the boys drifted away from her, down the dark side street, a glowing ember hovering between them. "Bacon on the hoof," one of them shouted. He followed the comment with a squeal. Maureen glared into the dark, because the kids expected it, but the taunts of cowards, they didn't do much for her. Never did. When you motherfuckers get stuck up at gunpoint for your hardbegged cash later, she thought, you'll be crying that I wasn't around.

The girl in the buzz cut set down her banjo, balancing it carefully across the plastic bucket. She walked over to Maureen, leaving the other kids behind. She wore knee-high black leather boots with the buckles undone, and a black-and-white-striped bodysuit under gray overalls cut off mid-thigh. As she got closer, under the shadow of her hair, Maureen could see an elaborate tattoo winding around her skull. A dragon, or an alien, maybe. One of those snakes eating its own tail? Maybe it was an alligator? Something ugly, Maureen thought, whatever it was. The girl had another tattoo in the center of her collarbone, something dark and blurry that Maureen couldn't make out. A bat? A raven? Bad work, whatever it was. Three tiny barbells pierced her right eyebrow. She wore a silver stud in the vertical groove of her upper lip.

"I'm looking for a drum," Maureen said to her. "A snare drum. The young man in the car left it behind earlier this evening. I was hoping it was around."

"He was forced to leave it," the girl said, "by that other nasty cop. They weren't bothering anyone, you know. They're pretty decent. People in this town actually like live music, I don't know if you've heard. It's kind of a tradition."

"So you've seen it?" Maureen said. She wanted the drum, not an argument about city culture.

"We have it." The girl smiled, her teeth surprisingly white. She had a streak of lipstick on one of her canines. "We held it for him, for when he came back."

Maureen turned and signaled for Marques to get out of the car. The girl in turn made a gesture, and a skinny, dreadlocked boy of no more than nineteen, his long fingernails painted black, appeared out of the dark and brought forth the drum, holding it out for Marques to receive. Marques took the drum, turning it over, holding it up in the streetlight, looking for damage. With a nod, he pronounced it fit and tucked it under his arm. Maureen felt as if she'd presided over some ancient tribal peace negotiation. It seemed to be a success. Peace achieved, she moved on to other business.

"Did you or any of your friends," Maureen asked, "catch the name of the cop who picked up Marques and busted up the band?"

"You can't find that out yourself?" the girl asked. "You need us for that?"

Just my luck, Maureen thought. I got the halfway smart one. "I'm just asking."

"Like I want him down here looking for me next." The girl grinned, shaking her head. "Cop problems are cop problems. Don't even."

Maureen turned to Marques. "And you have no idea who he was?"

Marques shrugged.

"Y'all all look the same to us," the girl said.

Maureen turned back to the girl. "You said you don't want him down here looking for you next. Did he bust up the band, or was he looking for Marques by name? Has he done this kind of thing before? He a regular down here?"

The girl pursed her lips and made a "talk to the hand" gesture.

"Can we go?" Marques asked. He'd forgotten his worries, Maureen noticed, about riding in a cop car or facing his grandmother.

The girl sucked her teeth, rocking on her heels. Maureen pulled a five-dollar bill from her wallet, offering it.

"Five whole dollars? Seriously?"

"The next thing I hand you is a summons," Maureen said.

"For what?"

"I'll find something. You want me searching your pockets?"

The girl took the money, moving smooth and quick as a rattlesnake strike. Maureen wasn't sure she'd seen it happen. Her hand was just suddenly empty. A pickpocket, she was, Maureen thought. And a good one at that. The girl said, "I believe the exact quote was, 'Which one of you punk-ass motherfuckers is Marques Greer?'"

"Dammit, bitch," Marques said. "Mind your fucking business."

The girl lunged for him. Maureen stepped in between them. The girl bounced off her. She weighed nothing, Maureen thought. Thin skin and hollow bones under those ragged clothes. Two hundred pounds of attitude in a ninety-pound body. I could break her in half, Maureen thought. *I* could. "Okay. Okay. Back off, both of you." Everyone separated. "Marques?"

"I don't remember it like that," he said. "I remember it like I told it to you at the district. She looking for another five dollars. Maybe she can buy some soap with it."

"Marques, put your drum in the car. Wait for me there." Marques had the attention of someone in the NOPD, Maureen thought, the wrong kind of attention. That someone had the pull to make Quinn and Ruiz their errand boys, and authority enough to make Hardin, a sergeant like Preacher, nervous and sneaky about his defiance. Who could that be? Whoever it was, Maureen knew she didn't want their attention on her.

"Whatever she say to you, OC," Marques said, "don't believe her. She a punk-ass dope fiend. And she a thief. You know me."

"Marques, please," Maureen said. She was getting a headache, from the aggravation or the patchouli and body odor it failed to mask, she couldn't tell. "Take care of your drum. It's what we came down here for, right?"

He headed for the car.

"OC?" the girl asked.

"Officer Coughlin," Maureen said.

"I know you," the girl said to Maureen. "I never knew your name but I recognize your face. I remember your elbow. And your shoulder. You don't remember me, but I know you."

"I don't think so," Maureen said, not turning around. "I don't work down here."

"You really don't remember, do you? You nearly busted my skull open behind Café du Monde, back in the spring. And you don't even remember me. My ribs hurt for two weeks."

"That was you," Maureen said, all statement and no question. She circled her finger around her head. "You didn't have this business up here then." As if the tattoo somehow made a major difference in the girl's appearance. Her name popped into Maureen's head. On the day she'd graduated from the police academy, with her mom and Nat Waters visiting, Maureen had broken up a bathroom purse snatching not far from Café du Monde. This girl had been the thief. Maureen had laid her out on the pavement.

"Dice," Maureen said. "That was what Hardin called you. You still stealing, Dice? Tattoos ain't free. Neither are banjos. And from what I remember, heroin ain't free, either."

"Why you gotta be like that?" the kid with the one-string ukulele whined from the shadows. He was the only one who'd stuck around. He had eye shadow over only one eye. He was sweet on Dice, Maureen could tell. It radiated from him like light. She felt something twitch in her gut. Envy again? Of this? Of these two? What was wrong with her?

"We were nice to your friend here," the kid said. "We shared our space with him. It was a *cop*, like you, that busted up his gig and almost lost him that drum. We *helped* him."

Both women turned and stared him down. He looked away, tuning his instrument, mumbling under his breath. Dice, for her part, hadn't blanched at Maureen's insult.

"I'm off that shit," she said. "And I've *been* off it." She shoved her hands deep in the pockets of her overalls and cocked one hip out to the side. "And don't you worry how I make my money, Officer. I got talents and I use them, just like any other God-fearing American."

"I'll take that as a yes on the stealing," Maureen said.

"Just like you, Officer," Dice said. "I do what's necessary to survive."

"Indeed," Maureen said, eyebrows raised. "Y'all have a good night."

She headed for the car. Marques sat on the bumper, drum on his knees. The radio on her belt crackled. "Attention, fourteen-twelve."

Maureen keyed the mic on her shoulder. "Fourteen-twelve here, go ahead."

"Fourteen-twelve, duty sergeant requests your presence at a thirty-C, five hundred block of Lyons. Code One."

Marques looked up at her, wide-eyed. "A thirty call? That's a murder, yo. Can I come? Please? I won't tell my grandma."

"Dispatch, show me on my way. Fourteen-twelve out." She led Marques away from the car, back to the kids on the corner. "Dice, come over here."

Dice took her time, sauntering in Maureen's direction. "Good thing you were down here hassling us over playing music while someone got murdered uptown."

"Marques here *needs* to get home. Please help him catch a cab."

Dice put out her hand. "Cabs ain't free."

"For fuck's sake." Maureen dug some cash from her pocket. She pulled out a twenty, handing it to Marques as she spoke to Dice. "He gets a cab home to his grandmother. That is the only acceptable option."

"I look like a babysitter?" Dice asked.

"He doesn't make it home," Maureen said, "and I'm coming back with friends. We clean out and shut down this corner and nobody gets to play here. Not tonight. Not ever. Do not try me on this. Next time I won't *almost* bust your skull."

"Daaaaaaaaaaamn," Marques said.

"Enough outta you," Maureen said. "We had a deal. I hear bad news about you, and you can forget about playing anymore with Roots of Music. I know Mr. Dodds don't let anyone march in an ankle bracelet."

"That's cold, OC," Marques said.

"It is what it is," Maureen replied. She took out a business card, scrawled her number on it, and gave it to Dice. "Help him out and I'll owe you a favor."

"And what's that worth?" Dice asked. "Can't eat a favor. And I don't get up the Sixth District much."

"Use your head," Maureen said. "Marques is on the street and not in juvie because he had a name to mention. You already said there's a cop coming down here hassling this corner. You don't want a name to use if you need one?"

She walked back to the cruiser and slid behind the wheel.

She backed the car off the sidewalk and hit the lights, palming the wheel as she hung a hard turn off Frenchmen and onto Chartres, headed for Elysian Fields, engine revving.

She'd come to the Eighth District to get Marques out of trouble. Instead, she'd left him on the same corner where he'd been arrested hours earlier by a cop who'd come hunting for him, only now he was in the company of an antisocial vagrant thief with a grudge who may or may not be a junkie. What could possibly go wrong?

9

Maureen found only one other unit on the scene when she turned off Tchoupitoulas Street and onto Lyons. With each week, she knew less what she was going to get when she rolled up on a scene, half the district or a single car could be waiting. The other unit was parked on an angle, closing off the street, its light bar pulsing. But Marques had correctly recognized the police code he'd overheard as a murder. Somewhere near that one other police car was a dead body.

A crowd had gathered on the corner outside a brick-faced, windowless late-night bar called F and M's. Maureen knew the place. It was popular with Tulane and Loyola students current and recent, with a few LSU folks thrown in for flavor. She'd cruised this corner before, answering neighborhood complaints about kids doing everything from fighting to fucking in the dark spaces along Lyons Street. The same shit she used to see, and sometimes do, when she was younger. She parked her cruiser.

Climbing out of the car, Maureen recognized the familiar shadowy forms of Quinn and Ruiz, the orange embers of their cigarettes glowing in their hands. The young spectators across the street nursed drinks and cigarettes. They were close to the river, across Tchoupitoulas from the docks, and the air was damp and heavy with humidity. The street smelled like cigarette butts, stale piss, and staler beer. Fraternity-approved hip-hop throbbed from inside the bar. No crime lab techs, no coroner or ambulance, not even a detective had arrived yet. The homicide machine, with its multiple moving parts, took its time getting up and running late at night. Still, unlike on Magnolia Street, at least the body hadn't lain undiscovered for a week.

From under the sagging eaves of the bar, curling clouds of cigarette smoke over their heads, kids called out questions to her. She ignored them as she approached the other two cops.

Quinn met her in the street, halfway between the cars. "You done with babysitting duty?"

"I traded him in," Maureen said, "for babysitting you guys." She lit a smoke of her own. "Preacher sent me up here. Special request. Y'all getting lonely?"

Quinn glanced over his shoulder at Ruiz, who leaned on the hood of his unit, arms crossed over his chest, watching them. "We asked for you. We had Preacher put the call out. We got something here you're gonna want to see."

His blue eyes were electrified, though his mood was dark. He'd taken something, Maureen worried, in an effort to counteract the drinks she'd smelled on him earlier. She hoped it wasn't more than one too many Red Bulls. She had her doubts.

"You guys finished your errand downtown pretty quick," Maureen said, loud enough for Ruiz to hear. She knew she shouldn't push the matter, shouldn't be antagonizing them. If Quinn and Ruiz had gone downtown looking for Marques, they'd never admit it to her. Not after she hadn't played along outside the Eighth. But maybe if she pushed the right button on one of them, and Quinn was her best bet, she thought, they'd show her something. "Quick enough to get it done and be first on scene at this thirty call. Nice job. Everything work out?"

"What? Yeah, yeah, fine. Some bullshit thing Ruiz had to double-check. Nothing worth talking about. Don't worry yourself over it."

Quinn flicked his cigarette butt, arcing it over the street. He watched as it tumbled through the air. He gestured for Maureen to follow him. She did. It wasn't like him to be this somber. And it wasn't being at a murder scene that bothered him; she'd seen him cutting up and joking at worse locations, in the aftermath of worse crimes than an isolated homicide. Something heavy was on his mind. Was it Marques, maybe his trip to the Eighth District with Ruiz? She decided that picking at him, that treating him with suspicion, might backfire. It certainly wasn't a tactic, she realized, that would work on her. If she took a different approach, talked to him like a coworker, like a teammate, she thought, maybe she'd get more out of him. Maybe the ex was at him again over his son. Maybe the kid had struggled through another bad day at school. She fought to recall the child's name.

"How's your boy?" Maureen asked. "He okay?"

Quinn frowned at her as though seeing her through a haze. "Who? Ruiz? I dunno, ask him."

So much for creating a bonding moment, Maureen thought.

They stepped around the police car, approaching a pea-green VW bus, its paint job measeled with rust. The bus leaned to one side on two flat tires. Close to the vehicle, on his back, with his eyes open, lay the dead body, a white male with bad skin and a crew cut, his throat slashed. Even through the sheet of dried blood, and there was plenty of it, Maureen could see the fatal wound: a gaping smile cut across his throat, running under his jaw and an inch or two above the Adam's apple, not terrible deep, but deep enough to get the job done. Blood was everywhere, which meant he'd been killed where he lay, and not dumped there after the deed.

Maureen recognized the victim as Clayton Gage, from the previous night's traffic stop. Her eyes flicked to his crotch. At least this one had his pants pulled up. There was nothing remarkable about his belt buckle. "What the fuck? How is this joker not in lockup?"

"We only hit him with misdemeanor charges," Ruiz said over her shoulder, by way of explanation. Maureen hadn't heard him approach from behind. For a big man, he moved quietly. She was furious with herself; he shouldn't be able to do that to her. She moved away from him.

"We never heard from you about anything more serious," Ruiz went on, "about the woman and such. We had next to nothing to book him on, especially if the woman stole the bags. Bond couldn't have been much. And the hold on misdemeanors is twenty-four hours max. Judge or no judge."

"So he got kicked right on time?" Maureen glanced from Ruiz to Quinn and back to Ruiz. Neither spoke. "How often does that happen? He had no priors? No warrants?" Neither man answered her. "I woulda sworn he had a file as thick as the Bible." She shook her head, hands on her hips, looking down at Gage. "Go figure. The one time the system works like it's supposed to, this is what we get. Waste of fucking time, the whole fucking traffic stop."

"You're an English major," Ruiz said. "Isn't this what you call irony?"

"You got the stolen purses back," Quinn said. "Your instincts were pretty on point about pulling over the pickup truck."

"Just smart enough," Maureen said, "to not see this coming."

"I don't see a connection," Quinn said, "between what we did with this guy last night and what happened to him tonight." He held his hands a foot apart. "Two separate, unrelated incidents. How the fuck you gonna see this coming?" He turned to his partner. "Back me up here, Rue."

Ruiz shrugged.

"I'm not saying we should've seen this coming," Maureen said. "That we should've been able to predict it. I just really thought this guy, the feeling I got off him—I don't know what I'm saying."

"Fucking prove it," Quinn said. "That's all *I'm* saying. You can't connect last night to this mess. No way."

Maureen said nothing, running the beam of her flashlight over the body at their feet. She understood Quinn's point, but thinking the previous night's events might not matter was foolish. Gage had gone from police custody to dead on the street. Someone, an NOPD detective most likely, would be interested in the time in between. And then would come family, the lawyers, too, probably. If there was a way to implicate the NOPD in his death, Maureen thought, specious connections or not, somebody would find it. Preacher told no lies. The NOPD were a fallible group. One with a bad reputation. She looked down at the body. Thanks for nothing, motherfucker. You couldn't get killed on someone else's beat?

Gage wore dark cargo pants, unbuttoned at the waist, his white belly exposed over the top of them. Auburn hair crusted with blood spread across his flesh like ivy crawling from his belly button. The amount of blood spilled down his front told Maureen he hadn't collapsed right away. He'd stumbled or staggered, blood pumping out of him. His hands were painted red from clutching at the wound. Bloody handprints from his efforts to stay upright, as if that would somehow save him, smeared the dirty side of the VW. His platinum necklace and diamond earrings were gone.

"Another throat slash," Maureen said. She turned to Quinn. "Like our one over on Magnolia. Two in a week? That's kind of fucked up."

"Agreed," Quinn said, with an authority that surprised Maureen. "This is fucked up. We don't get 'em much like this. Not out in the street like this. Everything's gunplay now. Shit like this is usually indoors, domestic. Some dickhead gets a steak knife in the ribs."

Maureen pulled on plastic gloves and squatted down beside the body. "Similar wound."

"Ixnay this junior detective stuff, Cogs. Leave it for the dicks. They like it better that way. I'm telling you for your own good. I heard the four-one-one on the Magnolia vic. Crazy. Think about him. Be glad you didn't fuck around with him."

Maureen ignored him. She was thinking of Preacher's hopes for a spark from the Sixth. Similar vic, similar wound. If there was another connection, she wanted to be the one to find it. If no connection existed, she thought, if the resemblance of this killing to the other murder was coincidence, no harm done. "Similar vic, too. White, kinda trailer-parkish. Killed on-site with a single wound to the throat."

She waved the flies away from Gage's face. She hung her forearms over her knees. She took several deep breaths, leaning over and around the body.

"What was he doing back here behind this van?" Maureen asked. She clicked on her flashlight, moving the beam over the ground around her.

Quinn shrugged. Ruiz had wandered off into the dark. Maureen didn't like not knowing where he was. She disliked harboring worries for her safety around a fellow cop.

Trying to disturb the body as little as possible, she rummaged through Gage's front pockets.

She found his wallet, the well-worn nylon-and-Velcro billfold with a faded Mötley Crüe logo on the front. He'd probably had it, she thought, since the eighth grade. Inside, he had lots of singles, a few fives, and a card for half off a lap dance at a Downman Road strip club. The other stuff Maureen figured he bought at the club, kitchen-sink crank from the look of his teeth and parking-lot hand jobs from the look of the rest of him, he paid full freight on those, if not double.

Mixed in with the dirty, wrinkled bills was a ticket stub for a gun-and-knife show about three weeks earlier, held west of the city out in Kenner. She found a pocket calendar listing the year's remaining gun shows like the schedule for a sports team. He had no credit cards or debit cards. He had no cell phone. Tucked in a wallet pocket were business cards from several gun shops. She looked at one off the bottom of the stack, for a store outside Baton Rouge. Its logo was an assault rifle. The store motto read *Worried about the next four years?* Mixed in with the cards was a yellow Post-it note folded closed.

"You believe this shit?" she said, passing the business card over her shoulder to Quinn. "Subtle."

"It sells guns," Quinn said. "They know their market. I'll give 'em that."

Maureen opened the Post-it note. Written inside, in a childlike scrawl: *Heath. 718 St. Peter Street. Eleven p.m. Sunday.*

"And then there's this," she said. "That's Pat O's address. Gage had Pat O's go cups in his truck. I met a guy named Heath the other night on Magnolia Street."

"On Magnolia Street? A guy named Heath? You sure about that?"

"He arrived right after you guys bailed. He owns the house where the body was found. He's some kind of slumlord, a total douche bag, too. No surprise there." She'd detected an odd note in Quinn's voice. She turned and looked up at him. "You know the guy?"

Quinn blinked a few times. "I know *of* him, his family. They're old-school New Orleans. His dad's a big shot. Just that kind of thing. You see their pictures in the society pages, they're always doing charity shit that involves wearing tuxedos and ball gowns. Good people." He handed her back the business card and took the note from her, frowned at it as he reread it. "Maybe we leave this business alone, Cogs. Let Homicide handle it. Seems complicated, a lot to sort out."

She put out her hand, gestured for the return of the note. Quinn didn't give it back.

"Let me bag this," Quinn said. "It is evidence. I should do something useful around here."

"Suddenly you're interested," Maureen said, only half kidding. Quinn didn't respond. He was already walking away from her. Maureen turned her attention back to Gage's wallet.

She checked his driver's license again. Three years expired. She stared at the picture. Gage looked healthier in it, though not a whole lot. Not much to compare, his corpse and his driver's license photo. Neither would flatter him. She should have run his name through her computer herself last night, not left everything to Quinn and Ruiz, who she knew could get lazy. It was her stop, her scene. She should've kept control. Leary and the stolen purses had commanded her attention. She'd been too impressed with her own detective genius, and with exerting her physical authority over Gage, with feeding that adrenaline need.

Quinn had returned. She looked up at him. "Mr. Gage was visiting our fair city from LaPlace. At least that's what this license says."

"A country boy," Quinn said. "I'd never have suspected."

"What are the odds that whoever killed him took his phone, his credit cards, and his big bills, and put his wallet back in his pocket? Pretty long, I'd think. We can probably rule out a robbery." She stood. "His jewelry is gone, though we don't know that he was wearing it."

She stretched her back then lifted her right foot, rotating her sore ankle until it cracked. She'd left her Percocet at home. Maybe after this business here she'd swing by her place real quick. She looked up and down the street. "Where's his truck? We should check and see if he claimed it out of impound. What was he doing out here? He wasn't hanging with his old college buddies at F and M's." She turned to Quinn. "This doesn't make any sense. This is such a weird place for him to get murdered."

"How the fuck should I know?" Quinn asked, impatient. "Where are the fucking detectives? Maybe he liked college girls. Pat O's was full of them last night." He moved closer to Maureen. "Cogs, one more time, not to pull the experienced officer card, but you can dial it down. You *should* dial it down. We're already working above our pay grade here."

"C'mon, aren't you curious? Stringing yellow tape, herding drunk kids, it's fucking boring. My brain falls asleep."

"You've been a cop since August," Quinn said. "It's October. You can't possibly be bored already."

Maureen reassembled Gage's wallet and set it on his hip. "You heard the brass, you were at the same meetings and roll calls I was when they read the memo from HQ last month. More investigative initiative from the uniformed officers. It's encouraged." She paused. "Don't you wanna know if we missed something last night that could've prevented this? Or that could lead to the killer? Could be good for us."

"You're new," Quinn said, "but you should know by now that there's what the brass says for the reporters and the mayor and then there's the real world we live in. Having the Justice Department hanging around doesn't change that. And now because of this first dead guy, the marshals and the FBI are on their way? It's gonna be a fucking circus around here. Guess who's gonna get stuck playing the clowns? Fuck that. The dicks are gonna be crazy nervous. I gotta deal with them regular. Now is not the time for us to get uppity. Especially if this murder and the Magnolia Street murder are connected. We want no part of that. None."

"I think it's too late for me as far as being uppity," Maureen said. "You got that note?" She wished she hadn't handed it over to Quinn. She'd made the same mistake she made with Gage, letting go of something important too easily. "You'll make sure the detective gets it?"

"It's in the car," Quinn said. "It's safe." He pointed across the street. "That there's the kid who discovered the body."

Maureen saw a young man, early twenties, dressed in khakis and a yellow polo shirt. He wore his shirt collar popped. He leaned against the brick building, his head hanging, his hands on his knees, a big watch hanging loose on his left wrist. He had on boat shoes with no socks, wore his sandy hair in the goofy, bushy style favored by boys—young men, Maureen corrected herself—these days. These prep school kids, Maureen thought, they all looked the same to her. He was, she thought, a younger, slimmer version of Caleb Heath. "What's he got to say for himself?"

"Not much," Quinn said. "Claimed he was headed for his car, meant to duck behind the VW for one last piss and literally walked right into our boy back there."

"So the body's been disturbed," Maureen said.

"Not much."

"He left footprints?"

"Nobody's pulling anything useful from that gravelly mush," Quinn said. "And who knows who else has been back there tonight before Gage got done."

"The kid call it in?"

"Nope," Quinn said, laughing. "He went back inside and told the bartender about it, yelling about it over the fucking music. Which was awesome, because that guaranteed the whole bar knew there was a dead body outside. Must have been ten of them standing around, polluting the scene when we got here. Fortunately, these kids chase easy, like pigeons. We didn't have much of a time getting them herded back across the street." He shrugged. "Which is good. It's our asses getting chewed by the detective if the Junior League over there sours the scene."

They both turned as the crime lab van came around the corner, blinding them for a moment with its headlights. It made a K-turn on the street, throwing its lights on the shrinking crowd of kids, and backed up to the scene.

Clad in dark blue cargo pants, ball caps, and their matching NOPD polo shirts and windbreakers, the techs climbed out of the van and read-ied their equipment. Ruiz went over to greet them. A few kids wandered into the street and up to the edge of the scene, watery cocktails in one hand, smartphones in the other, craning their necks to see through the shadows and to take pictures, attracted to the new arrival and activity, deciding if any of it was Facebook worthy.

Maureen moved toward them, sweeping her flashlight beam across their faces, yelling at them, backing them up onto the opposite sidewalk and against the wall of the bar. Quinn was right. They were easy to push around. Not quite the same crowd, she thought, as Magnolia Street. At least no one was throwing bottles at her. Not even any insults or wise-cracks like in Frenchmen Street. Not yet, anyway. She thought of the previous night's tedious and fruitless Magnolia Street canvass. She was not looking forward to another one.

"Are we gonna have to interview the whole bar?" she asked, return-ing to Quinn. "All of these kids, there's probably fifty more inside. It seems pretty obvious to me that Gage was killed on this block, right where we found him. Who knows who saw what coming and going? Did any of them see him inside the bar?"

Quinn sighed. "What we do next depends on what the detective says. We can take the initiative and ask around, but I don't know that we're gonna get any kind of useful statements from a barroom full of hammered college kids. Unless the detective is hard core, I'm thinking it's too late at night for a neighborhood canvass."

"We did one on Magnolia Street," Maureen said. "Most of those guys were drinking and smoking all day."

"They're used to us in that neighborhood," Quinn said.

"I cruise this block twice a week on noise complaints."

"Atkinson was in charge on Magnolia Street. Unless we get her for this one, day shift'll get stuck with the door-to-door in the morning. It's gonna be fucking useless anyway. No one saw anything. I guarantee it. That way, every neighborhood is the same."

Maureen chewed her thumbnail. "I wanna know what Gage was doing back there. Hiding? Waiting for someone to come out of the bar? Maybe Heath stood him up the other night at Pat O's. Maybe Gage hooked up with Leary and blew off the meet." She looked at the mop-headed kid, who was now texting something on his phone. "Heath struck me as the arrested-development overaged frat boy type. I could see him digging this place. You think so?"

"Maybe Gage was taking a leak behind the van like the rest of the neighborhood," Quinn said. He closed his eyes, pinched the bridge of his nose. "Was he smoking rock? Maybe he was beating off to college-age pussy? The fuck should I know?"

"You think he was with the person who killed him?" Maureen asked. "You think they knew each other?"

"Then why do it here?" Quinn asked, exasperated. "Why kill him in a place where the body might be found before he even bleeds out? According to Eli Manning over there, this VW's been around as long as anyone can remember. Back behind it is a popular spot for plenty of wonderful things. Techs'll find an old condom or two back there, I figure."

"I could've done without that bit of intel," Maureen said. She fought back a smile. No matter how hard Quinn pretended not to care, she'd noticed, he had answers, or theories, at least, for every one of her questions. His brain was working the scene, she thought, even if his heart wasn't in it. Why hadn't he ever gone out for detective? she wondered. Another time, she decided, she'd ask him that. "Maybe Gage didn't know this bar, this corner. Maybe the killer didn't know it, either."

"It's fucking F and M's," Quinn said. "It's infamous. People know it. Besides, it only takes half a minute to figure out that there's plenty of foot traffic on this block."

"Gage wasn't from here, remember?" She looked up and down the block. "The killer could be in the neighborhood. Could be in the bar, even."

"I doubt that," Quinn said. "There's a lot of blood here. A lot. He'll be wearing a fair share of it. After a job this messy, he's got to go to ground and clean up."

"The body's fresh. The killer is bloody. He can't be far. I wish we had more urgency here."

"Tell it to the detective," Quinn said, nodding at the dark sedan pulling to a stop in the middle of the street. "Fucking finally."

Maureen watched as a short, jowly man in a gray suit climbed out of the driver's seat. He had a heavily gelled gray and wavy pompadour, and thick lips. He looked like a lounge act's bass player's dad, Maureen thought. Quinn spat in the street. "Awesome. I love this guy. Really. I do. What a great fucking night we're having."

"Fuck me," Maureen said. "At least we won't have to work too hard tonight."

"You got that right. Let me see how Rue's doing with the techs. You wait here for His Majesty. Remember now, all he needs is the basics. The facts, no theories. The bare minimum. Keep it simple in the Sixth, Cogs. That's how we roll."

Maureen watched the detective, Ronnie Drayton, also known as Defective Drayton, hitch up his trousers. He surveyed the scene, puffing out his chest for the chirping co-eds in short skirts and high heels now whispering behind their hands. Rumor had it he was sleeping with the new crime-beat reporter from the *Times-Picayune*, a recent Brooklyn émigré fifteen years his junior.

"Thanks for nothing, Quinn," Maureen said.

Quinn raised his shoulders high, palms upturned. "Hey, you're the one with the big-time professional aspirations. We drew the Lead Defective, the guy who couldn't catch herpes in a whorehouse. That means you'll have a shot at nabbing the killer yourself. The brass will love you. You'll get a medal and a promotion. It's totally a glass-half-full type of scenario for you. Enjoy."

10

Drayton walked around the front of his car, somehow looking right through Maureen as he approached her, unbuttoning his suit jacket then adjusting his crotch with one hand. She'd worked other murder scenes that had become his cases. She didn't follow up, but she wasn't sure he'd cleared a single one of them. She didn't like him and was far from the only one on the force, uniformed or otherwise, who felt that way. She wondered who or what he knew that allowed him to linger, indifferent, ineffective, and entitled while the rank and file got gutted by the merciless new regulations. A part of her wanted to come right out and ask him who he was blowing to keep his job. She kept her questions to herself. Instead, she met him in the street, her hand extended. "Officer Maureen Coughlin."

Drayton stopped, leaving her hand hanging in the air. Behind them, the cameras flashed as the techs took photos of the body and the scene. He stood motionless for a moment, posing, Maureen thought, just in case someone was taking his picture. He sucked his teeth and gave Maureen the slow and deliberate once-over with his eyes, a smirk curling one corner of his mouth. She noticed he had fat fingers and wore a pinkie ring.

"I thought there was a body to check out around here," Drayton said.

"Other side of the van."

Drayton nodded. "You new?"

"Relatively," Maureen said.

"What makes a striking young thing like you want a dirty job like this?"

"Assholes," Maureen said after a beat. "I get to do something about them, rather than just helplessly tolerate their shit. It's empowering."

"The body's behind the van, you say?" Drayton stayed where he was. "Messy?"

"I do," Maureen said. "A bit."

She noticed the number of kids on the corner had dwindled. She couldn't say how many had gone back inside the bar and how many had wandered off into the night. How many potential witnesses they'd lost. The music from inside the bar was louder. She couldn't be sure, and her knowledge of hip-hop was minimal, but she thought she'd heard the same song playing on Magnolia Street. Welcome to New Orleans. Above all else, on went the party.

"Detective," she asked, "would you like us to secure the bar, start doing interviews? Names and numbers, at least?"

Drayton chuckled. "Collins, I doubt the murderer came out here, shot this guy, and then sauntered back in the bar for a Jägermeister."

"The COD is a throat slash," Maureen said, knowing as she did it that she shouldn't correct a detective. He'd find out soon enough how his vic had died. "And as for the bar patrons, I was thinking witnesses more than a perp."

"A slash? What did I say? Isn't that what I said?"

"My mistake," Maureen said. "The bar, Detective? The witnesses?"

"Eh. Sure. If you need something to do." Hands in his pockets, he wandered around the front of the VW, checking out the van and jingling his change. "Haven't seen one of these in a while. Classic. Damn shame, the state of it. This is why we can't have nice things."

Maureen watched him observe himself in the dirty windshield, acting again as if the cameras on scene were for him and not the dead man on the ground. He released a long, low whistle when he saw the body, now illuminated under the bright white light of the crime scene lamps. Maureen could more clearly see the blackish-red wound across the throat, the exposed viscera, the apron of deep red blood down the man's front. The blood pooled around him on the street glistened on the dirt and gravel like leaked oil. Flies alighted in it, more of them on his face and chest.

"Will you look at that," Drayton said, tucking his tie into his shirt, pulling on latex gloves, and squatting beside the body. His new leather shoes squeaked as he moved. "A dead white boy. Go figure. Haven't seen one of those in a while, either."

"We had one in Central City just last night," Maureen said. She waited for a response from Drayton. "Throat cut like this guy. Dead about a week." She waited again. He didn't even look at her. He was humming to himself. Was that Sinatra? She felt her own throat tighten with rage. Quinn had warned her to keep it simple. This was why. What he'd meant was "lower your expectations." "We found him in a vacant on the dead-end block of Magnolia. Detective Atkinson caught it. It was in the twenty-fours."

She looked at Gage's wallet, balanced right there on his hip, waiting like a book to be opened. Pressure built behind her eyes. Her ankle throbbed. She was tempted to go back to her car. She thought she might scream if Drayton didn't pick up the wallet. Instead, as if to taunt her, Drayton picked up a stone from beside the body, studied it, put it back where he'd found it. Maureen thought she might give him one more nudge.

"There's things about this vic that you might want to know," Maureen said. "Like, for starters, the fact we arrested him last night."

Drayton looked up at her, his hands draped over his knees, one eye closed. "Maybe you should secure the bar, after all, Costigan."

"It's Coughlin," Maureen said. "Coughlin."

Drayton waggled a finger at her. "Wait a minute, I know you."

The lascivious glint had returned to his eyes. While flies buzzed over a throat wound, Maureen thought, not two feet away from him, he beamed like a college kid who'd recognized a local stripper in the grocery store.

"You're that redhead," Drayton said. "From the drug dealer thing, with the dead kid in the car. I heard about you. You're Atkinson's girl. We did that thing together on Jackson and Annunciation, that daytime shoot-out with the car crash about three months ago. Weren't you there for that?"

Maureen caught her breath, stunned. Girl? She wasn't anybody's fucking girl. And she sure as shit could not see Atkinson, who outranked Drayton not just on the NOPD, but also in every discernible human quality, tolerating Drayton's condescending lounge singer clown show for one second. He wouldn't have the balls to talk to Atkinson, or to look at her, or to not look at her, the way he did those things with Maureen.

"Listen, Detective," Maureen began, "maybe there are some things, some information that you're missing, things that happened last night that I should—"

She felt a strong hand grip her elbow. Quinn. "Hey, Cogs. Great work here. Fantastic. Just who I was looking for. Now that everyone's up to speed, let's leave the hard work to the high pay grades. All right then. Nice seeing you, Detective, thanks for coming out. Cogs, let's do something else, way over there away from here."

Maureen allowed Quinn to lead her away.

"Yeah, sorry about that," Quinn said. "I forget he's a whole 'nother level of intolerable with female cops. We think of you as one of the guys, sometimes it gets in the way. It's a compliment, in a weird way."

"Oh, I get the feeling he's intolerable with females in general," Maureen said.

"So we gotta canvass the bar?" Quinn asked. "What did Drayton say?"

Maureen blew out a long sigh. She needed to be smart. She was swimming against the current here. On Magnolia Street they'd talked to every person they could find willing to stand still in front of them. But now? Nothing. No interest. True, they'd been shut out for leads on Magnolia Street, but, at least, unlike this time, it wasn't the cops doing the stonewalling. Why should she nag and beg to make more work for herself? She was tired. Her ankle ached. She'd get no help here from Quinn or Ruiz. The detective was on scene. Useless asshole or not, he was in charge now. He was responsible. When she was a detective, she could run things her way. Until then, maybe there were some benefits to being an injun and not a chief. "He was noncommittal."

"Then that's a negative, Ghost Rider," Quinn said. "I promise you, we ain't missing anything. Nothing those kids say is gonna be worth shit."

"I have noticed," Maureen said, "that no one's come running outside to offer us their assistance."

"Astute," Quinn said. "You feel me?" He looked around, shaking his head. "Man, it sucks to be here for this. I used to hang at this joint, back when I was younger. High school and after. Now and then I'll work a detail out here for some private party in the back barroom. Nothing's changed. Place doesn't get going until after midnight. Lots of drunk girls, not one of 'em over twenty-five. A pool table used strictly for dancing on. Killer cheese fries."

"I hadn't heard," Maureen said. "I can't believe I missed this place."

They watched as workers from the coroner's office loaded the corpse onto a stretcher, zipping closed the body bag after tucking in the head.

"Yeah, I'm surprised Preacher let you get through training without sampling those fries," Quinn said.

"I guess he left me some local treasures to discover for myself."

The stretcher went into the back of the van with as much care as an old couch headed for Goodwill.

"Where *do* you hang, Cogs?" Quinn asked. "What's your thing? Me and Rue were trying to figure that out the other night."

"I don't get out much," Maureen said.

"I got that impression," Quinn said. "Rue thinks you have secrets."

"I mean, I do some stuff," Maureen said. If she wanted Quinn to warm up to her, to trust her more, she had to give something. And in the back of her mind, despite her recently formed suspicions about his agenda and his loyalties, she didn't want Quinn seeing her as a friendless loser. Even if it was true, she didn't need him knowing it. "I go to Parasol's for the games. I've been to Bon Temps, seen the Soul Rebels there a couple of times. I've been down to Frenchmen, to DBA and the Blue Nile. Brass bands are cool. Nothing like that where I come from. I like the Spotted Cat. I like watching the jazz dancers through the window."

"Funny," Quinn said. "I never figured you for a dancer. Who do you go with?"

Maureen shrugged as an answer. She went out alone, though she sometimes didn't go home alone. She wasn't telling Quinn any of that; she'd already told him too much. That thing about the Spotted Cat was stupid. Maureen's cell phone buzzed in her pocket. She grabbed it, grateful for the distraction. She checked the number. Atkinson. No doubt she'd heard about the similar murder. Maureen knew she was that on point. Bit of a difference, Maureen thought, between her and that tool Drayton. She let the call go to voice mail. She didn't want to talk to Atkinson around Quinn and Ruiz. She didn't like feeling that way, but there it was, a strong signal from her gut.

"Listen to me," Quinn said. "Maybe you and I should talk about last night."

"Oh, no."

Quinn raised his hands. "It's no big thing, it's not. It's just that after you left, Preacher kind of squashed taking Gage to jail."

"Squashed?" Maureen asked. "What do you mean squashed?"

"We had the woman. We had the stolen goods. You did good work."

"The guy was a witness," Maureen said. "At the very least. At worst he was dangerous. I didn't like him. I told Preacher that at the time. You never even ran his record, did you? I could've been right about him. We could've put a real threat back out on the street."

"He ain't dangerous no more," Quinn said.

"Really? That's what you have to say."

"We didn't have anything serious on him. He was useless baggage, Cogs. Best possible outcome, you ask me. Look forward, think ahead. You fill a case file with a bunch of random drunken white-trash bullshit, you think anybody important appreciates it? You think the DA's office wants a case like that? There aren't enough PDs for the killers and dealers already locked up. Think about it. People remember, Cogs. Lawyers, judges, brass, they remember people who make their jobs more difficult. People who muck up the works."

"So that fairy tale about him bonding out so quick?"

"Don't get mad at Rue," Quinn said. "He didn't think we should bring you into it. He was covering for me. He was being a good partner."

"I can't believe you let me stand there and tell Drayton stuff that wasn't true."

"Good thing he ignored you," Quinn said. "And I pulled you out before it got worse."

"Fuck you, Quinn. And the pickup truck?"

"Gage drove away in it, far as I can tell."

"We never got a decent look around inside it," Maureen said.

"Looking for what?" Quinn asked. "What are we gonna find? You pulled him over because he was a dirty white boy. What we got on him was dirty white boy bullshit. Who knew some crazy other shit like this would fucking happen? I could see this coming, I'd be down in Jackson Square with a bunch of pretty rocks conning the fucking tourists. And this murder would've happened anyway. What Rue said about the bond is true, you know that. You know the rules if anyone does. Gage would've been out by tonight. No doubt. He'd be dead anyway, even if we had arrested him. It was out of our hands the whole time."

"I have to tell Drayton about Leary," Maureen said.

"Do you?"

"Christ, Quinn, they were together the night before Gage was murdered. According to her they had sex. You don't think that's relevant? Worth looking into?"

"You dealt with her," Quinn said. "You really think she's relevant to this? Did Gage express any real concern or interest in her? You think she's anyone's *lover*? That she'd be helpful or credible in any way? She's the one who got locked up. She's in jail. She's got a better alibi than *us*, for chrissakes. C'mon."

"I'm not saying she's the killer," Maureen said. She didn't see the point of correcting Quinn concerning Leary's whereabouts. "But she's a person of interest."

"Only to you. Save yourself the trouble. And think about if you wanna waste Drayton's time with that dirtbag Leary. Use that busy brain of yours to make *less* trouble for once. That broad was some local hustler skank he talked into the truck for a five-dollar blow job. We both seen worse."

"I'm not having it come back on me," Maureen said, "that I had info a detective could have used and I held it back. I'm not taking that weight."

Quinn lit a cigarette. "Preacher was rank on scene. He said squash the thing, so we did. No paperwork, no nothing, you know what I mean? You can't bring Leary into it without putting Preacher in, too. We can all be in this mess, or we can all be clear of it. How is this even a hard decision for you? Why is this conversation ongoing?"

"Why would Preacher do that? What's he care about Clayton Gage?"

"You got me," Quinn said. "We were following orders. Me and Rue, we're covered. You, too, I'm sure. Talk to Preacher if you got a problem with the way it played out."

"I will," Maureen said.

"Good luck with that. Don't forget that he agreed to send you here tonight. You don't think it was 'cause he knew we should have this exact conversation? Maybe he wanted you on board with us when this case, and Gage's name, started making the rounds? You got a good rep going around the district. Here's some free advice: don't blow it over low-rent dirtbags."

"Is that a threat, Quinn?"

"It is what it is. I don't understand why you're so hostile. We're only trying to help you out." Quinn leaned close to Maureen, "Listen, I'm gonna remind you of something important here. Don't throw Preacher under the bus with Drayton. You'll come out of that the worst. Going over your duty sergeant's head will look bad. And I know you got this teddy bear image of him 'cause he was your training officer and he smoothed some things over for you so you could get out of field training with a clean record. He's done it before. He's a pro. He knows how to look good. But fuck with the guy's livelihood and you can enjoy a new career being a meter maid in Houston. He's got juice up and down the ladder. He's a player. We've all known him longer than you. We all know him better than you. Believe it."

"Gimme a little credit, Quinn. I'm not *that* hotheaded. I'm not a rat. I know I owe the guy. I know I'm better off on his good side."

"Nobody's trying to hurt you," Quinn said. "I swear. This guy Gage doesn't get offed, none of us are even talking about last night. We're friends. We're a team. We had us a minor miscommunication. Nothin' to it. Remember that."

"The note from Gage's wallet?" Maureen asked.

"What note?"

"I'm gonna remember this, Quinn," Maureen said.

"You should," Quinn said. "Trust me on this, Cogs. I'm looking out for you. For all of us. Forget any ideas about connecting Heath and Gage. Don't cross Preacher, don't cross people like the Heaths, and you'll have a good life in this town. They do more good than harm. A lot more good. Trust me for a little while. I'll prove it to you."

They watched as Drayton headed their way.

"I'm sure this douche canoe has cracked the case by now, anyway," Quinn said. "Without our help."

"Colligan," Drayton called out.

"Seriously?" Quinn said, eyebrows raised.

"That's the third different one," Maureen said, shrugging. "Collins, Costigan, Colligan. At least they're all Irish, I'll give him that."

"The ID on the stiff, give it to me again," Drayton said.

He hadn't asked for it a first time, Maureen thought, but she let it go. She glanced at Quinn. "Clayton Gage. Thirty-six years old. LaPlace address on his driver's license. Could be old, though. The license is expired. ID's in his wallet."

"You went through his wallet?" Drayton asked.

"You didn't?" Maureen replied.

"So what the fuck's he doing in New Orleans?" Drayton asked Quinn. "Let's start there."

"Saints game yesterday," Quinn said. "Party trip into town." The quickest glance at Maureen. "It's a possibility."

"So he gets from alive yesterday in the Dome," Drayton said, "to dead tonight outside F and M's. How's that happen?"

Maureen studied her shoe tops. Think about Preacher, she told herself. She was wary of both Quinn and Ruiz after the past two days, but Preacher she trusted. If he'd asked for a favor from Quinn and Ruiz, he had his reasons. Couldn't be smart, she thought, helping Drayton at Preacher's expense. And there was no helping Gage now. Any connection between the Cooley and Gage murders was for the detectives to investigate. Atkinson certainly didn't need her help and Drayton clearly didn't want it. Why make useless noise? And how could Preacher know Gage would turn up dead? The guy did keep questionable company. Going by his wallet, Gage's life's pursuits were strippers and guns, and if he was connected to Cooley, maybe much worse. Maybe the real mystery was not that he'd been murdered, but how he'd survived as long as he had. And maybe Quinn was right. Maybe Heath and Leary had nothing to do with any of this. Maureen didn't quite believe that, though, and she was pretty sure Quinn and Ruiz didn't, either.

11

In response to AtKinson's message, Maureen met the detective at the St. Charles Tavern, a grungy twenty-four-hour corner restaurant on St. Charles Avenue in the Lower Garden District, and the closest thing Maureen had found in her police district to the Staten Island diners she haunted back in her waitressing days.

The setup of the place was simple: a big square room with a scarred and dirty linoleum floor, a low ceiling, and bad lighting that turned everyone's skin yellow, though some blamed the food for that. A bar crowned by silent TVs and neon beer signs stood against the right-hand wall. Video poker machines huddled against the back wall and a jukebox glowed in one corner. No matter the time of day or night she was in there, the air smelled of old kitchen grease, moldy air-conditioning, and cheap ketchup. The dim tavern was popular with night shift folk, Maureen's kind of people, with service industry workers, cabdrivers, cops and firefighters and EMTs, the occasional Uptown insomniac hunched over a paperback or a crossword puzzle. Most nights, a few tourists wandered through on their way home from the Quarter to the St. Charles Avenue hotels, looking to satisfy their late-night drunken munchies.

That night, as Maureen sat eating with Atkinson, three cabbies huddled close together at the bar, chattering in a guttural Middle Eastern language Maureen didn't know, throwing hostile glares at her table. Earlier that night, a fellow driver had been pistol whipped and robbed out in Gentilly. They resented the fact, Maureen figured, that she was in the tavern eating instead of out hunting for the assailant or protecting the next potential victim. Two ambulance crews in uniform, young, clean, and loud, surrounded a big table in the back.

At a nearby table, a group of tourists, their store-bought, out-of-season plastic beads draped in bunches around their sweaty necks, argued over whether or not it was appropriate to order Bloody Marys. The affirmative side argued that since it was now technically morning, Bloody Marys were the way to go. The negative side did not buy into the "it's so late, it's early" argument. Since they hadn't been home yet, the counterargument went, it was still "last night" and Blood Marys were for, and only for, everybody knows, the morning after. Nobody suggested that everybody had had enough to drink already.

Atkinson smiled at the argument, shaking her head, her curly blond hair falling about her cheeks and shoulders in chaos as usual, the sleeves of her shirt rolled up over her muscled forearms to avoid the gravy into which she dipped her mushy, thick-cut French fries and her rubbery fried shrimp. "You used to cocktail, Coughlin. You have an opinion on this great debate we can't help but overhear?"

"Negative," Maureen said. "I try to tune it out."

She'd ordered her usual: a bowl of pungent gumbo with two fried eggs on the side and a bottomless cup of black coffee. She drowned the eggs in Louisiana Red Dot, dipping the fork-cut slices into the gumbo. For a late-night hole-in-the-wall, the tavern had killer seafood gumbo, at least according to her limited experience, with a dark roux and always half a crab's jointed legs poking out. She wondered what their secret was. Probably never cleaning the gumbo pot. One day she'd learn to make it. She'd do it the old-fashioned way, where the roux was hand stirred for hours. As a practice in patience and delayed gratification, she told herself. As a practice in commitment. Maybe she could get Patrick to give her a recipe. She had a real kitchen now. She could do those things. Or maybe she could call him up, invite him over, fuck him without the bullshit pretense that embarrassed them both, and get the recipe off the Internet. Maybe she should forget about Patrick altogether. It was going nowhere, had already *gone* nowhere; they'd been hooking up as exes for longer than they'd been dating. She could head off that humiliating and inevitable moment when he stopped answering her texts. It was coming. She could feel it. She pushed her food away and reached for her coffee mug. The tavern also served their coffee the way she liked it, old and burned. Or as she liked to tell her coworkers, hot, black, and bitter like her heart.

"Earth to Maureen," Atkinson said. She dipped a shrimp in her gravy, held it dripping over the bowl. "So what was it Drayton called you?"

"A girl," Maureen said. "Your girl, to be precise."

"And this bothered you?"

"I know, right?" Maureen said. "Not his associating me with you. But the word *girl*?" She blew out a long breath. "Normally, I'm not like that." She raised her hands. "I admit, I'm still getting used to every other person around here, man or woman, calling me baby and honey and sweetie, but I get it's a local habit. It's not personal. And I guess I'm a feminist or whatever, but I never got hung up on bad vocabulary, on whether I was a girl or a woman or a lady. It was pointless and a waste of energy, considering the places I worked.

"And I don't make a big deal of it on the job, when it happens. Every now and then one of the older guys calls me dear or missy. Who cares? Think of what I get called on the street."

Atkinson raised her right hand. "Been there, bought the T-shirt."

"Exactly." Maureen wrinkled her nose, as if a bad smell had drifted up from under the table. "But something about him, about the way

Drayton said the word, it made the hairs on the back of my neck stick up—and not in a good way."

"You're not the first to have that reaction to him," Atkinson said. "Give him as wide a berth as you can. He's got a rep for scapegoating the rank and file when his cases go south, which, you may imagine, happens fairly often. Keep me in the loop. I don't know what I can do, but . . . with the similarities you saw to the Magnolia Street killing, I may want to take this one from him."

"How's Drayton going to feel about that?" Maureen asked.

"As long as we keep it quiet, he and I," Atkinson said, "and protect his ego, make it look like he's doing me a favor, like he's giving it to me and I'm not taking it from him, it won't be a problem. Matter of fact, if the case doesn't turn into a slam dunk in the next twenty-four to forty-eight hours, he'll be only too happy to give it up. He might be calling me." She paused. "Not the kind of thing I should really be sharing with a platoon officer, but there it is." She dunked and ate another shrimp. "I heard you saw our boy Marques tonight. I've been meaning to talk to you about him."

Maureen slowly set down her fork. She shifted her eyes away from Atkinson. After weeks of what she felt was departmental failure to look out for the kid, a lot of people were interested in Marques tonight. "Do I wanna know why?"

"Mother Mayor called me earlier," Atkinson said. "She told me Marques showed up at home a couple of hours ago, perched on the handlebars of some dirty, bald-headed white girl's bike, with his drum tucked under his arm, asking for change for a twenty. And telling her the whole situation was *your* idea. She was less than thrilled."

"That I kept her grandson out of jail?" Maureen rubbed at her temples. "That woman."

"Oh, come on," Atkinson said. "You're gonna act surprised Marques didn't tell his grandmother he got arrested? She said Marques told her he had to help you out with something on Frenchmen Street, and that's why he was coming home so late. So now she's thinking we're the reason he keeps sneaking out of the house, that we're encouraging it, and dangling him out there as bait for Bobby Scales. She's talking about calling my boss. And yours. And her city council rep. And the mayor."

Maureen shook her head. "Good Lord."

"You want to tell me what really happened?"

Maureen told the story about picking up Marques at the Eighth District, about their trip to Frenchmen, and about how she had to leave in a hurry to help with the body on Lyons Street on Preacher's orders. For the time being, she left out running into Quinn and Ruiz outside the Eighth District and their open hostility to Marques, though she would've liked Atkinson's input. Any concerns she had about her fellow officers had to go through Preacher first. Preacher knew Atkinson had taken Maureen under her wing, and he liked and respected her. But Maureen knew that wouldn't stop him from resenting her taking squad problems outside the squad. Quinn and Ruiz would like it even less. Atkinson herself would notice the breach in protocol. Maureen didn't want to undermine Atkinson's trust or confidence in her.

"That kid kills me," Atkinson said, rolling her eyes. "Maybe we oughtta forget about looking out for him and hire him to work for us."

"I'll stop by his grandmother's place," Maureen said, "or over by Roots of Music rehearsal tomorrow and straighten him out."

"Don't waste your time," Atkinson said, chuckling. "If he's not listening to his grandmother, no way he's listening to one of us, even you, OC. Besides, what're you gonna tell him that he doesn't already know? That he didn't do what was smart, he didn't do what he was told, he didn't do what he promised you he'd do, but things turned out okay anyway. Where have I heard that story before?"

Atkinson wiped her mouth with her paper napkin, refolding it before tucking it under the rim of her plate. "It's good. It's good that Marques and his grandmother trust us enough to call us, especially after we let them down on the Bobby Scales case. I'll put up with her paranoid theories and her threats if it means they'll keep in touch with us."

"That 'we' who let them down being the detective squad," Maureen said, the challenge popping out of her mouth before she even knew she'd thought it. "And the district commander's office. Us out on the street, we're banging heads whenever we get the chance. We're still after him."

Atkinson laughed out loud. "Blaming the higher-ups without a second thought. You are becoming a tried-and-true platoon officer."

Maureen felt a rush of blood to her collarbones, old frustrations surfacing inside her. She did not like being laughed at by anyone, especially Atkinson. "I'm just saying, the rank and file could've used some backup from the suits and the brass while the case was still hot a few weeks ago. We took our eye off the ball too soon. We had him on the run and we let him go to ground."

"The rank and file being you," Atkinson said, smiling. "Listen, we don't need to have this conversation right now."

"The guy is a killer," Maureen said. "Everyone knows it. And *somebody* in this town knows where he's holed up. The case oughtta be getting more resources, more attention, is all I'm saying. I've been telling Preacher the same thing."

"You know why that case was allowed to cool off," Atkinson said, a hint of warning in her tone. "Marques is unreliable."

"Marques is a fucking kid," Maureen said. "A thirteen-year-old boy. We're the adults. We're the ones who are supposed to fix things. What the fuck kind of department is this that it can't take a killer off the streets without the help of one teenage boy? We can't find another way?"

"The other way is what I want to talk to you about," Atkinson said, "before you get your back up any further. Marques is our only witness on the murder beef. We have no other good evidence he killed Mike-Mike or that he was even the shooter at Mother Mayor's place. Whatever resources we shifted off another maybe stronger case now, over to Scales, would be wasted because Marques won't testify, or even make a useful statement. You said it yourself, Marques is a thirteen-year-old kid. We can't count on him. I appreciate your enthusiasm, but your way isn't the best way."

"The brass was too eager," Maureen said, "to get a dead kid out of the headlines and off the evening news."

"You don't really believe that," Atkinson said. "You're just being contrary. You think we'd let Scales walk over bad publicity? At the rate kids are killing each other in this city, you really think I would let that happen?" She waited for an answer. "Maybe you forgot I was, I *am*, the lead on Mike-Mike's murder."

"No," Maureen said. "I didn't forget." Her breathing had become quick and shallow. She felt sweat breaking out along her hairline, and it wasn't from the hot sauce. It was time to dial it back. Nothing productive came of picking fights with Atkinson. They were on the same side. "Of course not."

"You haven't been a cop long enough to be *this* cynical," Atkinson said. "I mentioned Marques for a reason. And it wasn't to call you out over how you handled him tonight. While you've been out knocking heads in the Sixth District, have you heard anything about Scales going around? Has Marques? Rumors? Stories? What's the word around the neighborhood?"

"Not a fucking sound," Maureen said. "Not a sighting, not a rumor, not a whisper, nothing. No sign of his pal Shadow, either. I figure maybe they're not running together anymore. Shadow's not famous for his loyalty."

"You asked Marques about it."

"Of course I did," Maureen said. "I got the snitches-are-bitches song and dance." She waved for the check. "Maybe Scales is dead and we haven't stumbled over the body yet. One can only hope." She paid. "No change," she said to the waitress.

"Okay, good," Atkinson said, nodding. "So it sounds like there's nothing on the streets about it. I ask because we have an address for Scales. I'm waiting for the warrant to come through."

"A murder warrant?" Maureen asked. She felt the tension in her back and shoulders, in her neck and behind her eyes, release. She was elated and embarrassed at the same time. "I'm giving you grief for letting him skate and the whole time you know you're gonna fucking nail him."

"I tried to head you off," Atkinson said. "You're tough to reroute once you get worked up."

"Tell me about it," Maureen said. "I'm working on that."

"Grab your coffee," Atkinson said. "Let's go outside and smoke."

Maureen and Atkinson took a small sidewalk table set against the tavern's front window. The sky was lightening, but not enough yet to switch off the streetlights. As they sat, a streetcar rumbled by on the neutral ground, headed toward Lee Circle and downtown, half full of sleepy-eyed riders in the various modest uniforms of the downtown cafés and hotels. Another day shift readied itself to get under way, Maureen thought. She checked the time. She had little more than an hour before the end of her night tour.

"This address you have on Bobby Scales," Maureen said. "Where did you get it? I've heard nothing about this."

"We've been keeping it very, very quiet," Atkinson said. "I'm glad nothing has hit the streets about it, that's a good sign."

Again Maureen thought of Quinn and Ruiz. "You're worried about a leak inside the department."

"Not that," Atkinson said. "I had some concerns because of how the lead came to us."

"Which was how?"

"Hell indeed hath no fury like a woman who's found out you've been fucking her cousin on the side. And knocked her up while you're at it."

Maureen clapped her hands. "You've got to be kidding me."

"She came *straight* downtown to HQ," Atkinson said. "Five years ago, her uncle got shot out in Hollygrove. I got the guy who did it. She remembered me. Hair up to here, makeup out to there, big gold earrings. She took some *time* getting ready for this. The girl was spitting fire. She was talking so fast I had to confirm the address three times. Took me twenty minutes to get her to get around to it, and she came in ready to give it." Atkinson waved her hand, as if waving away a cloud of fluttering words in the air. "I know more about Castilla Roget's love life than I would ever need to know. But she gave him up. She's called me twice at

HQ to see if we got him yet. She wants to make sure she gets to tell him it was her that gave him up. I was hoping she wasn't out bragging on giving him up before we could nail him. She seemed pretty thrilled with herself."

"So as soon as the paper comes through," Maureen said, "you're taking his door?"

"With my steel-toed boots on. Which brings me to my next question: You want in?"

Maureen nearly leaped across the table and planted a big, fat kiss on Atkinson's lips. "Do I want in? Do I want in? Are you kidding me? Yes! Yes!"

Bobby Scales was a twenty-something Uptown thug, amoral and vicious. He was the prime suspect in the strangulation and burning death of one of his thirteen-year-old soldiers, Mike-Mike, and in the attempted murder of another one of his former soldiers, Marques Greer, in a drive-by that had put three bullets in Marques's grandmother's house, while she, Marques, Maureen, and Preacher were inside. Scales was the first hard-core criminal Maureen had come up against on the job. Scales was the first killer, the first deadly predator she'd found within her reach since her entanglement with a sociopath named Frank Sebastian on Staten Island. And Scales had eluded her. Vanished like smoke on the same day she'd first laid eyes on him. She couldn't bear letting an evil like that slip away, not when she'd faced this one with her badge and her gun and the power and force of the law behind her. But after the drive-by the NOPD lost track of Scales. He vanished into the small city and the network of loyalties and connections he knew so much better than she did. And after a few weeks of halfhearted searching, interest in the fates of both Marques and Scales had faded from the NOPD's collective imagination. Other crimes and killers and victims took their place. None of them were in short supply, unfortunately. This address Atkinson had was the first hard lead on Scales since the night he'd vanished.

Maureen realized that at some indistinct point in the recent past she had started doubting Atkinson's assurances that Scales would surface, and that the cops would be ready for him when he did. She feared that another murder, Marques's murder or that of his grandmother most likely, was the only way Scales would get back on the department's radar. Maureen again saw why cops throughout the department called Atkinson "the Spider." She saw designs and patterns invisible to everyone else. She believed in a good trap as well as a stealthy pursuit. Everything she wanted eventually came to her. Scales had tickled a strand in Atkinson's web. Now the detective was prepping her pounce.

"You're not worried," Maureen said, "that Ms. Roget will regret coming to us, or lose faith, and tip him off before we get the warrant?"

"She was angry," Atkinson said, "but she wasn't stupid. She came down three days after she found out, so it wasn't in the heat of passion, so to speak. And, yeah, she wants him to know that it was her that got him for stepping out on her, but she wants to tell him that when he's safely on the other side of some thick plastic or some steel bars." She shook her head. "I always knew Scales wasn't as smart as he thought he was. He fucked with the wrong girl. This Castilla, she's built like both Williams sisters rolled into one."

"Scales has a habit," Maureen said, "of fucking with the wrong women. I'm thrilled to see it finally bite him in the ass."

"I'm only going to say this once," Atkinson said, leaning across the table, making sure her eyes locked with Maureen's, "but I have to say it, and you have to hear it. This isn't getting a kid home after curfew, this is the deep-down serious, black-and-blue, bulletproof-vest dirty work of the job. We know Scales travels strapped. We know he isn't afraid to pull the trigger. I need to know I can trust you to take orders, to do what you're told. To keep your cool."

"You have my word," Maureen said. "I will be a good soldier."

"Good. Now about that body from tonight," Atkinson said, sitting back. She tapped her fingertip to her throat. "Let's go over it. Tell me about the wound."

"I left the scene thinking razor blade or something like it. Long and sharp. Box cutter is a possibility, but the wound was deep. Kitchen knife, if it was super sharp."

"Drayton thinks like you do?"

"I would think so," Maureen said, "though I can't say for certain. I would hope so. It seemed pretty obvious."

"And why is that?"

"Well, at first, in the dark, it looked like a thin red line and like maybe the assailant had gotten lucky and nicked an artery. But when we got light on it, we could see the wound was thin but it was deep, at least half an inch. And it was long. Not ear to ear, but close."

"Like when you gut a fish," Atkinson said. "Deep and straight."

"I wouldn't know," Maureen said. "I've never been fishing."

"Didn't you grow up on an island?"

"It wasn't that kind of island," Maureen said. "Anyway, I can imagine what you mean, and yeah, that could be accurate. Maybe a razor-sharp filet knife could've been the weapon. A long and narrow blade. We didn't find any kind of weapon."

"The vic's hands? Defensive wounds?"

"Nothing stood out," Maureen said. "But I have to admit, I didn't really look close. Maybe he was nicked, but I don't think so."

"Cooley wasn't cut on his hands, either. So it didn't look like Gage fought? Or that he saw it coming?"

"I don't think he saw it coming," Maureen said. "A wound like that would probably come from behind, right? Or face-to-face? You'd have to get close." She extended her right arm across the table, as if reaching for Atkinson's throat. "A slash, from arm's distance, like in a fight, you couldn't get a wound that deep or that long. Or that clean. If there was a struggle, the wound wouldn't be so neat."

"Could he have been unconscious when he was cut?"

Maureen shook her head. "The blood ran down his front. He was standing. And there are handprints on the van, like he tried to hold himself up. Blood everywhere on the ground."

"You didn't notice any kind of spray pattern?"

"Uh, no, can't say that I did."

"You want to look for those things," Atkinson said. She put her finger on the table, moved it in a growing spiral. "Radiate out from the body"— she shrank the spiral—"then back in again."

"Right." Maureen shrugged. "I'm not Homicide quite yet."

"True," Atkinson said, "but never assume the next cop will find what you missed, never leave it for the next cop." She sat back in her chair, her hands raised. "Because the next cop might be me—"

"But it might be Drayton," Maureen said.

"Yup. Ugly truth. So did the killer leave any trace of his presence on the scene?"

"None that we found," Maureen said. "Other than the body."

She thought of her strong sense that Gage was a predator. Had she been wrong about him? Had he been more scavenger than hunter? Or had he left a wounded creature on the loose in the past, one that had slipped his grasp and had come back for revenge, either luring him to or stalking him at that bar? She thought of Sebastian having met his own end trying to bring about hers. Every now and then it happened that way, the balance of power fatally tipped in unexpected ways. What a revenge killing didn't explain, though, was the resemblance between Gage and the other victim. She recalled the business cards and the Post-it she'd found in Gage's wallet. She wanted to tell Atkinson about them, but hesitated. What was the risk, Maureen wondered, that something she missed in Gage's wallet could somehow lead back to the meeting at Pat O's, or back to the note that Quinn had destroyed, or even back to Preacher?

She shifted forward in her seat. "Is this normal?" Maureen asked. "One detective sitting down with a platoon officer and going over another detective's case? Even as a weird, morbid, really cool tutorial?"

"I don't know if can list five things that qualify as normal in this department," Atkinson said. "If it makes you feel better, no, I'm not using you to check up on Drayton's work. I'm going over the murder with you, not Drayton's casework on that murder. If I had a problem with him, I'd go to the source. You're the only one in the department who's seen both bodies."

"True," Maureen said. "So why didn't you come by the scene tonight, see it for yourself?"

"I show up and Drayton feels undermined," Atkinson said. "You think he was ugly the way you saw him tonight, imagine what he's like with a woman looking over his shoulder, which I can actually physically do, I don't just mean that metaphorically."

"I'm surprised, I guess," Maureen said. "I wouldn't think Drayton's feelings mattered here. Catching the killer matters."

"I couldn't give a shit about Drayton's feelings." Atkinson sipped her coffee. "But why make an enemy when I don't have to? Why make him want to get in my way? Look, we're operating, in case you hadn't noticed, in a pretty testosterone-heavy environment. Going around stomping the primitive macho egos under our boots may make us feel better, but in the long run it won't get us what we want.

"If Drayton thinks I want the Gage case because I think I'm a better cop than him, he'll never give it to me, which is not what we want, because he won't catch the killer. And what we want, what we always want, is to catch the killer."

"So if Drayton reaches out to me about the case," Maureen said, "I won't tell him we talked."

"That would be best. They're fragile, these men and their egos, Maureen. We have to ease them gently to one side, not roll them off the edge of the table. Refer him to me."

"So, do you think the same person committed both of these murders?"

"What do you think?"

Maureen hesitated. "I don't know that I'm qualified."

"First thought," Atkinson said. "Yes or no. Just for fun."

"Yes," Maureen said, before she could talk herself out of her answer, or out of answering at all. "The victims are so similar. And the cause of death is the same."

"Another thing I thought of, I did have a body drop the night of the drive-by at Mother Mayor's place. A close-quarters throat slash, this one in Armstrong Park. A redneck vic from out of town, though this one was female."

"I don't know," Maureen said. "Lots of people get shot. The same kind of people, with the same types of guns. We don't go around thinking there's one person behind every shooting because of it. Because we have three similar people killed the same way doesn't mean it's the same killer."

Atkinson drew her finger across her throat, a frown on her face. "Razor blade. Or any kind of blade. It's an odd way to kill people, even in this city. Maybe especially in this city, the way we are about guns. It speaks to something personal. It's intimate. Penetrative. Three throat slashes in three months? That stands out to me. If I were Drayton, I'd be looking for someone with a debt or a grudge, and I'd be looking for a connection between the victims. Not that he'd ever ask me. God forbid."

12

The following evening, Maureen sat at a small metal desk, her face in her hands, fingers digging into her hairline. She squeezed two fistfuls of hair. She was in the security office for the Interim LSU Public Hospital, searching their computer for evidence that Madison Leary had passed through their doors. She had found none so far. Beside her, a hospital security guard paced in a tight circle, saying for the third time, "But you said night, you didn't say morning. Technically it was morning when they brought her over. Or said they did. I wasn't working that shift. I wasn't here. It wasn't my responsibility."

"I'm well aware of that," Maureen said. "I know you weren't here. I only care that she was here. I'm not blaming anyone for losing her, I just want her found."

Maureen moved her hands away from her face, splayed them on the desk, pressing them flat on the metal until her knuckles turned white. She knew she sounded like a junior high guidance counselor when she spoke. She had to do better than that. "Okay." A deep breath. "Okay.

Let me rephrase the question. You're right, I'm not being clear. Do you have any security video from yesterday *morning* of the hospital receiving a female prisoner from the sheriff's department, most likely through the emergency room?"

"Well, I have to look."

"Can you do that for me?" Maureen asked. "Please?"

"Can I sit in front of the computer?"

Maureen pushed up from the desk. "Of course."

The security guard sat, wiping his palms on his thighs before sliding the mouse around on the desk and clicking keyboard keys, sweating and frowning as he searched the hospital's digital video archives for the early-morning footage. She wanted to find Madison Leary, Maureen realized, if for no other reason at this point than the woman was lost and no one else was searching for her. Somebody should know where she was.

"And the nurses in the ER?" the guard asked. "What did they say?"

"Not much help," Maureen said. "Anything that happened on another shift may as well have happened on another planet. They're overwhelmed."

"They wouldn't even take you to the beds?"

"They did," Maureen said. "But there are only ten psych beds in the ward. Two were empty and the other eight were men."

"You're sure?"

"I'm not a detective yet, but I can tell women from men. Would've been hard getting out of the academy otherwise."

"I'm only asking," the guard said. "People come in here looking pretty rough sometimes."

"I believe it," Maureen said. "Any luck with the video?"

"I'm working on it, please. You checked the other hospitals?"

"These are the only emergency psych beds in the city. This is where the sheriff told me the ambulance would take her. Only game in town, they said."

The guard turned in his chair. "What about the north shore?"

Maureen drew her finger across her throat. "Closed down over the winter. State budget cuts."

"So there are ten beds for psychiatric emergencies," the guard said, "in all of Orleans Parish."

"And Saint Tammany, too. Don't you read the paper?"

"I quit reading it when they went down to three days a week." The guard shook his head. "Ask me again why I moved to Jefferson Parish. Good Lord. Where do the crazy people go?"

"Elysian Fields, borders of the Treme. Under the I-10 overpass seems pretty popular these days. I'll look there next." She nodded at the computer. "Any luck finding our prisoner here, the place where she oughtta be?"

"What do you need her for?" the guard asked, turning back to the computer.

Because she's a thief and person of interest in a murder case, though apparently I'm not supposed to care about that.

"Police business," Maureen said. "She's not like a serial killer or a jewel thief or anything like that, but I really can't say."

The guard pointed and clicked, shaking his head. "I really think my supervisor should be here for this. You really should talk to him."

"I would *love* to," Maureen said.

"He's in Cancún, at a conference. He should be back by Monday."

"My prisoner is missing today!"

The guard flinched when she shouted. She could see him melting into a pout. As much as she knew she needed to, she doubted she could rally the personal warmth to coax the man out of it. As bad as Theriot from the sheriff's department, this one. Jesus. These soft fucking men were making her crazy. They could each of them take lessons from Marques.

"Are you sure you don't need a warrant for this?" he asked.

Maureen wasn't sure if he was being vindictive or if he was that ignorant. "I'm not asking for anyone's personal information or file or medical records. I'm not asking to leave with anything. I don't even want to leave with the prisoner. I just need to confirm she made the six-block trip from lockup to here like I was told she did. Is there a way, any way at all, we can do that?"

"Not if she didn't make it here." The guard turned in his chair, back to the computer. "Sounds to me like your problem is with the sheriff's department, but what do I know?"

Over his shoulder Maureen watched the fast-forwarded version of the morning in question in the emergency room. She was about to give up when a flash of blue, Madison's T-shirt, caught her eye. "Stop it, stop the video."

The guard did so. There, seated at the end of the row of plastic chairs in the ER waiting room, was Madison Leary, slumped forward, her hands upturned in her lap, looking much like she did seated in the white pickup.

"Son of a bitch," Maureen said. "Let it roll. Not too fast."

The sequence played forward at an accelerated pace. With a view from above, Maureen watched Madison and the time stamp in the corner of the video. Leary sat motionless like a turtle in the bottom of an aquarium, the nurses and doctors and patients flowing around her like colorful fish. After about twenty minutes, Madison stood, stretched, turned around, and walked out the sliding glass doors of the ER, as if an invisible spirit had entered and animated her body. She disappeared into the night. "You have got to be fucking kidding me."

"That would explain why she's not in one of the beds," the guard said.

Now it was Maureen doing the pacing. "Can I, uh, can I sit there a sec?"

"I don't see why. You found what you needed. She's not here. She was, but she's not anymore." He sounded giddy with relief. "It's not our responsibility."

"I'm going to have to ask you to step aside," Maureen said, "and let me have a look at that computer."

"Or?"

"That woman is a fugitive," Maureen said, which was an exaggeration, she knew, since Madison had never officially been in custody. "And this computer documents her flight. I will come back with six more cops and seize it, and take it down to the DA's office, and you with it, where they will pore over every file looking for more evidence of her escape from custody. And then he'll grill you like a fucking sausage. You want that? You want to call Cancún and explain that hot mess to your boss? You been looking at airline tickets, at Craigslist for another job, we're gonna see it. Been playing poker, looking at porn, we're gonna see that, too."

"You can't really do that," the guard said. "Can you?"

"Fucking try me. Please. Because this seems to be the week for that."

The guard jumped up from the chair. "Fine, have it your way, but I'm putting this whole episode in the shift log. My boss is going to want to chat with your boss."

Maureen squeezed the back of the chair. "Officer Maureen Coughlin, Third Platoon, Sixth District. Badge number fourteen-twelve. My duty sergeant is Preacher Boyd. Put it on my permanent record."

"I'm getting coffee." The guard turned on his heel and left the office, slamming the door behind him.

"I didn't want any anyway," Maureen yelled after him.

She sat at the computer, rewinding the video prior to Leary's appearance in the waiting room. She knew what had happened, but she wanted to see it with her own eyes. After a few minutes of video, the automated sliding doors opened. In came Theriot and another deputy dragging Madison Leary, limp and barely staggering, her feet stepping then dragging. Each man held one of Leary's arms. Leary seemed only half conscious, a long line of spit hanging from her bottom lip, unaware of where she was or what was happening to her. She was tiny, hanging limp and broken between the two men escorting her. Why hadn't anyone gotten her a wheelchair?

The deputies dumped Leary in a chair, wiped their hands on their uniform pants, and hustled out of the waiting room, looking like two frat boys leaving a drunk date on the doorstep. Maureen watched them closely. Neither of them spoke, not to each other, to Leary, or to anyone else in the emergency room. Neither man even glanced back at their charge on his way out the door.

Not long after Leary's arrival, the emergency room erupted into a frenzy as a man with blood pouring from his abdomen and down his lap, an obvious gunshot wound, staggered into view. He turned in a slow circle before collapsing in a tangled heap of limbs not three feet from where Madison sat. Though Maureen couldn't hear it, she knew shouting and screaming rang off the walls. Leary didn't react to anything around her. She didn't even look at the man who'd been shot. She slumped like an exhausted child snoring through a boring TV show. A pack of people in different-colored scrubs rolled over a gurney and addressed the man's wound. They loaded him onto the gurney and wheeled him away out of the picture. From there, the footage Maureen had already seen. She stopped the video.

She leaned back in her chair and scratched at her scalp. Why? Why abandon a prisoner in the middle of the emergency room? That was an easy one. Because she wasn't a prisoner, Maureen thought. She wasn't even a person. She was a problem, a stray on the wrong doorstep, nothing more than that. She was bodily fluids and physical effort and cavity searches and paperwork. She scared the deputies. So they ditched her in a way that left no paper trail back to the department. Just in case that scary, skinny little woman turned out to be dangerous. Or know a lawyer.

Maureen got up from the desk, left the security office. The guard was nowhere to be found. She passed through the bustling emergency room and out into the hospital parking lot. Two smoking EMTs at the back of an idling ambulance gave her the once-over. She gave them the finger and they giggled like children. An old woman in a wheelchair stared at her, hostile.

Maybe she was being too harsh, Maureen thought. Maybe the deputies got caught up in the drama surrounding the gunshot victim outside the camera angle. Maybe they'd run outside to help someone. Maybe they'd meant to turn over Leary the right way and lost track of things. She could believe that, if she wanted to give the deputies the benefit of the doubt, if she tried real hard to fool her own instincts and her own eyes.

As for right now, Maureen thought, climbing into her patrol car, Madison Leary could be passed out under a car in this hospital parking lot, or behind a nearby Dumpster. She could be miles away by now. She could have leaped from the Crescent City Connection and into the fucking river. Maureen wondered if there was anyone other than her who cared. She wondered why *she* cared, and how much she really did, now that the effort had become draining.

Leary wasn't the only person in New Orleans she'd proven unable to help, Maureen thought. She had a job shot through with failure. Failure of genetics, of governments, of systems and institutions, of parents and schools, of morals and souls. Failure was why she had a job. Shit, if the world ever got its act together, she thought, she'd be back waiting tables.

Maybe she should take a page from Atkinson's book, she thought. Maybe the thing to do was sit back and wait for vibrations in the web, see what happened around her instead of always forcing the issue. She studied her own eyes in the rearview mirror. They looked strange to her. Old. Tired. That was what she would do. She'd hang back and see how things shook out. Nobody was asking her for anything. In fact, Preacher had warned her off Leary's trail. She dropped the cruiser into drive. Marques and his grandmother, Quinn and Ruiz, Heath, Gage, Cooley, and Madison Leary: she'd let them go, all of them, let them fend for themselves at least for the night—as soon as she straightened out that lying motherfucker from the sheriff's department.

13

Maureen threw open the heavy door to the intake and processing center, storming past a glum-looking family of four seated in the lobby. She slapped her palm several times on the protective plastic at the reception window. The same female deputy she had dealt with the previous night, when she had first come looking to find Madison Leary, rose from behind a desk. She stood with her chin raised high, her shoulders drawn back.

"Excuse *me*, Officer," she said, not moving from behind the desk. If she recognized Maureen, she gave no sign.

"You need to come to this window," Maureen said, "or buzz me through that door. Y'all have some questions to answer."

Taking her time, the deputy edged around the desk and sauntered to the window. "Bad night on the streets?"

"Always better to be out there working," Maureen said, "than to be sitting on my ass in the air-conditioning."

"But you keep coming to me for help," the deputy said.

Someone in the seated family caught their breath.

The deputy leaned toward the window. She lowered her voice and raised her eyes to Maureen's face. "You *need* to stop talking to me like I'm some corner punk. Now."

"You *need* to stop dumping my prisoners out onto the street because you feel like it." Maureen leaned her elbows on the counter, her nose inches from the protective plastic window. "What ambulance company was it that took my prisoner over to LSU Public the other night? You remember that? The woman, Madison Leary. Can you look that up for me?"

Maureen saw the flash of recognition in the deputy's eyes. She hadn't worked the night Maureen had brought Madison in, but she was a witness to the lies the other deputy told. She had no interest in protecting her coworker, Maureen knew. She'd be plenty pissed at him for putting her in this mess. She'd give up anything to get Maureen and her attitude away from the window, and to excise herself from the rest of the story.

"I want to talk to Theriot," Maureen said. "The big, bald guy. It's important. Where is he?"

"He's in the shed tonight."

"The what?"

"The guard shed, down at the end of the street, at the entrance to the construction site. The city wants someone in it twenty-four seven. Tonight, it's his turn."

"Don't call him," Maureen said, standing. "Don't tell him I'm coming."

She turned, almost colliding with the young mother from the family, who had come up close behind her. Her husband sat with a kid on either side of him, a boy and a girl, about seven years old, maybe twins. The man scowled, none too pleased his wife was talking to a cop.

"Excuse me, Officer," the woman said. "Can you help us?"

"Depends," Maureen said, in a hurry to get to Theriot. "The deputy back there can probably do more for you than I can."

"It's not that," the woman said. "We came to check on my brother. He got arrested last night. We got what we needed, but now our car won't start. My husband says it's the battery." She tossed a cold-eyed glance over Maureen's shoulder at the deputy. "Seems no one in the sheriff's department's got any jumper cables."

Maureen knew she had jumper cables in the cruiser. But this is how it starts, she thought. They ask for something small, then slowly raise the stakes. When the jumper cables didn't work, she'd be hit up for cab fare, or even a ride home, like a damn taxi service. She'd get the sob story of how the brother was a quiet neighborhood guy trying to turn his life around, was there anyone she could talk to for him? Then back in the neighborhood they'd motherfuck the sheriff's office and the NOPD to anyone who would listen. The next time NOPD came around asking questions, looking for help, no one would know a thing. Maureen took a deep breath. "Listen, I've got work to do. If you don't have a phone, I'm sure the deputy can call you a cab. Or make change for the pay phone."

"Tol' you," the husband grumbled.

"A cab from here to the Seventh Ward is expensive," the woman said. "We put up what we got extra for my brother. And then our car is stuck here. I got a phone. I left a message at my cousin's house 'bout an hour ago." She held up a glittery white cell phone. "But he at work and hasn't called back."

"Typical police," the husband said. "Quit wasting time, girl."

Maureen stared at him, stepping in his direction, but speaking to the woman. "I've got cables in the unit, ma'am. Get the kids a soda. Soon as I'm done talking with the other deputy, we'll see if we can't get your car started. Just hang tight for a minute."

"Thanks, Officer," the woman said, rocking on her heels, twisting her lips at her husband. "'Preciate you."

The husband kept his head turned away, frowning over his shoulder at nothing. The kids looked at the floor, swinging their short legs and sneakered feet under their chairs, embarrassed and confused by the adult hostility over something as simple as a ride home.

Maureen left the cruiser parked, walking the two blocks to the construction site, silent and locked up for the night. The looming square of the new jail stood tall against the highway and the stars, a black cube aglow in the faint lights from the nearby cranes. Plastic banners bearing construction company logos wrapped the box like a half-opened birthday present. Their loose edges flapped in the wind. One of the banners caught Maureen's eye. There it was, like Atkinson had told her, HEATH DESIGN AND CONSTRUCTION. Big white letters against a blue background. She hadn't noticed it before.

"Well," she mumbled, "would you look at that."

She'd seen the company banner elsewhere around the city. They'd recently finished a shiny new four-story building, lots of metal and glass, on Earhart Boulevard in her district, corporate offices or something. The building's sleek modern look was out of character for the surrounding industrial area, which was otherwise old warehouses and tumbledown shacks lined up along one of the outfall canals from the lake. There was a bakery on the ground floor. Other cops in her district had high praise for the bakery's coffee, but the place was never open during her night shifts.

In the guard shack, Maureen could see Theriot's jowly profile illuminated by a laptop computer. As he stared at the screen, he methodically fed potato chips one at a time into his pink mouth. From the look on his face, she guessed he wasn't watching the video feed of the deserted construction site. Maureen had the impression that had a giant spacecraft descended from the night sky and airlifted away the new jail, Theriot would never have noticed. He didn't react when she shouted his name. When she got closer, she saw the white wires of his earbuds dropping from the side of his head. She picked up a piece of gravel from the street and bounced it hard off the side of the guard shack. Theriot ducked at the crack of the stone on the metal shed, throwing his earbuds to the floor with a shout and looking around.

"Over here, Theriot," Maureen said.

"That was you? What the fuck?" Theriot's eyes widened as he recognized Maureen. "You."

"Yeah," Maureen said. "Me. You remember me. I'm the one who should be asking what the fuck. Guess why I'm here."

Theriot closed his laptop and squeezed through the narrow doorway of the guard shack, meeting Maureen in the street, his keys jingling as he moved. "How should I know?"

"Guess where I'm coming from."

Theriot shrugged. "Again, I should know?"

"How about LSU Public," Maureen said, "where I watched video of you and some other toolbox dumping my arrest in the waiting room and disappearing like you're pulling a high school prank. How about that? You told me you sent her over in an ambulance, but you took her over yourself. You left her in the waiting room and didn't even tell anyone she was there, or what was wrong with her, or where she came from. How is that acceptable?"

"You don't understand what had happened," Theriot said.

"How did you think I wouldn't follow up on this? That I wouldn't find out?"

"Because you're a cop?" Theriot said.

His answer, Maureen realized, was genuine, not a joke or a shot. She watched as the delayed understanding drifted across his face like daylight across a dirty room, the realization that Leary had gone missing, or maybe worse.

He squeezed his temples with one hand. "Shit. I knew it. Fuck. Man, I can't catch a break. What did she do?"

"Yeah, shit," Maureen said. The wind kicked up, swirling dust and grit around her legs. "It just so happens we need her now, as part of a homicide investigation, and now she's fucking gone. I watched her walk out the fucking door." She cut her hand through the air. "No trace."

"I called for an ambulance," Theriot said, wiping a big hand down his now-sweaty face. "It started out right."

Whatever modest hopes he had for his future in the sheriff's department, Maureen knew, he felt they were quickly disappearing. She let him keep thinking it.

"I did call," Theriot insisted. "I swear, but they were gonna make me wait an hour at least. Unless somebody's bleeding or having a violent seizure or something, they hate coming to the jail. Not for mystery shit like her. I'd have better luck with United Cab. A psych case like her, there's no place to put her hardly. Our psych beds at the jail are full every night. Nobody wants her. It's a major pain in the ass for everybody."

"It's your fucking job," Maureen said. "It's what the sheriff's department is for. To take care of the jail and the prisoners. Did I miss a memo?"

"What do you think happens," Theriot said, "if I put a stone-crazy broad like that in my holding cell? You know what that does to the other prisoners? To those other women? Then I got a whole night full of maximum crazy and nobody gets any help. Not me, not you, not her."

"How is any of this my problem?" Maureen said. "You're worried about your prisoners. What about the detective I have to tell is short one material witness in a homicide case? What about that? You think I'm gonna eat this shit for you? You think I'm gonna cover for you at my own expense?"

"I'm not asking for that, but have a heart, Officer. Most of our male general population is living in tents, like it's a fucking war or something." He jerked his thumb over his shoulder. "Try doing my job for a week. You're breaking my balls over one crazy lady? The city's infested with crime, and we don't even have a fucking jail."

"Look, Deputy," she said, "whether or not I have a heart, you fucked up, and we have to do what we can to fix it. The woman's name is Madison Leary, and how about you lay off calling her a broad, for starters."

"Whatever you say, Officer."

"Did Leary say anything, anything at all, that might indicate where she's gone?"

Theriot shook his head. "She was mumbling some shit about rabbits, I think. Nothing that made any sense. And then she went blank and limp. I mean, I thought for a minute she'd up and fucking died on us." He looked around, as if someone else, maybe Leary herself, could be eavesdropping on their conversation. "To be honest, she made me real nervous, she made us all real nervous, all the deputies. I've been doing this a while. I've seen some shit that'll straighten your short and curlies.

This was something new. We were afraid to touch her, like a wire lying in the street and you don't know if it's live or not."

"But you touched her," Maureen said.

Theriot raised his hands. "Nothing bad. Nothing inappropriate. We couldn't leave her lying on the floor, drooling. Me and another deputy, we carried her out to the car, and laid her down in the backseat and drove her over to the hospital. It's only six blocks. It was best for everybody." Theriot licked his lips. "When she was lying there in the backseat, she was singing. All the way to the hospital. Real quiet, the words were hard to make out. Something about a butcher's boy. And the devil. I swear. Gave me the shakes."

An idea floated across the back of Maureen's mind. According to what she'd learned tonight, Madison Leary had been on the streets when Gage was killed.

"I didn't come here for a fucking ghost story," Maureen said. "Jesus. Grow up."

"If you saw the security video, you saw the shape she was in. It never even occurred to me that she would wander off. She didn't seem hardly capable of it. Then some car dumped that shooting victim outside and all hell broke loose after that."

"And you got caught up in helping the shooting victim," Maureen said.

Theriot hesitated, thinking for a moment, Maureen knew, that she was throwing him a lifeline. He realized she wasn't. "He was already at the ER. I don't know what other help we had to offer. We came back here." He shook his head, as if he couldn't believe the situation had turned out as bad as it had, either for him or for Leary. "Listen, are you going to jam me up on this? Did this Leary woman, like, *see* somebody get killed? How important is she?"

Maureen shrugged. She lit a cigarette. "If it's between me and you taking the fall, it ain't gonna be me."

She couldn't pinpoint why she was making Theriot squirm the way she was. Because he whined, she thought. Because he whimpered and showed her his soft underbelly without a fight, a weakness that always brought out her claws, cop business or not. She'd hidden Leary's existence from Drayton. Hidden the whole story of the traffic stop. She'd let Quinn make off with the Post-it note from Gage's wallet. She was as guilty as Theriot of ass-covering behavior. Was she any better, any different, than this guy? She had no right putting the screws to him.

Theriot licked his lips again, blew out his breath. "C'mon, Officer, cut me a break. I need this job. I got alimony. I got a mortgage."

"I can't make any promises," Maureen said. "You fucked up, that's on you. You have to live with the consequences. If I have to answer for what happened to Leary, I'm pointing in your direction. I'm not gonna lie to anyone for your sake."

"I was trying to make the best of a bad situation."

"You mishandled a prisoner and then lied about it to me," Maureen said. "You're lucky you're not up on charges right now. You realize the break I'm cutting you?"

"I wear a uniform, too, you know." Hands on his hips, Theriot kicked at the gravel in the street. His eyes glistened with tears. "That's the problem with you cops. You make everyone you talk to feel like a fucking criminal."

When she reached the cruiser, Maureen unlocked the trunk and pulled out the jumper cables. She slung them over her shoulder, walking up the wooden ramp and into the intake and processing office. She got as far as the soda machines before she realized the family with the broken-down car was gone.

Alone in the lobby, the deputy reassembled the pages of an abandoned newspaper that had been spread over the chairs.

"The cousin finally showed up," she said, not looking at Maureen. "How much you wanna bet they never come back for that piece-of-shit car and leave the city to tow it and take care of it, try and chase 'em down for the bill?" She stood, folding the paper and tucking it under her arm. "No wonder I can't get a damn raise."

Maureen said nothing, oddly upset and disappointed that the family had solved their transportation troubles without her help. She felt pretty fucking useless, in general.

She turned and walked outside.

As she tossed the cables in the trunk of the cruiser, her phone buzzed in her pocket. She slammed the trunk closed and answered the call. "Coughlin."

"Where are you?" Preacher asked. Maureen could tell he was unhappy. Lovely.

"Following up on something," she said.

"I been trying to raise you on the radio for ten minutes," Preacher said. "You need to tell dispatch if you're gonna be out of service."

"Took longer than I thought," Maureen said, pulling open the car door. "I'm sorry. I'm back at the car right now. What's going on?"

"Drayton is here," Preacher said. "Looking for you."

Maureen's insides froze. She tried to keep her voice relaxed. "And what did he want?"

"You. He's hot, Coughlin. Breathing fire."

"I'm guessing this isn't a social call."

"Are you not hearing me? He's at the district. He didn't call. He came to our shop for no other reason than to talk to you. Don't take it as a compliment, it's not."

Maureen sat on the bumper of her cruiser, phone at her ear, forehead in her hand. "Is it about the Gage case?"

"He didn't specify," Preacher said. "But I can't imagine another reason he'd be looking for you, can you?"

"No, no, I can't." Maureen moved the phone away from her face. She let out a long breath before returning it to her ear. "So he's waiting there for me?"

"Yes, indeed," Preacher said. "He's waiting for you in the break room. But before you talk to him, you're gonna come see me. I'll be waiting for you in the parking lot."

14

Maureen parked the cruiser in the motor pool lot behind the Sixth District building, among several other dinged and dirty units along the chain-link fence topped with razor wire, the cars waiting for washing and maybe touch-up repairs. She spotted Preacher right away, standing over by the trash cans, off to the side of the garage and the building's back entrance. He gave her a silent nod when she got close. He held a lit cigar between his fingers.

"Give me another minute," Maureen said. "I gotta pee."

Another nod, his eyes away from her. Maureen hated it when Preacher didn't talk.

In the bathroom, she spent a couple of extra minutes on the toilet, elbows on her knees, face in her hands, hiding in the stall. She took long, slow, deep breaths, visualizing her rib cage expanding and contracting, and trying to map out in her head what she'd say to Preacher.

She needed to protect herself, starting right now, from Drayton and whatever he had planned for her, but from Quinn, too, and possibly from Preacher, which may have been what worried her most. And Preacher, Quinn, and Ruiz, they'd be expecting *her* to protect *them* from Drayton. She was the buffer between him and whatever it was they were up to. She feared Drayton had somehow found out that she and her coworkers had withheld information from him about Gage and Leary, though she didn't know how that could be the case. The fuckups at the jail and the hospital meant no paper trail existed of her traffic stop the other night. A few standard radio calls no one would remember. The witnesses involved, on the NOPD and in the sheriff's department, none of them wanted the truth coming out. Preacher's possible questions for her bounced around in her skull. She couldn't settle her mind on one. She thought of what Quinn had said, that they had known each other long before she had arrived. That she should be careful about crossing Preacher, especially.

She thought of advice she'd heard public defenders give their clients, and that prosecutors had given to her before she faced a cross: answer only the question you are asked, offer nothing, anticipate nothing. Simply react. Calmly. Thoughtfully. She wiped, flushed, and stood. She reassembled her uniform.

Before heading back outside to meet Preacher, she washed her hands, taking a moment to study herself in a mirror. She had bags under her eyes, tiny wrinkles had appeared at their corners. Her lips were pale and dry. The edges of her nostrils were bloodless and white, as always when she was upset. She recalled the couple of times she'd testified in court, staring into the mirror like she was doing now, what little makeup she owned scattered on the restroom sink, unsure if it was better for the city's case that she look like a cop or a pretty girl. Juries these days trusted pretty girls, even average to moderately attractive ones with New York accents, more than they trusted the police. They trusted *anyone* more than they trusted the police. Even the police didn't trust the police.

Tonight, she felt more like the defendant than a witness for the prosecution. She considered putting on some makeup for the meeting with Drayton, she kept the basics in her locker, but decided against it. Wasn't worth the trip down the hall. Not for him. She would give him nothing. Show him nothing. She needed more than lipstick could do for her. And Preacher had waited outside long enough.

She tucked stray strands of hair back up under her NOPD ball cap. She dampened a rough brown paper towel under the faucet and used it to polish her round, silver badge, wiping away the dust and coffee stains. With the palms of her hands, she tried to press and smooth out the bags under her eyes. She tossed the paper towel in the wastebasket and pushed out through the bathroom door.

Preacher stood under the eaves of the building. A light rain had started to fall. He had a particularly smelly cigar going. For a moment, Maureen had confused its aroma with that of the trash cans a few yards away. Preacher looked tired, his hooded eyes narrow and creased at the corners. Maureen lit a cigarette and leaned against the building beside him.

"Is Drayton gonna be okay with this?" she asked.

"Okay with what?"

"With you briefing me before the interrogation."

"I don't know what you're talking about," Preacher said. "Briefing? You're on duty. I'm your duty sergeant. I'm having a cigar out by the garage like I often do. Your rolling back through the district on police business. We're shooting the shit about another night in the Big Sleazy. I don't see what's suspicious about that."

"So Drayton's unhappy with us. Do we know what about?"

Preacher turned his cigar between his teeth, speaking around it and puffing smoke. "There isn't much 'us' to it. He's pretty focused on *you*. Something about the integrity of his homicide investigation. He wouldn't discuss it with me. So I wouldn't discuss you with him. I left him stewing. *Integrity*. It's a funny word for that man to be using. I bet any one of his ex-wives would get a kick out of it." He shrugged, a small, sly smile on his face. "He doesn't seem to trust me. It's an insult to me." He lowered his cigar, serious now. "Do you trust me, Coughlin?"

Maureen blew out her breath. "I do, Preach. You've never given me a reason not to."

"Took you a minute to answer there."

"It's a serious question."

Preacher leaned forward, spitting shreds of tobacco onto the pavement. "I want you aware of the stakes. This conversation, in some form or another, the one you're about to have with Drayton, might end up being discussed in front of a federal judge. With the decree signed, Her Honor has access to whatever and whomever she wants, whenever she wants it." He paused, shrugged. "The cases that go sideways, the ones that stand out for the wrong reasons, the *anomalies*, as you like to say, those are the ones the judge will look into. This case cannot go sideways, Coughlin. I'm not having my district, or my platoon, being the first lambs to the slaughter. Let that happen in someone else's shop. I won't be a disgrace to the department. Believe that."

"I did not do anything to fuck up that crime scene," Maureen said. "Or my paperwork. Same as with Cooley at Magnolia Street. I did nothing to screw up any arrest that Drayton might make, or charges he might bring. And neither did anyone else on the scene. I promise you, Preach. I'd take that to the judge right now, tonight."

"But you were not first to arrive," Preacher said.

"I was not. That was Quinn and Rue." She thought of Quinn, of the note to meet Heath. Evidence he'd secreted away from the crime scene, a small and quiet act that had made criminals of both of them when she'd looked the other way. What else had he done before she'd arrived? Anything? How deep in it was Ruiz? She took a deep breath. Pretend that brief moment with Quinn hadn't happened, she told herself. Pretend. Fake it. She'd done it her whole life. "I have complete confidence in how they handled the scene. I'd vouch for them. It looked like it should have when I got there."

Preacher wouldn't play coy with her about Quinn, Maureen thought. If he knew what Quinn had done with the note, he would've said so. He wasn't asking about that. The less Preacher knew, Maureen thought, the more protected he'd be if that judge came calling. She kept the secret note to herself.

"Anyone who tells you we blew it," Maureen said, "Drayton or any-one else, is either misinformed or a fucking liar. We did it right, me, Quinn, Ruiz, all of us."

"I spoke to Quinn," Preacher said. "He told me you mentioned your traffic stop to Drayton."

"That was before I knew y'all had let Gage go," Maureen said. "No one had caught me up yet. Had I known he'd never been arrested, I'd have kept quiet from the beginning."

"What did Drayton say?"

Maureen chuckled. "Nothing. He ignored me. I don't think he heard a word I said about it. It was then that Quinn pulled me aside and rec-ommended I drop the subject."

"And did you?"

She felt ashamed in front of Preacher. Not because she'd sided with Quinn, but because she'd done so out of fear of being rejected, of Quinn turning against her. Because she wanted even the burning-out, tainted cops to like her, to think of her as one of them. "I did. And I haven't spoken to Drayton since."

"And whatever happened to the woman?" Preacher asked. "The one who was in the pickup?"

"You told me to give that up."

"Did you?"

"No."

"Why am I not surprised? Well, then. Out with it."

"Sheriff took her over to the hospital as a medical," Maureen said. "She had some kind of breakdown or seizure while they were processing her at intake. She never even made it into the parish records. There's no record of her. No paperwork, nothing in the computer. She's gone, like a ghost, like she was never there to begin with.

"The sheriff's deputy, a guy named Theriot, he lied to me about how Leary got over there. He told me she went in an ambulance, but I found out when I followed up on his story that he and another guy dropped her off in the waiting room on their own. Left her sitting there and didn't even point her out to anyone. She recovered after they left, or she was acting the whole time, and she got up and walked out. A gunshot came in right on their backs. Leary disappeared in the chaos."

"So this mystery person who Drayton might need," Preacher said, "this direct connection to his dead guy, who he doesn't know exists because nobody told him about her, she's in the wind now, she's gone. They fucked it up at the jail *and* the hospital. Incredible, even for this sheriff's department."

"That's correct. Though I have to say, I don't know how much of an asset she'd be to an investigation."

"We tend to let the detectives decide who's an asset to their case and who isn't," Preacher said. "Usually." He wiped his hand down his face, blinked a few times. "And this follow-up visit to the hospital you made, that would be why I'm getting phone calls from security guards at LSU Public. It would be why I'm getting screamed at about rogue platoon officers threatening subpoenas and property seizures and such."

Maureen said nothing.

"Wouldn't it?"

"I don't know if *rogue* is the right word."

"Holy shit, Coughlin. Do I sound concerned with semantics right now?"

"No, sir. Yes, sir. That visit by me would be why hospital security is calling you. He gave me a hard time about the security footage."

"So we're clear," Preacher said, "there is a record of this Leary woman. Unofficial, but a traceable record that leads back to you. It's the trail of people you've pissed off trying to keep track of her. People are much more likely to forget you if you're nice to them. Feel free to use that knowledge in the future."

"Theriot lied to me, sir, about custody of a prisoner. That's illegal."

"So the fuck what?" Preacher said. "What makes you so special that people gotta tell you the truth when you ask for it? *You* lied to *me* when it came to Leary. By omission, at least. You disobeyed my orders. I told you to forget about that woman, didn't I? I told you not to play social worker. You told me you wouldn't anymore."

"They threw her away like trash," Maureen said. "The deputies, they may as well have thrown her in the fucking gutter."

"And we're lucky they did," Preacher said. "Face reality. She's a missing link to the traffic stop that needs to stay missing."

"Stray dogs get treated better than she did. And what about us? We let the guy who put her in that truck, who was taking her God knows where, we let him walk. All I asked of those guys is that they do their fucking jobs, so that I can do mine, like you asked of me outside the jail."

"You gotta show more respect for people outside the department," Preacher said. "I know it's hard for you out there. You're from out of town. You're new. You're female. It's a ballbusting trifecta. But you can't go around like you're the varsity QB and everyone else who's not a cop is the JV goddamn water boy. People resent it. People who resent you won't help you. They look to get even, to fuck you, in fact, and not in the good way. Nobody likes a crusader. The moral high ground gets pretty fucking lonely. And as cops, we're useless on our own. We need all the help we can get from other people. Understand?"

"I do," she said.

"At least pretend to care how other people feel," Preacher said. "Even when they piss you off, *especially* then, in fact. You'll get more done. Who else knows about this mix-up with her?"

"In the department," Maureen said. "Me, and now, you."

"It is a shame about her," Preacher said. He thought for a long moment, collecting himself. "For the record, I don't condone how she was treated. I'm not unsympathetic."

"Why is it so important," Maureen asked, "that Madison stay lost, and that Drayton not learn about that traffic stop?"

She knew Quinn's answer, that Gage was somehow, in some shady way, connected to Caleb Heath, a connection that Quinn was motivated to keep hidden. She wanted to hear Preacher's explanation. She hoped it was better, or at least different. She didn't want to hear that even the irascible, proudly selfish Preacher Boyd was beholden to the mighty Heaths.

"This Clayton Gage she was with," Preacher began, "the feds got a hit on him. Drayton has to meet with the local FBI in the morning, and the U.S. Marshals are waiting in the wings to talk to him, which is why he's reaching out to you suddenly tonight. They're only interested in Gage as far as I know, but Drayton's worried it's more than that, and that the Gage investigation is a pretense to get him in a room where they can hit him with something else." He paused, thinking, Maureen could tell, about how much further he should go. "I'm not saying Drayton's got *reason* for the feds to make him nervous, far be it from me to make aspersions, but, you know, it is what it is. He's pissed as a wet cat that Gage led the feds to him. Don't count on him being a reasonable man."

"I knew it," Maureen said. "Didn't I tell you? Gage's a kidnapper, right? Or some kind of serial killer."

"He's on the federal terrorism watch list," Preacher said.

Maureen was taken aback. She hadn't seen that coming. "Another one? Jesus, he's got to be connected to Cooley."

"Gage was a wanted man in Tennessee and North Carolina. For gun crimes and threats and assaults against law-enforcement officers. They've been looking for him for over a year and a half. They're thinking he might have been down here running with the new offshoot of the Louisiana chapter of the Sovereign Citizens, but they couldn't get a solid line on him. They were looking for him out in the river parishes when he turned up dead in New Orleans."

"LaPlace," Maureen said, "the town on Gage's driver's license, and where his truck was registered, that's out that way, correct?"

Preacher nodded. "Two federal fugitives with hate-group connections dead within a week in our district? Can't be a coincidence. They're thinking maybe Cooley was connected to the Citizens as well."

"I'm not familiar," Maureen said.

"Sovereign Citizens is an antigovernment thing, mostly they work in

the courts, bizarre privacy and antitax stuff, lots of paperwork and protest, but there's a history of violent, militant offshoots growing off the
main branch of the movement. Seems we have one of those here in
Louisiana, a gun-happy splinter group called the Watchmen Brigade.
These militant groups share a particularly violent attitude toward law
enforcement. We're a favorite target."

"Cop haters? That's nothing new."

"Cop killers," Preacher said. "To hear the feds tell it."

"A cop-killing hate group? How do I not know about this already?"

"We haven't had them here in Orleans Parish, not that anybody
knew about till Gage got his throat cut. A Sovereign Citizens militant
wing killed two cops in West Memphis three years ago. Another killed
two in South Carolina over some land about a decade ago. Now they're
moving into Louisiana."

"So it's a Deep South thing?" Maureen asked.

"The Citizens are nationwide," Preacher said, shaking his head, "as
is the devil's work that comes with them. The feds busted some nutbag
in Alaska planning on going after cops and judges. He had grenades.
One of them pulled a gun on a cop in Ohio, got himself shot dead by
the side of the road." Preacher puffed on his cigar. "When you searched
Gage's car, you check the glove box?"

"No, I did not," Maureen said, her mouth dry. "I saw the handbags. I
got distracted. Christ, he reached for it at one point. Said he was going
for paperwork. I feel sick."

"The feds are feeling pretty queasy about the whole thing, too. Get
pulled over and open fire, pull the pin on a grenade when the officer
is alongside the car, that's the MO. Total ambush. They've done it
before. Like a fucking suicide bomber at a checkpoint. It's what happened in West Memphis and Ohio. Idaho and New Hampshire, too.
Personally, I think these guys count on lowered suspicions from cops
since they're white. I heard they put bounties on specific cops in certain departments—minority officers are a favorite target." He stopped,
patted his caramel forehead with a handkerchief. "I spent some time

catching up on the Internet while trying to contact you. This is why I hate computers. They've been more busy than ever since we got us a black president." He wiped the corners of his mouth. "Seems we got white boys turning Taliban all across the country, including right here in the sportsman's paradise. And now these trailer-park Taliban are turning up dead in New Orleans. Crazy times."

This news about Gage explained the gun-show ticket, Maureen thought, and the business cards. She was willing to wager every one of those dealers exhibited at the local gun shows. Gage was a local boy who knew his way around the southern part of the state, and who knew which dealers didn't run background checks. There were two gun shows a month in the New Orleans area alone. He probably had a whole network set up from New Orleans to New Iberia. That made sense. He'd be the perfect point man for a group looking to arm themselves to the teeth on the QT, as long as he didn't do anything stupid like drag strange women out of bars. But they always did, didn't they? Cooley would fit into this somewhere, maybe as Gage's point man in New Orleans, maybe as an assistant of some kind. Maureen figured that whoever had killed them knew how the two men fit together.

Maureen also knew she had to make sure Drayton had found those business cards and the ticket, and was making use of them. He could lead the feds back to a whole network of illegal gun dealers. Goddamn, she thought. How did a murder this important land on Drayton's plate? She'd have to talk to Atkinson, who, as far as Maureen was concerned, needed to take over the Gage investigation posthaste.

"Wait a minute, let me get this straight," Maureen said. "We had a guy involved in a potential cop-killing conspiracy, a federal fugitive, a fucking *terrorist*, in the backseat of one of our cars, and instead of taking him to lockup, where the feds would've found him when he hit the system again and been able to use him against a domestic terrorist organization, an organization that's maybe out to murder New Orleans cops, we let him go."

"Not the NOPD's best day," Preacher said. "I'll grant you that."

"And now that the wannabe cop killer got murdered," Maureen said, "we're covering up the fact we ever knew him?"

"Forget you and me, what do you think this would mean for the NOPD if word got out we had him and let him go, without even bothering to run his name through our computer? We're talking national humiliation. *Again.* Just when the department's getting Katrina behind them. You didn't run his ID, did you?"

"I did not," Maureen said. "I left it to Quinn, who obviously never followed through. I fucked this up. Did I? Did I fuck this up? I got distracted by Gage's tough-guy attitude, and then Leary and the handbags, and then you guys showed up. We had this motherfucker. We *had* him. Oh my God, I fucked this up."

"Not that it would matter if the shit hits the fan," Preacher said, "but none of us thought Gage was anything more than a drunk coon-ass when we had him by the side of the road. The Superdome and the French Quarter were full of 'em all day. And, don't forget, nobody knows we had him but you, me, Quinn, and Ruiz."

Maureen looked up at the sky, biting down hard on her bottom lip, trying to blink her vision back into focus, her heart racing. *I told you so,* she wanted to scream. It was not *none* of us who had underestimated Gage. She'd said he was dangerous. Who cared if she was wrong about exactly why he was trouble? She'd insisted they needed to hang on to him. *I told you, I told you, I told you. I told you he was trouble.* She also knew that if there was one thing Preacher didn't want to hear right then, it was *I told you so* from her. There was no point to it. She'd accomplish nothing by reminding him of her suspicions.

"If this case somehow ties into people planning to kill cops," Maureen said, "how can I lie about that? Why should I? We didn't do anything wrong, not really. A couple of minor mistakes at the traffic stop, a miscommunication at the Gage crime scene."

"No one is asking you to lie," Preacher said. "I would never. I'm only asking for some finesse from you."

Maureen laughed. "You do realize who you're talking to."

"Were it another detective in charge of the Gage murder," Preacher said, "I might even say we should come clean. But I don't trust Drayton, not one bit. He will hang the NOPD losing track of Gage and getting him killed on you if he can, Coughlin. He might do worse."

"Hang what on me? I told him about the traffic stop, it's not my fault he ignored me."

"Anyone else witness that conversation?" Preacher asked.

"Excuse me?"

"If it comes down to your word against Drayton's," Preacher said, "who can vouch for your version of the story?"

"You're not serious."

"Who?"

"Quinn, maybe," Maureen said. "I'm sure he was near enough to hear me talking to Drayton."

"The same Quinn whose idea it was to let Gage off the hook in the first place?"

The same Quinn, Maureen thought, who absconded with evidence linking Gage and Caleb Heath. She knew what Preacher was asking her: was she willing to stake her career and maybe her freedom on Quinn having her back? Did she trust him?

"Wait a minute, Quinn told me it was *your* idea to release Gage."

Preacher hesitated. "I approved it as ranking officer on the scene. There's a difference. Maybe you misunderstood Quinn."

"Maybe," Maureen said, but she didn't believe it.

"Drayton will blame you," Preacher said, "for letting someone conspiring to kill cops get away. He will use you. When you get upstairs alone in a room with him, he will accuse you of queering his scene. He might accuse you of much worse. Cooley and Gage are in the system.

"Someone, a clever cop, say a thorough cop with ambitions, who crossed paths with them and knew where to look could find their names in the computer. What if that certain cop figured out these Sovereign Citizens and the Watchmen were moving into New Orleans? What if that cop decided to forgo the usual channels and take matters into her own hands? These fugitives are in league with cop killers, they're wannabe cop killers themselves. Using an untraceable weapon like a blade instead of something that leaves a trail like her service weapon would be smart. Throw off suspicion. What if she had co-conspirators on the night shift? Who wouldn't want to help ice a bunch of cop killers and defend New Orleans?"

"Enough already," Maureen said. "I get your point. The amount of thought you've put into this makes me nervous. Christ almighty, I'm half convinced I did it. Would Drayton go that far, to accuse me of vigilante murder?"

"We've made it easy enough for him. You said it yourself, we had Gage in the car and we let him go. He was dead less than twenty-four hours later. Now why would we do that? How could that happen? Drayton'll make you look like a fuckup at best and a corrupt cop at worst, and he'll leave it to the feds to figure out which one you are. He'll hang the rest of us, too, if it makes you look more guilty. I'm convinced that's his plan."

"I couldn't have killed Gage," Maureen said. "I was at the jail looking for Madison Leary and then I was at the Eighth dealing with Marques. None of that is hard to prove. I had no idea who Gage fucking was, or where he was. I thought he was in jail the whole time."

"So what?" Preacher said. "If Drayton needs a face for the news, it's gonna be yours. And then he's the one in front of the cameras as the one who caught you. By the time the internal inquiry gets around to confirming your alibi, it'll be too late. You won't go to jail, but you'll be done in the NOPD. Being innocent doesn't mean you can't be damaged goods. I don't know what Drayton knows, or what he thinks he knows that's got him upset. I do know that he will toss you to the feds to get their attention away from him."

"He's dirty, isn't he?" Maureen asked. "That motherfucker, he caught federal attention long before this. That's why they're making him squirm, not telling him what the meeting tomorrow morning is about. They want to see what he does under pressure. They want to see if he'll give up someone worse. He's got something to hide. He's got a guilty conscience."

"Who doesn't? To you, it doesn't matter why Drayton is extra twitchy about the feds. He might very well know about Gage's past, but it only matters that he's nervous, and that he's looking for something shiny, like you, to distract them, especially if he ends up feeling cornered."

Maureen took a deep breath, let out a long sigh. "Okay. What do I tell him, Preach? What do I do? How do I play it?"

"You keep cool. You answer every question he asks. Nothing less. Otherwise, engage him as little as possible. And do not let it slip that you know the feds have come sniffing around him."

"You tell me this stuff I'm not supposed to know and expect me to act like I don't know anything. How do I do that?"

"That's the easy part," Preacher said. "Act like everyone we arrest. Act like everyone we interview at the scene of a crime. They do a great job of acting like they don't know a damn thing, despite the fact we all know better."

"And offer nothing more than what he specifically asks for," Maureen said, more to herself than to Preacher.

"Trying to be useful to him will be tempting," Preacher said, "but it won't help you. Don't worry about me, or Quinn, or anyone else. We can take care of ourselves. If we have to, if it comes to that, we can talk to him another time. Off the record, so to speak. Let's hope it doesn't come to that." Preacher stuck his cigar in the corner of his mouth. "Now, go talk to the man before he comes looking for you by looking for me and finds us commiserating. He's waiting upstairs in the break room. Anything he wants to know . . ."

"Only that and nothing more."

"You said it, not me. You can do this, Coughlin. I believe."

15

Maureen opened the break room door to find Drayton waiting for her. He stood in the far corner of the room, his hands folded over his stomach, one knee bent, his heel propped on the pale green wall behind him, directing his most smoldering stare across the room at her. On the table in the center of the room, beside a pile of newspapers, take-out menus, and district memos sat Drayton's BlackBerry and a half-empty cup of coffee. One chair was pushed away from the table at an angle. Maureen knew that Drayton had been sitting at the table, probably texting, until he heard her coming, at which point he'd gotten up to strike what she was sure he believed was an intimidating pose. She shut the door behind her without acknowledging him. She rinsed a coffee mug in the sink and poured a cup from the pot on the counter. It wasn't that he was such an actor, she thought, ripping open one sugar packet after another, it was that he so sucked at it. Hadn't any of his male coworkers taken him aside and clued him in? More proof, she thought, sipping the hot coffee, that not only female cops disliked him.

Stirring her coffee, she thought of Quinn and Ruiz maybe making moves behind her back. Preacher said he had faith in her. Waters did, too. Christine Atkinson had everything she wanted, at least professionally, and seemed eager to teach her, but Maureen often worried she was headed more Drayton's way, toward being the one nobody liked. She worried she'd gotten into the club and now was blowing it. That she'd be the one others mocked and kept in the dark, smirking and rolling their eyes and talking behind their hands when she arrived on the scene, like the men on Magnolia Street had. She didn't think her coworkers saw her that way, but Drayton didn't think it, either.

She leaned against the counter, cupping her hot coffee in both hands. Here's your chance then, she thought, to prove yourself a team player. "Detective, you wanted to see me?"

Drayton dropped his propped foot hard to the floor and sauntered over to the table. "What happens in this room stays in this room. It stays between us."

Maureen didn't answer. Drayton didn't seem to care. He reached into his suit jacket, producing something from the inside pocket. A rolled-up plastic bag. An evidence bag. Her heart stopped. The Post-it from Gage's wallet, she thought. Quinn had turned it in, putting her on the spot for not mentioning it to Drayton when she'd briefed him about Gage.

"Can you explain this?" he asked.

Maureen looked closer at the bag, resisting the urge to reach for it. She didn't see the yellow paper in it. "Explain the fact that you've got what appears to be an empty evidence bag in your hand? Or the fact that we're standing here?"

Drayton wiggled the bag at her. "You've got a reputation, you know. A hard-charger. A go-getter. You're a girl in a hurry."

"You've been reading my third-grade report card," Maureen said.

She could tell Drayton wasn't amused. A voice in the back of her head scolded that this behavior was exactly *not* what Preacher had instructed. But the way Drayton said that word: *girl*. It sounded in her ears like *child*. She inhaled the steam from her coffee, hoping the warmth and the scent would soothe and level her. Drayton was a detective, Maureen reminded herself. Asshole or not, he outranked her and everyone else involved by a lot. He could hurt her in the department if he wanted without going as far as framing her for murder. He could fuck Preacher and Quinn and Ruiz, too. He could hurt them with the feds, as Preacher had warned. He could wait until the Gage thing had blown over and hurt them later.

She took a hit of coffee. The fluorescent light overhead started to flicker, setting off a twitch under her left eye. She wanted to escape whatever snare Drayton was setting. She didn't need to make an enemy of him to do it. She was smarter than that.

"You're a clever girl," Drayton said. "I've heard that, too. Strong, independent streak. I've heard that you struggle with being a team player."

"I'd ask who told you that," Maureen said, "but I get the feeling you'd never tell me." She paused. "And it's not true. I can go along to get along." She hated herself for saying it. "So I'm thinking nobody's told you those things. Not really."

"I hear stories."

"I'm sure you do. So do I." She wouldn't back down to him, either.

With a snap of the wrist, Drayton unfurled the evidence bag. "Don't change the subject. Explain this to me. This is your one shot at it in front of only me. Make it count."

Maureen could not see what was in the bag, if anything. "Due respect, Detective, but what the fuck are you talking about?"

"You secured the scene at the Gage murder," Drayton said. "Or, I guess I should say, you were *supposed* to secure the scene. You know, do basic police work."

"Technically, I was second on the scene," Maureen said. "I assisted in securing it. Quinn and Ruiz arrived first, which, even if you don't remember last night, is the way it's written in the reports. Why do I get the feeling they're not getting the same shitty hard time over this that I am? Have you even talked to them about the crime scene?"

That was quick. So much for standing by your teammates, she thought. She waited for Drayton to throw it back at her. She hated him for how he made her feel. Contradictory. Hypocritical. Confused. Inferior. Like a nervous, bumbling rookie.

Drayton tossed the plastic bag at the table. He missed and the bag fluttered to the floor. Cursing under his breath, he snatched it up and slammed it down on the table.

"Look at that," he said, raising his voice now, pointing at the bag. "There's your answer why I'm coming after you and not them."

Maureen studied the bag. The note wasn't in it. That was a relief. Was something else supposed to be in it? Was it theatrics, Drayton using the empty bag to make a point? She'd seen other cops put on a show. She'd done it. Drayton's career was one long performance, Maureen thought. Maybe tonight was part of it. He held his arm outstretched, pointing at the bag. Drayton had come across as sexist, silly, and dim, not exactly a surprise in the modern workplace, law enforcement or otherwise. But now, with the way this episode was escalating, Maureen saw Preacher's concern that he could be treacherous, manipulative. Bullies could be as dangerous, Maureen knew, and as lethal, as the brilliant. She knew this firsthand.

She set her coffee down on the counter. She stood up straight, raising her shoulders and her hands in exaggerated confusion. Drayton wasn't the only one who could act. "I'm sorry, Detective. I'm not trying to be difficult, but I'm not sure what you're asking me. Can you help me out?"

"Did you handle the body?" Drayton asked. "Who was with you when you did?"

"*Handle* is a strong word," Maureen said. "Quinn and I, we checked it out. We looked around the immediate area. The usual. See if the weapon is recoverable, stuff like that. I found his wallet and checked his ID. But we didn't move him or anything, if that's what you're asking. Why would we do that?"

"People have their reasons," Drayton said, looking away from her, rueful tones creeping into his voice. "Sometimes they even have good ones, at least to them. They don't see the bigger picture."

He sat at the table. He picked up his BlackBerry and checked the screen, without real awareness he was doing it. He did a similar thing with the evidence bag. Slouching in his seat, he scratched at something sticky on the table. He was the image of a man steeling himself for something unpleasant, but necessary. Drayton was shifting tactics, Maureen could tell. She could see it happening. Intimidating authority figure hadn't gotten him the results he wanted. Now he'd emulate the burdened public servant. Bad cop first, now the good cop. She'd let him play it. The more moves he made, she thought, the more he'd reveal about his true motives. She recalled a piece of advice she'd gotten from Atkinson. Once someone starts lying to you, she'd said, don't interrupt. Lies could tell plenty.

"You've put me in a difficult spot here, Coughlin."

Maureen's ears perked up; he'd used her name, gotten it right. Warning bells rang in her head. Had he been playing her with his thickheaded behavior? Was his act better and more complicated than she thought?

"That's not my intent," she said.

"It's no good," Drayton said, "when one cop has to go up against another cop, put himself at odds with her, or him, whatever the case. It's bad every way around, for the whole department. People get forced into choices they don't want to make."

Maureen moved to the counter and topped off her coffee. She wished she hadn't brought Quinn's name into the conversation about the body. She didn't want to put Drayton on a coworker's scent, or to be accused of trying to do so.

"I think we're miscommunicating, you and me," she said. "Men are from Mars, women are from Venus, that kind of thing. We're on the same side. Tell me what's gone wrong. I'll do what I can to fix it."

Pouting, Drayton waved a limp hand at the room. "This, this is not what I'm talking about, you and me in here." He stabbed the evidence bag with his finger. "This, in here, is what I'm talking about. This is what's wrong."

Maureen reached for the bag. "May I?"

"Please."

Maureen picked up the bag. Pulling the corners tight to smooth it out, she held it up to the light in the ceiling. She could see faint brownish red smudges on the inside of the bag. Blood. Dried blood. Okay, it wasn't empty. That was kind of a relief. And she saw a thin dark line running through each of the smudges. Hair. Bloody strands of long hair. She didn't know what to make of them.

"These are hairs, right?"

Drayton nodded.

"And they're from the Gage crime scene?"

That she was stalling, she knew, was obvious, and the hesitation only made her look bad. Time was running out, Maureen thought, to come clean about the traffic stop, about how those hairs got on Gage's hands and clothes. Even if those hairs led back to Madison Leary through some law enforcement or social work database, she wondered, could they lead Drayton to the traffic stop? She hated that Drayton knew more than she did about what was happening. She remembered Preacher's advice not to give Drayton *anything* he could use against her, or against them. She decided to trust the advice. It was certainly a lesser gamble than trusting the man in the room with her. She set the bag on the table.

Drayton stood, nodding again, sliding his hands into his pockets. "Here's the thing. The coroner pulled those hairs from Gage's shirt. He had others in the blood on his hands. A couple had been torn out at the root. The only way that happens, the only way those long hairs end up in his bloody shirt, is if Gage has close physical contact with the source of those hairs. If he was fighting back, say."

"Against his killer," Maureen said.

"Correct. The hairs we recovered that are not in that bag, I've sent them to the lab for tests. We'll know soon enough whose head they came from. I'm a good guy, I have love for my fellow officers of the law, so I'll give you one chance at this."

"You're not serious."

"Where were you during the time immediately before Gage was found?"

Maureen took a step back, put more of the table between her and Drayton. This was what Preacher had warned her about. "Due respect, Detective, but are you out of your fucking mind? Are you accusing me of killing Clayton Gage? Are you crazy?"

"You were out of pocket when he was most likely killed," Drayton said. "Off the radio. I checked." He moved closer to her, leaning over her as he would a suspect under interrogation, asserting his authority, taking away her space. "You have to admit, it's suspicious. And it's not the first time, either, dispatch has lost track of you. Not this week. Not this month. You have ideas of your own. You like to wander out of the schoolyard. You're not afraid to put your hands on people. What're you doing out there alone in the dark?"

"Alone in the dark?" Maureen asked. "I'm not fucking Batman. I'm riding around in a cop car, in a police officer's uniform. This is bullshit. Who said those things about me?"

Drayton didn't answer her. Don't step into the silence, she told herself. Don't do it. You don't know what he'll be able to use against you, she thought. Don't step into the quiet he'd set there like a bear trap. She couldn't help herself.

"I was at the Eighth District," Maureen said. "I was down on Frenchmen Street in full view of a hundred people, and probably a couple of security cameras. I have multiple witnesses, including an Eighth District duty sergeant and two officers from my platoon. I'm a suspect in the Gage murder? Fuck, no. I call bullshit. I don't know what this is about, Drayton, but you take even half a step more with this weak sauce and I'm going to the union. I'll press charges. You don't frighten me."

"What this is about, Coughlin, is I've got long brown hairs coming off my murder victim and I've got you among the missing at the time of death. This is your second body in as many nights. Men with a history of violence. You had time and opportunity to rig either crime scene any way you wanted. What's *your* fucking explanation, Officer?"

"My *explanation*? For what? For me ending up around dead bodies? I'm a fucking *cop*."

Though she was ready to let him have it, she didn't, surprising herself. The brakes caught and she stopped talking. She'd finally caught on. Drayton was trying to do her like Preacher said the feds were doing him. Trying to knock her off balance, shake her up, and see if anything useful fell out. He didn't have to frame her as the killer, she realized. That accusation was only to shock and scare her into coughing up something else. Did she visit a bar when she should've been out on patrol, did she hide out somewhere and get high? Did she, like she'd heard he did, have trysts on duty, fucking some civilian, or maybe another cop in the backseat of a city-issued vehicle? Drayton needed something to make it look like *she* was the weak link when the Gage investigation came under scrutiny. Out of everyone on the scene, Drayton had picked her as the toothless animal in the herd. His mistake. Of course he had picked her, she thought. He couldn't help himself. Officer Maureen Coughlin was the only *girl* on the scene.

She saw how she made an easy target, how she would be a good scapegoat for Drayton to blame for his sins and his failure. She was so new to the job and to the city. She hadn't been around long enough to leave a memorable mark, to make friends or inspire deep loyalty. Would Atkinson take her side over another detective? Would Preacher fall on his sword to protect her? They might. Not that Drayton knew the nature of either relationship. But Quinn, and Ruiz, they had long, complex histories in New Orleans and on the NOPD. They had a network of friends and supporters. Drayton couldn't tell who messing with them would anger. He thought he knew who he had to fear for crossing Maureen. No one.

She believed now that he wasn't clever, he wasn't a grand actor. He was a lousy, inferior cop, a mean and frightened man, an old façade worried that everything propping him up was about to be yanked out from behind him. Men like that were dangerous when scared, she thought. Petty and cruel, they could do a lot of damage before they finally lay down and died. To him, she was red meat he could use to keep the federal fangs out of his hide.

She wasn't about to be anybody's easy meal. Never had been. And if he kept trying it, and Maureen decided he very well might, she'd make sure he choked on her bones.

"This is the best you've got for me?" she said. "This is supposed to rattle me? Take this theory to the FBI tomorrow. Please. I fucking *dare* you. Waste of my fucking time."

Maureen took off her baseball cap, tossed it on the table. She pulled out her ponytail and held up a fistful of hair. Fuck finesse. "For the record, Sherlock, as for your brown hairs, I'm a fucking redhead, you fucking genius. Everyone but you knows that. And if you ask me if the carpet matches the drapes, I will knock you the fuck out."

16

Maureen sat in her cruiser, the engine running and the windows up. Her hands trembled on the steering wheel. Runners of sweat trickled down her temples. She breathed deeply as she processed what had happened in the district break room. Was there any way she had it wrong? No, she thought. No way Drayton lets her out of the room, out of the building, if he thinks he has a murder case against her, no matter how much venom she spat. No way Drayton gets alone in a room with her, she thought, if he believed her a killer. She chewed her bottom lip. If only he knew. She hadn't hung around to hear Drayton's reaction to her dare. He hadn't followed her out of the room. She hadn't seen him exit the district. The coward was probably waiting inside for her to leave.

When she'd burst through the back door into the parking lot, she'd glanced about for Preacher, who, no fool, was nowhere to be found. She didn't go looking for him. She didn't want to see or talk to him. She didn't want to be seen, by Drayton or by anyone else, running for the shelter of a man or a superior. She checked the time on her phone. She forced herself to take deep breaths, one after the other. Approaching midnight. She dropped the patrol car into reverse. Time to get back to work.

Tonight was her turn to watch over closing time at Commander's Palace in the Garden District, the highest of the high-end restaurants in New Orleans. The posting was a favorite gig of hers. She enjoyed keeping a watchful eye as the waitstaff in their vests and ties and long white aprons, and the valets in their dark pants and blue polo shirts, flush with cash from a night's hard work, dispersed to their cars, talking and laughing and smoking, tiredness tugging at the corners of their eyes, bending their backs. The Commander's gig was what she needed to get her mind right after the sordid business with Drayton—a simple, quiet task that made her feel useful and good. She turned to back the cruiser from the parking space.

Through the rear window, she spotted a dark figure standing behind her car, his face hidden in shadow, his blue uniform glowing red in her brake lights. "Where y'at, Cogs? Watch where you're going."

Fucking Quinn, Maureen thought.

"Sorry," she said. "Didn't see you."

Quinn came around to her window. "Some drunk asshat got punched out by a cabbie for puking up the taxi's front seat. Then said asshat barfed all over *our* backseat when we hooked him up. We came to switch out cars. Another hotshit night in fuckstick paradise."

Maureen couldn't think of a single thing to say.

"You all right?" Quinn asked. "You look pale. I mean, even for you."

"Long night. These twelves get to me sometimes. Sorry about your car. I gotta roll."

"I just gotta talk to you real quick," Quinn said, squatting beside the car, wrapping his fingers over the top of the door.

"Not right now," Maureen said. "My turn at Commander's tonight. They call and complain if we're late."

"Fuck them," Quinn said. "Nobody's robbed that place in a hundred years. Even the skells know better than that. That used to be a paid detail, you know. We used to get something for that, for the effort, instead of bitchy fucking complaints when we get distracted by crack and murders and shit and have to be fifteen minutes late for babysitting."

Maureen raised her shoulders. "Yeah, well, from what I hear, not much about paid details is gonna be the same anymore, not even the name."

"That's what I want to talk to you about," Quinn said. "Not everything's gone to shit in that department, not yet anyway. You got a smoke?"

Maureen reached her pack on the dash, gave one to Quinn, lit one for herself.

"I feel bad," Quinn said, "about doing you wrong over the traffic stop. It would've been no kind of thing if not for that murder, but even if that hadn't happened, we shouldn't have gone behind your back like that."

The way you told it to me at the murder scene, Maureen thought, everything was on Preacher's orders. Now it's different? Why? She let Quinn keep talking.

"It was a disrespectful thing," Quinn said. "And yet you kept it close around Drayton last night when you could've punched us in the dick. I owe you a solid. I want to make it up to you."

"It's nothing," Maureen said. "Trying to be a team player. Buy me a beer."

"For true," Quinn said. "Players look out for each other, though. Ain't none of us getting rich out here. You're off duty tomorrow night, right? I got a sweet detail, a fat charity gig in one of the mansions out by Audubon Park. I usually do it with Rue, but his daughter's in this school play or some shit and his wife has to work. He tells me this and I think I might ask around, and then I think, why hand an easy three hundred cash to some other bum when I can lay a little well-deserved payback on my boy"—he smiled at his mistake—"excuse me, on my podna, the Cog that turns the wheel?"

"Quinn, I appreciate this, I do," Maureen said. "And I'm not judging, I swear I'm not, but with the feds around and all—these details, they're like one of the first things the feds and the brass are going after. Probably not something I should get into."

"I hear you," Quinn said. "But this gig ain't like that. Me and Rue, we've done it six years in a row. It's no secret. It's on the up-and-up. No worries. It's for *charity*, for chrissakes. The mayor will probably *be* there. The chief, too. Let him come out and send us home if he's worried about the feds." Quinn flipped open his notepad, scratched something down with a pen. He tore the sheet off and passed it to Maureen. "Next year, yeah, the gig goes to a couple of captains, or we get taxed on it or whatever, but this year people who need it get it." He stood. "I'll see you there tomorrow evening. Regular blues. Six thirty."

Maureen folded the notepaper, tucked it into the pocket of her shirt. "Thanks, Quinn. I appreciate the hookup. Now I really gotta roll. I don't want my night being the first night in a hundred years that shit goes wrong."

"No doubt," Quinn said, standing. He looked pleased with himself. He tapped his fist twice over his heart. "Roll out, soldier. Protect and serve like a motherfucker."

17

Maureen arrived at Commander's Palace to find Preacher waiting for her. He had parked across Washington Avenue from the restaurant, sitting in his NOPD Explorer with one arm hanging out the window, fingers drumming on the door. The truck leaned to one side, with two wheels up on the curb. Maureen parked the cruiser a few yards ahead of Preacher, beside the whitewashed walls and the piked black iron gate of Lafayette Cemetery, under the canopy of a sprawling live oak a century older than either the cemetery or the restaurant. As if to protest the intrusion, a handful of acorns panged off the roof of the cruiser.

Maureen climbed out of the car, slamming the door behind her, and walked over to Preacher. The sweet, syrupy smell of bread pudding hung in the air. Frogs chirruped in neighborhood yards. The street was covered in smashed acorns. They crunched under her feet. She wasn't used to it yet, October acorns on the ground while warm breezes rustled the huge green and leafy branches overhead and sweat dampened the small of her back.

"I'm not that late," she said, approaching the Explorer. "No more than five minutes. They couldn't have called already."

"I didn't know how long you'd be with Drayton," Preacher said. "Figured I'd go ahead and cover it until you got here. I wanted some air, anyways." He put his cigar to his lips, puffed on it. "Everything went okay?"

"Yeah, fine," Maureen said, looking away. She watched a cab go by up Washington, the driver chattering on his phone, making a rolling right turn at the red light. A stray cat, a mangy orange tabby, strolled across the street, fearless, looking right at them before slinking under a parked car nearby.

Preacher said nothing. He turned his cigar in his mouth, looking at her with narrowed eyes.

"Okay, enough already with the eyes," Maureen said. "Our meeting went poorly."

"I had a feeling," Preacher said. "Tell me about it."

Maureen knew Preacher could have sent another unit down to Commander's to cover for her. He had concerns, naturally, and he wanted to give them a chance to talk about the meeting away from any eavesdroppers or interruptions, and away from Drayton. If the detective had it out for her, if that meeting tonight was the beginning, she needed to build her defense. She needed Preacher to stay on her side. She wondered if Drayton would push back against a group of cops, male cops. Would he have the spine for it?

She patted her uniform pockets, looking for the pack of cigarettes she'd left on the dash of the cruiser. "I don't know what there is to tell. He and I, we don't like each other."

"You don't know what you *want* to tell," Preacher said. "There's a difference."

"I'm not a perp in a box, Preach. Ease off."

"I'm here to help you, Coughlin. It's my job. You're in my platoon. Relax."

"He comes at me mysterious, like some stupid high school teacher with this 'we both know why you're here, don't we?' game. When that doesn't work, he gets hostile. And *then*, you were right, he starts asking me where I was and what I was doing at the time of Gage's death—like I'm a suspect. Like he expects me to wilt under that bullshit."

Preacher pinched the bridge of his nose. "Is his blood on the walls?"

"It didn't get *that* bad. Close. But he got nothing from me he can use."

"So these crazy accusations," Preacher said, "what was his ammunition?"

"He had an evidence bag," Maureen said, "with bloody hairs pulled from the blood on Gage's shirt, and from his hands. Long brown hairs that he said could be mine."

Preacher tapped his temple. "And you corrected him? About your business up here?"

"I don't think he'll ever forget I'm a redhead."

"I swear to Christ, Coughlin, you're the only reason I come to work sometimes."

Preacher shifted in his seat as if pain had crawled through his gut. He looked at his cigar as if it had been the thing to pain him, stuck it in his mouth for a few puffs, removed it.

"You know what? I think we're okay for now." He stuck his cigar in his mouth. "Anyway, keep me posted on this."

"One more thing," Maureen said. "Speaking of the feds, Quinn asked me to work this detail with him tomorrow night. This charity party out by the park."

"You off duty tomorrow?"

"I am."

"Knock yourself out," Preacher said. "It was me that told him to give it to you when Rue bailed, anyway. He owes you." He hung his elbow out the window. "How tight are you with Ruiz?"

"I can't say I am," Maureen said. "I like the guy well enough. He's a good cop. He makes me nervous, though. You want to know about Ruiz, Quinn is the guy to ask. You know that."

"Do you have any idea," Preacher said, "why Ruiz would want out of the Sixth? He talk to you about it?"

"This is the first I've heard of it. He asked for a transfer?"

Preacher nodded. "Out of the Sixth, and off the night shift until the transfer goes through. And he wants it kept quiet."

"Quinn told me it was his idea for me to work that detail. He told me Ruiz had a family thing and that's why he couldn't do it. That prick."

"Calm down," Preacher said. "Quinn's repeating the excuse that Ruiz gave him. Ruiz asked especially that Quinn be kept in the dark till the transfer goes through." He shook his head. "Quinn was gonna give the detail to Hollander. He asked me about her schedule."

"She's got bigger boobs than me," Maureen said.

"Some people's motivations remain elusive," Preacher said. "Quinn, not so much. Though I have to say he didn't fight me when I told him to give it to you. As for working details, you'll hear when the serious changes come. The cries of the aggrieved will echo in the halls, believe me. Don't worry about it till then. You're covered."

"In the midst of this symphony of ass covering," Maureen said, "are we giving any thought to who might've killed Gage and Cooley? That seems to have gotten lost."

"Not our problem," Preacher said. "We've done our part. It's Atkinson and Drayton's problem now."

"Preach, we both know who that brown hair probably came from."

"Anybody find any trace of her at the Cooley murder?" Preacher asked. "No."

"You think that woman's a killer?"

"No."

"Me neither." Preacher started the truck. "Forget about Leary. She's the only woman in New Orleans with long brown hair? Even if it is hers, by the time Drayton gets the lab work on that hair sample I'll be dead and you'll be long retired. Cops who the lab techs actually like pay off mortgages before they get lab work back, forget about cocksuckers everyone hates."

Preacher shook his head. "Let it go. We're not private investigators. We're not social services. We've been through this. Not your problem." He tapped his badge. "Not *our* problem. Don't make it so. Mark my words, someone will end up suing you for something. That'll be the thanks you get. Don't you have enough problems?" He dropped the truck into reverse. "You hearing me?"

Maureen stepped away from the truck, her hand in the air. "See you back at the district."

Preacher backed up. He pulled out into the street. Instead of driving away, he stepped on the brakes and waved Maureen over to him. "One thing I want you to remember." He held up two fingers. "This is twice now."

"Twice what?"

"Twice that you've been around Drayton, discussing this murder he's working, and twice you've failed to mention your knowledge of people of interest to the case. One of whom actually has long brown hair. If it's not a cover-up, it'll do till the cover-up gets here."

Maureen froze inside. "Are you kidding me? You *told* me to stonewall him. You shot down my idea about Madison Leary thirty seconds ago."

"I'm not criticizing or accusing," Preacher said. "I'm reminding you of the facts at hand. We're not out of the woods, is what I'm saying. Don't relax, and don't tell Quinn or Ruiz about your meeting with Drayton. They might think he was asking about them. We don't need the suspicious vibes going around. That's exactly the kind of thing Drayton finds useful."

Maureen felt light-headed. She couldn't keep up. "What's that supposed to mean? You don't think Drayton's gonna keep trying to drag us into his problems?"

"It means," Preacher said, "that if Drayton wants to step on his dick on this case, you need to let him. Stay clear of it. Stay clear of Leary and anything else connected to the Gage and Cooley murders. Breach of duty and moral conduct are terminable offenses. Remember what the chief said, 'Lying is dying on the NOPD.' Remember that you're on probation until next August. We're not even required to give you a termination hearing."

He swung the truck around Maureen and headed down Washington toward the river, finishing the block on the wrong side of the road and leaving Maureen standing in the street, marveling and terrified at how effortlessly she was losing control of her life.

The mangy tabby she'd seen earlier sat on the hood of a parked car, looking at her, its tail twitching, its eyes aglow with reflected light.

18

The next morning, Maureen tumbled out of bed five minutes before noon. She'd gotten four hours of sleep. As she walked out of the bathroom, she realized she'd swallowed a couple of painkillers before checking to see how her ankle felt. Wearing satin pajama bottoms and a loose-fitting NOPD tank top, she brought her phone and her coffee onto her porch, where she drank sitting in her rocking chair. Across the street, today dressed in baby blue, the little girl worked her pink tricycle up and down the broken sidewalk.

A group of sparrows wet their wings in a rainwater puddle on her walk, one bird keeping a single eye trained on her while the others washed and preened. The ornaments in the miniature jungle that was her neglected garden reminded Maureen of a bizarre set of ruins hidden in a colorful rain forest. The plants buzzed with bees, butterflies, and dragonflies. Lizards of every shade of brown and green hunted insect prey among the leaves. Maureen enjoyed imagining the lizards as tiny dinosaurs stalking the tropical wilds of her front yard.

She glanced through the newspaper, skipping the headlines and checking the forecast for signs of the October cool. There was none, but no rain was expected for her detail that night. The Gulf remained blessedly clear of late-season storms. She'd almost survived her first hurricane season. She folded her paper, set down her coffee mug, and rubbed her eyes. At some point in the afternoon, she'd catch another two hours of sleep. No matter how late into the night she'd worked, sleeping into the afternoon left Maureen depressed. Waking up even at five to twelve made a world of difference in how she felt. She stretched and yawned, rocking in her chair, breathing in the humid air. The streets washed with rain, her garden aglow in the light of another hot and sunny day, made the events of the previous night feel less sinister.

She pulled one of her own red hairs from the front of her tank top.

She thought of Drayton's evidence bag.

Leary had claimed a sexual encounter with Gage in the pickup. The hairs had been left behind then, or if there'd been a struggle getting Leary into the truck. Made perfect sense. She didn't need lab work and DNA for that. And it wasn't outlandish to think Gage hadn't showered since the traffic stop. She was pretty sure he hadn't changed his shirt. She wouldn't ask Quinn or Ruiz or Preacher if they remembered what he'd worn at the traffic stop. She didn't need to remember. She needed to stop thinking about it, to follow Preacher's advice—no, she corrected herself, his orders—and leave the matter be.

She understood Preacher's warning about her sins, about her lies of omission. His admonishments about duty and moral conduct were not jokes. They were not hyperbole.

As big a dick as Drayton was, Maureen thought, she was the one obscuring by omission the murder victim's recent history. Hell, she'd stood by while Quinn had destroyed physical evidence of the victim's possible associates and activities. She was guilty of multiple fireable offenses. She was quite possibly a felon. A criminal. She'd fucking *handed him* that piece of paper. She couldn't be more complicit had she tried to be, had she meant to be. She needed to remember that she was only as clean as the cops around her. By protecting them she was protecting herself. She sipped her coffee. And she'd had such high hopes for her new career, her new life.

The police superintendent had instituted what he called an "honesty and truthfulness" policy not long before she'd enrolled in the academy. Any lie, the policy declared, about anything, no matter how minor, constituted grounds for termination. She'd seen three dismissals in her short time on the job already, one of them an officer, over things much less significant than impeding a homicide investigation. She could probably stay out of jail if what she was doing came to light. The NOPD had seen enough of its own people go to prison over the last few years. But keeping her job would be impossible. She'd be a washout. A failure and a reject.

As a young girl she'd been kicked out of two junior high schools for bad behavior. Smoking, fighting, cutting class, abusing her teachers. Mostly, she had trouble with male authority figures, or they had trouble with her, depending on who was asking. She could be viciously hostile toward them; other times she was too welcoming of their attention to her misbehaving. She liked boys. Her mother, Amber, blamed Maureen's runaway father for everything. He'd disappeared when Maureen was eleven. Maureen blamed him, too, because it was convenient and none of the adults in her life were willing to contradict her. Most seemed willing to let her rage, as long as she did it somewhere else.

She'd squeaked through a third school when her mother, crushed flat by heartbreak, loneliness, a full-time department store job, and a maniacal offspring had threatened her with doctors, medication, and boarding school. After the eighth grade, somehow, Amber got Maureen admitted to a last-chance all-girls Catholic high school. She did better there, suddenly disdainful of the attention she used to crave, turning her anger inward in the school halls, and finding an outlet for it as a runner. She ran like mad, for miles, like something was chasing her.

She'd graduated, though as a senior she'd been bounced from the track team, despite setting school and Staten Island records as a long-distance runner. The nuns had no sense of humor about an athlete running on cigarettes and amphetamines. Not one that ran Cs in the classroom. After high school, except for running and cigarettes, she struggled to stick with anything, even drugs, unless she counted waiting tables. Which, she thought, sitting on her porch, there was a good chance she'd be doing again before Halloween the way things were headed. For the first time in fifteen years, for the first time in her adult life, she didn't want to be on her own anymore. She wanted to be part of something. Something bigger and stronger, something that made her *feel* bigger and stronger, than she was alone. Something she had *chosen*. In the NOPD, in New Orleans, she'd found a place, finally, where she wanted to belong, to stay. Whatever happened to her in the future, she decided, it would happen in New Orleans. No fucking way was she going back to Staten Island. No way was she moving back into her mother's house. She'd walk into the Mississippi before she'd go back up north. This place, as brief as her time in New Orleans had been, this was her life now, for better or worse.

Across the street, two crows perched bobbing and cawing in the sunlight on the red-tiled spine of the roof. Preacher was right. He was always right. She needed to put some distance between herself and the Gage case, to get back to regular, standard, non-attention-grabbing police work. She activated her phone. She'd call Quinn, firm up their plans for the evening, see if there was anything she needed to bring with her. She saw that in the night, the early morning, really, while she'd slept, she had gotten a phone call. She thumbed her way to the lone message on her voice mail. The number was blocked, or unlisted. The caller had left a message.

At first, Maureen took it for a wrong number, or a pocket call. The message began with several moments of near silence, whispers, slow breathing, maybe the muffled sounds of distant traffic. Out of the background noise a voice arose, softly singing. A woman's voice, singing low, as if she wanted no one other than Maureen to hear her. *Look at that deep well*, the voice sang. *Look at that dark grave.*

The same lines, the same melody, repeated three times before the caller had hung up. Gentle, like a secret lullaby. Or a spell. Or a warning. The throaty voice was unmistakable. From somewhere in New Orleans, Maureen knew, Madison Leary was singing to her. Maureen looked at her phone, put it back to her ear. Beyond bizarre. The question was why. And how had she gotten the number? What else did she know? Maureen's address? Preacher would understand her pursuing something like this, Maureen thought. Handling it solo was the best way to keep it quiet, right? She wouldn't even wear her uniform. Where had Leary gotten the number? Maureen wondered again. Someone had given it to her. Maureen had an idea who, and where to find her.

19

Maureen found Dice in the Marigny, sprawled in the newly cut grass in a corner of Washington Square, a small, pretty, tree-dense park between Frenchmen Street and Elysian Fields, not far from the corner where she'd left off Marques.

In the center of the park, Dice's friends sat in a circle, passing around a thin joint. Dice sat off to the side of the group, cross-legged, plucking a slightly funky repeating riff on the worn strings of her banjo, tapping her booted foot in the grass. As Maureen approached the circle, she recognized a few faces from the other night. They made no attempt to hide their weed as they packed a bowl to follow the joint around the circle, daring Maureen to say something to them. She could hear the righteous diatribes percolating in their throats.

She ignored them. She headed straight for Dice.

"Afternoon, Officer," Dice said, without looking up from her instrument.

"We need to talk," Maureen said.

Dice looked up. "I don't know what about. I brought your friend home, like I promised. I watched him walk into his grandmother's house." She smiled. "That is one serious lady. She's not a huge fan of yours. I liked her."

"It's not about Marques," Maureen said. "It's about someone else." She gestured over her shoulder with her thumb. "Come to the Rose Nicaud with me. I'll buy you lunch and a coffee. When was the last time you had a salad? You could use one."

"What if I already had lunch?" Dice asked, peering up at Maureen from her pickle bucket, one eye closed. "And I hate salad. What else you selling?"

"Coffee and lunch. And I won't call for a unit to come by and kick your pot-smoking friends out of the park and run warrant checks on them on this beautiful sunny day. Best deal you're gonna get."

Dice stood, turning toward her friends. "Hey, I'm going over the dark side with lady law over here. I'll be back in a few."

A couple of the other kids grunted to show they'd heard. The skinny boy from the other night waved and grinned. The others glowered at him and he blushed. Maureen tried to remember the last time she'd been that high.

"Let's go, copper," Dice said, striding through the grass, her banjo over her shoulder.

"You don't want to leave that here?" Maureen asked.

"With those thieves?" Dice replied. "I wouldn't trust them with my worst pair of panties. If I wore any, that is."

Maureen and Dice left the park through the open iron gate and crossed Frenchmen Street. They took an outside table for two on the narrow sidewalk, under the awning of the café. Big, cartoonish faces had been drawn in colored chalk on the concrete. Maureen thought she recognized one, by her glasses, as the city council president. Inside the café, she bought each of them a large black coffee and something to eat. Dice accepted a microwave-warmed slice of broccoli quiche. Maureen had a jerk chicken sandwich that left her sweating under her eyes.

"You mentioned the last time I saw you that you'd kicked the heroin," Maureen said, dabbing at the moisture on her cheeks. "Nice work. I can see the difference in you."

Dice scoffed at the compliment, catching a scrap of quiche in her palm as it bounced off her chin. "Yeah, that's why you didn't recognize me the last time you saw me, 'cause I look so healthy these days."

"You do look better," Maureen said. "You do."

"Officer, if this is gonna get weird," Dice said, "I don't roll that way. Pickin's are slim around here, a clean working dick is hard to find, but I do prefer boys nonetheless. Pretty much exclusively. And I don't do the gay-for-pay thing."

"There's something we can agree on," Maureen said.

"As long as we've got that straight," Dice said, with a wry smile. "So to speak." She studied her fork. "Tell you what else I haven't done in a long while, eat with real utensils. The metal feels weird in my mouth."

Maureen resisted the urge to crack wise about Dice's multiple lip piercings. "What is that tattoo on your head?"

"Smaug," Dice said, shoveling food into her mouth. She wasn't letting a crumb escape. "From *The Hobbit.*"

"I know it," Maureen said. "The greedy dragon with the mountain of stolen treasure. Very nice." She'd eat half her sandwich, she decided, and send Dice back to the park with the other half.

"So you saw the movie," Dice said.

"I read the book," Maureen said. "In junior high. And again in high school."

"A cop who reads," Dice said. "I'm about to fall out of my chair."

Maureen smiled. "Smaug. Huh. So you're the girl with—"

"Don't even," Dice said, raising her hand. "Don't go there. I'm so sick of hearing about that. I didn't know when I got the tattoo, okay? I was fucking high. Like for months. It's not my fault. You'd think living on the streets I'd get some kind of break from that kind of pop culture shit. But the fucking tourists . . ." She shook her head. "I'm gonna start telling people it's a dragonfly, or a magic eel or something. It's almost enough for me to grow my hair back." She rubbed her buzz cut. "Almost. I make decent dosh having my picture taken because of it. It's hard to reject a good revenue stream in a down economy."

"You ever get off the streets?" Maureen asked. "Like, what happens when the cold comes?"

"Depends," Dice said, rubbing her fingertip over the glass plate. When she noticed Maureen watching, she slid the plate aside. Maureen knew better than to offer her leftovers right then. Dice would throw them in the gutter. Dice lifted the lid from her coffee cup, sniffing the contents. "Some people go home. Not everyone out here has nowhere to go. For some kids it's an adventure out here, like backpacking across Europe.

"Those of us who stay, sometimes we try to move indoors. In the winter, there's plenty of vacants left, especially deep in the Bywater and into the Nine. Hard to keep warm, though, and not burn the place down, or strangle ourselves on carbon monoxide. And Deep South or not, it does get fucking cold down here some nights. And wet. For days. It gets in your bones. High summertime we go inside, too. This place stays fucking hot at night, and the bugs, and the rats. I'm not about to get rabies or that West Nile bullshit. And you know when late August comes people get cranky and start shooting. It's worse than the winter sometimes.

"We don't do shelters much. The older people don't like us, and straight couples have to split up. None of them take dogs. And the shelters can be more anal about wine and weed than you guys." She shrugged. "Some of those places, the staff are grimier than we are. And shady, quick with their hands. A couple of the hostels cut us a break sometimes, if tourism is slow and if we can scrape together a couple of bucks and do some work in the kitchen and shit."

"You ever do that? You ever stay in the hostels?"

"I can wash a dish," Dice said. "I'm not helpless. I can fold sheets and hot mop a floor if I have to."

Maureen sat back in her chair. "You talk like it's embarrassing to want to be warm when you're cold, or cool when you're hot. It's human nature to protect yourself."

"It's not that," Dice said, bristling. "It's getting warm yourself and leaving others in the cold while you do it. Sometimes we pool the money, try to work it so we each can get a night inside. A shower. A real bed with heat or air-conditioning. But those arrangements never last. They degrade with a quickness. People bitch, they jump the line. That's the problem with any larger money-based system, it condones that 'fuck everyone else, I'm getting mine' mentality."

She lifted her chin at Maureen. "Like y'all, doin' that devil's work, using people against each other, to rat each other out. Using their pasts and their addictions and troubles against them. You'd let us all kill each other with sticks if you could get away with it."

Maureen knew the credit she'd earned with her charm offensive and her ten-dollar lunch was maxing out. "I'm looking for someone. I thought you could help me find her. No ratting, no snitching. It's not like that. You'd be doing a good thing." The feminine pronoun snagged Dice's attention, as Maureen had hoped it would. She took Dice's silence as encouragement to continue. Thievery was the connection between Dice and Madison, that was Maureen's best guess. Like the cops who half-heartedly pursued them, the downtown pickpockets and petty thieves, which was most of the kids on the streets, knew and kept track of one another—who was in jail or rehab, who was on the run, who had left town, who had returned. They had a threadbare camaraderie that sustained them, a target-rich environment, places to get out of the heat and the cold, as Dice had said. It might have been Dice who turned Madison on to Pat O's in the first place.

Maureen knew she needed to be gentle with the question. Going right to the accusation would backfire. "In your travels, have you ever met a woman named Madison Leary? She's older than y'all, but I think she's spent some time on the streets. She's hard to miss. Her eyes are two different colors."

To Maureen's surprise, Dice broke out into a huge smile. "Madison?

The singer? With the long brown hair? Yeah, I know her. She's cool as shit." Dice's smile crumbled. She'd remembered, Maureen figured, that she was talking to a cop. "Did something happen to her?"

"You could say that."

Dice bounced her palm off her forehead several times. Tears welled in her eyes. "This fucking city, I swear." She picked up her fork, dug the tines into the denim over her knee.

"It's not that," Maureen said, resisting the urge to reach across the table and snatch away the fork. "Not yet. She's lost. And I'm trying to find her, *before* something terrible happens. She reached out to me. She called me. It was a strange call. Upsetting." She paused, giving Dice a window to speak. "Not a lot of people have my number, Dice. I can't remember the last person I gave it to, other than you."

"She said she knew you," Dice said. "That she was part of a case you were working."

"If that were true," Maureen said, "why would she need to get my number from you?"

Dice sat up in her chair. "I know, right? That's what I said. So *she* said that she had your number, but lost it, and that you were expecting to hear from her. She made it sound like a real crisis." She shrugged. "I mean, you're a bitch. I wouldn't be on your bad side. She said she didn't want the others knowing she was working for the cops, which was why she hid from you that night."

"What night?"

"The night you came for Marques's drum. She hid down the street, in the dark, mixed in with the other kids, but she was here. She saw us talking, watched us. That's how she knew to ask me for your number. She saw you give me your card. I used her red bike to take Marques home to his grandmother."

Maureen frowned. There was a piece of the story missing. "So she just walked up to you, this complete stranger, and offered the use of her bike?"

"She's not a stranger," Dice said. "That's why she was on the corner with me when you showed up. We met in the spring, panhandling, working the St. Claude traffic lights with cardboard signs. Hers said something about sick kids. Bullshit, natch. She was clever. She could work it. You could tell she'd been hard done by. It was us and a bunch of guys, so we stuck close, looked out for each other. And we hit it off. Musical backgrounds and shit. For a while we split a room at the Bend in the River hostel, over on Esplanade in the Treme? They reach out to people on the street. Not everyone in the charity business is a scumbag."

"Tell me what you know about her."

"She came to New Orleans from outside LaPlace," Dice said. She looked at the fork like she'd just found it, put it back on the table. "She'd been there a few months, but that wasn't where she was from originally. I think that was like North Carolina, or Virginia, someplace like that. One trailer park's the same as the next, she used to tell me." Dice smiled at the recollection. "Like the suburbs, she said. She was funny."

"She came to New Orleans to be a singer?" Maureen asked. "Is that what she told you?"

"I don't know if she told me that," Dice said, "or if I guessed it because she had such an awesome voice. She liked that dark Appalachian shit we're always pretending to play on Frenchmen, but she knew it for real, you know? But she had no instrument, which I always thought was odd. Showed up without one, far as I know. If I could get a banjo, I figured she could manage some old guitar or something."

"She ever get any gigs?"

"We'd talked about gigging together, playing on the corner for change, like a duo, that kind of shit. It was another way to make a little money. Her voice, it woulda stopped people in their tracks. We know a lot of the same songs. I can play some guitar, too." She shrugged. "Never happened. After a few weeks at the hostel, we lost touch. I was getting into the shit again at the time. I don't hide it real well. Bend in the River put me out. She might have tried looking for me over the summer, not that I would've known it."

"You think she stayed in the hostel without you?"

"She left, too," Dice said. "Not long after me. When I kicked again, I went to see her, but she was gone. No one knew where. She could have stayed as long as she wanted. She didn't need my income. That's another reason it was weird to me that she had no instrument. I didn't know it until we were living together, but she had cash. A good bit of it."

"This cash," Maureen said. "She made it how?"

"Brought it with her from LaPlace," Dice said. "She didn't have a job, unless you count the panhandling and the stealing, which can be more tiring than you would think. She had thousands, it wasn't St. Claude Avenue toll money."

Maureen said nothing. She let the silence hang.

"She gave me some from out of the box she kept it in." She looked away from Maureen. "I stole some. Not much. I think she knew. That was a reason I went back to see her."

"To pay her back?"

Dice laughed. "Yeah, from the pile of extra money I have. I went back to apologize for flaking on her."

"So she came to New Orleans," Maureen said, "to make it as a singer, but never had an instrument and never played anywhere."

"Happens more often than you'd think," Dice said. "I heard her sing around the hostel. I don't know why she never used it for more, but she had the voice."

"I believe it." Maureen took out her fresh pack of cigarettes, offered one to Dice, and lit them both. "She ever tell you why she left LaPlace, ever give you a reason? She ever tell you anything about her life there?"

"I don't know how much more I can tell you."

"Because I'm a cop?"

"Because I don't know anything."

Maureen knew Dice was lying to her, but she didn't push. She let the silence have its way. Dice looked away from her, running her eyes over the underside of the awning, over the motionless blades of the ceiling fans and the dead and empty wasp nests in the crossbeams. She studied the parked cars on the street, the clownish faces drawn on the sidewalk, putting her eyes anywhere but on Maureen. Dice smiled crooked, her eyes teary again. She'd lost people before out here, Maureen thought. She'd lost more than people.

"His grandmother doesn't like you," Dice finally said, "but Marques thinks you're the shit. He said you got in some trouble on his behalf. He talked my ear off about you. All the way to Grandma's house." A pause. "So what do you really want?"

"Here's the thing," Maureen said, leaning across the table. "The Madison you describe is not the person I'm looking for. That person and the person I'm looking for sound like two different people. Something happened to her. And now she's vanished. Is there anything you can think of that might help explain her disappearing?"

"Disappearing from where?" Dice asked, skeptical again. "No one gave a shit about her to begin with. Same as me, same as you without that uniform. How does someone who's already invisible vanish?"

"My heart bleeds for you and yours, it does," Maureen said. "You're getting defensive. You're hiding something. What are you not telling me?" She waited. "I'm looking for her now. She matters to me. Now. I can help her. Tell me about her."

"She had these orange medicine bottles," Dice said, "a bunch of them, a pill stash." She corrected herself, "No, it was not a *stash*. What I carried was a stash. She was on medication. I went through them when she wasn't around." Dice, for a fleeting instant, was embarrassed at her behavior. "Like I said, I was getting back into the shit around that time."

"What were the pills?"

"Not what I'd hoped for," Dice said. "That was for fucking sure. Clozaril was one. There were a couple of other kinds. I forget the other names. I asked around. Turns out it was scary shit. Antipsychotics. No use to a junkie. Not to take, not to sell. I left it alone. I wasn't that cruel or desperate. Not yet. She was rationing, anyway, by the time we moved into the Bend in the River. She was cutting the pills in half. I don't know if she ever tried for a new 'scrip." Dice shrugged. "Like there's anywhere for someone like us to go for that shit."

"And how did you feel about that?" Maureen asked. "When you learned your new friend from LaPlace with the pretty voice had a mysterious wad of cash and a collection of antipsychotics under the bed?"

"It's a strange world we live in." Dice rolled her shoulders, dismissive. "I mean, she stole the money, that was obvious, right? Drug money, probably. Nobody panhandles their way into a shoe box of cash money like that. Cash is like water through your fingers out here. We're not *savers*. I know plenty of people who've been on and off meds. And I know plenty more who should be on them. It ain't no thang. The money made me more nervous than the pills. Nobody chases after a few lost bottles of pills; they go out and get more. I never counted it, but I saw *stacks* of cash. Enough for whoever she took it from to come hunting for her. When I saw the money, it made more sense to me why she wanted to be off the streets and living indoors."

"Clozaril's no joke," Maureen said. "It's for severe cases of paranoid schizophrenia. *Severe* cases. Violent cases."

"Well, had I known that," Dice said, playing it casual while Maureen watched the fear in her rippling below the surface, "the fact that she slept with a straight razor under her pillow would've bothered me a whole lot more."

Maureen felt her stomach drop, as if she'd been standing atop a trapdoor. The LaPlace connection and now this. Add in the brown hair and strange old outcast Madison Leary became a murder suspect. At least she was to Maureen, the only one who knew enough of the details to assemble the theory. A razor would match the murder weapon at the Magnolia Street killing, too. "A straight razor. Under her pillow. While rationing her crazy pills. That didn't frighten you?"

"You're funny," Dice said. "You talk like Madison's so different from everyone else I live with. Like she's a, whadda you call it, an anomaly. Everybody I know, the women especially, carries something as a weapon. Who else is gonna protect us? Y'all?"

Maureen nodded. Women didn't accessorize their egos with weapons like men did. They carried them for practical purposes, for use. She felt her gun pressing against her tailbone. Before she'd become a cop, since she was a teenager, she'd carried a switchblade. She had used it for more than ornamentation, as a girl and as a woman. It had saved her life. She had killed a man with it. And until she had become one, she had never counted on the cops, either.

"The under-the-pillow thing was slightly weird," Dice continued. "I'll give you that, but it's not like she sat up nights sharpening and admiring it in the moonlight, doing tricks with it, or talking to it. She wasn't Gollum. She cut her pills with it. Seemed like a nice razor, too. Shiny blade. Clean. I could see my reflection in it when she showed it to me. She told me the blade was new, but the handle was real old. Said her grandmother gave it to her. That *her* father had carried it in the First World War. She said the handle was real African ivory."

"You believed her?"

"About the handle?"

"About any of it."

Dice thought for a moment. "It was important to her. But where it came from, her story changed about that. Same as the stories about where *she* came from. She told me when we were drunk one night that the razor had belonged to her daddy, and that she'd killed him with it, and took it with her when she ran off. She told me another time she'd killed a bootlegger that had come after her back in the woods, when she was living in a cabin in North Carolina. She was mysterious about herself."

"A bootlegger? Either she was mysterious or she watched too much TV."

"Bootlegger, meth dealer, something like that. Some dude who tried to rape her. A rapist is what he really was. Doesn't matter how he makes his money. Like I said, her story changed, her stories always changed depending on what kind of mood she was in or what level her meds were at when she was telling them."

"You think she killed the guy she took the money from?" Maureen asked. "Before she left LaPlace."

Dice shrugged and looked away, not eager to theorize about a possible homicide. Maureen thought maybe she could reach out to the La-Place authorities. Or better yet, use the computer in the car to check the St. John the Baptist Parish crime records. See if anyone there had had his throat cut in the past few months.

Gage hadn't come to town from LaPlace for the Saints game. He'd come looking for Madison Leary and her stolen money. He'd come to do business with or for Caleb Heath. They'd met at Pat O'Brien's to discuss it. That was where Gage found Leary, either by plan or by accident. Pat O's was a place someone like Heath would choose for a meeting, and that Madison Leary would choose for hunting. It was a target-rich environment for both overgrown frat boys and pickpockets alike, restocked every night with new packs of drunk young women. Had Cooley come after the lost money first, and when he went missing Gage came next? How did Caleb Heath fit in with an anarchist militia group? He did have plenty of the one thing Cooley and Gage and men of their ilk seemed to always lack: money. Madison Leary could answer these questions, if Maureen could track her down before the Watchmen Brigade did.

So she hadn't found Leary, but she'd found a possible weapon and motive in the Gage and Cooley murders, and had, in the process, pushed herself closer to returning to work with a confession to make. She'd lose her job. Quinn, too. And Ruiz. And Preacher. And Drayton would bungle the case in the end, anyway. But if Leary was leaving a trail of blood across south Louisiana, Maureen thought, she couldn't be ignored, right? No matter who she was killing. What had Atkinson said? It wasn't their place to judge the victims.

If Maureen connected the Cooley and Gage murders, Atkinson would take on both cases for sure. Drayton and his problems would be shoved aside. Maybe, maybe, Atkinson could, what was Preacher's word, help them *finesse* the situation. Maureen knew it'd be asking a lot of everyone involved. Could she, did she have the right to, make that decision on behalf of Quinn and Ruiz and Preacher? She'd have to go to them first.

"Do you think the money came from the rapist Madison said she killed?"

Dice raised her hands, and her voice. "Now you're putting words in my mouth. I never said Madison ever killed anyone. I never said anything like that. Don't write that down, don't tell any other fucking cops I said that."

"Okay, okay. I was asking your opinion."

"Like fuck you were." She took another of Maureen's cigarettes.

"Back to the razor then," Maureen said. "Why didn't you steal the razor and sell it? Sounds valuable. Shit goes missing in hostels and shelters. You're a thief."

"Up to a point." Dice looked away, thinking, watching pigeons bobbing about in the gutter on Frenchmen Street. Lost in thought, she looked to Maureen about fourteen years old. She released a long sigh. "I thought about it. It did look like it was worth something. But she would've known. She would've known it was me who took it."

Maureen couldn't help but admire Dice's general lack of shame or guilt over her own survival methods. Her plans, her decisions were tactical, morals never factored in. What other people called ethics neither helped nor hindered. It was never personal. "And then?"

Dice shuddered, smiling at her recollected fear. "There was something about her, those crazy eyes, maybe. A vibration came off her. A hum. Deep, like an old iron bell." Dice raised her hand, made it tremble. "Or like a tuning fork. Even with the meds, you got the feeling she heard things the rest of us didn't. That she would, that she *could* do things if you crossed her."

"What things?"

"I decided to leave that space blank. We lived in the same room. I never stole from Madison again, after those first couple of bucks. Not another dollar, not a single pill. A good thief picks good targets. Soft targets. Maximum profit, minimum blowback. Madison Leary was not a soft target."

Maureen took out her wallet. She slid one of her business cards across the table. Dice palmed it, slipping it into her pocket. It was meaningful, Maureen knew, that Dice had so readily taken the card. Dice trusted her. Maureen knew she could come back to her. "If you see her, if you hear about her, anything reliable, call me right away."

"She's got your number," Dice said. "If I see her I'll tell her to call you."

"The card is for you," Maureen said. "She knows me, not in the way she led you to believe, but knows I'm a cop. She might vanish again if you tell her I'm looking for her. Reach out to me, and me only, no other cops, if she surfaces. I want to hear her side of the story, from her own mouth, before I make any decisions about what I can do for her."

"I'm not promising anything," Dice said.

"You don't have to," Maureen said. "I'm not promising anything, either. We're gonna do the best we can, you and me."

"And this is two favors you owe me now," Dice said.

"You haven't produced on the second one yet. Don't get cocky. You ever call Madison out on her changing stories? Out of curiosity. To see what she'd say. To see if she'd tell you the truth?"

"And call her a liar over her precious antique straight razor?" Dice said. "Ha. How dumb do you think I am? Besides, we were roommates. What if the worst stories were the ones that turned out to be true? Then what? I don't want her telling my story to the next girl." She paused. "I have a question for you."

"Ask," Maureen said. "But I might not answer."

"When Madison called you, what did she say?"

"She didn't say anything," Maureen said. She felt her throat tighten. "She sang to me. The same lines, over and over. Something about an iron bell and a dark grave."

Dice shivered. "Oh my God. That scares the *shit* out of me."

"I'll lock my door tonight," Maureen said. And sleep with the gun on the nightstand. She got up from the table, collecting their plates and silver and trash to take back inside.

"There's something else I've never seen a cop do," Dice said, rising as well. "Clean up their own mess."

"Why the buzz cut?" Maureen asked, heading for the café door. "You pull it off, but what made you do it the first time?"

Dice slipped the fork she'd been holding into her pocket. She reached for the door, stopped. She took a deep breath. "When I was a little girl, I had hair past my waist. Thick and gold like honey. My mother, she used to pull it when she lost her temper with me. My father used to wrap it in his fist, when he did the things to me that made my mother lose her temper." She ran both her hands over her scalp. "Can't neither of them do that anymore. Nobody can. Ever."

You have to protect yourself, Maureen heard Waters say.

20

Arriving early for her detail that evening, Maureen parked a couple of blocks away from the house hosting the party, an enormous, rambling two-story antebellum home on the edge of Audubon Park, sheltered under the moss-draped and twisted boughs of giant live oaks. Maureen had seen the place before. Every now and then, on her longer runs through Uptown, she added a couple of loops around the bayou at the heart of the park. Running through the park, she had seen and admired the house, one of several regal mansions skirting Audubon Park, with its tall, glinting windows and its high and wide wraparound porch. Tonight, though, along with the rest of the hired help, she approached the house from the back.

The caterers, solemn-faced black men and white women in black slacks and white jackets, dashed up and down the flagstone steps and in and out the back gate as they made last-minute preparations for the party. Two older black men in neat tuxedos chatted as they set up and stocked a small bar in the rear sunroom. Maureen knew that in her own uniform, carrying on it a fresh whiff of the dry cleaner's, with sharp creases in her pants and sleeves, she looked clean-cut and professional. Her badge shined on her chest. Her boots shined on her feet. She had her hair, damp from the shower, pinned up under her NOPD ball cap. She'd even touched on some makeup, on her cheeks and her eyes. Light lipstick. Less than she wore to court, more than she wore on patrol.

Outside the house, she lingered on the sidewalk, dodging the caterers, thumbs hooked in her gun belt, craving a cigarette and unsure of the event's nicotine etiquette. She looked around for Quinn, but didn't see him. She knew she'd arrived early. After the trip to the Marigny and the conversation with Dice, she'd had a long run and a shower. Even after that, with what she'd learned about Madison Leary, she'd had no luck trying to relax around the house.

The caterers nodded to her as they hustled back and forth from their vans to the kitchen, not meeting her eyes as they passed. More than one, she was sure, was on parole or probation. More than one had something in his or her pocket for after the party. Others were plain busy.

Quinn soon appeared at the back door, shouldering past a scowling woman headed inside carrying a covered silver tray. He said something to her that he thought was funny. Maureen couldn't hear it. The woman didn't laugh. Quinn had a half-eaten deviled egg in one hand. Food flecked the corners of his mouth. The top three buttons of his uniform shirt were undone. His cheeks shone with aftershave. He took his time coming down the steps and along the walk, surveying the activity around him with a smug grin and a cheek swollen with pilfered food, a spoiled-aristocrat swagger in his stride as if the surrounding bustle were happening at his behest, on his behalf, and with his blessing.

Maureen felt something at that moment she had yet to feel for a fellow police officer, a dislike so intense it bordered on disgust.

During her time as a cocktail waitress she'd witnessed and endured that contrived arrogance in the pinkie-ringed faux-gangsters who'd piss their pants in the presence of a real, blood-on-his-hands mafioso. She saw it in her current job from the wannabe gangstas who clutched the front of their baggy jeans and rolled their toothpicks across their teeth, making kissing noises as she rolled by their corner in her cruiser. And Quinn was hardly the first of her fellow cops she'd seen giving off that brat prince attitude like body odor. She'd never seen it from him, though. Not until tonight. Was it the environment that made him like this? she wondered. Did he think himself a member of the posh circle he hovered around? Was it the small amount of power he held over the rest of the hired help? He raised his chin at her from the steps, grinning, when Maureen caught his eye.

She wanted to go home. She'd made a mistake accepting Quinn's invitation to this detail. She couldn't imagine spending a couple of hours with this version of him. The only question remaining was how bad a mistake it would prove to be.

As he met her on the sidewalk, Quinn wiped his hands on his uniform pants. "What's the haps, Cogs? You wanna eat, now is the time. We're not supposed to be in the house while the party's going on. Food is good. Brennan's is catering. And it's free."

"I'm good," Maureen said. "I ate before I came. Quite a production, though. What's the party for?"

"Fund-raiser for the musicians' health clinic, the one they run out of Ochsner hospital. The New Orleans Musicians' Clinic. It's usually real quiet, this party." He laughed. "It's not like the musicians get invited." He started buttoning his shirt. His breath smelled like boiled eggs and cheap rum. He hadn't limited his indulgence to the catering trays, Maureen thought. Or maybe he'd had a taste before coming over to the party. She slipped him her pack of gum.

"For the eggs," she said. Quinn refused the offer.

He patted his pants, found a roll of mints, ate two. "I pack my own."

Of course you do, Maureen thought. As does everyone who drinks on the job.

"Bunch of wrinkly old rich folks stuffing their faces," Quinn said, "swilling free booze, and writing fat checks, making them feel good about themselves for saving New Orleans cul-cha." He shrugged, clipping on his tie. "Whatever. I'm not a cynical man. It's a nice payday for us, too. And it does do some good. It's not like playing the clubs comes with health insurance. That shit does cost." He grinned. "A night like tonight everybody wins. Those kinds of scenarios are too few in this business."

"And what is it *we* do while we're here, exactly?"

"Stand around and look pretty," Quinn said. "You're off to a good start on that, by the way. I wasn't sure you owned any makeup."

"Then don't make me get ugly," Maureen said with a smile, cocking back her fist, "and lay off."

Quinn raised his hands, chuckling. "Trying to be polite. Overreact much?"

They watched as two young men in matching polo shirts set up three folding chairs and a wooden podium by the curb.

"Nice," Quinn said, nodding in approval.

"Valet service," Maureen said. "Wow. They're calling this a *cocktail party*?"

"I know, right?" Quinn said. "The valet makes our job even easier this year. Past years, our main job was walking these boozy staggering old geezers back to their cars after the party. You know, so they could drive home. Now we don't even have to do that."

"What is it we *are* supposed to do? Seriously."

"Relax. This isn't a test, Cogs. We walk around. Keep an eye on things. Make the rich folk feel protected. We'll pass by the front a time or two, make sure no one's trying to crash the party by coming through the park. It's not like we're the first line of defense against a possible armed assault. We're ornaments, window dressing. Trust me, Coughlin. Tonight is the very definition of easy money. You'll see."

They both turned when a loud, deep voice called Quinn's name from the back door of the house. Maureen watched as an older man, tanned and fit, his cream dress shirt and brown trousers better creased than her uniform, and worth more than a month's salary, stepped out of the golden backlight of the kitchen and down the back steps. As he came down the walk, his gait was stiff, his arms swinging at his sides. Maureen recognized in his controlled stride the sufferer of perpetual back pain. She wondered what pain meds he took. His brown hair was full, though streaked with gray, and parted neatly to one side. He had small but bright and lively blue eyes behind thick-rimmed glasses. His eyes looked familiar to her. Maybe she'd seen him on TV? In the paper? He brought with him a whiff of woodsy cologne. His diamond cufflinks, large "H"s, glinted in the porch light as he extended a welcoming hand to Quinn. Had to be the host, Maureen thought.

"Officer, always a pleasure," the man said, smiling. "Thanks so much for helping out again this year."

Quinn shook the man's hand. "Anything for a good cause, sir, you know that. Happy to be of service."

The man turned to Maureen, again offering his hand. "And you must be Officer Ruiz's replacement."

"I am," Maureen said, shaking hands. "Pleased to meet you. Officer Maureen Coughlin."

"The pleasure is mine," the man said, looking her up and down. "You're quite the colt. Welcome to the party. We're always happy to have a new addition to the fold. My name is Solomon Heath."

Maureen didn't flinch. Quinn, you motherfucker, she thought. You set me up. "Of Heath Design and Construction?"

"The very same," Solomon said.

Heath's hand was soft and smooth, the knuckles hard and pronounced. It was a hand Maureen could tell that maybe decades ago had done day labor. For years now, though, that hand had clutched a high-ball glass while the mouth full of white teeth gave orders, or that hand had steadied the smooth stock of a shotgun or the handle of a golf club while the blue eyes tracked ducks scattering across the sky or the lay of the green. She got the feeling Heath hadn't gotten construction site dust on his fancy leather shoes in some time. She recalled his son's comment about not having the time for the minutiae. What was the point of being the boss, she thought, if it didn't keep you clean? Maureen tightened her grip on the man's hand, sparking a twitch at the corner of his right eye when he sensed the additional pressure.

"So you and Officer Quinn," she said, "y'all have known each other awhile, it seems."

"My entire life," Quinn said.

"That's true," Solomon said. "Officer Quinn and my son, Caleb, even went to high school together. St. Ignatius over in Bay St. Louis. They've known each other more than half their lives." He beamed at Quinn the way a man would a notably loyal dog. "The first year I had this party, I asked for Quinn by name when I asked for a detail. He's a good man. I knew his father, too. Another good man."

"That's wonderful. New Orleans really is a small town, in its way. And full of good men." Maureen released Solomon's hand. "Well, I hope it's a wonderful party. Certainly a great cause. I'm thrilled to meet you. Anything we can do to help, please don't hesitate to ask." She turned to Quinn. "A boarding school boy. I'd never have guessed. You hide it well."

Heath slipped his hands in his pockets, as if to hide something in his palm. Maureen wasn't sure if it was the age spots or the manicure. Or maybe his wedding ring. And where was Mrs. Heath? she wondered. He looked Maureen up and down, again, his appraisal no longer only physical. She could tell he was unsure what to make of her. He sensed her hostility, had no idea what had touched it off. He was savvy enough to see through her fake cheer. He didn't like her, and so mistrusted her, that was obvious, and not, Maureen thought, unexpected. But Solomon did expect people to want him to like them. The expectation came with having money, she knew, and power, and was an advantage he was used to exploiting. Not having it made him uneasy, a feeling she was sure he did not enjoy. Maureen suspected Solomon Heath spent little time around people he couldn't predict, if not outright control.

Heath turned back to Quinn, his smile reigniting as if he'd flipped it back on with a switch. "If y'all need anything, pop into the kitchen and ask one of the servers. They'll be happy to help. You should recognize some of them. We have the same crew every year. They count on it." He shrugged, embarrassed at the burden of his benevolence. "The guests should start arriving at any minute. Give my regards to Officer Ruiz when you see him again. I look forward to having him back next year."

With a nod, Heath turned and headed back into the house, pulling the kitchen door closed behind him.

Maureen grabbed Quinn hard by the arm. She dragged him a few yards down the sidewalk, away from the back of the house and from the valet stand, out of earshot of the help. She squeezed his arm twice as hard as she had Solomon Heath's hand. "You mother*fucker.* Trying to help me out, my ass. How many more times are you gonna bullshit me?"

"About what? What are you talking about?"

"I'm supposed to be scared of him?" Maureen said. "I'm supposed to be intimidated because your high school buddy's daddy has a big house and a pile of money? Why would you play it this way? What is wrong with you?"

Quinn yanked his arm free from her grip, rubbing at where she'd grabbed him, pouting. "I don't know what you're talking about. I've told you from the beginning, I'm trying to do you a solid. I'm trying to show you why we massaged the situation the other night. Why we should continue to do so." He pointed back over his shoulder at the house. "I'm hooking you up with a serious player."

"You could've told me about your connection to this family at the murder scene," Maureen said. "That would've been fine. You could've asked *me* for a favor instead of stealing that note from me. Do I seem like such a bitch that you can't ask me for a professional courtesy?"

"If I'd asked for the favor," Quinn said, "which was squashing a potential clue to the murder, would you have done it?"

Maureen hesitated.

"No, you wouldn't have agreed," Quinn said, "and then we're arguing in front of everybody. I look bad, you look bad. Maybe I did *you* a favor by not putting you on the spot like that. C'mon, you see what this guy's worth, you think Drayton is involving Solomon Heath's son in a homicide investigation over a fucking Post-it note?"

"You were looking out for me. I'm supposed to believe that?"

"I was looking out for everyone," Quinn said, his voice rising. "Christ, you talk the talk about wanting to be a team player, Cogs, but you really suck at walkin' it sometimes."

"Solomon knows, doesn't he?" Maureen asked. "He knows you got Caleb off the hook, and whose hook it was. You brought me here to show me off. Like a fucking trophy. You're serving me up to him. He calls me a colt, whatever the fuck that means, so I guess you're supposed to be the cowboy who broke me. Fuck you, Quinn."

"I brought you here," Quinn said, "to introduce you to Solomon. Yeah, he knows you could've connected his son to Gage, and didn't. You better believe I made sure of it. He said he'd take care of it. He's a good friend to have, and now *he* owes *you* a favor. Where else you gonna get a deal like that? It's how the city works. You did *good* that night when we found Gage. I keep trying to tell you that, but you won't hear me. You did the Heath family a solid, got them on your side. You made yourself look good, made the department look good. Nobody's trying to make you look broken. Let yourself reap the rewards for a job well done, for chrissakes. And lower your voice."

"No offense, but Caleb's not the first trust-fund douche bag I ever met in my life," Maureen said. "His type are no good, they use people, they never stop at one favor, and their parents are usually worse. It's their parents who teach them other people exist for their benefit. Ask the folks on Magnolia Street what good people Caleb Heath is."

"Fuck them. Why don't I ask them what they think about you, or anybody in a police uniform while I'm at it? Mr. Heath has been a good friend of the department. Of the city, too. Those new uniforms Roots of Music and your boy Marques marched in last Mardi Gras? Who you think bought that shit for them? You think Solomon needs to throw parties like this, for poor-ass saxophone and piano players? He kept genera-tors going twenty-four seven after Katrina. This house was one of the only places in town cops could get AC and a cold drink. Hot food. A shower. It was more than the fucking city or the state or motherfuckers shooting at us from the Magnolia projects rooftops or the fucking *feds* who now, suddenly, want to be in charge of shit, had for us. Those of us who were here, we remember who stood with us. There's no expiration date on that. You just got here. Why don't you try to learn something instead of telling everybody how it oughtta be?"

Quinn pointed at the house. "There are going to be half a dozen kings of Rex in there tonight. They throw charity parties like this all year long. They're the society big shots. The fucking *mayor* will be here tonight. Come Mardi Gras, you wanna be out on the fucking parade route every night, your back hurting, your feet hurting, dealing with drunk college kids and middle-schoolers from the 'hood with guns? Or do you want gigs like this, where people bring you hot coffee and jambalaya all night? I'm trying to be your *friend* here, Coughlin, and plug you into the circuit. No bullshit. No joke. That academy rigamarole ain't the job. You should know that by now. *This* is the job."

"I talked to Preacher," Maureen said. "He told me Hollander was the one you were looking to plug into."

"She's got four years on the job," Quinn said, "and you got four months. How's it look if I go right to you? There's a protocol. Yeah, I suggested Hollander first, but I knew Preacher would suggest you. That's why I went to him and not straight to Hollander. He knows the deal."

"You don't know Preacher's deal as well as you think."

"What'd I ever do to you," Quinn asked, "that you gotta talk to me like I'm a shithead?"

"The consent decree is going to change everything," Maureen said. "That old-boy-network stuff, that who-you-knew-in-high-school shit is going out the window. We'll have the same shot at these good details as everyone else on the job. And they'll have to take their turn on the parade route. And your big-shot friends will forget they know you when they have to start filing paperwork on hiring cops for their personal business."

Quinn laughed out loud. "Nothing's going out the window. Nothing's gonna change. Fuck the feds. Fuck them. You know who worries about the feds? The high brass that's gotta answer to their faces and the newbies like you that don't know any better. The rest of us? Goddamn, woman. This is New Orleans. Can't nobody change this place. This place is its own animal, learn to ride it or get eaten. Man, sometimes I forget you're not from here. This right here is not one of those times. You don't want a piece of some perfectly legal, perfectly legit good fortune, fine, don't take one. But word gets around, Coughlin, about who's in and who's out. In a hurry."

"Why does everything that starts out as a favor with you," Maureen said, "end up sounding like a threat?"

Both of them stepped aside as a dark Town Car rolled up the narrow street, easing to the curb by the valet stand.

"I got no power over how you hear things," Quinn said. "I don't. You don't want to do this, for whatever uppity, Yankee, Puritan, self-righteous reason, that's fine. Take off. I'll tell Solomon you got your period. I got a phone full of guys who can be here in three minutes flat, happy for the favor and a go box of finger sandwiches."

"Fuck you, Quinn. I said I'm doing it, so I'm doing it." Maureen took a deep breath, released it slowly. "And fuck you again for that crack about my period."

"I'm sorry," Quinn said. "You're right. That was outta line." A shining Porsche SUV rolled past. "The guests are arriving, we should get back. I'm gonna smoke one, take a stroll and secure the perimeter. When I come back, you do the same. Then, whaddaya say we finish the night like professionals? We do our job, take our money, and go home."

"I can live with that," Maureen said.

"You're a tough one to figure, Cogs," Quinn said, lighting his cigarette. "But you're okay in the end." He smiled, backing away from her. "And not bad in the front, either."

When Quinn returned, Maureen walked down the gravel pathway alongside the Heaths' property, weaved through the butterfly boxes, and wandered out into the darkness of the park. From under the boughs of a live oak, invisible frogs by the dozens hiccupping and chirping in the black bayou behind her, Maureen smoked and watched the party from a distance.

White lights had been strung through the low-hanging trees near the house. The guests milled about on the broad wraparound porch, gaslight shadows playing across their bodies. The men wore light, expensive suits. The women wore gowns and clutched thin wraps around their bony shoulders, their necks and ears and wrists dripping with jewelry. Older wealthy white people in formal wear being waited on by black people in cheap tuxedos. From where she stood, the night could've been October 1911, or 1811. That was an odd thing Maureen had noticed about New Orleans, the way the city, the way a scene you watched, could flicker from one century to the next and back again before your eyes, the past coalescing out of the shadows and mist like an apparition hovering for a moment over a grave then fading again, dissipating into the night. Anything could trigger the phenomenon: the distant sound of mule hooves on cobblestone, the scent of the river, a warm breeze through the rattling fronds of a dry palm.

She loved the effect, even when it showed her the less lovely reflections of the city. It was to her as if New Orleans lived suspended in a perpetual ephemeral present, a city in amber; nothing ever truly left, and nothing ever truly died. Everything slipped behind the veil until its turn came around again, like your favorite painted wooden horse from the other side of the carousel. Not that she was ever much of a carnival girl, she thought, but New Orleans made you wonder. The city had a way of making you rethink your priorities.

Overhead, Maureen tracked dark fluttering shapes against the indigo sky. Bats. Like leaves of the live oaks come to life and making a break for it.

She felt the presence moving up behind her before she could see who it was approaching. Without turning, her hand on her weapon, she said, "Sneaking up on a cop, in the dark, how smart is that?"

Caleb Heath emerged from the shadows. He kept a respectable distance. He held his hands clutched behind his back, smiled. "Making my way back to the festivities after a walk of my own. Didn't even see you standing there until the last second. Sorry about that, darlin'."

Maureen expected him to keep walking. He didn't. Dressed in pale pleated slacks and a dark silk dress shirt, Heath looked like what he was, a rich man's underworked and overindulged heir. It took Maureen a moment to realize it, but Heath did not recognize her from Magnolia Street. He had stopped, she worried, to hit on her. From the look and the smell of him, she knew he was stoned. Very stoned. That was what he'd been doing off in the park, smoking much better shit than they got on Magnolia or Frenchmen Streets. He'd had himself some fine bourbon, as well.

"Daddy does throw quite the party," he said. "So popular I can hardly stand it. He is an expert. You haven't worked one of his soirees before, have you? I'd remember you." He offered his hand. "Caleb Heath. The son."

Maureen let his pale hand hang in the air. Suspended in the dark between them, it reminded her of a white jellyfish adrift in the night sea. Caleb did not have his father's hands.

"Officer Maureen Coughlin. This is my first Heath party, you're right about that, but we have met before, as it turns out." She gave him a moment to remember. He didn't. She offered a clue. "Magnolia Street."

Heath shrugged. He finally lowered his hand.

"The man we pulled out of your house the other night," Maureen said. "Turns out he had quite a history."

"That means nothing to me," Heath said. "I have no idea who that person was."

Maureen wasn't sure he knew what she meant and wasn't humoring her.

"He may prove to mean something to the FBI," she said.

"Then I wish them luck," Heath said. He had a mystified tone and a confused look, as if he couldn't believe they were still talking and she was not yet on her knees and blowing him behind the nearest oak tree. "They have a very difficult job. Is this what you want to talk about? It's a lovely night. All work and no play and all that. Let's enjoy the dark and the quiet. I don't have to go back to the party just yet. It's not like it's for me."

"When you met Clayton Gage at Pat O'Brien's," Maureen asked, "was Madison Leary with him or did he meet her there?"

That hit home. The events and people of Magnolia Street, they hadn't registered, but those three names—they got an instantaneous re-action from Heath as clear as the sound of breaking glass.

"Shame about Mr. Gage," Heath said, looking away from her. "It's a dangerous time in New Orleans for out-of-towners."

"So you heard about him?"

"Quinn and I, we talk. We talk about lots of things. We keep each other well informed."

"Gage was a friend of yours?" Maureen asked.

"Nonsense," Heath said. "Never met the man. I only know what Quinn told me about him. He seemed to be a man of questionable decision-making. His end, though sad, seems predictable."

"What makes you say that?"

Heath chuckled. "Quinn told me y'all met his date for the night. You tell me."

"So they were a couple, Gage and Leary?"

"You're asking me questions I couldn't possibly know the answers to."

Maureen watched as Heath began the long, slow process of digging a single cigarette from deep within his shirt pocket. He'd brought it with him, she figured, to mask the smell of the marijuana. Good luck with that, she thought. When he finally got the cigarette to his lips, Maureen lit it for him. While Heath smoked, she pondered her approach to him. Here was a chance, she thought, to get something substantial out of this night, to flip Quinn's subterfuge on its head. She needed to maximize these accidental moments with him, before his head cleared and he realized both that he wasn't getting in her pants and that he was better served not speaking with her.

Dice's stories playing on her mind, she wanted to nail down the Gage–Leary connection. She suspected that Gage had tracked Madison to New Orleans, maybe with Cooley's help, in search of her and the money she'd stolen from the Watchmen. Gage couldn't alert the authorities to his troubles. He'd have to get the money back himself. Had Gage somehow tracked Madison to Pat O'Brien's? If he'd known she was a thief, he'd have known her style, and he could have found the target-rich spots she'd work. Or had Leary set a trap? Had she let him find her? Had she worked Pat O's because she knew Gage would be the one to come after her, and that he'd know where to look for her? How deep into the Watchmen had Leary been hooked, Maureen wondered, before something, maybe her own demons, had driven her away from them?

After the lunch conversation with Dice, Maureen was questioning who had gotten in whose way at Pat O'Brien's that Sunday night. She had figured Leary for the wild card, and that she had queered the business meeting between Heath and Gage. But had Heath been the monkey wrench in Leary's plan? How ironic would that be, Maureen thought, if both Heath and Leary had picked Pat O'Brien's because it was full of drunk college girls, making a decision that would get Gage killed. Whose life was in danger in that truck? Maureen wondered. After Maureen had messed up Leary's chance to kill Gage that night, after Leary had managed to escape both the jail and the emergency room, she'd arranged another meeting with Gage.

Making an offer of surrender and a shoe box full of money would be how Leary had lured Gage into meeting her alone outside F and M's—another bar popular with drunk and oblivious college-age kids, another spot rich with, what had Dice called them? Soft targets. Madison might have known it and picked it herself. Her range might extend far beyond downtown.

Cooley had come first, Maureen decided. And after he had fallen down the rabbit hole, Gage had been dispatched by the Watchmen to find Leary. Madison had killed Cooley, too. Maureen was sure of it. If she went back to Magnolia Street, and asked the right people the right way, she could find someone who saw a red bike parked outside that empty house. One question remained. How had Leary and Cooley found that property in Central City?

Maureen wondered if she wasn't looking right at the answer.

"And you've got nothing," Maureen said, "that you want to inform *me* about while we have the chance to keep this conversation casual and off the record? Such as *your* whereabouts the night Gage was killed. I can protect you with that information. I know your father does a lot for the city, if I can help him out, or you, I guess, the more I know, the better."

Heath narrowed his eyes at her. "What makes you think I need protection?"

Maureen could tell she unbalanced him. He was like his father that way. The rich, she thought, who could figure them? They toughed it out through city-swallowing hurricanes then came undone over the smallest of things, like people underwhelmed by their big money and minor depravities. Right now, she was a buzzkill to him, nothing more. He wasn't sure what to do with a woman if she wasn't tugging at his wallet, his zipper, or both. His name alone should have done it for him. Her calm irked him. She thought of Preacher and of Atkinson, of their reliance on the patient, steady, almost gentle approach. Something to be said, Maureen thought, for underplaying the role sometimes. And she knew that because she stood there with tits and without a dick, Heath would never suspect she'd figured him out.

She decided to push only a little.

"What if I told you," she said, "that the police have material evidence of a prior relationship between you and Gage? That we have hard evidence of a planned meeting. A meeting about guns and money."

"I'd think you were a liar," Heath said, sniffling. Maureen could see him struggling to navigate the fog in his head. "In fact, I'd know you were lying, because if you had a sliver of a scrap of anything that could put me in danger, like maybe a Post-it note with my name on it from someone's wallet, I'd be in an interview room right now, having this conversation with a real detective. I sure as hell wouldn't be standing in the park with a glorified security guard who was *playing* detective while waiting on the crumbs that fall from my father's table. That's what I would say."

She hadn't expected a flinch from Heath over her revelation of the note. She hadn't expected him to own up to anything, even in his addled state. The test, the trap she was setting, it was for Quinn, to ascertain once and for all whether she could trust him with anything that she'd learned from Preacher or Dice. Destroying the note was one thing. Telling Heath about it was another thing entirely, a worse thing. Quinn had failed the test, and his supposed friend had betrayed him. The sad thing was that she couldn't even tell him.

"Quinn and I," Heath said. "We've talked about you."

"Nothing but nice things, I'm sure."

He shrugged. "He's impressed with you, but you make him nervous."

"We're working some things out, the two of us," Maureen said. "But he's got nothing to worry about. Tell him that, the next time you two talk. What was the real nature of your relationship with Clayton Gage?"

"You have a temper, Quinn says, and a propensity for violence. For snap judgments, too. You're quick not to like people. I can vouch for that. He wonders how long your career will last. You're a bit of a hazard. To others. To yourself."

"Not a lot of people to like, the business I'm in," Maureen said. "And my career will last at least as long as Quinn's does, if not longer. I can promise you that."

"Violence," Heath said. "Is that why you left New York?"

"Excuse me?"

"Like I said, Quinn and I talk. He says you're a native New Yorker. Long Island, is it?"

"Staten. Staten Island. Two totally different places."

"Don't meet many people around here from that particular place," Heath said, kicking at a thick tree root bursting up through the soil. His wits were returning. "Not sure I could find it on a map, which says more about the place you're from than it does me. You're a long way from home. I'm curious about how you got from there to here. I'm interested in people's stories. Actually, no, I'm not. That's bullshit. I couldn't give a flying fuck about other people's stories, but I do like useful information. It's always surprising how much of someone's story you can find out with a last name, birthplace, and a few other basic facts."

"I got here by car," Maureen said. "Like plenty of other people." And like hell, she thought, are you doing your own research. Had Quinn done it for him? Would he do that, Maureen wondered, plot against her, a fellow officer, with a civilian? "I got what I needed from you. You've told me plenty. I'm sure it's time for you to get back to the party. Your daddy is calling you."

"My father has plenty going on around him," Heath said, "to keep him distracted. Surgically enhanced wives and widows abound at these things. He doesn't need me to catch his next trophy. I can stand out here with you for as long as you like. We've talked about my friends. Let's talk about yours. Isn't that what women like? To be asked about their lives? How's your young friend Mr. Marques Greer? How's his grandmother? They like their new place in the River Garden? We built that, you know. I pretty much own it. Maybe I'll visit over there, ask how they're getting on. See if anyone from the old neighborhood needs to find them. Maybe they miss their old friends."

He recited his lines like a bad actor in a worse TV drama. Someone had armed him with them, Maureen thought. Who? Quinn again? Maybe Ruiz? Someone concerned she and Heath might end up talking. Had to be Quinn.

"This park closes at dusk," Maureen said, "which was some time ago. I'd hate to have to cite you for trespassing. And I get the feeling that if I searched you, I'd discover contraband. Then we're talking jail. I'd have to perp walk you through your father's lovely party. He wouldn't like that. Why don't we not go there?"

Heath stepped closer to her, making a show of his fearlessness, swinging his foot wide, hands clasped behind his back. "How far do you think you'd get, really, with me in cuffs? At my father's house? How do you think that would play back at the district when my father called? Last week, my father won the redevelopment contract for the row of old storefronts *across the street* from the Sixth District. Whose playground do you think you're in, Maureen?"

Maureen closed the distance between them, her hands clasped behind her back. "I know you, Heath. I've known you my whole life. You're as common and as tedious as herpes. So fucking impressed with yourself. You're a titty baby, living on an allowance, everything bought and paid for by someone else's brains and hard work. Never made anything in your life but a mess."

"There's the New York," Heath said, smiling, leaning back. "It comes through so much clearer when you get angry, Maureen. I bet it comes out real strong when you fuck. I bet you fuck hard."

"You don't get to call me Maureen. You speak to me, you call me Officer Coughlin. I took shit from you people my whole life, I don't have to do that anymore."

"That badge is like your pussy," Heath said, looking her up and down. "You think it can't be taken from you with a few good slaps. This is New Orleans. That tin star may as well come with a popgun and a cowboy hat. It's a half step above a Mardi Gras costume."

"Walk back to the party," Maureen said. She pulled a compact black cylinder from her belt. "Or get carried back. Your choice."

Heath chuckled. "Pepper spray? Really?"

Maureen snapped her wrist. The cylinder released a telescoped, spring-loaded metal rod with a weighted ball at the end. Maureen held the weapon close to her thigh. Heath's eyes flicked to it before returning to her face. "It's called an ASP," she said. "It breaks bones. I can get a new job faster than you can get new teeth, or a new jaw, or two new knees.

Daddy's money can buy you new things, but it can't make the pain go away. Pain punches its own time clock."

Heath opened his mouth to speak, a smile playing in his eyes, but he decided to say nothing.

"You walk around alone in the park at night often?" Maureen asked.

"What if I do?"

"You might want to rethink that habit," Maureen said.

"Has the NOPD given up on solving the murder problem? Shifting resources to the trespassing issues, are you? Or are you threatening me, Officer Coughlin?"

"If I wanted to get you, Heath, why would I warn you *not* to wander around alone in the dark? It's not us, or me, that you need to worry about. It's dangerous times in this city."

"Oh, it's been dangerous times in this city since there's *been* a city," Heath said. "You new arrivals are all the same. You act like it's some big revelation that New Orleans is a slippery place. The swamp and the things in it with wings and claws, with scales and teeth, they were here before you, and they will be here after you're gone."

"Mr. Heath," she said, "it's my sworn duty as an officer of the law to inform you, in the interest of public and personal safety, that the aforementioned Madison Leary, has, as of this moment, evaded capture. Her whereabouts are unknown. She could be anywhere. She is rumored to be proficient with a razor blade. We know she is familiar with Uptown."

"How fun and cryptic," Heath said. "We won't meet again." He turned away from her and walked toward his father's grand house, hands deep in his pockets.

Maureen watched him walk away as she lit another cigarette, her hands shaking. Quinn would be wondering what was keeping her. Heath never looked back her way, only throwing his hand in the air like a wave as he crossed from the park onto his father's property, the flab of his soft body jiggling under his expensive shirt. The people on the porch thought the wave was for them, and returned it, but Maureen knew the gesture had been meant for her.

She watched as he sauntered up the stairs, ignoring the line at the bar and getting himself a drink before hugging and handshaking with several guests who'd been waiting for cocktails. None of them minded deferring to him. She didn't know how much she really believed Madison Leary was out there in the shadows with her ivory-handled razor at the ready, waiting for her shot at Caleb Heath. She couldn't be sure Heath mattered to Leary, if a real connection existed, or if it was wishful thinking on her part that Leary would come after him. She'd given Heath what she could tell her conscience and her superiors was a warning, and, another part of her hoped, a nightmare or two. Men like Heath, though, she thought, could not imagine themselves being killed by a woman. Or a poor person. She wondered if they believed they could die. Wealthy, powerful men did die, though, Maureen thought. They could be killed. Same as everybody else. She had proved it. She had killed one herself.

Heath entered the enormous glowing house, a man vanishing into fire, the butler opening both of the tall oak doors for him like the gates of Heaven. She knew Caleb Heath was not another Frank Sebastian—a vain and evil man who had won his power with his willingness to do savage things others would not do. Caleb Heath by comparison was a weak-chinned bully, a capricious and spoiled man-child. Heath would never in a million years go himself to the River Garden to threaten Marques and his grandmother. He would pay someone else to do it for him. He could do damage, but he didn't have power, not really. People he paid would turn on him for the right price. What people like Caleb Heath had, what they mistook for power, Maureen thought, was permission. Permission to indulge their callous whims and bloated visions of themselves because of their names and their stations. Once you had power, Maureen thought, it was yours until and unless you gave it away. Permission, unlike real power, wasn't yours. Permission could be revoked by those who bestowed it, whether you liked it or not. You had no say. Maybe you were allowed the illusion of influence, but even that was a courtesy awarded from the outside. In that way, Caleb Heath, Maureen thought, was somewhat like her. Until her probationary period was over, she had permission from the powers-that-be to be a cop. When that time was over, when she was a real cop on her own, then she'd have real power.

Unlike her, though, left to his own devices, given nothing but a broken bottle and thirty seconds to fight for his life, Caleb Heath would die a pathetic, tearful, and lonely death. If you took away his checkbook, and the family name and money that made it more than a worthless pile of paper, Heath could not protect himself. That dependence, to Maureen, was the very definition of weakness. It was what separated them. What made Heath dangerous to her and to others, Maureen worried, was that on some deep, unconscious level, Heath knew his needs and weaknesses, too, and lived in mortal fear of their exposure.

Maureen rubbed out her cigarette in the dirt at her feet and tucked the filter into her pocket. At some point during her conversation with Heath the frogs had gone silent. The bats had flown away. Sticking to the shadows and the alley that took her around the back of the mansion, she returned to find Quinn to finish her shift.

Over the course of her night outside, she saw neither Caleb nor Solomon Heath again, though she could occasionally hear their voices and their laughter bleeding out into the night from the house. She did not tell Quinn of her encounter with Heath. He'd probably know about it soon enough. She knew it wasn't true, but at times she felt that Caleb laughed extra loud so that she would hear him. He knew she was out there, patrolling the yard like a good dog.

At the end of the night, after the last of the guests had left, a young man in a suit who Quinn didn't recognize came out the kitchen door and handed each of them an envelope.

Maureen tucked her envelope in her back pocket, tipped her cap to Quinn, and headed for her car. She wanted to sleep on what to do next with him. He'd tried getting tough with her at Gage's murder scene.

Then he'd gone the other way and sweetened the deal with the offer of this detail and the others it would lead to. He'd let her know he was hooked into important people who, at least to hear Quinn tell it, could do things for her in the future. Quinn was slick. She had to give him that, the way he played bad cop, good cop with her, better than Drayton did, feeling her out for what would work. She did have things of her own to hide. Quinn might know what some of them were. She couldn't trust him. He wasn't an ally anymore, if he ever had been, but making him an enemy wouldn't do her any good.

21

Around midnight, Maureen sat in her rocking chair, the night cooling around her. The last of the cicadas buzzed in the crepe myrtles and palm trees. A sweating glass of cold white wine rested on the table beside her. She watched the haloed streetlight, waiting as she often did for the flitting silhouettes of hunting bats. She had never seen one in the Irish Channel, not that she would swear to, only possibilities out of the corner of her eye, but her general environment seemed so damn tropical Gothic, they had to be out there. The evidence was too strong to resist. She watched for bats nearly every night.

Next to her wineglass, a cigarette burned in the ashtray. Next to the ashtray sat her phone. She was thinking about calling Quinn, hadn't yet worked up her plan.

He'd promised her three hundred dollars for working the party. When she'd checked the envelope at home, she'd found thirteen hundred dollars, thirteen crisp one-hundred-dollar bills so new that they stuck together. She couldn't accept the money. She wouldn't. The question was what to do next. The cash had come from Solomon but had to do with Caleb. A son tangled up in a homicide case had to be pretty fucking counterproductive when it came to landing city and state construction contracts. Especially when word got out, and it surely would, that both Cooley, who'd died in a house he owned, and Gage, who he'd planned to meet at Pat O'Brien's, were active in a domestic terrorist organization. Strong circumstantial evidence indicated that Caleb was guilty of the same. Evidence all around her, she thought, suggested the night sky be full of bats, and yet she'd never seen a one.

Was the money advance payment for whatever was coming next? she wondered. An invitation, maybe, over to Solomon Heath's way of doing things. Or was the extra thousand a threat, a "look at how little a grand means to me, Officer" kind of gesture. A "think of what I pay people a lot more powerful than you" message. One thing it wasn't, Maureen knew, was a no-strings-attached gift.

When she had waited tables and a certain kind of high roller left a big tip at the end of the night, it wasn't for the service he'd already received, it was for what he expected next time he came calling. It was a demand, an expression of power. Solomon Heath was that kind of high roller, the kind who slid his hand down your hip and over the curve of your ass while you took his order, looking you in the eye while he did it, daring you to respond. Making sure you knew, because he had money, he could touch you wherever he wanted. Making sure you knew he could cost you your job.

Nobody ever asked, she heard Preacher say, for only one favor. No. Fuck no. She was not about to go to work for the Heaths.

Considering what she now knew about the Heath family, Maureen believed that Drayton would never pursue the case and risk exposing them to association with Gage or Leary. So she and Quinn and Ruiz were covered there. She wasn't sure who had murdered Gage, but she knew his connection to Heath killed the investigation into his death. So why pay her, then, if Caleb was already protected by Drayton? Because, she thought, a thousand dollars was nothing to the Heaths, a dollar bill tossed in the bucket of a French Quarter tap dancer, and having another cop in their pocket couldn't hurt, especially with a son like Caleb on the loose. What if they needed her a week, a month, a year from now? They wanted her paid for and safe on the shelf.

Had Quinn been paid the same as she had? Maureen wondered. She knew that if she asked Quinn, she wouldn't get the truth. He'd tell her what he'd told her at the party, that she should enjoy her good fortune, that these breaks were part of being a New Orleans cop, compensation for the unrelenting onslaught of insanity-inducing bullshit they faced every day. She'd considered calling Preacher, but couldn't think of a way to talk to *him* about the money without feeling like she was ratting on Quinn. Like more tales of shady shit was what Preacher wanted to hear from her anyway.

And what to do about Leary? Maureen had to do something. Right? Wasn't it her duty? Circumstantially, with what Dice had revealed, Leary had emerged as a viable homicide suspect. The Gage murder was Drayton's case. How much, exactly, was she in a position to tell him about Leary? Maureen believed the things that Dice had told her about the money and the pills and the razor blade and where Leary had come from. But Maureen also believed that Drayton wouldn't even take an interview with a tattooed homeless woman, if Dice could even be persuaded to give it, something that Maureen knew was very much in doubt.

She thought she might go down to the Eighth District and give a description of Leary to Hardin, ask him to let her know on the quiet if Leary surfaced. That was how she was most likely to turn up again, getting busted. It was how criminals lived, committing the same crimes in the same neighborhoods and getting caught at it by the same cops, until they died of their addictions or got killed by rivals or put away by police. When Leary popped up, Maureen could deliver her to Atkinson. Dice might even talk to Atkinson. Maureen thought she could persuade her.

Maureen shook her head. She kept forgetting that she was better off with Leary missing. She didn't want things to be that way, but . . .

The FBI, though, in its pursuit of the Sovereign Citizens and the Watchmen Brigade, would harbor no qualms about pursuing Heath's history with Gage. Maureen picked up her wine, swallowed half of it. She took a long drag on her cigarette. So let them, she thought. Let the FBI do what they wanted with the Gage and Cooley cases. What was it to her? The odds of the FBI finding their way back to her and her mistakes surrounding the traffic stop were infinitesimal. Neither Gage nor Leary was around to rat her out. And who knew if the feds even cared about her? She hadn't been around long enough to get dirty. Let Quinn protect his rich-kid friend, she thought. And if Drayton tried throwing her to the feds, she liked her chances against him. She had no desire to fight Quinn, Drayton, and the Heaths for the chance to get herself in trouble over a minor glitch in the investigation. She'd be keeping the dust of her mess off Preacher's badge, too.

Maureen drank down the last of her wine. She grabbed her cigarettes, got up from the rocking chair, and went into the kitchen. She rinsed her wineglass and set it upside down in the drying rack beside the sink. Time to get ready for bed. She reached into the cabinet over the counter and pulled out a bottle of Jameson. In a juice glass with a blue palm tree painted on the side, she poured herself a double shot. She drank it down, took a moment to catch her breath. She splayed her hands on the kitchen counter, pressed her weight into them, feeling the muscles in her arms harden, watching her knuckles whiten as the blood drained from her fingers under the pressure of her weight.

The truth of it was, Maureen thought, she didn't care who'd killed Clayton Gage, or his buddy the white-trash Nazi. Gage was an operator for domestic terrorists and probably a rapist who preyed on the mentally ill. Cooley was shit-kicking trash, worse than trash, and Louisiana was better off without them. If they weren't killers, they supplied the weapons to people who killed. Even if Leary had cut their throats with her granddaddy's straight razor, and Maureen thought now she probably had, she knew she could live with letting that go.

In fact, she'd be more comfortable covering for Leary than she would

for Heath. Not that she'd sacrifice herself to let Leary get away with murder, but if everyone around and above her was more concerned with
protecting themselves and their important friends, Maureen thought,
why not let Leary slip through the cracks? Let being invisible and forgotten play in her favor for once. Unless the phone calls kept coming, Maureen thought. As long as Leary lost interest in her, they could coexist.
Maureen liked her odds. She figured homeless schizophrenics weren't
known for their attention spans. On the other hand, if Leary had killed
Cooley and Gage, she'd shown focus and cunning. Maureen sniffed, sa-
voring the lingering whiskey burn in the back of her throat. She figured
she should go lock her front door. She stayed at the kitchen counter. She
took the neck of the whiskey bottle in her fingertips, rotated the bottle
on the counter.

She walked to the fridge, opened the freezer, and stood for a moment enjoying the cold air on her face. She broke one ice cube free from
the tray, put that cube in her whiskey glass, and poured some more
Jameson over it. She sat with her drink at the kitchen table, and lit up a
cigarette. She recalled then decided to ignore her promise to the landlord not to smoke inside the house.

She'd left the envelope full of money on the kitchen table, trying not
to look at it as she moved around the house earlier, showering and pouring her wine. She shifted her glass and laid her hand over the envelope.
There was one possible way to gain some insight about the money. She
could confront Solomon Heath. Knock right on his front door. Ask him
what he thought he was buying. His answer would let her know how
cheap he thought she was. Bribery and extortion were tough accusations
to make, though, with no one around to hear them, especially against
one of the richest and best-respected families in the city. Most likely,
now that Solomon had made his move, she'd never get face-to-face with
him again, no matter what time of night she showed up or what door
she knocked on. She thought of the little girl across the street from her,
with her braids and her raggedy tricycle. Her family could use that
money. Marques and his grandmother could use that money. They

could pay their rent with it, Maureen thought, putting the money right back into Solomon's pocket.

But she wouldn't do it, give up the money. She might return it, if she thought that could hurt Solomon Heath, or if he could hurt her with keeping it, but she wouldn't give the money away. She knew that. She wasn't that generous. She never had been and didn't aspire to be. She was a cop, a city employee saving to buy a house of her own. She was not a charity worker. A thousand dollars was a thousand dollars. She had the nerve to keep Solomon's money and give him nothing in return for it. That wasn't even a hard question. She looked forward to it, actually. She knew the power of saying no, of defying expectations. And she'd been broke so many years of her life that her conscience laughed at the moral quandary.

Outside on the porch, her phone rang. She hesitated to get up and answer it. A call coming after midnight was probably important. And probably bad news. She trotted through the house, answered the call right before it went to voice mail. "Coughlin."

"How was your detail?" Atkinson asked.

Maureen sat in her rocking chair. "It was fine."

"Our paper came through," Atkinson said. "We're taking Scales's door at dawn. You want in, right?"

"Abso-fucking-lutely."

"Good to hear," Atkinson said. "We're meeting at oh five thirty, in the Jazzy Wings parking lot, on South Galvez and Felicity, to strategize and go over the details. Find us there. Don't be late."

"I won't be," Maureen said. Her heart was pounding. She could feel it in her throat.

"Any questions?"

"What do I wear?"

"Civvies," Atkinson said. "Something you can run in, if need be. Bring your cap, and your weapon, of course. I'll have a windbreaker and a vest for you. Anything else?"

"I'm good," Maureen said. "See you there."

"Indeed." Atkinson paused. "I'm glad, that after what he put you through, and after what he did to those kids, and to Marques especially, that you're gonna get to see him stuffed in the back of a cruiser."

"I am, too," Maureen said.

"Now get some sleep. I'll see you in a few." Atkinson hung up.

Maureen stared at her phone, her hand shaking from the adrenaline rush. Sleep, she thought. Good luck with that. She'd need a little help. She got up to top off her whiskey.

22

Maureen showed up at the Jazzy Wings ten minutes early, the low buzz of a hangover in her head, spearmint gum in her mouth, a travel mug of coffee in one hand and a thermos in the car. She wore a tight black T-shirt under her leather jacket, better to fit under the vest, and soft, old jeans and her running shoes. Her hair was pulled back in a tight ponytail that spilled out through the back of her NOPD cap. Her department-issued Glock was holstered on her hip. She wore her badge on a chain around her neck. She'd left the house hoping she looked at least halfway like a badass. Those hopes withered and died as she crossed the parking lot. Despite being ten minutes early, she was the last cop to arrive.

Atkinson, all six feet of her, leaned on the hood of her dark sedan, several large photos spread out in front of her. She was talking to half a dozen other cops surrounding her in a loose circle, five men who looked like the linebacker corps for the Saints and a redheaded woman built like a power lifter, broad shouldered with heavy arms and thick across the rump and thighs, her color significantly more flaming than Maureen's and her face more densely freckled. Every one of the officers looked like they could roll up Maureen like a magazine and tuck her in their back pocket. Instead of the regular uniforms, they wore combat boots, dark blue cargo pants, and matching shirts, NEW ORLEANS POLICE in big white block letters across a heavy cloth patch on the backs. Military utilities, basically, Maureen thought, in one color: midnight blue. The other officers were part of the Sixth District's special task force. Each of the city's police districts had a unit dedicated to serving warrants on violent offenders and making arrests on hard targets in dangerous neighborhoods. These cops were the big guns, the badasses, the department hammer. They dealt in violence and mayhem, an exclusive unit and a closed circle that rarely socialized with other cops. Maureen wanted to be promoted to that unit, to be in their club, with an almost sexual intensity.

Atkinson looked up from her photos as Maureen approached the circle. "This is Platoon Officer Maureen Coughlin. She works here with y'all in the Sixth. She'll be assisting with the raid this morning. She has some experience with the target."

Atkinson made no other introductions.

Maureen nodded, unexpectedly embarrassed, and mumbled a greeting. The other cops said nothing, not even looking at her, but the circle loosened enough to admit her and allow her a view of the photo array on the hood of the car. The photos showed front, side, and rear shots of a rundown shotgun house, painted dull gray, the unpainted shutters pulled closed, dark green vines growing up the back and sides of the house. That house, she thought, could fit five times over inside the mansion where she'd worked the party the previous night.

In a couple of the shots, Maureen saw Bobby Scales entering and exiting the front door. Much thinner than the last time she'd seen him, he looked haunted, tired. He looked more like prey than predator. Her heart jumped at the sight of him. Her embarrassment before the bigger, tougher cops dissipated. She liked seeing Scales this way. Vulnerable. Alone. Fearful. She liked thinking she'd had a hand in his dissipation.

She licked her lips. She enjoyed the thought of him dead asleep, oblivious to the forces aligning against him at that very moment, her among them.

Atkinson caught Maureen's eye before she resumed her briefing. "As I was saying, we've been running surveillance on the house since we got the statutory complaint. Scales always rolls in by three or four in the morning, always alone. We never see a sign of him, or anyone else, before noon. We know he's in there now. We will surprise the shit out of him when we crash through, which as you know could make things easier, could make things worse. We won't know till we're in it."

"He's always seemed like a runner to me," Maureen said.

Now the other officers looked at her, their heads slowly turning in her direction, their eyes hooded, like a pride of lions hearing a faint sound in the distance, deciding if whatever had made it was worth killing.

Maureen's throat dried up.

For a moment she was a high school freshman again at the first day of track practice: the bony, awkward, and stumbling new girl who smelled like cigarettes and coffee, mixing with a pack of sleek and feline upperclassmen who smelled like vanilla and strawberries, their bodies strong and curved, supple and grown-up, their eyes narrow and their claws at the ready. Tough days followed after that one, a couple of tough years, actually. But they couldn't make her quit, and by her junior year, they couldn't catch her, either. The pride chased *her* now, runners from her school, from other schools watching the soles of her shoes, her ponytail bouncing yards ahead of them like an uncatchable cat toy. It was the reason she wore it. A built-in taunt.

"I'm just saying," she said, "the three run-ins I've had with him, he's bolted every time, including him and me one-on-one in Jackson Square. He's never stood his ground and fought."

"I heard about that," one of the cops said, an olive-skinned dark-haired guy with veins bulging in his biceps. *Sansone* was stitched in white thread over his heart. "Heard you got put down pretty hard."

"I got suckered," Maureen said. "I got set up. He had help."

"That don't make it better," Sansone said, glancing at his comrades, "that makes it worse. He got over on you and got away." A chuckle rumbled through the group. "Lived to shoot at you, another cop, your training officer to be exact, and some civilians to boot, from what I heard."

"And he hasn't been heard from since, by the way," Maureen said.

"Exactly how many doors is it," Sansone said, "that you've kicked in at first light? On a multiple homicide suspect considered armed and dangerous?"

Maureen opened her mouth to speak.

"Dark house," Sansone went on. "Lots of blind corners and hiding spaces. Trouble spots for you, I've heard."

"None," Maureen said. "I'm looking to learn what I can. This is my first time doing something like this."

The redheaded woman smiled at her. "You'll be fine, Cherry. Just try not to bleed on the sheets."

"Now that we're friends here," Atkinson said, "can we get on with our work? I have the chiropractor at nine and I want to shower first." She lined up the photos on the car. "Pretty standard procedure: three busting in the front, two coming in back, one each by the windows in case of a jump out, and a freelancer on the street. We're on the corner, which is good, there's no alleyway crammed with junk or dogs or whatever between houses. No dogs on the block, so no barking. No fence around the backyard. The house is a double, but it looks like the other side is vacant, so no next-door neighbors. However."

Atkinson paused, looking over the group.

"However. There are neighbors up and down the block. None of them seem to have anything to do with our target, but most of the other houses are occupied. Our activities will draw attention. People will be leaving for work, maybe even coming home from the night shift. We should be early enough to avoid the schoolkids, but be heads-up, anyway. If this thing pops off, we cannot, I repeat, we cannot, have civilian casualties. No pets, no cars, no potted plants, either. Bullets go places.

In windows, through walls. Remember that. No bullets in anything but the target. And only then under the most extreme circumstances. If it gets that far, we've failed."

"No disrespect, Detective Sergeant," one of the cops said, "but you've confused us with beat cops. We don't miss."

"Today is not the day, then," Atkinson said, pointing her finger into the cop's wide chest, "for *your* first time." She turned to Maureen. "No blood on the sheets from you." Then, to the bragging cop, "No blood on the streets from you."

She collected her photos, slipped them into a folder, and slid a new one out, laying it down on the car. It was a crime scene photo. A dead young black boy, curled up in the trunk of a car. Marques's friend Mike-Mike, one of the homicides Scales was wanted for. Maureen had been there when the photo was taken. She'd chased Mike-Mike across a ball field earlier that day. In her sleep some nights, when she slept, she still chased him.

"Twelve years old," Atkinson said. "Fucking *twelve*. The statutory warrant is a tool. He's the reason we're here. Any questions?"

The group was silent, serious, their eyes fixed on the photo, recording it, recording the narrative behind it. Maureen felt she could hear the skin of the other officers stretching tighter over their muscles, like a leather gun belt tightening in the heat.

"Strap up, then," Atkinson said. She pulled open the back door of her car. "Here, Coughlin. Terranova, help her suit up."

In the backseat Maureen found a bulletproof vest and a blue windbreaker.

She dropped the vest over her head. Terranova, the redhead, grunting, pulled tight the Velcro straps on the sides along Maureen's ribs. She was so thin, getting the vest snug was a challenge. Normally, she hated wearing her armor. Today, the weight felt right. Once the vest was secure, Terranova pounded Maureen's shoulders twice, hard, as if she wore shoulder pads and was preparing to take the football field. The other officers did it to each other, nodding, muttering. Maureen thrilled at the dull thumps, though Terranova had walked away before Maureen could return the gesture, leaving her observing, but not participating in, the ritual. Her pulse was picking up, her blood crackling with adrenaline, charged. The windbreaker she pulled on over the vest upped her excitement. The jacket was the same deep, dark utility blue as the task force uniforms, NEW ORLEANS POLICE in big letters across the back. Atkinson wore the same jacket, one corner of it tucked behind her gun. Maureen mimicked the gesture. Now she felt full-on badass.

"Let's get this fucking done," Atkinson said, checking the safety on her gun. "I want this motherfucker in a cage. I'm tired of him breathing free air."

Maureen rode to the house with Atkinson, the other cops following close behind in their own dark-windowed and unmarked units, no lights and no sirens. Despite these efforts at discretion, Maureen knew that speed and the early hour were their best allies. There was no mistaking their identity. Three cars full of white people in that neighborhood couldn't be anything but a parade of cops.

"I guess I kind of stepped in it back there," Maureen said. "Sorry about that."

"They don't feel that training, or welcoming, for that matter, new officers comes under their purview. You should already be a wrecking ball when you get to them."

"I see their point," Maureen said.

Atkinson shrugged, her hands at ten and two on the steering wheel. "Look at it this way, they wouldn't have liked anything you did. Standing there scared and quiet wouldn't have gone over any better. They smell blood, they bite. It's part of what makes them good at what they do. Might've been worse. It's not personal, you're not one of them. As you may have noticed, this job is like any other, with hierarchies and prejudices and cliques. You'll learn to negotiate them."

"Believe me," Maureen said, thinking of Quinn, "I've noticed, and

I'm learning as fast as I can. I hope I didn't make you look bad for bringing me along."

"Do your job," Atkinson said, "and we all come out of this looking great."

"What is my job?" Maureen asked.

"You're the freelancer."

"I figured. So I'll be outside the whole time." She knew Atkinson heard the disappointment in her voice.

"If everything goes according to plan you stay outside," Atkinson said. "If you have to come inside the house, things are going very badly."

Two cruisers, seemingly out of nowhere, appeared in front them. The parade was now five cars long. The cavalry was rolling, and Maureen was part of it. She could hardly sit still. Atkinson accelerated. She checked the rearview. The other cars stayed close. "I know it sounds like the shit assignment," Atkinson said.

"I didn't say that," Maureen said.

Atkinson threw her a skeptical glance.

"Okay, yeah, I was hoping to be going inside. I wanna put the cuffs on him. Is that so wrong?"

Atkinson smiled. "Not wrong at all. But you have to wait your turn."

They were close, Maureen thought, two or three blocks now from the house. She felt sharp and clear-headed, her hangover gone, wide-eyed, as if pure oxygen were pumping into her system. She felt she could jump from the car and sprint there.

"A few quick things before the fun starts," Atkinson said. "No civilians on the street once we go in. No one comes outside, not even on their porches to watch. For damn sure no one approaches the house. Be courteous but firm. No explanations beyond we're serving a warrant. Use no names. As best you can, don't hurt any feelings. Don't bias anyone. We don't know who we're gonna need later as a witness."

They'd reached the corner. One cruiser went on ahead. It would circle the block, Maureen knew, closing off the street at the far end. Atkinson jumped the car up on the sidewalk, slammed it to a stop. Maureen nearly bounced off the dashboard, her seat belt snapping tight. She and Atkinson sprang from the car, slamming their doors in unison. Maureen watched as the other cops piled out of their cars, double- and triple-checking their weapons and vests. None of them spoke. Sansone rolled a toothpick in his teeth. Terranova breathed heavily through her nose, nostrils flaring like a racehorse in the starting gate. Maureen feared she'd start drooling from the anticipation. She wiped her sweaty palms down the front of her vest. Atkinson knocked her fist on the hood of the car to get her attention.

"You hear shots, you call it in first," she instructed Maureen. "Then you come in with the other uniforms when they get here. You do not come rushing in alone into an unknown situation. Under any circumstances. Understood?"

"Yes."

"If he somehow slips by us, run that motherfucker down. On foot, in the car, whatever. Do not let him get away." Atkinson beckoned Maureen around to her side of the car. She reached inside, got out a radio, handed it to Maureen. "If you have to chase him, make sure we know where you are."

"Count on it," Maureen said.

"Should you fail to follow any of these instructions," Atkinson said, her finger inches from Maureen's chin, "you will never take another door with me ever again. You'll be wearing shorts and a bike helmet and riding a Segway up and down Magazine Street. Understood?"

"Yes."

"Tell me you understand, Officer."

"I understand. I hate Segways."

Atkinson pressed her fist into Maureen's vest, over her heart. "This is gonna be a good day."

Maureen bounced on her toes, grinding her gum in her teeth, as she watched the others fan out over the property and around the house. She felt like a lame or sick little girl stuck at her bedroom window, watching the other kids play her favorite game outside. She couldn't remember a time in her life when she'd been more excited, more jacked up, her chest heaving under her bulletproof vest. No track team race, no handsome and groping boy, no drug, no whiskey, had ever cranked her up like this. Her adrenaline spiked again. She felt it shoot down the backs of her legs like cold lightning when Atkinson, crouched by the front door, her weapon drawn, yelled, "NOPD! NOPD! We have a warrant!"

Maureen watched two of the other cops, weapons raised and tight against their shoulders, position themselves under the shuttered windows. Sansone's voice echoed Atkinson's words from the back of the house. Atkinson stepped to the side of the front door. One of the boys rose up on one foot and shattered the front door of the house with one brutal kick.

Another crash came from the back of the house, and the task force poured inside, weapons drawn, yelling, "NOPD! NOPD! Nobody fucking move!"

Maureen caught her breath. In her head, she could see the crouched officers moving through the dim house, muscles tensed, eyes darting in every direction. More bangs and crashes from inside. A loud, panicked "What the fuck?" that Maureen knew had come from Scales. She knew she shouldn't be so transfixed, she knew she needed to be wary of some girlfriend or relative who might come running and screaming up the street, but she couldn't break her attention away from the action inside the house.

She heard Atkinson command Scales, "I said on your fucking face!" Furniture got knocked over or tossed aside. Something fragile broke.

Things were coming to a climax. The raid would end any second or would explode to a whole new level, depending on what decisions Scales made. Maureen drew her gun. She let it dangle against her thigh, the weight of it pulling at her shoulder. She took a couple of steps toward the house. She backed off, checked the block. She saw some curtains and shades move in their windows, but nobody came outside. The house went quiet. The cops under the window stood frozen, listening for that one sound, a cry or a command, a shout or a shot, that would tell them to move.

Terranova came out onto the front steps. She took a quick look around and turned back into the house. "All clear."

Atkinson came out next, lighting a cigarette as she came down the stairs.

Maureen slipped her gun back into her holster. She exhaled.

After Atkinson came Sansone and another cop, each holding one of Scales's ropy arms as they dragged him down the stairs, his hands cuffed behind his back. When they got him to the sidewalk, they stood him up. He wore filthy gray sweatpants and laceless Timberlands. His head was shaved clean. Bright red bloodstains dotted the front of his torn and dirty wifebeater. One eye was already puffy. He leaned forward, letting a long trail of bloody spittle fall onto the sidewalk, some of it staining the toes of his left boot. He'd put up enough of a fight, it appeared, to catch a beating, breaking no one's heart. Maureen did worry for a moment that he'd have to go to the emergency room instead of jail, but she couldn't see Atkinson letting her prize out of her sight, never mind her immediate custody. She had a lot more authority than Maureen or Preacher or the sheriff's office did about who went where. Whatever she wanted to happen to Scales would happen.

Maureen couldn't wait for the moment Scales laid eyes on her. She couldn't wait to tell Marques and his grandmother Scales was off the street.

"Put him in my car," Atkinson said, leading the way. Maureen figured that if she could, Atkinson would have Scales strapped to the hood.

Scales regained his balance and his ability to walk, shuffling along between the officers holding his arms. He tipped his head back, showing his teeth, grinning, acting casual and amused by what was happening to him. Just another day, motherfucker. Neighbors wrapped in robes and housecoats had started to appear on their porches. Maureen opened the back door of Atkinson's car and stood beside it, goose bumps running up her forearms and the back of her neck.

"Officer Coughlin," Atkinson said, "would you like to do the honors?"

Maureen took hold of the cuffs. Scales's one good eye swiveled in her direction, expressionless, thoughtless, unfeeling. She was reminded of the lizard she had seen the other day perched on her fence. If Scales recognized her face or her name, he gave no sign. Maureen saw no point in reminding him of their history. Cops were all the same to him. She'd wanted a big *I got you* moment, had thought about it many times since Atkinson had told her about the warrant. She knew now she wasn't going to get it. Scales's breathing was loud and labored. He sucked a wad of bloody snot to the back of his throat.

"Swallow it," Maureen commanded.

He did. That would have to do, she thought. For now. Maureen palmed the crown of his skull, pushing him down into the backseat of the car. "Watch your head."

She slammed the car door as hard as she could. She turned to Atkinson. She couldn't stop smiling. "Wow. I don't know that I've ever felt as good as I do right now."

"Oh, you have no idea," Atkinson said, cigarette smoke curling from her mouth. "It gets so much better. We're gonna break this guy to pieces. It's gonna be *easy*."

Atkinson called over two officers to keep an eye on Scales. Maureen joined her and the rest of the task force in the house search. The inside of the house was close and musty. The stale air put a tickle in Maureen's nose. Scales was not much of a housekeeper. To-go containers and empty forty-ounce and Big Shot bottles covered every flat surface, the bottles half full with cigarette butts. Dirty clothes covered the floor. Maureen tried to imagine Scales at the Laundromat, reading a book or watching daytime TV while his clothes spun in a machine. She couldn't make herself see it. A few flies buzzed high in the corners of the ceiling.

"We'll take a quick walk-through," Atkinson said, looking around. "We'll get techs in for more detailed stuff, fingerprints, fibers, that kind of stuff, later."

"What is it we're looking for right now?" Maureen asked, pulling on a pair of latex gloves, wishing she'd thought to take off her vest. By now, her T-shirt was a warm, wet rag against her skin. Sweat pooled at the small of her back, dampening the waistband of her jeans.

"Leverage, really," Atkinson said. "Big-ticket items. Officially, we're looking for physical evidence that connects him to sleeping with that underage girl. What I *want* is a connection to Mike-Mike's murder, which, I admit, is going to be hard to come by. I've never thought he killed Mike-Mike here. Anything that connects him to Mike-Mike in any way will be useful, though. Most important, we're looking for evidence of a crime or of criminal behavior, anything we can pound him with in the box. Anything to convince him the shit he's standing in is chin deep and we have the only lifeline."

"I'd bet anything he's got pictures or sex videos around here somewhere," Maureen said. "I doubt he's got a computer, but he's got a phone. You know he's got copies of those photos and texts that girl showed you. He seems the type, fancies himself a conqueror. He'll have trophies."

"And you're familiar with this type of asshole?"

"You're not?" Maureen asked.

Atkinson shrugged, conceding the point.

"I've seen similar acts before," Maureen said. "Predators are predators."

Sansone called Atkinson's name from the bedroom. Maureen followed her through the house. They found Sansone and Terranova standing by the closet, a large seaman's trunk between them, the lid thrown open. Where would a guy like Scales, Maureen wondered, get something like that?

"Found this in the closet," Terranova said. "Come have a look."

Maureen and Atkinson peered into the trunk. Semiautomatic rifles, AR-15s it looked like, had to be twenty of them. Silver and black handguns, both full and semiauto, were tossed in with the larger guns, as if they were merely packing material. High-capacity clips and drums, boxes of armor-piercing and hollow-point bullets. Everything in the trunk looked new, unused. The guns smooth and shining, the boxes of ammo sealed. This was not a collection for personal protection, Maureen thought. And no matter how great Scales's personal criminal ambitions, she thought, these weapons weren't for him. This wasn't merchandise for illegal retail on the street, either. Not this many rifles, anyway. These were different weapons than what they saw on the street.

"What the fuck was this guy planning?" Sansone asked, incredulous laughter in his voice. "A fucking revolution?"

"Not this mope," Atkinson said. "He's holding for someone else."

The bedroom was silent. This is an arsenal for a terrorist cell, Maureen thought. This is a trunk the Taliban would pay good money for. And this might not be all the weaponry in the house. It was only what they'd found so far. She agreed with Sansone's question. The AR-15 was the civilian version of the military's standard-issue M16. Every gangsta wants to be strapped, Maureen thought, but what in the world was Scales doing with this kind of firepower? And expensive firepower at that. Where had it come from? Where had he gotten it?

"You wanted leverage on Scales," Maureen said. "I think you found it."

"I'm calling for more help," Atkinson said. She looked over at the other officers. "We're gonna tear this place to fucking pieces."

23

"I want a lawyer," Scales said. "I ain't done no murders."

"We heard you the first three times," Atkinson said, seated across the table from him, her sleeves rolled up, her folded arms draped over the back of a turned-around chair. "We're working on it. We've got calls in to the courthouse. Budget cuts have everyone short staffed. It's tough. They might even be off today. What's the word? *Furloughed*? Who knows anymore? We might not hear back until tomorrow. It's not our fault you don't have a pay lawyer." She shrugged. "Your guess is as good as mine when the city gets back to us. As for the murders you *ain't done*, we'll see about that."

Maureen observed their interaction from the far corner of the interview room, where she leaned on the wall with her arms crossed over her chest. She'd shed her bulletproof vest, her cap, and her sweat-soaked T-shirt; Atkinson had rummaged up a clean department polo shirt. She looked almost like plainclothes, and could pass for a detective if you didn't notice her shield wasn't gold. She wasn't out to fool anyone, but didn't mind looking the part. She was thrilled to be in the room with Atkinson and Scales. She'd been sure as Scales was brought in, fixed with leg irons, and cuffed to the table that Atkinson would make her watch the interview from the other side of the two-way mirror. That was if she let Maureen participate at all.

"I want you in there," Atkinson had told her instead of sending her home. "I want him to see you. I want you standing in front of him repping Mike-Mike and Marques and his grandmother. I want you to bring them into the room with you."

"I'm not sure he remembers me," Maureen said. "Nothing registered when I put him in the car."

"We'll make sure he remembers," Atkinson said.

Back in the interview room, Atkinson pulled an unopened pack of Newports from her pocket, tossed them on the table for Scales. Scales scoffed at the offer. "Bitch, please. You think you gonna buy me with that?"

"I'm trying to show some courtesy," Atkinson said. She retrieved the cigarettes, put them back in her pocket. Scales looked surprised at the move.

"Courtesy? Nigga, please. Like y'all showed me at the house?"

"You need to learn to listen."

"I don't have to listen to y'all about nothing. And I damn sure don't have to talk to you. I know more than you think about how this here works."

"You've made your feelings clear," Atkinson said. "But this is one of those rare days where I don't need you to talk to me much. You're going to want to talk, but I don't need you to. What you want to do right now is listen to what I say—very fucking carefully. We're not sitting here for my benefit, Mr. Scales, we're sitting here for yours."

"'Cause you're cool like that," Scales said, pouting, looking away from her. "That's why my mouth is bleeding on the inside."

"Maybe I am cool like that," Atkinson said. "Maybe I'm the reason your liver isn't bleeding on the inside. Maybe this is your lucky day.

Congratulations. You got busted by the last cool cop in the department. Make sure you get yourself a Powerball ticket on the way home."

"So I will be getting out of here." Scales smiled. Maureen saw that his teeth remained bloody. At some point, he'd need stitches inside his mouth. "See, y'all done fucked up already, letting me know that."

Atkinson laughed. "What? Oh, no. You're not going anywhere. Not at all. I was making a point." She moved her seat closer to the table, the chair legs scraping on the floor. "You know who's on the other side of that mirror."

"More fucking *po*-lice, I figure."

"But do you know what kind of police?"

"Secret police?" Scales said.

Maureen could see the mud-stuck wheels straining to turn in his head. He looked exhausted, and was probably hungover. She knew that Scales was also not as savvy as he thought he was, which made not being able to nab him sooner so frustrating. His misplaced confidence worked against him at every turn, yet they'd needed a vengeful girlfriend to find him.

"If I told you about them," Atkinson said, "they wouldn't be secret, would they? Sex crimes, that's who's behind the glass. Why, you might ask, if I'm Homicide, would I have sex crimes watching my interview with you?"

She gave Scales a moment to reply, or to let his thoughts catch up to her. To Maureen, there seemed to be minimal activity behind his eyes. He was trying hard to stay shut down, to freeze them out, as if he were trying to ignore a stubborn pain. He said nothing.

"So, here's the million-dollar question for you, Bobby," Atkinson said. "Why today? How is it that we finally found your sad and dirty hideout?"

Scales shrugged. "The fuck should I know?"

He fidgeted in his seat, rubbing his hands up and down the backs of his arms, as much as the wrist chains would let him, looking away from them now. He tried hiding his fear, but it seemed to Maureen that the mention of the sex crimes unit unnerved him, undermining his bravado. It added an unknown element to the proceedings. A murder beef he knew how to handle. The police accuse, he denies, and around it goes. Being a murderer, he'd somewhat anticipated ending up where he was. Adding the sex crimes unit was something else, though. What that something was he hadn't figured out yet. He wouldn't figure it out, Maureen knew, without more help. He certainly didn't feel guilty of anything.

"You ain't got nothing on me," Scales insisted. "Some snitch a'yours tryin' to get over on you. This is some kind of setup."

"You could put it that way," Atkinson said. "But it's not us that set you up. Wasn't even one of our snitches. That's the beautiful part. This one is all you, asshole." She held up a plastic evidence bag containing a cell phone. Maureen thought of Drayton and his sad attempt to intimidate her in the Sixth District break room. She had a feeling that Atkinson would have better luck getting what she wanted.

"Recognize this?" Atkinson asked Scales.

"It's a phone."

"Is it your phone?"

"You gonna say it is if you want it to be."

"I hope it's your phone," Atkinson said, "because we took it from your nightstand, and because there are twenty pictures of you having sex with two different women on this phone."

She got up from her chair, walking around the table, getting close to Scales, who shrank from her. "Those two women, they know about each other. They do. And that's not the best part. You wanna guess what the best part is?" She actually gave him a moment to guess. He didn't.

"I see how this is," Scales said. "Bitches stick together and shit."

"The best part is," Atkinson said, "you know what those girls have in common, other than you? They're both fifteen years old. Well under the age of consent. You know what that makes you, other than a two-timing asshole and a poor judge of romantic companions? It makes you a felon. A child rapist, twenty times over. A sex offender. Against juveniles."

Scales shook his head, squirming against his chains, the ropy muscles of his arms flexing, terrified by Atkinson's accusations. "No, no, no. Those girls was about it. Steppin' out on them ain't against the law. Whatever they saying I did, they just mad because of the other girl. See? That's all this is. They just mad. They playin' you and me both. Man, I can't believe you fell for that."

"Oh, they're mad, all right," Atkinson said. "Mad enough to hand you right over to us. I don't see anyone taking a fall here but you."

Atkinson squatted on her haunches. She was so tall, and Scales so slumped in his seat with defeat, that they were nearly eye-to-eye. "So don't cop to murdering Mike-Mike. Please don't. That's fine. I'll hand you over to sex crimes. All I got is a witness who says you gave him the keys to a car with a body in the trunk, with orders to burn that car, a car you told the whole neighborhood was yours. Who knows if I can even get that witness to testify? You know this city, it's tough getting anyone to give the police the time of day, never mind testify in court. Except, except for these girls. Photos, signed statements, DNA. They are hot. They are pissed. It is *personal* with them. They're looking to put your dick in the meat grinder. I wonder if one or both of them ain't pregnant."

"Bullshit, I use rubbers every time with those bitches. See how they lie?"

Maureen blinked. Hardly even trying, Atkinson had gotten Scales to confess to multiple counts of statutory rape, and he didn't even know he'd done it. It had happened so fast, so effortlessly, Maureen was half surprised she hadn't missed it. She knew Atkinson hadn't.

Atkinson stood, leaning over Scales to deliver the hammer blow. "You see now why I got sex crimes people in the next room? I hand you to them, *they* charge you, *they* book you and jail you as a sex offender, son. As a *child molester.* How you think that's gonna go for you? You just confessed."

Scales's head whipped around, his mouth hanging open in disbelief. His brain finally caught up to what he'd said about using rubbers. It was almost unfair, Maureen thought, watching Atkinson work him over. Almost. She thought of how Scales had pressed his own advantages over boys smaller and younger than him, his size, his menace, his physical power. He'd pressed one into hiding, one out of town, and one into the grave. Now Atkinson was showing Scales what real power looked like. Every day of the rest of his life was in her hands. Where he would spend them, and what would happen to him while he was there. No, it wasn't unfair what Atkinson was doing to him, Maureen thought, or even unethical. It was justice. The sight of it thrilled her.

Atkinson turned away from Scales, shaking her head at the pity of the whole unfortunate situation. "And now we're stuck using these temp jails while the new one gets built. Security is a mess." She spoke now to Maureen, leaving Scales foundering. "Seems like once a month somebody's dying up in there. Nobody even knows why, half the time. Some prisoners we have to send halfway across the state, out to the rural parishes. Anybody told you about that? It's a tough gig, New Orleans baby gangstas jailing with trailer-park, swamp-living, meth-cooking Nazi white boys. There have been reports of conflicts. Of violent incidents. Some of our prisoners are coming back to the city in pretty rough shape. Casts. Wheelchairs. A couple haven't made it back at all. And I don't think we've sent them a black child molester yet. Maybe they'll send us a prize." She turned to Scales, looked him up and down. "Wanna guess what that prize might be?"

Scales sat up straight. Maureen could see the lightbulb finally starting to glow for him.

"I ain't no rapist. I ain't no child molester. Y'all can't make me one."

"It ain't us doing it to you," Atkinson said. "It's the law."

"You seen them photos," Scales said. "It's normal old sex. Those girls don't look fifteen. You can *see* that. If they been in your office, you seen 'em in person. I'm supposed to check IDs?"

"What I see," Atkinson said, "is fifteen getting you twenty, over and over again. I think every time you messed with them is another rape count. We're not even going to talk about what *you'll* be getting while you're doing those multiple twenties."

Maureen stepped out of the corner, nervous about what she had to say. "Detective."

Atkinson raised her eyebrows, as if surprised to learn Maureen had a voice. "Not now, Officer."

"I'm sorry," Maureen said. "I know I'm only supposed to observe, but the way things are going, it makes me nervous. Bad nervous." She glanced at Scales, who focused on her with startling intensity, pleading with his eyes for the lifeline he hoped was coming. "I have to say something."

She gave Atkinson a beat to answer.

"Your concerns, then?" Atkinson asked, sounding impatient.

"It's already rumored, and pretty much believed around the city, that Mr. Scales here killed at least one of his teenage soldiers while trying to revive a drug ring over the summer. It's rumored he tried to kill another boy, and that boy's grandmother, and a couple of cops. There are rumors that maybe he'd flipped, that he'd been seen doing business with a cop, and that was why we couldn't nail him. Those rumors were the main reason he's so toxic even to the local criminal community that he was squatting in a dirty hole when we found him."

"Your point, Officer? You're very eloquent, but we have shit to do here."

"Everyone we've talked to," Maureen said, choosing her words with care, "thinks he's a rat, and a child killer. I'm concerned that if we lock him up as a sex offender, what happens if those accusations get mixed up with the new charges? What if it gets through the system that he was raping these underaged boys before he killed them? And that's why he killed them. No jail in the state could guarantee his safety. You said yourself it's a mess throughout Louisiana. He wouldn't make his arraignment, never mind live to see trial."

"So you're interrupting my interrogation," Atkinson said, "to express your concerns for the safety of the prisoner?"

"I'm not real worried about him," Maureen said, looking at Scales, who was so panicked now she feared he'd hyperventilate, "but a lot of good police work, and a lot of potential information, which could lead to more good police work, goes up in smoke if he gets shivved in the lunch line and bleeds out screaming for his mommy on the tile."

"What the fuck are you talking about?" Scales hollered. He squirmed in his seat, rattling his chains. "You can't do that. You can't be telling people inside that I been raping and killing little boys. While I been snitching at the same time? What the fuck is *wrong* with you? Why you doin' me like this? You the police. You're supposed to pro*tect* people."

"I wouldn't do you like that," Atkinson said, "but the officer here has a point. Jail is worse than high school for rumors, worse than the neighborhood, worse than the police department or the courthouse, even." She paused, tapping her fingertip to her chin. "I just thought of something. You've never jailed before, have you, Bobby? Some juvie shit, but never with men."

Scales shook his head.

"My, oh my," Atkinson said. "Wow." She paused. "I almost feel sorry for you."

Maureen backed into her corner.

Atkinson returned to the seat, and the position, where she had started the interview, arms folded over the back of the chair. "You know how much we have on you. About the murder. About the girls. And now there's those guns, and how you got them, and your plans for them, which can change things for you. That looks to me like a federal beef. Now, taking a federal charge is no picnic, it doesn't bode well for your long-term future, I'm not gonna sugarcoat that. However, as we all know, your short-term future is looking mightily, brutally fucking grim right now. The feds do have more resources for prisoner protection than we do at OPP." She inched her chair a few inches closer to Scales. "Gimme a reason, Bobby. Gimme a good reason not to jail you as a fucking rapist child-murdering molester. A really good fucking reason. Because you know that's what I want to do. Talk me out of it."

Scales slumped in his seat again, a puppy cowering from the snapping jaws of a larger dog, hoping for mercy through submission. Maureen waited for Atkinson to tear open his soft belly. She watched and waited, chewing the inside of her cheek as Scales's brain worked harder than it ever had in his brutish and short life. "I—I could tell you about those guns. I do know some shit."

"Give it up."

"You gotta promise me. No rape charges. None of that child-molester shit."

Atkinson barked out a laugh. Maureen nearly jumped out of her skin. She wasn't sure when it had happened, but she was, at the moment, deathly afraid of Christine Atkinson. "Promise you?" Atkinson said. "I don't have to promise you shit. I have all the cards, remember?" She pointed her finger at her face. "Look at me. I own you. This is me promising you nothing. You go in the Orleans Parish system, and you go in on child rape and murder, in which case you leave on a stretcher or in a pine box, or you go in federal on guns, and leave walking upright with your blood on the inside—that's your choice here."

Scales's eyes kept flicking over to Maureen. She felt for the first time that he maybe recognized, and remembered, her. That's right, motherfucker, she thought, it's me, here to watch you go down in flames.

"Don't look at her," Atkinson commanded. "Look at me. She can't do anything for you. The whole rest of your life is with me. Me. What's it gonna be?"

"The guns," Scales said. He hesitated.

"Be special here, Bobby," Atkinson said. "Be fucking extraordinary."

He glanced back and forth between Maureen and Atkinson. Atkinson let her silence do its work and Maureen followed suit, her heart thumping against her sternum. They were gonna get something, she thought. Something really good, something beautiful. Life-changing, career-changing shit. She could feel it.

"Do not fuck with me," Atkinson said.

Maureen leaned forward, her weight on the balls of her feet.

"I ain't," Scales said.

"That trunk," Atkinson said, "where did those guns come from?"

"Some coon-ass cracker named Gage."

Maureen hiccupped. Atkinson threw her hands in the air. "And Gage is fucking dead. Literally a dead end. Holy Christ. You get more worthless by the second, Scales. I can't stand it."

"I didn't do it," Scales said, panicking again. Maureen could tell he hadn't known that Gage had been killed. "I didn't fucking do it. I didn't."

"Nothing, Scales," Atkinson said. "You've given me fucking nothing but a headache. For this I got up at the crack of dawn. So you could pin your shit on a dead guy."

"Wait, wait," Scales said. "Gage, he just one of the players, he a front. For some like crazy white-boy survivalist militia gang or whatever, from out in one of the other parishes. They was strapping up to fight y'all, is what he kept telling me. He used to talk all kinds of crazy-ass shit. I was like, whatever." He shrugged. "Long as your money be green and I don't hafta leave the house, or fuck with no cops myself."

Maureen thought of Gage's shitty pickup, of the discount cigarette butts and fast food wrappers littering the front seat. How had he paid for the expensive jewelry and the custom Saints jersey he'd been wearing the night she'd pulled him over? Where had he gotten the cash to buy those guns?

"People like that," Scales said, wonderment in his voice, "I thought it was always niggers they hated, Klan and white power and shit, but these dudes, it was y'all they had it in for, they hate cops with a passion. Always fuck-the-government this and fuck-the-government that. They changing with the times, us having a black president, I guess."

Maureen thought of the faded and disintegrating wallet she'd found on Gage's fresh corpse. Of the gun-dealer business cards and the gun-show receipt.

"Where did Gage get the guns that he brought to you?" she asked.

Atkinson turned and Scales looked up at her, both unsure which of them Maureen was addressing with the question.

"All that weaponry," Maureen said to Atkinson, "that shit costs money. Gage didn't have that kind of cash. He's not buying AR-15s twenty at a time without help. He may have been the deliveryman, he may have even bought the guns at pawnshops and gun shows, made the physical purchase, but someone else put up the cash for a stockpile like that, I promise you."

She had a name in mind, but couldn't decide if she wanted to hear it or not.

Atkinson turned to Scales. "All those guns come to you at once?"

"They arrived a few at a time. More supposed to be coming. After that next gun show out in wherever-the-fuck outside the city, next month."

Maureen thought of Gage's name on the federal watch list, of his criminal record. None of that would matter at the gun shows. No ID check, no background check, no purchase limit. Nothing needed but cash and connections and a handshake. Maybe the right tattoos, depending on who he was buying from. He didn't look like a terrorist, not to the people who sold him his guns—he looked the same as them. He looked like any average harmless guy walking down Bourbon Street drinking a Hand Grenade or a Hurricane. She took a couple of steps across the room. "Why? Why get involved with those guys? Why let them use your closet?"

Scales chuckled. "Why the fuck else? Like you said, cash money." He looked around the room, as if looking for an audience to share his humorous disbelief. "Rent out my closet to a bunch of white motherfuckers out to kill cops instead of niggers for once?" He chuckled again. "Nigga, please. Where do I sign up? Are you kidding me?"

"Who paid you?" Maureen asked. "Was it Gage?"

"That broke-ass tweaker? He had nothing." He shook his head, grinning. "Gage. That pussy. I heard his bitch stone robbed him blind 'fore he left for New Orleans. Took it all from him. That's why he was hanging 'round town instead of going back to his fucking trailer park to wait for the next gun show. He was looking for her." He chuckled. "He try to not show it, Gage, but she scare him, too. I don't know how hard he was really looking. He told these crazy stories about her. But he a man, and she took him off." Scales shrugged. "Can't let that shit go, I guess."

He looked at Atkinson and Maureen, his eyes half closed, a smile lingering on his lips. "Bitches, man. White ones, black ones. Nothing but problems, all a y'all. Nothing but devils, doing the devil's work, all a y'all. Man, all y'all *do* is ruin a man."

"Who paid you?" Atkinson demanded. "Who handed you the cash for keeping the guns?"

"The guy who paid me is the same motherfucker that paid for the guns, the guy who owned that house you found me in." Scales took a deep breath. "A big-timin' white boy named Caleb Heath."

And there it was. Maureen's heart, which had been pounding for what felt like hours, stopped. She could feel the blood drain from her face, the air burst from her body. Atkinson threw her the briefest glance. The name had surprised her, too. More than it had Maureen. She recovered faster.

"Gage was all talk," Scales said, "but Heath, he got juice. I could see that from the jump. He try to play it hard, try to play it street, he got this whole collection of ugly-ass, off-brand Saints jerseys. Man, but money like black, it don't cover up and it don't wash off, ya heard me?"

Leaning closer to Scales, Atkinson said, "Now you're making shit up. That fucking annoys me. Here I am trying to help you out. What makes you think I got the patience for this?"

"I *know* that motherfucker," Scales insisted. "He been in my house. Shit, he *own* that house, run-down piece of shit that it was. Part of the deal was I didn't have to pay no rent. He handed me spending money, like I said. Cash money from his hands to mine."

Scales had picked up on the mood change in the room, Maureen could tell. He knew the weight of that name he'd dropped. He'd gained confidence from it, wanted to ingratiate himself and capitalize on the connection. He straightened in his seat, and then described Caleb Heath perfectly. He crossed his arms over his chest, self-satisfied. He again reminded Maureen of Drayton, changing tactics to match the mood of the room.

"How else a broke-ass nigga like *me* gonna know a rich-ass white boy like *that*, unless *he* doin' dirt? I know that. *Y'all* know that, ya heard?" Scales shrugged. "Just another white boy who wants to be gangsta. Nothin' new. City full of 'em. Don't tell me you don't know."

Scales had a point, Maureen thought. No way he had picked Caleb Heath's name out of thin air. He was a scared and cruel punk scrambling under heavy pressure, selling out someone he did business with, someone he resented and had never liked or cared about.

"Who'd you meet first?" Atkinson asked. "Gage or Heath?"

"Gage," Scales said.

"Tell me about your first date," Atkinson said.

"I get a text, see, from my boy Shadow. He tell me to go by the daiquiri place by Claiborne and Louisiana, the one by the check-cashing place, at a certain time and all that. So I do it. I'm thinking maybe he got some new girls with him or something. Shadow there, but he ain't with no girls, he with this skinny white dude named Cooley, belt buckle as big as his head. We make the arrangements. I started out dealin' with him, but then this other white dude, Gage, I think he was Cooley's boss or whatever, stepped in. What the fuck happened to Cooley, I don't know. So if he dead, too, that ain't on me."

"What was this gang called?" Maureen asked.

"The Watchmen Brigade," Scales said, rolling his eyes. "Corny, right? Motherfucker talked about it constantly. Gage, he's hard-core *into* it, this militia thing, tells me over and over that there's an army comin', a war comin', they got money, they got guns, and I need to pick the right side."

An army was coming, Maureen thought, and Caleb Heath had their guns and their hideouts waiting for them.

"I'll hold the guns," Scales said, "babysit the stash in one of Heath's houses, and guys will come get the guns from me. When that happens, I'm supposed to give them up, no questions asked. I get paid for running the warehouse. Maybe get some smaller pieces to sell off on the side. Gage come by with a couple of guns at a time. Sometimes Heath was with him, sometimes not. I don't think Heath needed to be there, but he liked to be, you know? Maybe him being the landlord covered for the other white-boy traffic in the neighborhood. Like I tol' you. Maybe it made the boy feel gangsta. Made his dick hard, I guess. The rest, you already know."

Maureen listened to Atkinson's heavy breathing. She knew the detective wondered how much to believe, and what to do about it. With each new name, with each new lead, the case got more problematic, not less.

"Are there more houses like yours?" Atkinson asked. "Do the Watchmen have stashes around the city?"

Scales shrugged, getting bored now. "Fucked if I know. I don't ask, they don't tell."

Maureen was sure that in Scales's mind, no harm awaited Heath, rich and protected as he was. He thought he'd gained the upper hand by dropping that name. In his mind, he knew who and what he was to the cops—a black kid who fucked with other black kids in his run-down black New Orleans neighborhood, which made him not of much value to the NOPD. Who he was was worthless, but what he knew made him valuable. He figured feeding the white powers-that-be one of their own would stop any case, any investigation dead in its tracks, which would protect him, as well. The cops would choke on the Heath name and money, and have to spit out Heath, and Scales with him. And it would be back to business as usual for everyone in a few days, Scales, Heath, and the NOPD. Maureen swallowed hard. Heath and the NOPD would get back to business, but Scales? He'd be gifted to the cops by the Heath family like a tip slipped without a word into the valet's hand. He'd be a consolation prize. Unless the Watchmen got to Scales first for ratting out one of their moneymen. Scales was done, Maureen thought. Done. In jail. On the street. Didn't matter. He was done. A dead man. The finality of his fate, the certainty of his death, came so clear to her, so sure, that the idea's arrival made a snapping sound inside her brain that she could hear, like the breaking of a bone somewhere in her body—the difference being what she felt. Not panic, not pain. Nothing.

She watched Atkinson pace the small room, hands on her hips. At-kinson rolled her shoulders, working a kink out of her back. Even after this long interview, Maureen thought, Scales didn't know who he dealt with in her. She was a cop and a woman. He could never see her for real. He didn't comprehend the Heaths, and he didn't understand Atkinson. But Maureen did. She understood them both. Atkinson was another fatal flaw in Scales's plan. With her in charge of the case, there was no chance of anything going away. Atkinson didn't choke; she broke bones. Atkin-son would never bend to political pressure, from inside or outside the department. Never. Maureen couldn't see it.

Nobody, she thought, not Bobby Scales, not Caleb Heath, not Mau-reen Coughlin, would get off easy when this mess was done. She knew something else, too. Something that Atkinson didn't know. The clock was ticking.

Word would get out that Scales was in custody, not only through his neighborhood, but through the police department, too. Word would spread around the Sixth and reach Quinn. That meant Caleb Heath would hear before long that a detective had Scales in a box and was sweating him. That a big stash of guns had been found. Forces would align to protect Heath. Who knew how deep into the department Solomon Heath could reach on behalf of his only son? Who knew who Solomon could squeeze? Maureen didn't want to know, didn't want to end up in the grip of those soft and spotted hands.

"Do you know if Shadow set up other meetings like the one between you and Gage?" Atkinson asked.

"Like I already said, I don't know."

"Where do we find Shadow?" Maureen asked.

Scales chuckled. "Don't nobody ever know where to find Shadow. He just appear."

"Are there men out there right now hunting New Orleans cops?" Atkinson asked. "Are there more stashes of guns?"

"I don't know," Scales said. "I swear on my mother. I don't know."

"Guess."

Scales thought for a long moment. "I mean, if I was them, I wouldn't have one stash house for my gear, you know? If it gets hit, you outta business."

"*You* hook them up with anyone?" Atkinson asked.

Scales shook his head. "I don't know no one in the game like that no more. They came to me. I wasn't even looking. I was trying to lay low. Trouble just find me."

"Everything," Atkinson said. "I have to have everything you know."

Scales nodded his head. "Everything. I don't know what else there is, though."

Atkinson turned an empty chair around and sat with her arms draped over the back. Intertwined with her fear, Maureen felt an admiration for the woman that bordered on worship.

"Talk," Atkinson said. "Now. About whatever comes to mind. When I want you to stop, I'll tell you."

24

Maureen held out her coffee cup, which Atkinson filled. They were in the break room. Scales had been taken away. She hoped he didn't end up on Theriot's watch. Maureen's right hand ached. She had filled half of her flip-top notebook with the Scales interview after it ended. Her head spun from what she'd heard. Atkinson was eager to get moving on the information. Maureen wanted her to have everything she needed. What Scales had told her was not enough. Maureen had things to say as well.

"Is there some place private we can talk?" Maureen asked. She wanted to be away from the interview room. The thought of Atkinson bearing down on her like the detective had on Scales terrified her.

She wished Atkinson hadn't seen her face when Scales dropped the name Caleb Heath. She was grateful no one had been watching behind the glass, either, which she had known going into the interrogation. Atkinson had used the statutory rape accusation to get the warrant cut by the judge, glossing over the fact that Scales's accusers had only come in to give up his location and didn't intend to file charges. A good job of putting opportunity to use, Atkinson had declared. A gifted bit of gaming the system, Maureen had thought, with admiration for the idea, and gratitude for what they'd learned after the bust.

Maureen thought again of the thousand in cash sitting on her kitchen table. It had been meant for a moment like this one. She'd be expected to intercede on Heath's behalf. Maybe let it slip to the right ears that there'd been some sleight of hand behind the Scales warrant. Well, Solomon Heath was going to be pissed. Maureen planned on being the worst investment he had ever made. She wasn't concerned for him, or for his terrorist of a son. But she did worry for Preacher, and for herself. She loved being a New Orleans cop.

"You don't look very good," Atkinson said. "You all right? It takes a lot out of you, this stuff."

"I didn't sleep well last night," Maureen said. She sipped her coffee. "I was excited about this morning. I dreamed about it last night. I'm really grateful to you for including me."

"You did a great job at the house, and especially in there, with the good cop, bad cop stuff about the jail rumors," Atkinson said. "You played it perfect, better than we talked about." She sipped her coffee. "You may have a future as the good cop."

Maureen gazed into her coffee. It was lukewarm and weak, hardly darker than tea. Her hands shook. Exhaustion, she figured. Residual adrenaline. Fear. She had to come clean about Gage to Atkinson. She would. Today. In the next few minutes. The question was how best to do it.

"Was I really the good cop?" she asked. "I threatened him with jail-house rape. Seems like it was more like bad cop, worse cop."

"You did what was necessary," Atkinson said. "A lot of these guys, the ones who crack, they get pathetic. They're soft on the inside. They get needy and desperate and they want their mommies. Don't let that fool you. That man in there is a murderer. You know it, I know it, and he knows it. If he thought he could get away with it, right this minute he'd stick a screwdriver in your ribs first chance he got. He'd do the same to me, and to your buddy Marques. He tried.

"We were playing a role in there, and so was he, and we played ours better than he played his. Forgive yourself for being smarter than him."

"What happens to him now? Will we ever put Mike-Mike's murder on him?"

"I'll lock him up on the guns." Atkinson scratched at her scalp. "May as well. There's no hiding him from the feds. We have to give him up, for the greater good. Besides, they're gonna take him from us. This whole case is going to go federal. It has to. He's got info on domestic terror, on gunrunning by federal fugitives."

"He won't even do any time, will he?" Maureen said. "The feds will cut him a deal."

"It'll take a while," Atkinson said. "Who knows what can happen while they work everything out."

"But, ultimately," Maureen said, "he'll walk. He'll be hanging on a Central City street corner in no time. I'll be arresting him for the rest of my life."

"We don't know that," Atkinson said.

"We don't?"

"There's a good chance they'll put him away for a *long* time, without Marques even having to get involved. Marques will be better protected this way, so there's that."

"I don't believe you," Maureen said. "And you don't believe what you're telling me, either."

"It's out of our hands," Atkinson said. "My powers are pretty limited."

"What we did in there with Scales," Maureen said. "How much of that was legal?"

"That's for the lawyers to sort out later," Atkinson said. "I know you're still figuring things out, but let's keep our eyes on the prize. Someone has been putting up guns and money to hunt and kill cops, and now we know who it is, before any of us got shot. You were in on it.

You were part of it. That's going to be real good for you. Huge, possibly. I'll make sure you get your due."

"I know that," Maureen said. "I know what's important. I feel like I'm constantly fighting to keep my balance."

Atkinson peered at her. "Let's get out of here. Let's get some air, go get your car, and find someplace we can talk. You can tell me the real reason you're so twitchy and pale." She poured her coffee down the sink. "Tell you what, let's get us a drink."

Maureen glanced up at the clock on the wall. It was nine a.m. A drink sounded like a great idea. Insubordinate. Decadent. It was exactly what she needed. She could taste it already.

"I thought you had a chiropractor's appointment?"

"My chiropractor is Ms. Mae." Atkinson unfurled a Cheshire grin. "I won't tell if you won't."

Everyone inside Ms. Mae's, a smoky twenty-four-hour dive bar, booed when Maureen and Atkinson entered the bar. They had let the daylight in. Maureen had spent time in Ms. Mae's before, knocking back cheap and strong drinks with her platoon after particularly grueling night shifts. Once the black curtains fell back into place over the front door and the hazy, timeless half-light of the bar was restored, people returned their attention to their conversations, their drinks, and, in the center of the barroom, their pool and air hockey games.

Leaning over the rounded backs and shoulders of two men seated at the bar, Atkinson ordered two double Bloody Marys. Maureen recalled the argument she and Atkinson had overheard at the St. Charles Tavern. No bead-wearing tourists hung out in Ms. Mae's. Not mid-morning on a weekday.

Maureen took her drink from Atkinson. She removed the straw, dropped it on the floor. She took several deep swallows, downing half the cocktail. Her throat burned and sweat beads popped out under her eyes, both from the heavy pour of rotgut vodka and the generous dose of hot sauce in the Bloody Mary mix. Her nose started to run. Warmth bloomed in her chest like black ink in a bowl of water. She followed Atkinson through the mostly male crowd of bikers, stevedores, and late-night service industry people just off of work, and of hard-core drunks who never saw quitting time. They walked past the Pac-Man machine and the jukebox, to a booth in the back corner of the bar.

Maureen tossed her cigarettes on the table as they sat. Both women lit up.

"Getting your balance back?" Atkinson asked.

"I have to work tonight," Maureen said. She scratched at her scalp with both hands, trying to bring some feeling back into it. The vodka was already working on her. When had she last eaten? "I'm wondering what we're doing here. I'm confused."

Atkinson took a long drag on her smoke. "About what?"

"Why are we not going after Caleb Heath? Why are we not kicking in his door right now? Or at least giving the FBI his address."

"Caleb Heath isn't Bobby Scales, Maureen. He's Solomon Heath's son. That everyone is equal before the law is a glorious idea. It's also a complete farce."

"I know that," Maureen said. "I know who Caleb Heath is. But Bobby Scales told us that Heath is a terrorist." She fought to keep her voice low. "He told us that Heath is providing the Watchmen Brigade with cash and guns to come after cops, to come after us. You and me."

"I know this," Atkinson said, getting testy. "I was in the room. After I dropped you at your car, I made some calls. I have some things working. This situation is very fucking delicate."

"So you went to the FBI."

Atkinson looked away, her cigarette frozen on its way to her mouth.

"You didn't call the feds," Maureen said. "Who did you call?"

"I do declare," Atkinson said, "are you questioning how I do my job, Officer Coughlin?"

"No, Detective, I am not. I wouldn't presume. I don't understand what's happening here."

"I took you along on the Scales raid as a courtesy," Atkinson said. "Because you have drive and talent and the postacademy training in this department, where it exists, is fucking atrocious. I don't want to see you go to waste. I don't want to see you dragged down. I let you stay for the interview with Scales for the same reasons, and because I needed a foil and I thought I could trust you."

"Of course you can trust me," Maureen said. "Why does everyone always ask me that? I've never given anyone in this department reason not to trust me. It's not my fault I wasn't born in New Orleans, or that no one recognizes where I went to high school. It's not my fault I haven't been a cop for ten years, or that I wasn't here for Katrina."

Atkinson got up from the table, walking away from the booth. Maureen thought she was leaving, and nearly jumped from her seat and cried out for Atkinson not to go. When Atkinson shouldered her way to the bar, Maureen slumped in her seat, grateful she had restrained herself.

She lit her next cigarette off the end of her current one. She was dying for that next drink. Butting heads with Atkinson shook her. She felt short of breath, struggling for control of herself. She needed to be bigger than this, more grown-up.

Atkinson returned to the booth, two more Bloody Marys in hand. Maureen drank down the rest of her first, gasping again at the jolt of the hot sauce, even watered down as it was now with melted ice. That burn went so well with a fresh cigarette, she thought. She set that cup aside and slid her new drink in front of her. A sadness tingled inside her as she thought of her impending night shift. She'd have preferred sitting in that booth for the entire day, drinking Bloodys and chain-smoking. With what she was about to tell Atkinson, she might soon have plenty of time for exactly those activities.

"I have information," Maureen said. "I have information that you are going to need going after Caleb Heath. That's why I wanted to talk to you in private. It wasn't to question your decisions about how you handle him and what we found out."

Atkinson, Maureen could tell, had no interest in the apology. "What kind of information?"

"For one thing," Maureen said, "I have further proof that he and Gage knew each other."

"What is this proof?"

"I made a traffic stop the other night. A white pickup on Claiborne Avenue. There were two people in the truck. One of them was Gage."

"And the other?"

"A woman named Madison Leary. A petty thief. She'd stolen a bunch of handbags in the French Quarter. I learned later that she and Gage knew each other before that night. It looks like they knew each other in LaPlace, where the Sovereign Citizens and the Watchmen Brigade are based. I think she's the woman who stole the money Scales was talking about."

"That's why you pulled the truck over? Because of her?"

"No, I found the bags when I did the search, and the woman confessed. I pulled the truck over because it looked hinky. Wrong people, wrong place, wrong time, that sort of thing."

"Where is the woman? Can we talk to her about Heath and Gage? Does she know anything about the Watchmen Brigade?"

Maureen took a long sip of her fresh drink. She half-hoped she could drink enough during this conversation that she'd forget it ever happened. Maybe she could forget she'd ever even been a cop. "I have no idea where she is."

"But you arrested her."

"She's got psychological problems. Severe, I think. Violence. Delusions. Schizophrenia, maybe. She had some kind of episode at the jail, before they could process her, so they moved her to the hospital. But she never made it to a bed. The sheriff's deputies left her in the emergency room and she walked out after they left. I've been looking for her, and I found someone who knows her somewhat, but I haven't been able to find her."

Atkinson dropped her head into her hand, massaging her forehead with her fingers. "So you arrested two people involved in a conspiracy to murder police officers, and lost track of them."

"That's not fair," Maureen said. "I'm not blameless here, but when I pulled the truck over they were two drunk rednecks in the wrong neighborhood. I only found out about this conspiracy when you did, this morning, in that room with Scales.

"I wanted Gage arrested. I asked for it. It wasn't my idea to let him walk. When my shift ended that morning, I thought Gage and Leary were in jail. Gage should have been in jail the night he was murdered. He's on the federal terrorism watch list because of his involvement with the Sovereign Citizens, before this new shit in Louisiana. Somebody would've seen. We might have been able to use him against Heath. But fucking Quinn had to let Gage go because he's high school buddies with Heath, and he knew they were connected. Even went behind my back to do it. And like an asshole I let him talk me into covering the whole thing up in front of Drayton, as a professional favor, to keep the sacred Heath name out of a murder investigation." She threw her hands in the air. "And now that's for fucking nothing because the FBI's coming for Heath, anyway. Big fucking waste."

Maureen lifted her smoke from the plastic ashtray. She tapped the ash from the end and set it back in its place. "I was gonna drop Madison's name on Drayton, somehow, maybe, as soon as I could figure out where to tell him to find her. But Drayton kept pissing me off and I haven't been able to track her down, anyway." She poked with her finger at the olive floating in her cocktail. "Christ, I stood not three feet from that fucker Caleb last night."

"Excuse me?"

"I worked a detail at their house by Audubon Park," Maureen said. "I met wise old Solomon himself. It was a peace offering from Quinn, 'cause he knows he fucked me with Drayton. He usually works it with his regular partner. He said he felt bad for tanking my arrest and then things going bad with Gage. I mean, it was a couple of simple favors, one cop to another. And now this fucking mess."

"This was a legit detail?" Atkinson asked.

Maureen thought about the extra money, tucked in its envelope. "It was legit. I got the okay from Preacher. He encouraged me to work it."

"Fair enough." Atkinson sat back in the booth. Maureen could see the long, stressful morning starting to show on her face. "Tell me about Quinn."

"He's in my platoon. He—" Maureen wanted to keep talking, but couldn't, her words heavy and dead in her throat. Shocking her, tears welled up in her eyes. She told herself it was the booze, and the smoky air. Her scroll of complaints against Quinn echoed in her head. Why couldn't, why wouldn't she ever shut up? She gulped a breath. "I did it, didn't I? I turned rat on my own platoon. Holy shit. Marques does better keeping quiet over people that are trying to kill him. Look at me."

"Maureen, we're dealing with people now who are trying to kill you, and me, and maybe Quinn, and any other cop they can get in their crosshairs. We have to act. We worry about the fallout later."

"Quinn's one of the main reasons," Maureen said, "that I was so hot for us to get after Heath this morning. Quinn will hear, sooner rather than later, that we have Scales in custody. The bust was in the Sixth, after all. I know he'll tell Heath. When we inspected Gage's body, there was a note, a note that showed a planned meeting between Heath and Gage at Pat O'Brien's. Quinn took it from me. He told Heath about it."

"You're sure about this?"

"Heath told me himself," Maureen said.

"What happened in that interrogation room," Atkinson said, "it has to stay between us. You can't discuss it with anyone. Quinn can't know what we know. When we're done here, I'll reach out to the task force, tell them to keep it close. Hopefully, they haven't spilled too much."

"I won't talk to anyone," Maureen said.

"Not even Preacher."

"Not even Preacher," Maureen said. She was happy to leave him out of this mess. Preacher she would gladly protect. "Agreed."

"How well do you know Quinn?" Atkinson asked.

"Not as well as I thought I did a couple of days ago. Obviously."

"Do you really think he'd cover for someone involved in hunting cops over some old high school connections and a couple of lucrative details?"

"I can't see that," Maureen said.

"Can't see it," Atkinson said, "or won't."

"I can't," Maureen said. "Quinn is crooked. I see now he's probably dirty. Maybe he's even corrupt. Maybe he got carried away. He's got problems with his ex, with his son. Maybe it's all fucked him up, made him make bad compromises. But covering for cop killers? That's evil. I don't think Quinn is evil."

Atkinson waited a long time to speak. "How is it you think low-rent hood rats like Shadow and Scales get business connected to an Uptown sociopath like Heath?"

"A third party puts them together," Maureen said.

"You think Gage just happened to know Shadow? From where? You want to guess my leading theory on who that third-party connection could be?"

"Shit."

"Heath paid Quinn well for the connection to Scales, I'm sure."

"And for keeping Scales apprised of our efforts to find him and catch him," Maureen said. "Heath has houses all over the city. They could've moved Scales and the guns around indefinitely."

"That, too," Atkinson said. "And I'm sure Quinn passed by Scales's place every now and then to make sure he was keeping his head down and behaving himself. He couldn't let Scales do anything that might threaten the larger operation."

"Good Lord, Scales has been living under police protection," Maureen said.

"Quinn knew about the guns," Atkinson said. "He at least had to suspect. I'm guessing that at first he tried to know as little as possible about what Heath, Gage, and Scales were really up to, but did Quinn ask any questions? He knew of a pipeline running heavy weapons into the city, and he did nothing about it. He said nothing to no one. He pocketed his cut and let it continue. You wondered if he was evil. Sometimes evil is inaction as much as action."

"So now we go after Quinn," Maureen said.

"No," Atkinson said, stubbing out her cigarette.

"No?" Maureen asked. "In addition to everything else, Quinn's been helping to hide the number one suspect in two of your open murder cases. We have to go after him. What about what you said about inaction and action?"

"Any move on Quinn flushes Heath," Atkinson said, "probably right out of the country. With his daddy's money, he can be on a jet to Dubai in an hour. You run into Quinn tonight, you have to play it cool."

"I can do that."

"I hope so," Atkinson said. "You've done a bang-up job so far."

"I cannot believe this shit," Maureen said. "Right under my fucking nose."

"Look at the upside," Atkinson said, pushing up from her seat, sliding out of the booth, "by keeping Scales under wraps, Quinn and Heath have protected Marques. No way Scales goes after him while under their supervision."

"He doesn't have to," Maureen said. She felt anchored to her seat, frustration and vodka weighing her down like liquid lead in her veins. "Quinn and Ruiz have been doing it for him.

"They were down at the Eighth the same night I was, running some mysterious errand they didn't want to talk about. We ran into them coming out a side door. Marques was terrified of them. Nobody's been protecting Marques. Not Quinn, not Heath. They've been harassing and bullying him, because he's the only person on the street who can really hurt Scales. He was safe at school and at home, and at Roots of Music. Now he's playing gigs out in the streets, exposed and unsupervised, where any cop can pluck him off the street for whatever reason he wants to concoct." She finally rallied the energy to push up from the bench.

"I'll go get Marques. I'll find him at Roots or out on Frenchmen and let him know to lie low. I'll tell his grandmother to keep him indoors."

"Still feeling generous about Quinn?" Atkinson asked.

"I don't know what I'm feeling, to tell you the truth." Maureen took a deep breath. "And I don't much care what I'm supposed to feel. All I care about right now is figuring out what to do."

"For now," Atkinson said, "follow me outside."

The bright morning sunshine pained Maureen.

Cursing, she fumbled for her sunglasses, slid them on. Taking a moment to get her bearings, she tightened her ponytail, overcome with the urge to wash her hair. Traffic backed up at the Napoleon and Magazine intersection. Across the street, laughing middle school kids in uniform ran in circles at the corner playground, watched over by chatting teachers. On the corner where Maureen stood, middle-aged black ladies, overweight and weighed down with white plastic grocery bags, waited for the bus. Lord only knew, Maureen thought, what those women made of her and Atkinson stepping out of the bar at a few minutes before eleven, reeking of alcohol and cigarettes. She had a feeling that if they used that bus stop with regularity, these ladies were used to the variety of flotsam that washed up outside Ms. Mae's. The situation, to Maureen, felt both comfortingly and disturbingly familiar. She'd staggered out of bars into the daylight many times in the past, usually with a pocketful of tips, sometimes with a head buzzing with cocaine. Never before, though, had she made that daylight stagger with a badge in her pocket. She decided to not decide what this ignominious first said about her.

Before she and Atkinson parted ways, she had one more thing she wanted to discuss. She had a feeling they'd inched over the top of the roller coaster's first hill, their weight stacking behind them, and that coming events might twist and turn far too quickly for another chance at private conversation. Atkinson had her own sunglasses on and was thumbing a breath mint from its foil package. She offered it to Maureen, who took it, cracking it between her back teeth.

"You gonna be all right to drive?" Atkinson asked.

"Fuck no." Maureen savored the cooling sting of the mint on the back of her tongue. "I can walk it from here. I might stop at Slim Goodies and treat myself to breakfast. I'm never up before they close these days."

"Stop by your car, put your 'on duty' card on the dash," Atkinson said. "Avoid the ticket and the tow."

Maureen nodded. "One more thing."

"No more things," Atkinson said. "Wait to hear from me."

"It's not about Quinn, or Heath, or Gage, or anyone else. It's about me."

"Why am I suddenly really uncomfortable?"

Maureen set her hand on Atkinson's forearm. She led them away from Ms. Mae's door, past a small coffee shop to the next storefront, a costume shop that didn't open until noon.

"I did a bad thing," Maureen said. "I took a bribe."

"Sweet Jesus. Officer, you need to be careful here."

"It was an accident. After the detail at his house, Solomon Heath overpaid me by a thousand dollars. The money is home, in the envelope it came in. Some guy was handing out envelopes after the party, to the help. I put mine in my pocket without checking it. Quinn said three bills, so I figured it was three bills. When I got home, I saw it was more."

Atkinson was quiet for a long time. "And then what did you do?"

"Nothing. I had a glass of wine on the porch, thought about calling Quinn, see what he got paid."

"Please tell me you didn't do that."

"I didn't," Maureen said. "I already knew by then I couldn't trust him."

"What was the money for?" Atkinson asked. "What did you do for him?"

"Nothing," Maureen said. "Nothing, I swear. I figured it was gratitude for helping Quinn squash Caleb's connection to Gage. Or maybe he was greasing me for times like this, so I'd be on his team when Caleb got in trouble again."

"Or maybe Quinn asked him to do it," Atkinson said, "in case *he* ever needed anything on you. The bribe wasn't about Solomon, it was about Quinn."

"Good Lord."

Atkinson took off her sunglasses, rubbing the back of her wrist against her cheek. Maureen saw again, under the makeup, the dark black circles like storm clouds under her eyes. She said, "You have the money."

"I do." Maureen took a deep breath. A shard of the breath mint caught in her throat. She gagged for a moment and coughed it up, spitting it onto the sidewalk. "Can we use this? Trying to bribe an officer? Maybe to go after Solomon somehow? We're going to need to get through him to get to Caleb."

Atkinson laughed. "Maureen, you took the money, and didn't tell anyone right away."

"I didn't *take* take it," Maureen said, her voice growing hoarse from exhaustion and cigarette smoke. "I didn't know I had it until I got home. This was only last night that it happened."

"You withheld information about Caleb Heath's relationship to a murder victim from Drayton at the crime scene," Atkinson said. "You withheld that information again when he came after you at the district, about that murder. That *next night* Caleb Heath's father gave you over a thousand dollars in cash, which you pocketed and took home. And we're gonna use this situation *against* the Heath family? Maureen, you're smarter than this. Who do you think gets fucked in this scenario if it comes to light? Not the Heaths, that's for damn sure. Christ, you look like an extortionist." Atkinson raised her hands. "I can't believe I brought you into this. You're a mess."

"I haven't done anything," Maureen said, "except try to be a team player. And this is what I fucking get. I'll return the money. I'll bring it back to Solomon this afternoon."

"Absolutely not," Atkinson said. "Do not interact with that man."

"You're telling me to keep it?" Maureen asked. "I don't want it. I won't take it. I'm not like Quinn. This is how he got the way he is, by doing it that one time, but it's never that one time, not for the criminals, not for the cops, not for anybody."

"Maureen, please shut the fuck up. I want you to listen to me. If you ever speak of this conversation, ever, to anyone, including me, I won't stop with running you off the police force, I'll run you out of the state of Louisiana. I am not playing." She moved in closer to Maureen. "This thing with the money, it never happened."

"You mean get rid of it?"

"There. Was. No. Money. There never was."

"So if I get asked about it, if it comes up anywhere in what comes next, I lie. If it's the feds asking the questions, if it's Preacher, if it's you, I lie."

"There was no money," Atkinson said. "Never happened. Understood?"

"Affirmative, Detective Sergeant."

"Go home. Go to bed. Go to work tonight. You can be a great cop, Maureen, as long as we can keep you out of jail. Not another word, not another move, until you hear from me. You get inspired, you get a brilliant idea about how to fix everything, before you do anything, think about how much better you look in NOPD blue than you will in OPP orange."

25

While paying her tab for her eggs and pancakes at Slim Goodies, Maureen heard police cars flying down Magazine Street, one after the other, their sirens screaming. They'd turned most of the heads in the diner. As the sirens moved into the distance, she'd said a silent prayer of thanks that she was no longer on the day shift, and that, with her belly full of pancakes and fried eggs, she didn't have to go racing through the neighborhood at top speed.

She left a big tip and pushed open the front door of the diner, slipping on her sunglasses, lighting a cigarette, and looking forward to a few moments of peace during the slow walk home. She had time to squeeze in a few hours of sleep before her shift that night, and let the vodka wear off. Her ankle would be sore from the walking. She'd need a couple of Percocets to get through her shift. Maybe she could find a quiet place to park the cruiser, avoid everyone and everything as much as possible, and lie low for this one shift. New Orleans would survive.

She turned off Magazine onto Sixth Street to discover her block bursting at the seams with cops and emergency vehicles of every kind. That was where everyone had been headed. Two cruisers with their lights going sat nose-to-nose at her corner, closing off the block. One more guarded the other end. An ambulance was parked in the middle of the street, its back doors flung open. A fire truck idled on the far side of the ambulance. Maureen didn't see or smell any smoke. Her next thought was that a medical emergency had occurred. Something had happened, an accident that had scared her neighbors into calling every emergency number they could find. She put her hand to her hip, found her weapon there.

Those neighbors milled about on their porches or out on the sidewalk, many of them talking to either uniform or plainclothes police officers taking notes. The firefighters hung around their truck, chatting with one another. Whatever had happened appeared to be over. Maureen knew the look of a crime scene when the drama had ended and the task of gathering information about it had begun. She removed her gun from her hip, tucked the holster into her jeans at the small of her back. She couldn't walk into a crime scene smelling like booze and openly armed.

She trotted down the middle of Sixth, slowing as one of the officers standing near the parked cruisers walked up Sixth to meet her. "You're Coughlin, right?"

"I am," Maureen said. "What happened? What's going on?"

"You're to wait here," the officer said. He held up his hand as Maureen made to move by him. "Just for a minute. Sergeant Boyd is here. He's going to escort you through the scene."

He keyed his mic and announced Maureen's arrival.

She knew that Preacher was the scheduled duty sergeant for the night tour, and wondered what he was doing at a late-morning crime scene. She couldn't imagine he had good news. Preacher emerged from the crowd, walking her way with his head down. He was dressed in civvies, which Maureen realized she had never seen before. He wore a pressed, oversized, merlot-colored guayabera shirt and neat, dark jeans, the cuffs rolled up to expose black socks and brown sandals. At first glance, despite his chaotic surroundings, he looked ready for an espresso and a game of dominoes. Mirrored aviators hid most of his face, but Maureen saw that his usually busy and expressive mouth was a hard, tight line.

She squeezed between the bumpers of the patrol cars and entered the scene to meet him. "Preach, what's happening?"

"For fuck's sake, Coughlin," Preacher said, the stink of his cigars enveloping him, "is it too much to ask that you answer your phone?"

Maureen fumbled through her pockets and found her phone. She checked it. Preacher had called eight times in the last thirty minutes. "I had the ringer off," she said. "I was eating at Slim Goodies. I always turn it off when I eat out."

"Since when do you go out to breakfast? I've heard you talk a million times about straggling out of bed at noon. Today you decide to be the early bird?"

"I had that detail last night," Maureen said, thinking fast, eager to follow Atkinson's instructions not to talk of their morning and not to lie to Preacher at the same time. "I was in bed earlier. I like Slim Goodies. I like diners. I like breakfast, sometimes in the morning. What happened here, Preach? What the fuck is going on?"

"Slim Goodies got a liquor license?" Preacher asked.

Maureen blushed. She couldn't look at him. "Listen, Preach, it's kind of a private thing."

"I don't even want to know."

Preacher took off his sunglasses, wiped his face and the back of his neck with a black bandana. In her next-door neighbor's front yard, three EMTs knelt in a circle. Maureen couldn't see who was getting their attention. The EMTs worked deliberately, their faces calm. She tried to take comfort in that, anxiety eating at her insides. "What happened at the neighbor's place?"

"About forty minutes ago," Preacher said, "somebody shot up the block. Bad. One of their Great Danes got hit. The black one, I think."

"Oh, no."

"Winged in the shoulder," Preacher said. "Calm fucking dog, considering he got shot. Better than most people. That's him the EMTs are working on now. He should be fine. I think it was flying debris that got him, shrapnel, not a bullet. We need to talk to the family before we can let them take him to the vet, so we're doing what we can for the poor guy here."

"Any people get hit?"

"Thankfully, no," Preacher said. "They shot fast, with some heavy-duty firepower. Maybe even military grade. Close to it, anyway. We already ran out of those plastic cones to mark the casings. We'll pick up over a hundred, easy." He paused. "Their efforts were concentrated on a specific target."

"Jesus."

"They were after you," Preacher said. "Your house got the worst of it, by far."

"Me?" Maureen said. "My house?"

She looked past Preacher down the street. She realized that most of the police action was focused on her place. Crime scene techs stood in the middle of her garden, trampling the plants while photographing the front of her house. Her ginger plants now wilted in every direction, the red flowers gone, as if someone had decapitated the stalks with a weed whacker. She could see that the front window of the house had been shot out, and that the front wall was peppered with bullet holes. Big ones. Her wooden rocking chair and little metal end table had been obliterated.

"Come with me," Preacher said. "I sent some guys around to Seventh Street, by the way, checking for stray shots. No collateral damage so far. So that's good news."

Cops and techs stepped aside, saying nothing, not meeting Maureen's eyes, as she and Preacher moved down the street and approached the house. She felt like the mourning widow at a wake being led to the side of the beloved deceased. The closer she got to the house, the worse the damage appeared. Her knees felt watery.

"A white minivan," Preacher said, holding open her gate. "They stopped, threw open the door, and let loose. Covered plates. Guys in ski masks. That's everything we got from the neighbors on the block. Can't say I blame them for ducking, must've sounded like a fucking war zone."

"That van is already burning somewhere," Maureen said.

"They'll wait until after dark," Preacher said. "But, yeah, I don't see us lucking into nailing them in a traffic stop."

Passing through her front gate, Maureen searched for but couldn't spot her black and gold flamingos. Vaporized, she figured, in the on-slaught. Thankfully, miraculously, the Drew Brees statue had escaped damage. The front window of the house had drawn most of the fire. Not only had the glass been shot out but the frame and the woodwork had been destroyed. The bamboo shade had been shredded and blown into the front room, along with a lot of the glass and wood from the window frame. Numerous deep holes the size of tennis balls punctured the wall surrounding the window, as if giant toothy jaws had bitten into the house. She knew the inside wouldn't look any better, and wondered how deep into the house the damage extended.

"AR-15s," Maureen said. "Modified. I'm willing to bet."

"That's what I'm hearing," Preacher said. "Or worse."

Maureen lit a cigarette. She took a deep inhale of smoke, furious and committed to not tearing up in front of so many neighbors and coworkers.

"Jesus, Preach," she said, tremors of rage in her voice, letting the smoke trail out. "This is one step shy of a rocket attack. Like fucking Fallujah."

She turned, looking over the crowd and entertaining the thought that whoever had done this was observing her, wanting to watch her see the damage done to her house. She looked for Madison. She saw faces she didn't know, but nobody paid special attention to her. The shooters weren't out there, weren't watching her. She said, "This wasn't a warn-ing, was it?"

"No, no, it wasn't. Somebody tried to kill you this morning. Some-one who knows your schedule, who knew you'd most likely be home mid-morning." Preacher scratched his chin. "We found something on the porch. You should have a look at it."

For a moment, Maureen's thoughts turned to the envelope of cash from Solomon Heath. Where had she left it? In the kitchen. She spotted a large upside-down bucket by the front door. Something dark, it looked like blood, was smeared on the door. That had to be what Preacher was talking about. "This is a bad day."

"It's nothing that'll make you lose your lunch, or your breakfast," Preacher said. "The bucket was for the flies. We took it from a neighbor's yard." He stopped at the foot of the steps. "Go ahead, have a look. It's nothing alive, or human, if that makes you feel any better."

Maureen walked up the stairs onto her porch. She wedged the toe of her boot under the lip of the bucket and flipped it over. A bloody pink pig's head stared up at her. Flies rose up in a cloud, buzzing. She stepped back, waving her hand in front of her face. That explained the blood-stain on her door. She looked back at the street. Someone had thrown the head. It had hit her front door and come to rest on her porch. Hell of a toss from the middle of the street, she thought. Someone had taken the time to get out of the van, aim the head, and make a good throw. With the whole neighborhood in duck-and-cover mode from the gun-fire, she thought, that someone would've enjoyed plenty of time and had no worry about witnesses.

Maureen stepped to the edge of her porch, looking down the steps at Preacher. "They want us to know," she said, "want the neighborhood to know, that *they* know I'm a cop, and that they were willing to do this any-way. They want us to know that's *why* they did it. They want us to know they're not afraid of us. It's got to be the Sovereign Citizens and the Watchmen."

"That's about how I see it," Preacher said. "This is a first, though. Usually one cop is as good as any other to them. We're all the same. They ambush, or take advantage, like cowards. They don't outright hunt. I'll double-check, but this is the first I've seen or heard of them coming after a specific cop. And with a vengeance, it seems."

"Fucking hooray for me," Maureen said. "I always wanted to be somebody's first time." She thought again of the guns found at Bobby Scales's house. "We're done worrying about them moving into the city. They're already here. We're behind."

"We should have a look around inside the house," Preacher said. "If you feel up to it. A quick walk-through. For safety issues, in case there's a gas leak or some such. We checked around the outside, didn't find anything dangerous." He made his way up the steps. "We'll have to let the techs in soon for a close look at the bullets and the bullet holes. Evidence recovery. Can't imagine they'll find anything different from what's out front. It's gonna be a while before you can start to clean up. Probably not till after dark. I'm sorry about that."

"I can live with the mess," Maureen said. "I'll manage. As long as we can make a few extra passes tonight on patrol. I'm not sure I'll be able to lock the door."

Preacher laughed. "You can take the night off. We'll get by without you for one shift. New Orleans will survive."

"Fuck that," Maureen said. "I'm not changing a fucking thing. I'm not missing a night of work, and I know the next thing you're going to say. I am not getting a hotel room and hiding out, either. No how, no way. This is my place and nobody's driving me out of it."

"I'll put someone out front," Preacher said, "while you're at work and after. Till we make some headway on this."

"Why? So they can get shot at, too? Maybe that's what they want. A cop parked alone in a car would be a sitting duck. I'll be fine. I'll be better than fine. Now I know they're coming. They blew their element of surprise."

"We know you're tough," Preacher said. "Don't show us how stupid you can be. I don't want to make that phone call to your mother."

"I've been run out of my house before," Maureen said. "Never again."

"This matter is not resolved," Preacher said. "Don't think of it as such." He put his fingertips into a bullet hole by the front door. He shook his head. "Rounds this size, coming in this hot, you're lucky the place didn't catch fire and burn down. I don't know what they used, but it was more than what they needed."

"I'm fucking standing here," Maureen said. "So whatever they used, it wasn't enough."

"You got renter's insurance?" Preacher asked.

"Probably not enough," Maureen said. With her foot, she pushed the pig's head away from her door. "Those motherfuckers. Ridiculous theatrical bullshit. Fucking coward redneck farm boys. Shooting at a woman in her bed. You know they're having a big circle jerk somewhere, Preach, grabbing their dicks and cackling about what big men they are."

She wanted to pick up the pig's head and hurl it into the street. On second thought, maybe she'd keep it. She'd bleach the bones and hang the skull over her front door. Like a trophy, a warning. "You ever see anything like this, Preach? Ever see someone come after one of us at home?"

"No," Preacher said. "Can't say I have. Even in this town. Never thought I'd see the day, to tell you the truth."

"You'd be so bored without me, Preacher," Maureen said, trying to inflect her voice with humor. Her hands shook as she opened her front door. She flinched as the door swung open, lilting on its hinges. "You wanna come in? Escort me around my own house?" She reached around her back, pulled her gun. "I have my weapon on me."

"This tough-gal talk," Preacher said. "It makes you sound frightened, is what it does. You'd be smart to be frightened. I'm fucking frightened."

Maureen felt the pressure building behind her eyes. "Knock it off. Stop."

"I won't come in," Preacher said. "The district commander is on his way, and a community relations officer to deal with the press. I'm going to brief them, and to keep an anti-fuck-up eye in general on the proceedings out here. They're both gonna want to talk to you, so brush your teeth. I'll be in to check on you before any of that. And if you need me before you see me, holler. Don't hesitate."

"I never do," Maureen said. "What're you going to tell the DC?"

"That some backwoods militia group has moved into the city. That they're hunting cops, one Sixth District officer in particular. I'll make sure he knows if he hasn't heard already about the connections between Gage and the Sovereign Citizens group. I'll direct him to the feds from there. I'd imagine the FBI will want to talk to you about this, too." He patted at his neck with his handkerchief. "Maybe that's why the Citizens went for you, because of that traffic stop from the other night. Maybe they blame you for Gage getting killed. It would suit the conspiratorial, victimized mind-set those humps seem to favor. Maybe they've been planning this for a while, waiting to pick one particular cop, raise their game, and you stepped into the crosshairs."

He looked at her for a long time, as if processing a change he'd only now recognized. "Jeez Louise, Coughlin, you're the victim of an act of domestic terror. This is what al-Qaeda does in Afghanistan, blow up cops." He patted his forehead again. "What the fuck is this world coming to?"

"Gage lived long enough to tell someone about me pulling him over the other night," Maureen said. "I guess that's possible. If the Citizens and the Watchmen are already set up here, they'd be able to arrange a hit by now. But how would they know where I lived? I'm not listed. My name isn't exactly uncommon."

"New Orleans is a small town," Preacher said. "You'd be surprised who knows what."

His radio crackled. The DC was on-site, a voice announced, and looking for him. "Let me get with him and get things moving. Go nowhere without talking to me first."

"Wouldn't dream of it," Maureen said.

Something told her that busting Scales had touched the match to this particular fuse. Maureen knew that she was the only person involved who knew everything, about Leary and Gage, about Scales and Gage and Heath and Quinn and Ruiz and the Sovereign Citizens and the Watchmen Brigade, and how they all connected. Preacher knew some things. Atkinson knew most of the story. But only Maureen saw the whole web.

She wondered what kind of bounty that knowledge made her worth. Four figures? Five? Six, even? How high was the price on her head? Would it go up, she wondered, now that the Sovereign Citizens had come after her and missed? Later, she'd ask Quinn. She had a feeling he might know. She wondered for a moment if he'd come after her himself, but she knew he didn't have the nerve. She'd known killers. Quinn wasn't a killer. But he'd hand the killer a weapon and look away. Quinn would do that.

She walked into her house. Her cell phone buzzed in her pocket. She answered, heard Atkinson's stern if sleep-fuzzy voice. "I heard what happened. Are you okay?"

Maureen stood in her living room, looking over the internal injuries her house had sustained. Upsetting. Gruesome, but survivable.

"I'm somewhere between enraged and distraught," she told Atkinson. "I don't think the idea of that many bullets being meant for me has entirely sunk in yet." She paused. "I've been shot at before, but this is a different thing."

"We can assume that news of the Scales bust has hit the streets," Atkinson said.

"Keeping a lid on that information was doomed from the start," Maureen said. "We both knew that. Between the task force, the other uniforms on the scene. We'd been after him a long time. Nabbing him was a real score, we thought he was a dangerous man . . ." She let her voice trail off.

"As soon as I get myself together," Atkinson said, "I'm going over to the Tents and I'll take another run at Scales. See if there's anything else he can give us to help track down the shooters and where we might find them. If it's in there, he's gonna give it up."

Maureen didn't see the point. Why would Scales know of plans to blow up a cop? Why would anyone tell him? But arguing with Atkinson was pointless in its own right. She wouldn't do anything she thought was a waste of time. Atkinson didn't believe in going through the motions for somebody else's feelings.

"Multiple shooters," Maureen said, "in an unmarked white minivan. That's the full extent of what we've got."

"It's a start."

"I gotta go, Detective," Maureen said, pushing shards of glass and bamboo splinters across the living room floor with her toe. "I need to restore a semblance of order here before my night tour, for the sake of my own sanity."

"I completely understand," Atkinson said. "Reclaim your space. If it helps, think about it this way. If they thought you could be bought, they'd have come to you with money. If they thought you could be frightened or intimidated, they'd have come after you with threats. The fact they came with loaded guns? With intent to kill? Somebody is afraid of you."

"It doesn't feel like a compliment," Maureen said.

"We'll make them pay," Atkinson said, very matter-of-fact about it. Maureen envied her confidence, and not for the first time. "And I'm not talking about the damage to your house."

With that, Atkinson hung up.

Maureen slipped her phone into her pocket. Get moving. That was the key.

What to do first? Avoid any more damage. That was first.

She walked into the kitchen. Debris blown in from the living room littered the floor but her table and chairs and her appliances remained intact. On the table sat the envelope full of money. She snatched it up. She counted the cash quickly, thirteen hundred, and shoved it deep into her front pocket. She walked into the living room, surveyed the wreckage. She ran her fingers into her hair, interlacing her fingers over her skull, squeezing her head between her palms. Her throat was tight. The dust in the air tickled her nose. Her life had been perforated. Violated.

Holes everywhere. Puncturing the walls. Blasted into the planks of the beautiful hardwood floor, into the stone façade of the rebuilt fireplace. Splinters and chips of stone and plaster had sprayed throughout the room, mixed in with the pulverized glass from her front window. The air in the room glowed with sunlight reflected off the hovering particles of dust. A breeze off the river fluttered the shredded window blinds. She tried to imagine the sound of that destruction. The house was not hers, she had landlords, but she felt as if she owned what she saw, the house and the damage. She felt responsible for putting it right.

She had moved out of her mother's house when she was eighteen. For the next dozen years on Staten Island and then in New Orleans, she'd made do with either furnished apartments or secondhand stuff donated by coworkers, bought at garage sales, or rescued from the curb. Home was a place to wash off the world and crash after work, to get high and get laid between shifts. It had never been a place to live. Until she'd rented this house. On this house, for the first time in her adult life, she had indulged. For the first time, she had planned to stay.

Her first investment in her new home life, her first prize, her big reward, payback to herself for innumerable sleepless nights on her feet as a waitress, was her beautiful queen-sized bed. She'd bought it in a Royal Street antique shop. She had spared no expense. Not on the hand-carved wooden headboard depicting a trio of pelicans aloft under a crescent moon. Not on the box spring, the mattress, the sheets, or the pillows. She'd never owned a bed like that. Never owned anything bigger than a double. Never in her life had she thought about thread count, or pillow shams, or bed skirts. Or silk versus satin. The bed was her main luxury, her primary indulgence. Her island. Well, so much for that.

From where she now stood in the living room, with the freestanding fireplace blocking her view, she couldn't see the bed, but she saw the evidence that bullets had reached her bedroom. Holes in the floor and the walls there, too. Exploded paperback books on the floor. Shards of mirror glinting in the sunlight.

She told herself, standing there, that she couldn't bear to enter the bedroom because she couldn't stand seeing a lovely piece of furniture terminally wounded. Over a hundred years that bed had lasted—through fires, floods, and plagues—she thought, until Maureen Coughlin got her hands on it. Then it hadn't lasted a month. Deep inside, though, she knew the real reason she couldn't look, couldn't move from where she stood. She didn't want to see how many bullets had hit the bed, and where. The damage they had done, the damage that would've been done to her. She didn't want to acknowledge that had she been home and asleep, like she so often was, that the coroner would be wheeling her dead body through the wreckage of her home, her corpse zipped into a cold black plastic bag. She thought of what Atkinson had told the task force outside Scales's house. *Bullets go places.* Indeed they did. She didn't want to think where the bullets in her bed might otherwise have gone. She didn't want to think of Preacher calling her mother with the news. Could not think of her mother receiving it. Would they ship her body back to Staten Island? Maureen wondered. Or would they bury her here in her new home?

She heard Preacher reenter the house. She didn't have to turn around. She knew him by his slow gait and his heavy breathing. His face was mournful when she looked at him. "The DC would like to see you. If you don't want to talk to him now, I can make arrangements for later."

"I want to talk to Ruiz," Maureen said. "Now. That's all I care about."

"Have you tried him yourself?"

"I haven't bothered. He won't answer me."

Preacher hesitated. "Why is that?"

"Because he'll know where to find Quinn. He knows that's what I want."

"Call Quinn yourself," Preacher said.

"He won't answer me, either," Maureen said. "He knows better. I've found some things out, Preach. Things I can't tell you yet."

"You'll see Quinn tonight," Preacher said. "He's working the night tour. We can talk then, the three of us."

"Not tonight," Maureen said. "Today. Me and Quinn need to do this alone. This afternoon. Now. I don't trust him with a whole day to cover his tracks."

Preacher came closer. He spoke quietly. "Coughlin, you're not saying he had anything to do with this? No. No way. Not this. Nothing this big. That's an accusation, if it leaves this house, that ends our careers."

"I want to see him," Maureen said. "I'm tired, Preach. I'm tired of everyone telling me how it should play, and what I should think, and patting me on the fucking head and telling me that I don't understand the way things work in crazy ol' New Orleans. I want to see some shit and make some decisions for myself. It starts with Quinn. I wanna hear, from him, what he knows and what he doesn't, what he's into and what he's not. Then *I'll* decide what *I* believe. And what I don't." She could feel the cash in her pocket, could feel the corners of the folded envelope digging into her thigh. "It's your turn, Preach, to trust me. On this one, I know more than you."

Preacher was quiet a long time. "I guess we'll both know after today, one way or another, if you're gonna make it with us or not." He looked away from her, scratching at the stubble on his throat. "Dispatch will have a twenty on Ruiz. I'll reach him for you. Should I tell him to meet you at the Sixth?"

Maureen shook her head. "Tell him to call me on my cell. I don't want anything out over the radio. We'll pick a place to meet when he calls me. And tell him he better not tell anyone else about it, especially Quinn."

Preacher sucked his teeth. "I don't think we have to worry about that. We both know Ruiz is cutting his ties with Quinn. That should've been the tell right there that Quinn had gone too far." Debris crunched under Preacher's feet. "The DC? What do you want to do about him?"

"I'll follow you outside," Maureen said. So she was going to talk to the district commander with a pocketful of bribe money. So be it. Why not? That cash would go a long way toward a new bed. She deserved it. "May as well get it over with."

Preacher stopped them in the doorway. "The TV people are arriving. DSU. WWL. We can do this inside."

"Fuck it," Maureen said. "The people who shot at me are going to be waiting for the news reports. I want them to see my smiling face. I want them to know they missed their shot at the title."

26

In the time it had taken Maureen to sweep the debris into a large mound in the corner of her living room and for Preacher to come through with info on Ruiz, the day had flipped personalities. The warm, sunny morning gave way to high gray clouds. A damp and chilly wind rolled in from the west. Though hours off yet, heavy rain was on the way. The city would get one of those cool and windy October nights that reminded everyone that there would finally, mercifully, be a fall.

Before leaving the house to recover her car and meet Ruiz, Maureen had pulled on a brown leather jacket over her long-sleeved T-shirt and jeans. The jacket covered the service weapon she wore tucked into her waistband at the small of her back.

Two miles away, on the border of the Sixth and Second Districts, Maureen found Ruiz in the St. Vincent de Paul No. 2 cemetery across the street from Newman High School, sitting alone on a white marble bench between two decrepit crypts, his elbows resting on his thick thighs, his fingers laced in front of him. His blue uniform was stretched tight over his big shoulders. A paper coffee cup sat at his hip. He was waiting for her right where Preacher had said he'd be.

At first glance, Ruiz appeared to be puzzling over the faded names and dates on the crumbling grave marker before him. Maureen realized that he frowned not at what he saw, but at the thoughts moving around like clouds in his head. She could only imagine what they were. He appeared contemplative, a mood Maureen had never witnessed in him, and something about the look of it on him struck her as sad. He was a living version of the solemn, mourning statuary that surrounded him. The ground hadn't shifted under only her feet in the last few days, she thought. Others she worked with had lost their bearings and their balance, as well.

She was, however, she reminded herself, the person getting shot at.

As she approached Ruiz, she considered asking to sit beside him on the bench. She decided against it. She had neither the time nor the inclination to make nice. No good cop today.

"You heard what happened," she said, looming over him, crowding him as much as her size would allow.

"I heard. I'm sorry." He turned his hands palms up, studied them. "I'm glad, everyone is glad, that you didn't get hit. Anyone get hurt?"

"The neighbor's dog took some shrapnel. He should be okay. That was it, thank God. I went out for breakfast. First time in weeks, maybe months." Saved, she thought, by the anomaly. "Can you believe that?"

"I'm sorry about that Marques kid, too," Ruiz said. "I've been meaning to tell you that. I'm sorry we scared him like we did over Scales. We never really meant him any harm. We wouldn't have hurt him. The way I figured it, we were doing him a favor, keeping him convinced not to testify. You have to admit, that was the quickest way for him to get himself killed. Our way, scared into keeping his mouth shut, he was protected. I know who we are, what we're supposed to be about, to represent, but who living in the real world believes any of that protect-and-serve bullshit anymore?"

"I'll explain it to him," Maureen said, "next time I see him. But I don't think he's gonna see it your way. I'm not sure I do, either."

"This thing with Heath got bigger," Ruiz said, spreading his hands, "way bigger than it was ever supposed to. And it went all crooked. You have to understand, those militia fucks, I didn't know a thing about them."

"Then why the transfer request?"

"Quinn was getting weird," Ruiz said. "Paranoid. Truth was, the worse shit got with his ex and the boy, the angrier he got. Bad things were happening with him and it started coming out in these crazy ways, him blaming everybody, anybody, for his life being fucked up, for him being broke all the time, for his boy getting knocked around. He was drinking on duty. Getting into other shit." Ruiz shook his head. "Quinn doesn't know I asked for the transfer. He thinks it was forced on me. I tried to use our splitting up to help him, to play it like people were getting suspicious of us, that maybe they were trying to break us up. I thought maybe he would take it as a warning to mellow out, that he would get the hint." Ruiz pulled out his cell phone from his pocket, looked at it, and set it on the bench beside his coffee cup. "I got a wife. I got daughters. I'm a team player, Quinn is my boy, but there's only so far I can go with his shit. I can't get fired, lose my pension, my benefits. I can't go to jail. Not for Quinn's weirdo friends."

"Quinn didn't get the message," Maureen said. "You need to tell me where I can find him. He can't get out from under this on his own. We both know Heath won't help him."

A long, shrill coach's whistle and the voices of shouting girls emanated from one of the school athletic fields, the sounds echoing off the stone surrounding Ruiz and Maureen. After-lunch P.E., Maureen figured.

"You know who the Mannings are, right?" Ruiz said.

"I'm from New York," Maureen said, "not Mars. One of them plays up there, you know."

Ruiz turned, looking over his shoulder at the back side of the school. "They went to that high school right there, Newman. I want my girls to go there. I went there, too. Matt did, for his freshman year."

"Matt who?" Maureen asked, confused.

Ruiz considered Maureen for a long moment, looking up at her, his eyes narrow and dark. For some reason, she had the feeling he was about to stand and walk away from her, that he had lost any hope of their conversation being useful. He checked his watch, looked away from her. She wasn't sure what she would do if he tried to leave the cemetery. He had a hundred pounds on her. She thought maybe staying engaged in the conversation, wherever it wandered, would keep Ruiz seated. "Matt would be who?"

"Matthew is Quinn's first name."

"I never knew that," Maureen said. It was true.

"I knew him since he and I were six years old." Ruiz chuckled. "Me and him, we grew up together, right over in the next neighborhood, in Broadmoor, two houses apart. He's got three brothers, they're named Mark, Luke, and John. None of them live here anymore."

"You're shitting me."

"I am not," Ruiz said, shaking his head. "No shit. His parents were like that. Super Catholic. Super devout. His grandparents were worse. Bible thumpers from the Irish countryside. That's why, when he got in trouble, he ended up in Ignatius instead of reform school."

"I thought that was some exclusive boarding school for big shots."

"What? No. Who told you that? It was a last-chance stop for rich white boys before juvenile detention and grown-up jail. Nobody admitted it, nobody talked about the school that way, but that's what it was. If your family had the dough to grease the juvie courts and the Church, and your son couldn't stay out of trouble in New Orleans, you shipped him off to the Jesuits in Mississippi. Nobody who could afford it wanted their kids in the city system with the blacks, you kidding? The public schools were bad enough.

"You ever been to Bay St. Louis? If you want to relax in the quiet by the Gulf, it's perfect for that. You're a teenager that likes raising hell and you don't know anybody in town, it's fucking miserable. That's where Gage came in. He was Caleb's go-to guy. He was a couple years older.

He'd flunked out of Ignatius but stayed in town, worked in the cafeteria, did odd jobs on campus, something like that. He was another Louisiana kid, small-town south Louisiana."

"They all know each other," Maureen said. "Gage, Quinn, and Heath. They've been a team for years."

"The three of them have been runnin' podnas for decades," Ruiz said. "In Bay St. Louis, Quinn was raising hell alongside them every step of the way. Even back then, as a teenager, Caleb had a way of sniffing out people useful to him and making them feel like his friend, usually by using his money. He really just wants to be worshipped. Gage was a delinquent, the kind of guy Caleb wouldn't spit on in New Orleans, but in Bay St. Louis he knew where to find the easy drugs and the easy girls. He'd find them trouble and Caleb would pick up the tab. But Gage was watching and learning.

"When Gage needed a silent partner to support the Watchmen, Heath was the first person he called. Heath couldn't hand out the cash fast enough. Caleb was a real swinging dick in high school. Think of the rich kid with the big watch outside of F and M's, the one who found Gage's body. Bankrolling a gang of badass gun-happy rednecks brings Caleb right back to his glory days cutting up in Mississippi. Quinn told me that Gage made him some ridiculous camouflage jacket with stripes on the sleeve and epaulets and some stupid Watchmen logo on the back. Got him a matching ball cap.

"Caleb wants to be like his old man. Always has. He wants to be a boss man, have people kissing his ass. He wants to preside over an empire. Only he doesn't want to work for it, he just wants to peel the bills off the roll. Say what you want about Solomon, he put his time in. He builds shit. Caleb just wants to tear down."

"The city's full of rich, spoiled white kids," Maureen said, "who aren't financing domestic terrorism."

"Maybe Caleb's a true believer," Ruiz said with a shrug. "Maybe he *believes* that Sovereign Citizens fuck-the-police Don't Tread on Me shit. Maybe he's been in it with Gage from the beginning. Maybe it goes all the way back to those days in Mississippi. I wasn't really tight with Quinn again till we were cops. All I know is some people, you look at them and you can tell they came off the assembly line with hollow, empty spaces where important parts should've gone. Caleb Heath is one of those people. So's your friend, whatshername, that woman from the pickup truck. Heath's got money; she doesn't. Otherwise, I don't see a whole lotta difference. They're not *whole* people. We should be glad we can't understand them."

"So when Gage tells Heath the Watchmen want to do business in New Orleans," Maureen said, "and that they need some local connections, Heath calls Quinn. That's the next step. Gage to Heath to Quinn."

"Exactly. Heath calls Quinn and says, hey, our old pal Clayton Gage is in town, he needs a guy who can hold some product till he can move it through town. Me and Quinn, we have Shadow on a short leash from a pot bust, we go to Shadow, and Shadow puts Gage's flunky Cooley with Scales. Now we have Scales, who everyone is looking for, under our thumb, and we figure we turn him over to Atkinson as soon as Gage is done with him. We've got the whole thing worked out. This is New Orleans, it's all who you know."

"Except," Maureen said, "Scales pisses off one of his girlfriends and she dimes him to Atkinson before the product has been moved. And your business deal with a gunrunning child killer goes up in smoke. What a fucking shame."

"We didn't know," Ruiz said, "that the product we were dealing with was guns. Anyone says product, we think drugs. I never heard about guns until the story of you guys busting Scales went around. We made introductions, we never saw none of it after that. I never saw Gage, never met him, until that night you stopped him in his daddy's pickup truck."

"And you never asked, did you?" Maureen said.

"I had no idea about the guns, and we were gonna give up Scales as soon as we were done with him, I fucking swear. Heath played us, all of us."

"I had no idea," Maureen said, "that Quinn came from big-enough money to roll with the Heaths."

"He doesn't," Ruiz said. "At the time Matt got in trouble, his father worked at City Hall, in zoning and permits. Solomon Heath paid Quinn's way through Ignatius, all three years, and got himself a helping hand in the system for his Christian charity. That's how Matt and Heath became friends. If that's what you want to call them. Their fathers put them together."

"They don't seem a natural pair," Maureen said.

"But they are, Quinn is his father's son," Ruiz said with a shrug. "Owned by the Heaths like his daddy. And proud of it. They use him. Like a farm animal. He needs them. He's been paying child support for ten years. He needs the work they hire him for. I know he does. And it's not like the old days in the eighties, nobody's doing hits for the mob anymore. We're not criminals. In Matt's defense, I think he decided to become a cop on his own. His dad was dead by then, grandparents, too, and his brothers left town, even before the storm. I always wondered if Quinn became a cop because he thought it was the best way to be useful to the Heaths. They're kind of the only family he has in New Orleans anymore."

"He needs to get away from them," Maureen said. "Forget the history. He needs to talk to me now. His buddy Caleb is in bed with cop killers, with terrorists, buying them their guns, helping them move into New Orleans. Caleb's not footing the bill for truck-stop speed and condoms in Bay St. Louis anymore, Ruc."

Ruiz said nothing.

"Rue, listen to me. I'm done keeping a lid on what we did, not with a house full of bullet holes. Compared to everything else going on, our cover-up is small potatoes. Forget the brass, forget the feds, what do you think is gonna happen in the department when word gets around that

Quinn is protecting cop hunters. A betrayal like that? Forget it. Cop or not, he'll be lucky to get out of New Orleans alive. What do you think happens to *us* when word gets around we covered for him?"

Ruiz stood. He was so close that Maureen leaned back, resetting her weight on her heels. He looked down at her, fear in his eyes. "You wouldn't spread that rumor. You wouldn't rat him out like that. Not to his own."

Maureen straightened her shoulders, holding her ground. "It's not a rumor. Whether he meant to or not, Quinn did what he did. What I'm trying to tell you, Rue, is that I'm not the one he needs to worry about anymore. This case with Scales is going federal. Quinn needs to come in with me, and you, so we can tell our story before someone else does, before everyone else starts telling it for us. It'll be too late then."

Maureen felt Ruiz's fast-food-and-cigarettes breath on her cheeks. They stared into each other's eyes. Maureen's phone buzzed in her pocket. She stepped back from Ruiz and checked the caller. Atkinson. She answered, keeping an eye on Ruiz, backing away from him.

"Coughlin."

"I'm at the Tents," Atkinson said. "You know who isn't here?"

"You have to be kidding me."

"One Robert Carter Scales," Atkinson said.

"Tell me they didn't fucking lose him." If Ruiz was listening to her, or was interested in going anywhere, Maureen noted, he wasn't showing it. She was furious enough to start jumping up and down in place.

"Oh, this one is not on them," Atkinson said. "This one is on us."

"How is that?"

"Scales left in the custody of the NOPD," Atkinson said. "In the custody of Sixth District Platoon Officer Matthew J. Quinn."

"I'm going to call you back in one minute," Maureen said.

"When I'm off the phone with you," Atkinson said, "I'm putting out a BOLO on Quinn. We need that witness. As for Quinn, he has crossed a bright and shining line. He's done."

"The shooting this morning," Maureen said, "it was cover for Quinn snatching Scales. Get the whole department in an uproar."

"It makes sense," Atkinson said, "but we need Quinn to know for sure. And, Maureen, I have to tell you, if you hide anything from me about Quinn's whereabouts, for even one minute, you are guilty of a felony."

"One minute," Maureen said, but Atkinson was already gone. She blinked at Ruiz. "What else do you know?"

"I've done my part," Ruiz said.

"That was Atkinson, a detective sergeant, calling me," Maureen said. "Right now, this very minute, she's putting out a BOLO on Quinn. He's taken off with Scales, but I get the feeling you know this already, that you knew about it when I got here, that you knew about it *before* I got here and that this roundabout sob story about your lost lamb of a pal is a stalling tactic. Where is he, Rue? Hiding him is a felony. You need to tell me. If I'm going down, I'm burning us all."

"Your house getting shot up was never part of the plan. Not as far as I knew."

"Don't make it sound like it was my house they were after," Maureen said. "They were shooting to kill me."

Ruiz took a deep breath, again gazing away from the cemetery and at the school. "He's taking Scales to the river bend, to the levee past the zoo at the end of Magazine Street, where people used to run their dogs before the Corps of Engineers closed it off for the levee work. No one is there anymore. The woods between the river and the levee are still standing. You can't see anything happening on the river's edge from the road, or even from the levee."

"You can't lie to me about this," Maureen said. "You can't. You're positive that's where he's going?"

"He called me a while ago," Ruiz said. "Not too long before you did. Asking me to meet him there, asking me to help him put Scales in the river. He didn't even tell me why. He just figured I'd do it, that I'd help him kill this guy and cover it up." He shook his head. "I got kids."

He sat back down on the bench, any aggression gone out of him. "I hung up on him. I've been sitting here since, wishing this shit had never happened." He turned, gazing up at Maureen, elbows on his knees. "Cogs, you know, you coulda let that goddamn pickup truck go on by."

27

Maureen emerged from the trees on the back side of the levee onto a sloped, gravelly patch of riverbank bracketed on one side by a leaning willow and on the other by a chain-link fence that ran several yards out into the murky river. She had called Atkinson from the car. She figured she had five minutes, maybe ten, alone with Quinn before more cops arrived.

Beyond the willow tree, the shoreline continued upriver until it ran into a tumble of flat boulders that formed the barrier between the woods and a maritime salvage yard. Through the trees, Maureen could see the tilted sections of storm-damaged derricks and oil rigs brought in from the Gulf of Mexico. Downriver, on the other side of the chain fence, was the Army Corps of Engineers shipyard, a mammoth dredging ship idle at anchor at the edge of the wharf.

The river was low. The rocky beach ended at a wide apron of pungent black mud littered with trash and driftwood left behind by the receding river.

In front of her, Quinn stood ankle deep in the sucking mud, along the edge of the water. He was breathing heavily, leaning over with his hands on his thighs. Sweat darkened the back of his uniform shirt, the fabric stuck to his body. Beside him, facedown, clad in his orange OPP jumpsuit, was Bobby Scales. His ankles were shackled and his hands cuffed behind his back. One of his black rubber jail shoes was missing. He writhed on his belly like an eel tossed up on the riverbank, struggling to keep his face out of the mud. Maureen could hear his panicked breathing. She could see the trail through the stones and the mud Quinn had made dragging the struggling Scales to the water.

Before she could say anything, Quinn turned his head in her direction, squinting at her. He spat into the mud. "Cogs? The fuck are you doing here?"

"You really need to ask me that?" She started down toward the water. The ground was soft and wet under her feet.

"Did Rue send you?" Quinn asked.

"Not in the way you mean," Maureen said.

Quinn straightened up, twisting side to side to work the kinks out of his back, casually, as if she'd found him moving furniture and not dragging a kidnapped prisoner into the Mississippi River. His movements seemed to sink him deeper into the mud. Maureen wasn't sure he was aware of it. From the state of him, Maureen could tell Quinn hadn't planned on doing this alone. "So you're not here to help," he said. His speech was slurred. Booze.

"Depends on what you mean by help." Maureen stood at the edge of the mud. Her foot sank as she stepped into it, the mud pulling at her boot with a sucking sound. She lifted her foot free and stepped back onto the stones. "I know about your friendship with Gage. I know about Shadow. This can't go down like this. It can't."

"Why not?" Quinn asked. "Because of what you think you know? That's the problem with you, Cogs. Your weakness is you have this idea that everyone cares what you think, what you think you know and see. Like you're so fucking important."

"You're not a fucking murderer, Quinn," Maureen said. "For chrissakes, think about what you're doing. Think about who you're doing it for. How are you gonna live with this?"

"Pretty easy, to tell the truth," Quinn said. "So you're not going to rat on me, you're only concerned about my conscience? You're here for me, is that what you're saying?" He laughed. "How'd you fucking find me, anyway?"

"Ruiz did send me here."

Quinn's eyes went wide with surprise. He was astonished his former partner had given him up, Maureen could tell, but he wasn't angry. He wouldn't use the word *rat*, no matter how betrayed he felt. "Don't be too hard on Rue," Quinn said. "Don't blame him. He never really knew how everything fits together. He never knew how deep it runs. He's not a bad guy."

"He doesn't want you to do this," Maureen said.

"Not bad enough to be here with you."

Scales had rolled over onto his back, and recovered his breath enough to speak. "Hey, hey, this dude crazy. Help me, miss. Help me. This man gonna kill me."

Quinn turned to him. "You shut the fuck up."

"Help me," Scales implored, panic raising the register of his voice. "Please. I don't wanna die. I don't."

I don't wanna die. Was that what Mike-Mike said, Maureen thought, before you choked the life out of him? Before you tricked his friends into setting him on fire? Scales kept begging. Maureen wanted to jam her fingers in her ears and her foot down Scales's throat. The more pathetic he sounded, the angrier Maureen got.

"Shut up, Scales," she demanded. "Shut your fucking mouth or I'll fill it with mud myself."

But Scales wouldn't be quiet. He was crying now, wailing wordlessly. Sound traveled far along the river. Maureen worried someone would hear. People worked in salvage and shipyards. It wouldn't be long before a tug or a tanker cruised by. What was happening wouldn't be tough to figure out, two sweaty, furtive cops and a prisoner in orange, facedown in the mud. A part of her wanted to turn her back on the scene, to let Quinn finish what he'd started long before she'd even moved to New Orleans, and to let him live with the consequences.

But then she remembered that the Watchmen Brigade gunmen had gotten her address from somewhere, from someone.

Quinn was swearing at Scales to be quiet as he struggled to free his feet from the mud. He grimaced in pain, one hand snapping to his back as if he'd pulled something. Instead of coming closer to the shore, though, Quinn stepped in Scales's direction, his feet sinking again in the mud. He lifted one foot, brought it down on the side of Scales's face, grinding the toe box of his boot into Scales's temple, driving his face down into the mud.

"Fucking shut it, you piece of shit," Quinn yelled. "I fucking told you."

Scales couldn't cry out now, his nose and most of his mouth pressed into the mud. Maureen could hear him gagging and spitting.

Over Quinn's shoulder, out in the river, a fish jumped. Pelicans reeled in the sky over the silent dredging ship. Upstream and down the river was empty of traffic. It wouldn't last. Maureen could see the swirling currents running against and into one another on the surface of the water. She needed to end this. For a long moment, she fought against the need.

"Quinn!" Maureen yelled. Her instinct was to rush him, but she stayed where she was. "Quinn, stop it!" Her hand went to her weapon. "Please."

Quinn lifted his foot. Scales drew one knee toward his chest. He was able to roll his face out of the mud, his weight forward on his forehead. His body heaved. He choked and spat, his nose full of mud. Maureen realized she felt nothing for him. She didn't care if he lived or died.

Quinn settled his foot back onto the mud, taking a wide stance to steady himself and distribute his weight. He'd seen her hand go for her weapon. He showed no interest in his own, made no move. Maureen was relieved. With the mud and the sweat on his hands, he hadn't a chance of beating her on the draw. She moved her hand away from her gun.

"Seriously?" he asked, almost smiling. "You think you could?"

"Easy," Maureen said. "You're a sitting duck stuck there in the mud."

"Oh, I know you've got a good eye," Quinn said. "I know you can hit the target. But could you pull the trigger? On a fellow cop?"

"If you made me."

"Over this piece of shit?"

"How about over what happened to me this morning?" Maureen said. She pulled her weapon from the holster, held it against her thigh with both hands. "You gave them my address, didn't you? Why would you do that, Quinn?"

He seemed genuinely perplexed, seemed to be thinking. He shook his head. "I didn't know they were gonna *shoot* at you. I swear to fucking God. I gave your address to Caleb. You took the money from the party. He told me you were on the team. He said he had more for you, that he had something he wanted to discuss with you. I was trying to help you, Cogs. All I've tried to do since you pulled that goddamn truck over is help you, and you won't fucking take it."

"Look at where it's got us," Maureen said. "Look at where we are. You're trying to murder someone, in broad daylight, to protect someone who tried to have me killed."

"You talk fucking endlessly, this romantic bullshit about how you love it here. Well, lemme ask you this. Who's worth more to this city? Scales or the Heath family? You know, the people who've been here for generations, who build shit, *useful* shit. People who stayed after the storm, who stayed *during* the storm, who fed and watered the police department you now belong to while this fucking baboon and his fuck-tard cronies took potshots at us from the project rooftops? The Heaths rebuilt *half* of this fucking city after the storm. They give to every fucking charity in the city. What's this murdering, cop-hating gangsta slab of shit here in the mud worth? Who's better for New Orleans? The builders or the asshole who only adds to the body count? Who's worth protecting?

"Use your fucking head, Coughlin. We have the power to make the trouble we're gonna be in go away. All we gotta do is put a guy who killed an old man and a twelve-year-old in the river. And the people we're protecting by doing that are worth more than him and me and you combined." He raised his shoulders, his hands spread out in front of him. "Christ. How is this hard for you? I don't understand."

"You're delusional," Maureen said. "No matter what good Solomon Heath does, his son is no better, no different than Scales. He bankrolls hate groups and militias. Armed gangs. For fun. To be a big shot. He gives people money that they use to buy guns that they're gonna use to kill cops. Think what he coulda done with his name and his money, and he's a fucking terrorist instead. He *chose* it. He's no better than some asshole in a desert cave. How is this hard for *you*?"

"There's no proof of any of that shit about Heath," Quinn said. "Nobody's got any proof of Caleb putting up that money."

"The proof is lying right there in the mud," Maureen said. "Isn't that why the three of us are out here in the fucking first place?"

"So he spits out some white guy's name he saw on the side of a building because your dyke rabbi is putting the screws to him. You wanna blame somebody for us being out here standing in the river, blame Atkinson. Me? I don't care what he said under pressure, I know what he's done, to that kid, to that old man, to you. I'm taking out the trash. Should've been done a long time ago."

"Why haven't you done it already?" Maureen asked. "You could've done what you're doing today at any time in the past few weeks, ever since you and Ruiz busted Shadow, when there was a lot less attention, and you didn't do anything. You criticize Atkinson. You've been putting the screws to Marques, scaring him into keeping his mouth shut. *Now* you decide to take out the trash? Come on."

"We woulda never hurt that kid," Quinn said. "Or let anyone hurt him. You believe that, right? What do you think I am?"

"What about me?" Maureen asked. "What about the innocent people who live on my block? Getting rid of Scales only lets things like that continue."

"What getting rid of Scales allows to continue," Quinn said, "is the work the Heaths do for the city."

"And the money they pay you, too," Maureen said. "That keeps coming. Stop with the benevolent-benefactor shit. You're gonna spend your life in jail for an extra few grand a year? You think Caleb is gonna protect you if you go down for this? You think he'll put up money for you? Pull strings? Pay your child support? Protect your boy from the bullies? His daddy is hip-deep in city contracts. What makes you think Solomon will let Caleb anywhere near you? What he'll do is send some crazy freak from the Watchmen after you for five hundred bucks and a fistful of pills. You think he'll return the favor you're doing him now? He'll cut you loose faster than he did Scales. He might cut your throat for this favor you're doing him."

"We've known each other over half our lives," Quinn said. "I'll talk to Caleb. He'll listen to me. I can get him to rethink what he's doing, if it's like you said, which I doubt. Even if it is, he didn't mean any harm. He's no terrorist, he's a rich kid that didn't know any better. They're part of the city. Always have been. They like to go slumming, these Uptown kids. Cheap drugs, bossing around black people, white-trash pussy. Caleb's always been that way. Makes him feel tough."

Maureen saw over Quinn's shoulder that, upriver, the awesome prow of a container ship had turned the bend in the river.

"He's not an Uptown kid drinking at F and M's anymore," Maureen said. "He's a grown man. You think it gets better from here? It won't work like this. I can't let this go. Atkinson needs Scales. She'll come looking for him, and she's not Ronnie Drayton."

"She'll fucking thank me," Quinn said, "for saving her the effort."

She could argue that the feds wanted Scales, Maureen thought, but she knew that strategy would backfire, only further persuading Quinn to kill Scales.

"And I know what you're gonna say next," Quinn said. "Fuck the feds."

Quinn rocked in place, losing his balance for a moment as one foot sank a few inches farther down in the mud. Scales had rolled onto his back again, and was trying to blink the mud from his eyes.

Maureen saw that the ship coming downriver had to be the size of a city block. Quinn hadn't noticed it. Or maybe, Maureen thought, he knew better than to be afraid.

"Besides," Quinn said, "if anyone really needs Scales, the current'll spit him back up in a day or so." He shrugged. "Or it won't. I don't much give a fuck. Now help me get him out there."

"Think," Maureen said. "Whether he surfaces or vanishes, the trail's gonna lead straight back to you. You're the one who checked him outta jail. Atkinson already knows it was you. She told me herself." She knew she should be watching Quinn, but she couldn't take her eyes off the approaching vessel. It seemed to be running so close to shore. An optical illusion, she told herself, caused by the curving riverbank. "There are witnesses at the sheriff's department, there are cameras everywhere."

"This is the same sheriff's department," Quinn said, "that dumped your crazy-eyed purse snatcher in the emergency room and went out for tacos, and then lied to you up and down about it. They're a bunch of lazy fucking amateurs. You think I can't cover a trail? That I haven't before? I'm pretty good at this shit."

"You think any deputies you buy or bully will hold up," Maureen said, "when Atkinson comes calling? Or the FBI?"

"All they have to do is play dumb. They're good at that." He kicked at Scales. "Help me here. Help me make this look like an escape. Prisoners slip out of the Tents with alarming frequency. Scales is another one lost. A minute or two facedown in the mud under my boot and he's finished. We pop the cuffs off, shove him out into the current, and let the mighty Mississippi do the rest. He vanishes, and nobody knows but us.

"If there's nothing left to do but bust a couple of cops for Scales's disappearance, Atkinson will back off, especially if one of those cops is you. She's smart. Don't let her fool you. She knows the game. She knows Scales isn't worth screwing over good people, like you, like the Heaths."

He paused, letting her think it over. The ship looked to be running too close to their side of the river, Maureen worried. Surely there was a reason for that, she thought, something about currents and river depth and navigation and whatever.

"Bring him in to shore," Maureen said. "Away from the water. Or leave him there, and you come in. Come closer. We'll talk about it some more."

Quinn looked over his shoulder, seeing the ship. "Is that what you're staring at? Forget it. Nice try. Good acting. You do look terrified. But watch when it passes, that ship won't be anywhere near us. Before she got knocked up, my ex and I brought her dog here once a week. I've seen this before. The river plays tricks."

She wanted to tell him it wasn't the giant ship that made her nervous, or even how close it ran to their bank. What unnerved her was the huge wall of water foaming at the peak of the ship's prow, and where that water would go as the ship passed their location and headed downriver.

"Before I come in," Quinn said, "you need to help me get him in the water. You have to prove you're on my side. Otherwise, I'm just surrendering."

Maureen said nothing. She didn't move.

"C'mon, Coughlin. Think of the bad shit Scales did, and the bad shit now he'll never get to do. Think of the good shit we get to keep doing. We're protecting ourselves here, and Rue, and Preacher. There's a hundred other routes for the FBI to take to the Citizens. Caleb will owe us huge. He'll shut down the Watchmen's New Orleans operation. Think about it, Maureen. Scales dies. Everybody wins. You can't deny it." His eyes got wide. "Okay, what about this? I can turn Caleb against them, right? I can flip him for us. I know I can. Wouldn't even be hard. That would be huge, us handing the feds a witness against the Sovereign Citizens like Caleb Heath. What he cares about is being the big shot, it don't matter to him who he gets to play it in front of. He can play at being an FBI secret agent. He'll love it. We'll get promoted. You could *walk* onto the task force at the Sixth or any other district. Preacher'll be fucking thrilled."

Maureen wanted to tell Quinn he was delusional about their futures, and about his friend Caleb Heath, but she'd be telling Quinn things he'd known and chosen to ignore long before she'd come around. She toed the mud, testing it, staring at Quinn, thinking about where she stood. From what she could tell, and she was guessing, she was at a safe-enough distance from the water. Quinn, on the other hand, stood at the edge.

"Me and you," Quinn said, "we could make a deal. We could make this work."

The huge black hull of the ship, a rushing thundercloud, seemed so close as it swept past them, sending fat, rising swells of gray water like bull elephants rolling toward the shore. Maureen marveled at how quiet it was, something of that size and speed going by. She imagined the giant propellers churning under the river's surface. She felt miniaturized. She took a quick step in Quinn's direction, her foot sinking into the mud. He'd been right about the ship. It was farther out on the river than it had appeared. Maybe she could reach him before the water did.

She looked at Quinn, who frowned back at her. He could feel it coming. Maybe, if she could free herself from the mud, she could pull him out of the water. Scales was screaming. He might be beyond saving.

The big swells crashed ashore hard and took everything out of her hands.

Quinn barked out a yelp as a wave slammed into his back, pitching him forward. Scales disappeared under the water without a sound, swallowed. Quinn's knees buckled in the undertow as his legs were sucked deeper into the mud. Knee-deep. Hip-deep. The deeper he sank, the faster he sank. He bent backward then forward in the rushing water, flopping about in the push and pull of the river like a stuffed toy in the jaws of a playful dog. His arms flailed. He had for some reason that Maureen couldn't fathom pulled his gun. He wouldn't let go of it. His hand was black. Mud and dark water ran down his arm. Another wave washed over his head and he went under, vanishing from Maureen's sight.

With the river curling and seething around her ankles, the swirling water black with mud, Maureen fell back onto the stones, her foot popping free, bootless. She scrambled back to her feet and retreated. The waves kept coming, each one bigger and louder than the last, driving Maureen stumbling farther back up the rocky beach. She tumbled over backward again, falling on her ass, her gun bruising her tailbone. As she fought for breath, watching the river, the swells subsided. The river settled a few long moments later, the last wave washing over the mud as quiet as a sigh.

Every trace of Quinn and Scales was gone from the riverfront, as if they had never been there. She couldn't find her boot, couldn't even locate the hole in the mud where she had lost it. Maureen got to her feet, hobbling across the stones.

She climbed out onto the dirt embankment that surrounded the leaning willow. She stepped up onto the exposed roots, and clutching a crooked branch, inched out over the water, searching the river for any sign of Quinn. She knew Scales was lost. Deep inside, she hoped she wouldn't find Quinn, either, that she wouldn't see him thrash to the surface a hundred feet from shore, calling for her help. She lacked the nerve to challenge the river on his behalf.

The river showed her nothing.

Atkinson came crashing out of the woods, two sweating cops in blue on her heels, their weapons drawn. She looked around, panting. "What the fuck, Coughlin?"

"They were here," Maureen said, "and then they were gone." She spoke standing on the exposed roots of the willow, as if the backdrop of the river added credence to her story. She was already thinking of all the things she could have said and done differently in the last few minutes.

"A giant ship washed them away. You can still see it. I couldn't get to them. There was nothing I could do."

Atkinson didn't respond. She called for backup, including calls to the Coast Guard and the state police for search and rescue. She named it a rescue mission, but everyone on both ends of the call knew the truth. It would be a recovery mission before sundown. Maureen knew it, too.

Her calls made, Atkinson didn't speak or reach out to Maureen to help her back to shore, as Maureen had suspected she might. Instead, she stared at Maureen, her radio clutched at her side, her blond curls blowing in the breeze, her eyes hidden behind dark shades. Maureen eventually had to look away from her. She watched from her perch under the willow as more cops appeared out of the woods. They wandered aimlessly, uselessly, along the rocky shoreline, shading their eyes in the cloudy haze as they looked out over the river for signs of life, whispering to one another.

Maureen knew, she *knew*, that her fellow officers understood her decision to stay on shore after the waves had died. They'd have gone into the river after Quinn, she knew, like she would have, if there existed any chance of bringing him back out alive, but they knew, like she did, the powerful river currents would have sucked them underwater. The Mississippi would have swallowed them, too, one after the other, like marshmallows tossed to the alligators at the zoo. No one on that rocky beach thought her a coward. Maureen knew that.

When she looked at the spot where Atkinson had stood, the detective was gone. It took Maureen a moment to spot her. She had turned her back and was walking away into the trees.

28

The second Saturday after Quinn was swept away, Maureen stood at the back porch railing of her rented bungalow, her hips pressed into the sun-warmed wood, watching a large blue heron stalk the edge of the canal cutting through the property. She was on Dauphin Island, a thin spit of sand in Mobile Bay, a few miles off the coast of Alabama. She was on hiatus from her house, her job, and her city. The Saints had beaten the Panthers by twenty last Sunday, remaining undefeated, and sat comfortably atop the division. Maureen eagerly anticipated watching this Sunday's game on TV by herself, a bottle of wine at her elbow, instead of in a crowded noisy bar. She would still wear her Pierre Thomas jersey, even if no one was around to see her in it.

Back in New Orleans, her landlords had come in from Houston to hire a contractor. Repairs had started right away. The landlords were sympathetic about her trauma, and tight-lipped about the condition of the house and what fixing it would cost. Maureen would be allowed to finish out her lease. No one was going to put a cop who'd been shot at out on the street, not even in New Orleans. Not right away, at least. She hadn't asked about their lease-to-own deal, figuring it was best to let the pain of paying the contractors recede before raising the subject. Just as well. She had to resolve her own concerns about her future ability to pay rent before she could go making any deals or offers to buy anything. She had wondered, at one point when she was feeling desperate and was deep into a bottle of whiskey, if maybe there was a bed at the Bend in the River. She could room with Dice. She struggled not to think about Dice.

The break from work had come at the orders of the police department's Public Integrity Bureau. She was suspended indefinitely, with pay for now, pending the results of their ongoing investigation into her recent activities. She'd given them her testimony in the days following the events by the river, and they'd left her waiting on their call. When they felt like it, they'd let her know if she had a job and a future with the NOPD. The possibility that her career had ended made it tougher for Maureen to part with the bribe money she'd taken from Solomon Heath, but she found good uses for it. The three hundred she was owed for the detail she kept. Five hundred went to Roots of Music, the citywide marching band for middle school students. The money covered one scholarship; another kid like Marques would learn to play, would get to march someday soon in Mardi Gras parades. The last five hundred paid the rent for her week at the beach. Fuck it, she thought. She deserved it.

Maureen enjoyed Dauphin Island, though she knew she would have enjoyed it more under different circumstances. The island was dead quiet. It had one restaurant and one general store, neither of which offered much beyond the basics or was close to her bungalow. Except for an older couple living across the canal in a raised two-story on the bay side of the island, and the yellow-eyed heron who visited mornings and evenings, she'd encountered nary another living soul. The freshly paved main road across the island made a perfect running track, with dunes stretching down to the Gulf at one end and a bird sanctuary at the other.

She'd run the island end to end each of the three days she'd been there so far, the salted breezes chapping her cheeks and lips.

On Thursday morning, the last day of Maureen's testimony for the PIB, Quinn's body surfaced three miles downriver, having come to rest against the barnacled hull of a tugboat. Little that was recognizable remained of his face or his hands, river denizens having had their way with the corpse. His uniform and his badge number helped identify him, as did the mother of his ten-year-old son. The woman remembered the cheap tattoo of a crawfish in the shape of a fleur-de-lis on his hip. She had been with him when he got it late one night on Frenchmen Street, and had counseled against it—speaking as if that mistake had been the first tumbling domino in Matthew Quinn's downfall. Caleb Heath was supposed to join them that night, the woman said, to get a matching tattoo of his own, but he had stood them up.

As a consequence of her suspension, Maureen was barred from attending Quinn's funeral. She and Ruiz and Preacher had missed it, the three of them prohibited from any contact with the department or with one another. Maureen found herself somewhat relieved at the ban. She wanted to reach out to Ruiz, but had no idea what to say to him. Of course, the ban on communication had not stopped Preacher from talking to her. He offered regular words of encouragement as well as updates about their respective proceedings fresh from his innumerable sources throughout the department. He was considering retirement, he told her in one booze-slurred message. He didn't need the NOPD. He'd work for a pit bull rescue organization, or open a doggie day care business of his own. He wanted to deal with personalities, he'd said, that understood joy and gratitude and simple pleasures. Maureen wasn't sure if it was cops or criminals he was looking to escape with his new career.

She'd heard nothing, from Preacher or from anyone else, about whether Caleb Heath had attended Quinn's services. She saw in the paper that Solomon Heath had announced a major financial contribution in Matthew Junior's name to a scholarship fund for the children of fallen and disabled NOPD officers. The amount was secret but far larger, Maureen was sure, than anything Quinn's fellow cops could afford to put in the donation jar at the Sixth District. The statement did not mention that Quinn and Caleb Heath had known each other since they were teenagers, only the Heaths' long-standing love of all things New Orleans. The whole article had been much more about the Heaths than about Quinn or his son.

Maureen had read Quinn's obituary online. It was short, accompanied by his academy graduation photo. The article made no mention of where he'd gone to high school—a strange omission for a New Orleans boy, born and raised. In the comments section following the article, which Maureen knew she shouldn't read but did anyway, Ruiz had posted a brief note telling about how he and Quinn had grown up together in Broadmoor. It was the only comment on the article that Maureen could stomach.

There wasn't much the department could do with the story of Quinn and Scales at the river. A cop kidnapping and murdering a prisoner was tough to hide without a hurricane blowing through town, so they didn't try. An unstable cop had gone rogue, they insisted to the media, and taken the law into his own hands with a suspect in a heinous set of crimes. As the caring father of a young child from whom he was estranged, one anonymous retired officer guessed, dealing with a child-murdering animal like Scales was too much for an already exhausted NOPD veteran to take. One who had endured the unspeakable horrors of Katrina and carried them stoically inside for years. Maybe he had first encountered Scales during those dark days, someone said. The retired officer expressed his wish, as did the superintendent and the mayor, that Quinn had availed himself of the numerous mental health resources provided by the police department.

Sometimes, the mayor said, shaking his bald head, we try to do too much by ourselves. No one serving our city, he said, should feel like they are on the front lines alone.

Maureen waited for those resources to be offered to her. At least, she thought, she waited at the beach.

Atkinson kept her distance. No calls. No drinks at Ms. Mae's. No meals at the St. Charles Tavern or Handsome Willy's. Maureen understood. She was damaged goods unless and until the department decided she wasn't. She hadn't expected, nor had she asked for, any help with her case. From a discreet distance, by omission, Atkinson had provided it, anyway. During Maureen's hearings, the bribe from Solomon Heath had not come up. That secret had been kept. Atkinson had also officially taken over the Gage murder case, folding it into her investigation of the body Maureen had found on Magnolia Street, and of an older case from the summer, a young woman found murdered, her throat cut, in Armstrong Park. Drayton had been only too happy to let go of the Gage case, and the federal interest that came with it.

By serving up Quinn as a rogue, the department had afforded Maureen good cover from outside eyes. Though the media had noticed her suspension, they called it "administrative leave," which meant they had accepted the department line that she was on leave for matters unrelated to the events surrounding Officer Quinn. Her house had been shot up by suspected cop killers. She had nearly drowned trying to prevent a fellow officer from making a terrible mistake. And she was so new on the force. Her district commander wondered aloud to any reporter who would listen, who could possibly question her need for some time off to regroup? If only the late Officer Quinn had been as wise, the media officers said, as Officer Coughlin. Maybe the department culture was changing for the better. No one in the media was talking about disciplinary action, no one in the police department was telling tales—not yet, anyway.

Through everything, Maureen kept quiet. She talked to no one who didn't wear the uniform. She took her union rep's advice. She answered the questions she was asked by the people in the department she was answerable to, nothing more and nothing less. Then she got the hell outta Dodge. She knew her future in the department depended very much on what the brass thought they could get away with letting her get away with. She knew the brass wanted the story dead and buried as fast and as deep as she did. They wanted to see if she would and could take one for the team. She hoped her silence proved her willingness to do so.

The FBI would make a run at her, Maureen knew, when she got back to New Orleans. They'd come to her quietly, when the story had started to fade from public and media consciousness, but they'd come. They'd want her help with the Watchmen. They'd want her knowledge of Madison Leary and her links to the militia. The loss of Quinn and Scales might slow the Watchmen Brigade's move into New Orleans, Maureen thought, but it wouldn't stop them. Why would it? They were winning. They'd be waiting for her back in New Orleans as well. When they came for her again, they wouldn't be quiet. But they wouldn't catch her by surprise this time. The FBI, the Watchmen, the elusive Madison Leary—Maureen had a lot of work waiting for her back home. She liked her chances of getting her badge back. She would be ready. She would blacken some eyes and turn some heads.

The body of Bobby Scales had yet to be recovered, though Maureen knew that the Mississippi could cough him up at any moment, or it could be weeks or months in the future. Or it could be never. No one had stepped forward to argue for a search, or to agitate for his body's recovery for burial. If anyone missed Bobby Scales, they kept their feelings to themselves.

Preacher had passed word of Scales's fate to Marques and his grandmother. He loomed large in their imaginations, though, and Maureen knew it would be some time before they were convinced of his death. She knew how those ghosts could linger. She'd visit with them when things around her had cooled, when she got back to the city. She'd never tell Marques she had argued for Scales's life.

Before leaving for the beach, in an e-mail, Maureen told Atkinson everything she knew about Madison Leary, about who Dice was, and about how Dice had known Leary and had helped Maureen with the case. Maureen had searched Frenchmen Street for Dice herself, but she had vanished. Her friends wouldn't talk to Maureen about her. Maureen told herself that Dice had simply moved on, as so many kids like her did, to another city where the weather stayed warmer through the winter months, or that maybe she had a home and a family she'd been able to return to, having had her fill of adventure on the streets of New Orleans. Maureen could not shake the deep dread she felt when she thought about sending Dice looking for Leary carrying nothing more than a business card. She hoped Dice had ignored her. At least there had been no more singing phone calls. Maureen was grateful for that. She'd thought about changing her phone number, but didn't want Dice left unable to reach her. Maureen figured she would've heard from Preacher if Atkinson had enjoyed better luck finding Dice or Madison Leary.

From the railing of the back deck, Maureen watched as down by the canal, in a flash, the heron speared something pale on the sharp point of its beak. The bird tossed its head back and gobbled down its wriggling prey, the lump moving down its long throat, the one glistening yellow eye that Maureen could see ever watchful of its surroundings. The bird lowered its black foot into the water and opened its wings, standing motionless and baring its breast to the sun. Maureen wondered if the heron could see her watching from the porch. It was a predator, Maureen thought, perhaps the island's largest, and it certainly was not afraid.

Those options for Dice, those possible explanations for her disappearance, Maureen knew, were the things she told herself to make herself feel better, to stop herself from obsessing on the whereabouts and activities of Madison Leary. Those thin fantasies, however, did nothing to repel or even dilute the regular visions she had of Dice lying in the dead bushes or the dry fountain of a neglected city park, or in the empty gullet of an abandoned house, or in the gutter by a broken-down van, her throat slit wide open, her dark shimmering blood pooling around her shaved head in the moonlight like a quicksilver halo, her empty eyes pointed up at the stars and the wide expanse of indigo sky, her mouth slightly open in surprise.

ACKNOWLEDGMENTS

Major thanks as always to my family and friends for their love and support.

Special thanks to my editor, Sarah Crichton, for always pushing and for knowing that it's never bad news if it makes a better book. Also a huge thank you to everyone at FSG, including Marsha Sasmor, Lottchen Shivers, Lenni Wolff, Abby Kagan, Spenser Lee (for unwavering support), and Alex Merto (for the eye-popping cover). Many thanks to Elizabeth Bruce and everyone at Picador.

Much gratitude to my agent, Barney Karpfinger, and his team at the Karpfinger Agency, including Cathy Jacque and Marc Jaffee. Warriors all, and people of infinite patience.

I listen to A LOT of music writing these books, including but not limited to New Orleans artists: Anders Osborne, Dr. John, the Soul Rebels Brass Band, the Rebirth Brass Band, Galactic, Truth Universal, Pleasure Club, Juvenile, the Revivalists, Kelcy Mae, the Hot 8 Brass Band, Trombone Shorty and Orleans Avenue, John Michael Rouchell, Shamarr Allen and the Underdawgs, and Allen Toussaint.

The music of Gillian Welch was especially important to this book.

The Roots of Music is a real music and educational program doing great work here in New Orleans. Learn more about them here: www .therootsofmusic.org.

All my love to my remarkable wife, AC Lambeth, as brave, talented, wise, and understanding a partner as anyone could ask for. Nothing good happens without her.

Read on for an excerpt from
Bill Loehfelm's *Let the Devil Out*

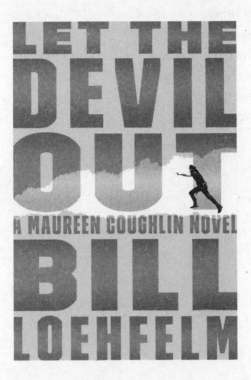

ISBN 978-0-374-29857-9 (hardcover)
ISBN 978-0-374-71172-6 (e-book)

"Bill Loehfelm, a rising star in crime fiction,
just keeps rising higher. . . . Maureen Coughlin is a
hero for the ages."—Laura Lippman

Available in hardcover and e-book in Summer 2016 from
Sarah Crichton Books, an imprint of Farrar, Straus and Giroux

1

Late November. The time of the silver-haired man.

These past weeks, every gray cloud charcoaled across the pale sky brought him back to her. Every cold breeze coming down the Mississippi felt like his hands under her coat. His shadow walked before her everywhere she went, painting the buildings and the sidewalks of New Orleans like the shadow of a great carrion bird. When she awoke in the mornings, she felt he'd only just stepped away from the foot of her bed. The bed with bullet holes in it. Late at night, he whispered the names of the dead, his victims and others, in her ear during her last conscious moments, when she felt helplessly paralyzed by the coming sleep.

Which meant that most nights, Maureen did her best to stay awake until morning.

Maureen sat alone at a corner cocktail table at d.b.a., a Frenchmen Street bar, thinking about the silver-haired man speaking names into her ear. So, she figured, sipping her drink, she was now officially hearing voices. So be it, then.

Maybe that was for the best. Maybe they would help. Hearing voices gave her something in common with one of the women she was out here looking for: Madison Leary, the woman who killed men with a straight razor and who sang old folk songs about death and the devil into Maureen's voice mail. Maybe the connection, this new empathy, would inspire an idea. Maybe it would change her luck. Lord knows, she needed *something* to shake things up. She needed something to break. A break in the case, as they say. At this point, she'd take going half-crazy, even if it was the second half, even if it meant she was going the rest of the way crazy. As long as Madison Leary was there at the finish line.

She lowered her eyes to the table, avoiding the faces in the barroom, and sipped her drink again, embarrassed even though no one was looking at her.

The time of the silver-haired man, she thought. Oh, please, girl-friend.

What bullshit. Melodramatic bullshit, Maureen. You know better. Get over it.

He was just a man, she told herself, over and over again. *Just a man.* Repeating that sentence as if it were a stone she threw again and again at the great black bird overhead. Of course, she could never throw it high enough. And the bird never got frightened and never flew away. But that didn't stop her from trying.

She thought of the Greek god condemned to roll his stone up a hill, condemned to repeat the same meaningless task for eternity. She couldn't recall what his sin had been. Or his name. Didn't much matter. It wasn't much of a story, and Maureen knew what her own sins had been. The silver-haired man was just that, a man. Not a devil. Not a god. Not a ghost. He'd had an ordinary name. Frank Sebastian. And he was dead. Maureen knew this for sure. She'd been ten feet away from him when he'd died.

The time of the silver-haired man? His time was over. She had seen to that.

Sitting at her table, Maureen tried imagining herself as someone else. A different person. With a different voice. This was a new thing she'd been trying in her head. A way to hear herself tell the story of what had happened to her before she had come to New Orleans. She studied her pack of cigarettes. American Spirit. A chief in a headdress was on the front of the box. He smoked a peace pipe. Maureen lit up.

She closed her eyes and envisioned herself not as the thin, short, pale-faced redhead she was, but maybe as a stout, dark-haired, and tattooed medicine woman, crouched on her haunches as she told her story, surrounded by openmouthed, wide-eyed squaws circling the longhouse fire. She tried to hear herself, tried to listen to herself tell them the story of the Silver-Haired Man, the November Man, the one who haunted her in these late weeks of autumn. The one she saw reflected in store windows along Magazine Street and turning corners ahead of her along St. Charles Avenue. The one who lived in the blind spot over her shoulder, who hovered in her peripheral vision. The man she had seen in the soulless eyes of a sociopathic rich boy outside a party at his father's Audubon Park mansion, who she saw everywhere around her in the bars and clubs of New Orleans at night, in the glittering ravenous eyes of brown and black and blond young men.

But when she tried *listening* to her other self tell the story, as soon as she started paying attention and seeing everything again, seeing Sebastian, the cattails at the water's edge, the headlights of the oncoming train, Maureen's invented self fell silent. The story ended and the vision disappeared into a tiny point of light, as if someone had pulled the plug on an old television. At the table in the bar, the medicine woman vanished and Maureen was left alone again with her ache and her fear and her ghost, and she had nothing to say and no one to listen to her not say it. I need to find a way, she thought. I need to find a way to tell the story to someone.

She had hoped that this first anniversary wouldn't haunt her. The first six months after Sebastian had tried to throw her in front of a train, she still lived on Staten Island with her mother in the house she'd grown up in, on the same streets where everything bad had happened, and so it kind of made sense that those events had lingered. But *this* November, she had a new life, in a new city. She was a cop now, for chrissakes. A cop on indefinite paid administrative leave, she thought, which made her a cop without a gun and a badge at the moment, which wasn't much of a cop, but a cop according to her paycheck. And she'd get her badge and her gun back. Soon.

The point was she had put a lot of work into becoming a different woman, into building herself into a new person. A *real* new person. And leaving behind that bastard and the places he'd taken her was a big reason she had done that work.

But then the weather had turned at the end of the month, and Maureen learned that November in New Orleans could be, if it wanted to, as cold and gray and wet and bleak as November in New York. And at the turn in the weather had come her dark turn of mind. This year should have been much different from the last. She had expected it to be different. She *deserved* it to be different. And when it wasn't, she got pissed. More than pissed. Angry. Incensed. *Furious.*

The woman Maureen had been watching for more than an hour got up from her barstool, bringing Maureen back to the present. This woman was not Madison Leary. This woman was not part of a murder case. This wasn't police work. This was something else. Something private.

Just for tonight. Which was what you said the last time, Maureen thought.

The woman pulled on her coat, flipped her long black hair out from underneath her collar, gathered her phone and her purse, and headed for the door. The bouncer opened it for her, letting the cold outside air rush into the barroom as he said good night. Maureen pulled the hood of her baggy black sweatshirt tight against the back of her neck. She longed for her father's old blue pea coat, the one she had lost last November. The one she had left in a bloody heap on the floor of a Staten Island emergency room, soaked in Frank Sebastian's blood.

She drew her hands into her sleeves. She carried a weapon in the front pocket of her sweatshirt. She savored its weight on her lap.

A man Maureen had also been watching emerged from the dim and narrow hall that led to the restrooms. He froze, his face scrunching in anger, when he saw the empty barstool. He looked around the bar. Maureen could tell it was all he could do to keep from screaming the woman's name. They'd arrived at the bar at different times, the woman first and the man about twenty minutes later. Right away they had fallen into a bad argument, quickly enough that Maureen knew it was the continuation of a previous fight, badly enough that the bouncer had come over from the door to check on them. Maureen hadn't been able to hear much of what they were saying, but she'd heard enough to know that the man had followed the woman here from another Frenchmen Street bar she'd left to get away from him.

After the bouncer's intervention, the man had moved away down the bar, pretending, Maureen could tell, to watch the funk band that had taken the stage during the argument. But throughout the set he had kept a close eye on the object of his ire, glaring at her over his shoulder, his silver-labeled bottle of Coors Light raised to his lips.

From where she sat in the corner across the room, Maureen could see the wheels turning in his head. She could read his thoughts. She didn't like what they told her. Her fears were confirmed by the fact that the woman had waited until the man was out of sight to make her move for the door. She wasn't leaving. She was escaping. She was fleeing.

The man gave up searching the bar. He made for the door, shouldering people out of his way. He hurried out in pursuit, Maureen knew, of the woman who had slipped away.

She grabbed her cigarettes and slid off her barstool, pulling on her gloves and moving for the door as quiet as a shadow. She raised her hood over her head, slipped her hands into the pouch of the sweatshirt, gripping the weapon hidden there, a telescoping baton with a weighted tip called an ASP. She kept her head down as she passed by the bouncer and out the door. A few paces ahead of her on the crowded sidewalk, she spied the angry man searching for the frightened woman.

Like she had with the others, she'd take him from behind, start with a quick strike to his knee. A man who can't stand can't fight back. Then, before he even hit the ground, she'd go for his throat. For control of his voice, his breath, and the blood rushing to his brain. Destroying the knee hurt him, and it gave her strategic advantage. But compressing his throat in the bend of her elbow, *strangling* him? That was what induced the panic; that pressure conjured the terror. The terror was what she wanted. Terror left a lasting impression. She knew that from experience.

Maureen would make sure he never found the woman he pursued. Not tonight. Not ever. And that he'd never know what hit him.

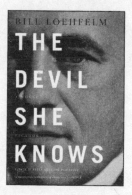